# ROBIN HOOD, 1192

# ALSO BY T.L.B. WOOD

# ROBIN HOOD, 1192

## THE SYMBIONT TIME TRAVEL ADVENTURE SERIES, BOOK SEVEN

### T.L.B. WOOD

Book and cover design by eBook Prep
www.ebookprep.com

July, 2021
ISBN: 978-1-64457-187-3

***ePublishing Works!***
644 Shrewsbury Commons Ave
Ste 249
Shrewsbury PA 17361
United States of America

www.epublishingworks.com
Phone: 866-846-5123

*For Raquel and Gabrielle*

*Up the airy mountain,*
  *Down the rushy glen,*
  *We daren't go a-hunting*
  *For fear of little men;*
  *Wee folk, good folk,*
  *Trooping all together;*
  *Green jacket, red cap,*
  *And white owl's feather.*

WILLIAM ALLINGHAM

# INTRODUCTION

Before the Normans arrived from France, the language spoken in England was Anglo-Saxon, otherwise known as Old English. This speech was an amalgam of different languages spoken by the tribes that invaded England over a large expanse of time. The Normans brought a French dialect to add to the mix, and consequently, Old English, French, and Latin were spoken. The languages were one part of the mixing of cultures, and the times were challenging and politically complicated.

This book is a creation of fiction and is a product of the imagination of the author. It is not an attempt to write a historically accurate account of the times. However, an attempt is made to keep the action within the boundaries of what would be realistic for 1192. Any resemblance to anyone other than documented historical figures is purely coincidental.

# ONE

"What's with *Ivanhoe?*" Kipp asked, pausing in his reading to stand, stretch and yawn, opening his mouth wide like a hungry alligator about to snap. "I'm trying to wrap my head around the culture of the day." He turned to glance at me. "And I don't think I'm making any progress."

It was spring in the piedmont of North Carolina, and I was taking full advantage of the lovely mild weather to sit on the steps of my front porch to watch the world go by. Kipp, at my side as always, had been staring at his Kindle for a good hour. Occasionally, the stylus would drop from between his teeth, and he would sigh like the biggest martyr in the world, hoping I'd turn the pages for him. A woman walked by with a small, energetic dog tethered to her side with a leash. She paused at the end of my walk to smile at me, fellow dog lovers, or so she thought.

"Your dog is simply beautiful!" she gushed, showing her teeth as she waited for me to return the compliment. Her furry companion stared at Kipp and became still as he realized that Kipp, despite his canine appearance, was not a dog. It didn't take much effort for him to become entangled in his human's legs as he sought cover from something inexplicable and therefore threatening in his world.

I murmured some appropriate, expected words, and after the

dog-loving woman managed to unwrap the leash from around her legs, she continued on with her walk. The sidewalk in front of my house was uneven, the concrete broken by the stubborn roots of old trees. I hoped the lady would not trip and go flying to the ground. Ignoring Kipp, I glanced across the street and noticed that both Philo and Peter's cars were gone from Philo's driveway. Last year when my friend and boss, Philo Marshall, decided to move smack dab in my neighborhood, I'd worried that too much closeness could breed discontent. But it hadn't, and I'd found I enjoyed his company.

"Hey, are you listening to me?" Kipp asked, turning his bright amber eyes on my face. He poked my side with his long, pointed muzzle to make a point, literally.

How could I not listen to Kipp, I wondered? He was my bonded partner and as fellow symbionts in a human world, that meant quite a lot. We'd traveled back in time on many occasions to unravel mysteries and smooth out the bumps in the historical record of humanity. And since we were telepaths, I had to listen to him. A year had passed since we'd been present at the assassination of Abraham Lincoln, but for us symbionts, such a passage of time was insignificant. We were long-lived, and I'd actually been born in 1604 and had managed, with my former lupine partner, Tula, to rack up quite an impressive record of fact-finding trips in my four-hundred-plus years.

Kipp, ignoring my lack of response, turned his eyes back on his Kindle as I stared at the top of his furry head. The sun, which was at its zenith, broke through the dense canopy of green leaves, and a shimmering ray of gold discovered Kipp, who looked like a puddle of molten copper. He was much older, technically, than I, but then again, not really when one takes into account the magic of time travel. Although he'd zoomed to contemporary times from some 70,000 years distant, he was maybe only two hundred years old in real time. I thought Kipp was sulking, just a little bit, and reached over to tousle the hair on his large head. He ignored me until I tickled the spot he couldn't reach between his upright ears.

"So, back to *Ivanhoe*," he huffed, exhaling loudly as if bothered. "Explain the culture, please."

"Kipp, the setting of *Ivanhoe* predates me, also, since I'm not quite that old," I said, lifting a dark eyebrow. I knew to humans I seemed to be a young woman, maybe in my mid-to-late twenties after a night of good sleep. It was following a time-shift, when I'd returned from a visit to the past, that I felt my age. Such things tended to be more difficult as I grew older. "So, it was just like anything else involving humans. Culture and societal mores change and evolve over time. The world now does not resemble what might have existed in, let's say, the year 1100." I knew he wanted more. "The French Normans invaded England and fought the resident Saxons, going on to establish dominance over the country. That act changed the entire relationship between the people and established new rules about land ownership and that sort of thing." There was more, but he'd become distracted.

A brown SUV was pulling into Philo's driveway, and that meant Peter and his lupine partner, Elani, were home. Four symbionts sharing one house seemed like a lot to me, I thought critically, before realizing I was in the same boat. I'd opened my home to Fitzhugh and Juno, elders in need of housing at the time. Shaking my head, I berated myself for the hypocrite that I was. Kipp tensed next to me, his muscled body feeling like a coiled spring. Elani, beautiful and sleek, had jumped from the SUV and was staring our way, her plumed tail waving. Even from the distance as the sun struck her dense pelt, the fur seemed to give off an iridescent shine, and she somehow managed to sparkle, like a rare gem amongst the ordinary. And although Elani was trying to control it, waves of her feelings towards Kipp wafted across the street in the mild breeze that also brought the sweet scent of flowering plants. Spring, it seemed, brought beautiful flowers and blooming trees, as well as love.

Kipp exhaled again, forcefully. He and I shared an unusual—for contemporary times—level of access to one another's thoughts since I'd encouraged Kipp to do what was natural for him. In our current symbiont culture, such a thing was considered rude, intrusive and possibly aggressive. But even with our constant enmeshment in each other's brains, I couldn't tease out the depth of his feelings for Elani. She was bright, beautiful and kind-natured. What was there not to love?

Peter, on the other hand, was no mystery. He turned and waved his hand at us before beginning to unload groceries. I'd reluctantly become a mentor and trainer of sorts for him and Elani, and that had morphed into our working as a quartet, which was very unusual in the symbiont world, since the usual configuration was a humanoid paired with a lupine partner. But our collective at Technicorps liked to be progressive and pushed the new way of visiting the past. I knew I could be stubborn and resistant to change, but it actually had been okay, and when forced, I would admit I'd benefited from the relationship. Their youth challenged me in ways I was just beginning to comprehend.

"Are you ever going to get a new car?" Kipp asked, dropping his *Ivanhoe* queries for a moment. "Philo has a nice SUV so that he and Vashti can ride in comfort. Peter and Elani have one, too. And look at your, uh…" he struggled, trying to find a word.

"Jalopy?"

"Yes, whatever that is. I mean, you can't even take Fitzhugh and Juno to work because we can't all fit in that little heap of rust with wheels." Kipp huffed again. "You don't like change."

A tiny breeze had curled around the side of my house to ruffle my hair, pushing a tendril across my face. As my hand went to stay the errant strand, I touched the thick braid of hair at the back of my neck and realized Kipp was right. I never changed my hair style and just pulled it back into a braid for convenience, too lazy to do anything else. Glancing down, my lips tightened as I took note of the worn, faded jeans I wore and the t shirt that had a yellow paint stain on the front. Maybe I was a slob at heart and didn't know it yet? Internally I began to justify my sloth. When traveling, I often had to wear clothes that were uncomfortable, restrictive, hot, heavy and all sorts of other unpleasant adjectives. At home, I did as I pleased. I almost snorted in defiance.

"I'm willing to look at a new car," I said, surprised to hear the reluctant words spring from my mouth. "But I enjoy our walking to work," I began, turning to look at Kipp.

"I do, too, but when it's raining," he began.

"Okay, Kipp, quit pushing," I grumbled.

The door behind me opened, and the tall figure of Fitzhugh

loomed, almost casting a shadow. I craned my neck back to stare at him. Odd, even when in a good mood, he had the appearance of a foreboding wizard, ready to cast a spell upon me. He'd taken a nap, something he'd learned to enjoy of late, and was daring me to tease him about his unusual activity, since he was not given to laziness or a lack of discipline. I noticed his eyes were still a little puffy from sleep, and his long, gray hair was mussed.

"Philo invited us over for a cook-out, and I wondered if you are going to change that stained shirt into something more presentable or just go as is?" Fitzhugh's voice took on a low rumble as he summed up his opinion of me without really having to say anything more.

"Yes, dad, I plan on changing my shirt." I laughed softly as he dug his toe into my back. He wasn't my dad nor anyone else's, but it was fun to tease him.

"And you promised to make a salad," he added.

With a groan, I finally stood. "First Kipp, now you. I was just trying to enjoy this pretty day, and he is bothering me about *Ivanhoe*, and now you won't let off about my shirt and a salad. And then there is the discussion about why my car is not as nice as the ones Peter and Philo are driving. In case you've not noticed, they have car payments, and I don't." I finished in a rush.

"You're just cheap," Fitzhugh remarked. "You won't spend money on anything if you can get by with less."

"Yeah," Kipp added for emphasis.

"Okay, you guys are ganging up on me, so I plan on working on a salad, preferably in peace." I gave one last look at my yard and the surrounding neighborhood. My house was shadowed by large trees; occasionally, when the wind would blow, the canopy of leaves would part like a door opening to allow light. The house was ordinary, small, with a parlor, two bedrooms, a kitchen, and a shotgun hallway with a squeaky wooden floor. But I couldn't think of living anywhere else. Something in my heart was soothed by a compact dwelling almost hidden by the surrounding trees and shrubs. I brushed past Fitzhugh and made my way to the kitchen, which, due to the row of windows stretching the width of one wall, was cheerfully well-lit. It was clear my home would never be profiled in a magazine, as it was filled with an eclectic assortment of mismatched furniture, some of which had passed the qualification of well worn. In addition, for many humans, my tendency to crowd my dwelling with collected artifacts and broken and forlorn pieces of junk would be disturbing. But what else would one expect from a traveler between the centuries? I suppose I find some degree of comfort from those items which, at one point in time, were connected to human beings. In my fantasy moments, I speculated the objects carried with them the experiences and even feelings of previous owners. Of course, I would then and still do deny any sentimentality in regards to my behaviors.

A large salad bowl rested on the chipped tile of my kitchen counter. Another mark against me, I thought, as my lips turned down. Many people would be annoyed by the lack of perfection in the surface of the tiles, but I rather liked the fact the damage made it unique. Maybe I was just an odd symbiont with a strange way of viewing the world?

"Yes, you are peculiar," Kipp said, having followed me into the kitchen. Juno, not quite as old as Fitzhugh but close enough, was resting on the floor, her tail thumping in greeting as I entered. Kipp touched her grizzled muzzle lightly with his before choosing a place where the sunlight pooled on the worn, wooden floor and, after circling, plopped down with a heavy thump. "But I love you regardless."

I was not to have any peace since Fitzhugh trailed a moment later, followed by Lily, a feline who'd adopted Kipp. She proceeded to wind her small striped body in and out of my legs, meowing loudly as she performed perfect figure eights.

"Have you not fed her?" I asked Fitzhugh, feeling cross for no good reason.

"No, she likes it when you do it," he replied smoothly, taking a seat at the battered old dinette table that served as my fine dining room ensemble. Fitzhugh was obviously aiming to aggravate me and was doing a magnificent job. I noticed he was tracing the burn pattern made by a pot in the past, his finger-tip dragging along the top of the table. He ignored me and turned his attention to Kipp. "What is your interest in *Ivanhoe*?" he asked.

"Well, as I was reading an article about an upcoming movie, I ran across a character named Locksley, and that translated into Robin Hood. So, I have done some research and found that the character of Robin Hood could never be verified as having been an actual individual who lived. He could have been a composite of many of the outlaws who existed over a period of many years, or there could have been a discrete person with whom the legend of Robin Hood began."

"And?" Fitzhugh was smiling at Kipp.

"I asked Victor to do a library search, and he found that no symbiont has ever tried to research the truth behind the stories." Kipp glanced at me briefly before returning his attention to Fitzhugh. "I find it interesting no one has made an attempt, despite the frequency and popularity of the legend throughout human culture for many years."

I knew what was coming and began to explore my own memories of some of our collective history. The notion of a time-shift that could be filled with such complexities was challenging, and I felt my shoulders creep upward with tension. My fingers began to tear at lettuce as I took a deep breath.

"And?" Fitzhugh said, again.

"I think I am going to propose a trip to medieval England to investigate the truth behind the legend of Robin Hood," Kipp replied.

# TWO

Darkness had fallen, and our group of symbionts was gathered in Philo's back yard, where he was grilling steaks and chicken. Even I, a vegetarian when I could manage such, had to admit the aroma was intoxicating, and I tried not to laugh at Kipp drooling in response to the odors that were caught in the wind currents, tantalizingly suspended in the air. We—Kipp, Fitzhugh, Juno and I —had made our trek across the street just as twilight was falling, and the sky had darkened to a shade of deep lavender that preceded the curtain of gray to come. On the western horizon, a last orange curve of the sun was clinging to life before disappearing for the evening, diminished and defeated for the day.

Philo grabbed me around the shoulders and gave me a hasty kiss on the top of my head as he waved hello to Victor, the newest addition to the library at Technicorps, and his lupine symbiont, Fyre. I knew the only reason he'd invited them was in consideration of Vashti—his son's previous lupine partner and now Philo's casual companion -- and her attraction to Fyre. I tried not to roll my eyes as the love bug would be biting all evening. First, there was Elani and her feelings for Kipp. Now, we had Vashti and Fyre. Of course, there was nothing to prevent two lupines from bonding in our symbiont way. Humans might not understand, but our lupines have the intellectual and emotional capacity to match that of their humanoid companions, and they can and do "marry" just as we humanoids do when all the stars align. But one thing was for certain. A decision had to be made about one's life choices, and that was either to bond, humanoid and lupine, for purposes of time travel or seek the stability of marriage with a like partner. I had done both in my long life and was content to go the traveling route, despite my occasional protestations and grumbling over proposed time-shifts. I actually liked my work and could envision doing nothing else.

In any case, I was glad to see Philo looking happy again. He was my friend of longest acquaintance, and that longevity had bred complete trust between one another. When his wife left him to join their son, Silas, on a new adventure in life, Silas's lupine partner, Vashti, remained with Philo. Vashti's ethics were in constant conflict against the lack of such in Silas. I wasn't sure if she would ever choose to bond and travel again. Smiling, I admired her lovely coat of gray mottled fur and was happy over how she'd recovered physically from the time I first met her in London in 1888. That had been a life-changing trip for me, too, since a trip to locate a missing Silas had morphed into a chase after Jack the Ripper. And I met a human man and fell deeply in love. I'd lost my zest for travel after that and occasionally longed to return to the side of one William Harrow. He'd given me a necklace of pearls; my fingers went to my neck to touch the coolness and alien feel of the tiny beads. But could a long-lived member of another species, no matter her human-like appearance, live with a human male? The odds would suggest the pairing would be a difficult one. A wet nose touched my other hand, which rested at my side.

"You okay?" Kipp asked, glancing up at me. Of course, he knew my thoughts had drifted to Harrow, and he felt the squeeze of my heart in my chest as if it had been his own.

"Yes," I replied, reaching down to scratch his furry, broad head, completing the gesture with a gentle tug on his upright ear.

Fitzhugh glanced up at me from across the small patio, and even though he wasn't accessing my thoughts, I believed he recognized the expression on my face and knew my heart. We'd discussed how long the pains of lost love lingered, and he was as clueless to answer that age-old question as was I.

Peter, to keep things lively, had found a Frisbee and decided to determine which of the lupines had more game. Juno, who'd outgrown her days of rambunctious play, took her place on the lawn, resting to watch the youngsters compete. But then a potentially awkward moment occurred, and several of us collectively held our breath to see what would happen. Fyre, although youthful, had a profound limp as result of a past injury. He would not have the ability to keep up with the others. Vashti, who enjoyed a good competition, had a crush on Fyre. So, what would she do? As Fyre, a very attractive lupine with some early gray touching his brown muzzle, lay down in the fragrant grass next to Juno, Vashti hesitated before walking over as if to rest with the two.

"No," Fyre said, gazing at Vashti, his tail wagging. "I want to see what you've got."

It said a lot about Fyre that he didn't begrudge her a bit of fun, nor was he envious of the other lupines who dashed after the flying Frisbee. We all had to laugh as Kipp began to struggle to keep up with the females who benefitted from their sleeker bodies. It was obvious that Vashti was showing off, more than a little, for Fyre. After one pretty vigorous clash that left Kipp rolling in the grass, I called a halt. I knew Kipp's competitive nature, and he didn't have a shut-off valve.

"Okay, guys. Time to cool down so that we can eat in a bit." I glanced at Juno, who nodded her grizzled head in approval. It was not difficult to see that Vashti was strutting, just a little, as she walked back towards Fyre. She'd managed to put the unconquerable Kipp in his place with a firm body check.

"Are you okay, buddy?" I whispered to Kipp, using our private form of telepathy.

"Yes," he said. "At least I think so. But I feel pretty embarrassed."

"Why?"

"I'm bigger and stronger," he began.

"And sometimes it is about calculation and leverage," I replied. "Remind me to put on a Bruce Lee movie."

"Who's that?"

"You'll see."

Kipp, as well as Elani and Vashti, plopped down in the grass, taking a few moments to recover before eating. Elani, beautiful girl, was taking covert peeks at Kipp, keeping her actions veiled, lest he catch her in the act. Kipp, who was technically her supervisor at work, tried to act unconcerned and businesslike. He actually began twisting his head, looking up at the sky, his eyes following a duo of brown bats which were chasing invisible insects. Yes, I thought. Act as if you don't care, Kipp. My money was on the persistence of Elani.

"Philo, Kipp had an interesting notion about a possible time-shift to research the truth behind the Robin Hood legend," Fitzhugh said. His words caught the attention of all of us.

Philo paused in his managing of the grill to stare at Kipp, his eyebrows lifted in surprise. "Really?"

"Yes," Kipp replied. "The story of Robin Hood is a very common theme in human culture, one that has persisted since the early middle ages. And I'm intrigued by the constancy of the legends and the fact no one knows if there was a man who began it all, or if he was simply a myth created by the authors of the day."

"I don't know how you would even pinpoint a time frame from which to work, Kipp. And that would be why no one has tried. The stories, as I recall, stretch over centuries and even the locations of his alleged activities are in dispute." Philo took a sip of iced tea; the condensation was rolling off the glass in shimmering beads of water. After replacing the glass on the table, Philo dried his hands on the seat of his blue jeans. "The tales of Robin Hood were even around during my early years, things we grew up on." Philo smiled at me as I nodded since I'd had a similar experience. "He was painted as a hero, and we used to play games imitating the legend when we were young."

"Well, I've thought about how difficult it would be to select a starting point and, with Victor's help, was able to do a little research and have an idea." Kipp was resting in the grass close to Juno. He often lay close to her, resting his muzzle across her flank. Kipp never stopped missing his mother, I realized, and Juno gave him some

21

sense of that earlier bond. She was like a gentle, wise, grandmotherly type of lupine, and she had the unique distinction of being universally beloved. One might have thought that any being who'd lived as long as she might have carried some negative baggage, but it was not so with Juno. As I gazed at her, I was pretty confident I had a lot of negative baggage in my trunk.

"A man named Joseph Ritson published what he thought to be the definitive history of Robin Hood. He, Ritson, was a friend of Sir Walter Scott, who went on to include Robin Hood in his book, *Ivanhoe*." Kipp reached his massive head forward to lick fastidiously at his right forepaw, where he obviously saw something he didn't like.

"And what would you do with that information?" I asked. As I spoke, I realized I was trying to modify my tone, careful not to sound negative or critical of Kipp's plan. Peter looked my way, clearly in the throes of excitement.

"I thought that someone could go visit Ritson and find out where he got his information, which was specific as to where Robin Hood was born, when he died, and his true name. Depending upon the outcome of that interview, we might conclude that we can reasonably pinpoint a time and location to visit." Kipp glanced up at me.

"Kipp, that's pretty vague," I opined. As I felt the eyes of all present on me, I became defensive. "And I'm not being negative, just for the record book. I'm responding to this as an experienced, responsible traveler." I took a deep breath, letting it flow out slowly. "You don't plan a time-shift without a definitive starting place."

"And that is what you are supposed to do, Petra," Fitzhugh remarked. He lifted a hand to smooth his mustaches and long beard, the gray hair stretching down to his chest. "No one here questions your experience or your gameness for the chase."

I knew if Fitzhugh continued with his kind, complementary words, that tears would follow along with my embarrassment. As loved as I felt in that small group, I didn't want to cry. I confess I sometimes felt like I had lost my zest for travel and didn't want to become a burned-out hulk at my relatively young age. The stress of traveling, however, had put a dent in my energy as of late.

Since the lupines had cooled down, we stood and gathered around the table where the food was placed and took turns both preparing bowls of the chopped meat for the lupines as well as fixing our own plates. I, for one, was glad for the distraction, since it gave me distance from the feelings I'd experienced when Fitzhugh dropped a love bomb on my parade. And I was grateful when the talk went to other topics, including a construction project pending at Technicorps and the fact Philo needed a new roof and didn't I need one, too. Between Kipp wanting me to buy a car and Philo being critical of my battered roof, I felt as if I might need to find a second job.

Victor, who I'd noticed tended to be quiet and listen to everyone before issuing an opinion, stirred, catching my attention. He'd actually made a good addition to the library as an assistant to Fitzhugh after the previous one left. It had, traditionally, been a difficult position to fill due to Fitzhugh's exacting standards and overbearing presence. But Victor seemed unfazed, and I'd come to appreciate his subtle but sarcastic wit and clever attention to detail. He was very good at his research and seemed content. I sometimes wondered if he missed traveling due to Fyre's infirmity, but he didn't appear restive. Maybe he was like me to a degree. He'd seen a lot—maybe too much—and it was good to not have the stress.

"In researching Ritson, I suggested to Kipp that a pair of travelers might travel to 1795 when he published his collection of ballads about Robin Hood," Victor said. It was clear he'd continued to think about the trip while the rest of us were easily distracted by a shiny new object of conversation. "They could request an interview and during that time attempt to discover what influenced his opinions about the legend." Victor smiled. "Even if Ritson is reluctant to share, we are, after all, telepaths, and can still access his thoughts on the matter."

"What were some of those conclusions?" Juno asked.

"He thought Robin Hood was born in 1160 and was active during the time of Richard the first. He also thought Robin Hood had some aristocratic background, was born in Nottinghamshire, and had the original name of Robert Fitzooth. He even was able to give an exact date of his death."

"That seems pretty specific," Juno remarked.

"That's what I was thinking," Kipp said. "He either made it all up or got his information from some source."

The evening began to wind down, and after Victor and Fyre departed for home, the rest of us were left to relax in the lounge chairs or on the grass and watch the stars overhead. I found gazing at the sky left me drowsy and fought my eyelids drifting shut. There was always something soothing about staring up into the blackness of night, a calmness that came as darkness fell. Victor, for all his positives, didn't share our collective history, and there were untold stories and even secrets that the rest of us maintained. Kipp, due to his raw genetic history, had displayed talents unknown to modern symbiont collectives. And we, those of us left around the remains of dinner, chose when and where to share those special talents. None of us wanted Kipp to become a sideshow attraction for Technicorps.

"So, if we were seriously to consider such a trip in search of Robin Hood, would it be reasonable to make a shift back to interview Ritson?" Kipp asked. "And if that didn't bear fruit, I understand there would be no basis to continue."

I glanced at Fitzhugh, who raised his eyebrows. Leaning forward, he picked up his glass of tea and took a sip before draining the glass. Silence followed for a minute, and the yard was filled with the soft sounds of the neighborhood settling down to rest as darkness became complete; the drumbeat thrum of unseen insects intensified as we became cocooned by the night. From a short distance away, we could hear the caterwauling of an owl in the nearby woods echoing against the backdrop of homes and habitation. Overhead, a silvered crescent moon was bright against an inky sky.

"I'd like to propose first we do more research on Ritson himself and see if we can, from reading his publications, divine more information." Fitzhugh nodded at Kipp. "Perhaps we can use the library to pull together some data and give it to you to study."

Kipp nodded his head, and I was happy to see he was being reasonable. I knew once he got a head of steam in his boiler, he could be a formidable presence to obstruct.

We finally put an end to the festivities, and Fitzhugh, Juno, Kipp and I returned home. I was enjoying the evening but noticed Juno was yawning excessively and pleaded fatigue since I knew she wouldn't. Fitzhugh and Juno almost immediately went to their room, while Kipp and I retired to ours, where I enjoyed the sounds that accompanied nightfall, sounds that carried a quality alien to the rest of us. My bedroom window was ajar, the aperture covered by plantation blinds for privacy, a gentle breeze rattling the wood. As always, Kipp lay next to me, his head heavy across my chest. Not all symbionts were as close, and as I recalled, Tula had preferred her old woolen blanket on the floor next to the dark void of my closet. I knew Kipp didn't think of me as his mother, but there was something in our relationship that met his need to be nurtured. I didn't mind, and obviously some need of mine was met, too.

We spent some more time digesting *Ivanhoe*, which was not a particularly easy book to read. Many of the references were archaic, and unless there were annotations, the meanings would be lost to contemporary readers. Fortunately, I'd lived during the times when *Ivanhoe* was written and could manage to plow through most of it. But the work had become tedious, and finally, I'd put the Kindle away. Kipp drifted off just before me, and I lay there staring at the ceiling, unable to sleep; my thoughts were busy considering a possible time-shift and all the positives as well as negatives.

Kipp was restless, moving in his sleep, moaning a little, his lower jaw sagging as he began to pant. In the tangled world of dreams, Kipp was back on board the *Titanic* again, and facing us was the young woman calmly walking her Great Dane as the deck began to tilt. Around us, people milled, anxiety and fear welling to the point of contagion. In Kipp's dream, the woman's eyes met mine and she smiled, thinking she and I were in the same boat, literally. Neither of us would be permitted to take our canine companions on board a lifeboat and neither of us would leave without our companions. Of course, I had another method of exit through the gift of time travel, and she didn't. The Dane's dark eyes met Kipp's, and even though he knew Kipp was no dog, he wagged his tail; he was a friendly, affable beast.

As the nightmare continued, I pondered my choices. There were three that I considered. First, I could do nothing and allow Kipp to struggle and, perhaps, resolve an internal issue. Second, I could enter his dream telepathically and change the outcome. Third, I could awaken him. I chose the latter, since I had not the heart to let him hurt and couldn't figure out a way to manipulate the dream to a happy ending. There was nothing about the *Titanic* that was happy.

"Kipp," I murmured softly, placing my lips next to his ear.

"What?" he awoke suddenly, filled with confusion. Kipp tried to sit up, but I gently pushed at his shoulder.

"No, it's not time to get up," I whispered.

He settled back and placed his head on my chest, allowing me to gently stroke his head.

"Petra, I know I've given you a hard time over your reluctance to take on some of these tougher trips, but I'm getting a better understanding of your feelings. These do take a psychological toll on us, don't they?"

I didn't answer his question since the response was obvious.

"And considering the fact you've traveled for many more years than have I, I can only imagine some of the, uh, baggage you carry with you." He pushed his jaw into my chest, almost to the point of pain. "I've been only consumed with the pursuit of the elusive goal and not attentive enough to the anxiety and pain that follows."

I tugged on his ears and kissed the side of his furry face.

"Juno talked to me the other day and tried to make a point so that I would be more sensitive to your feelings. I think this dream was, well, meant to be."

I smiled to myself. Kipp was always sensitive to me. He had to be, as entangled in my brain as was he. Kipp had the ability to know my thoughts and feelings as well as the true intent behind the words. We lacked the ability to hide from one another. I couldn't imagine life any other way.

"Go back to sleep, Kipp," I said softly. "It's still early."

He actually fell asleep within three minutes, but I was wide awake, staring at the dark ceiling above me. Outside, a soft rain had begun to fall; the sound of the water hitting the roof felt like a charm cast by a magician, lulling me into a hypnotic state. From what seemed to be a great distance away, thunder rumbled. Life for symbionts, just as with humans, was tenuous, uncertain and always in flux. Of course, we created much of our drama by inserting ourselves into past history and doing so with a soft footprint so as not to disturb the dust of antiquity. But it was what we did as a species. I suppose, like all other creatures, we were just carrying out what the Creator meant for us to do. So as not to awaken Kipp, I gently placed my hand on his chest, where I could feel his heart beat, slow, steady and strong. It was grounding, as was all contact with Kipp.

# THREE

It was Saturday, with no work responsibilities looming overhead, and Kipp and I had decided upon an early morning jog out into the countryside. I could linger in bed like anyone else, enjoying the smell of brewing coffee or steeping Earl Grey tea, compliments of Fitzhugh, but I admit I enjoyed sunrise. I'm not sure which I like best, sunrise or sunset. I guess I still possess enough of the adventurous spirit in me that sunrise, with its breathless, unspoken promise of the day, will always be exciting.

As we left the house, the birds, which seemed active as they, too, stirred, were making sufficient racket to awaken the whole neighborhood. Neither Kipp nor I spoke as the last of the houses fell behind, and we entered the softly rolling hillsides of the country. Since it was spring, the green hills were dotted with various wildflowers, which seemed to have been tossed to earth by a careless hand, and it delighted the eye to find a patch of blue here, yellow there, and some pink splashes in between. Nature had a way of making the unexpected and mismatched come together to form a perfect whole. As I breathed deeply, I could taste the sweetness of the blooming flowers lingering on the back of my tongue like a drop of amber honey. The sun had angled over the horizon and was on the rise, a large, orange ball against a cloudless sky that suggested a warm day to come. There was a flash of color overhead as a bird darted past, its wings bright red against a tablet of blue. There was no wind, and the trees seemed heavy and still, the branches bent with thick foliage.

We made our way without conscious planning to the graveyard where my young son rested. I'd once avoided going there, unable to stand the pain and finding that pretending nothing had ever happened suited me well. But Kipp, bossy as ever, had made me remember, and I was grateful. Going to visit with George was something I now appreciated. Stopping our jog, we walked slowly underneath the arching, iron entryway and made our way up the hillside. I'm not sure why, but it felt disrespectful to run, willy nilly, amongst the headstones, so I usually threaded my way carefully and with a sober attitude, gazing at the granite markers and their sentiments, occasionally nodding my head to acknowledge the love left behind. The artistry of old tombstones was lost in the modern day, I'd found. The thoughts of that loss of poetry mixed with grief and hope for an afterlife made me feel thoughtful, not quite sad, but just ruminative.

On the backside of the hill, there was a row of graves, unmarked, from the American Civil War. Kipp stumbled down that grassy slope one day and discovered he had a sensitivity to the souls who remain with us as ghosts. That discovery had led us down some places that were not comfortable, and collectively we and our small inner circle had put a stop to ghostly investigations for the time being. I noticed he didn't visit those graves anymore when we came to spend time with George. Although the day was bright, an unexpected shadow veiled the hillside in gray as a solitary cloud was chased across the sky, hiding the sun for a few moments until the sun emerged again, more brilliant and intense than before.

I sat on the grass next to George's marker, letting my hand touch the cold granite, which was damp from the early morning dew. My fanny would be equally damp when I stood to leave, but I didn't care. It was good to sit on that lonely hillside, and I was never sure why a graveyard did seem so quiet, but they always were. Not to be morbid, but they could be a good place from which to view the world. Kipp, after nosing around a few minutes, returned to my side, and I draped my arm across his broad back; his fur was warm from both the exercise as well as the rays of the sun that had been captured amongst the dense hairs of his pelt. His breathing, along with mine, had slowed, and the sounds of his soft panting diminished, leaving us in silence.

"Kipp, what did you get from Victor and Fitzhugh about Joseph Ritson?" I asked, having made a deliberate choice to be uninvolved. After all, if Kipp was interested in investigating Robin Hood, he needed to do the work. Elani had researched the last trip, so maybe it was time for Kipp to do so for the next one. I was comfortable being the caboose on that particular train.

"Joseph Ritson was born in 1752 and died in 1803. He published what many felt to be the definitive, to that day, collection of all the stories and songs, poems and ballads that had been compiled in folklore dating from the late 1100's. He was convinced that Robin Hood had his origins as an actual historical figure. Where his thoughts differed from some others, who thought Robin Hood was a yeoman, Ritson believed Robin Hood to be of aristocratic extraction who probably could have claimed the title of the Earl of Huntingdon. He was born in a village called Locksley in Nottinghamshire. Ritson felt he had sufficient information to claim Robin Hood died in 1247."

Kipp sighed and pushed close, wanting me to scratch his back where he had an itchy spot. There was an unexpected moving shadow, and I glanced up at the sky, my eyes following the path of a large bird circling overhead. It appeared to be a buzzard, looking for a meal. I hoped Kipp and I didn't appear inviting.

"Sir Walter Scott was influenced by Ritson, and the two met more than once over their lifetimes." Kipp took a deep breath. "There would be a tight window for us to interview Ritson. He published his collection in 1795, but in 1796 he had a mental collapse of some sort and barricaded himself inside his chambers in Gray's Inn in London and set the room on fire." Kipp glanced at me, and the sunlight was caught in his eyes, which seemed back lit by some internal energy source. "He was confined to a mental institution after that."

I sat quietly, lost in speculation, wondering what could have happened to a successful man to drive him to the edge of reason. Kipp responded to my thoughts.

"I couldn't really figure out what happened to him," Kipp said.

"So, what would be your angle of attack?" I leaned back, propped on my elbows, enjoying the early sun on my face. Later it would be too hot and too intense, but now was just right. Before I could stop myself, the mama bear analogy flooded my mind.

"Hey, you never did tell me about mama bear," Kipp whined.

"Another time, please. I'm concentrating."

"I thought that we could go back to late 1795 and concoct a way to finagle an interview with Ritson, using Peter as a reporter, perhaps, interested in his work. Hopefully, he will speak with Peter, and we can try and figure out how he obtained his information." Kipp sighed. "Even if we don't get what we're looking for, it would be good practice for Peter and Elani."

I sighed, closing my eyes against the golden sunlight. The warmth felt good against the thin flesh of my eyelids, and I almost imagined I could see the sun, bright, defined and staring back at me. "Kipp, that would be a lot of work just to see if we need to take a time-shift. You'd have to convince the Twelve of its worth since we'd have to be wardrobed for the times." I frowned. "I can almost see Karl's face."

"Well, I'm not worried about Karl," Kipp answered crisply. "It's his job to supply the correct wardrobe as well as other essentials, and if he has a problem, he can speak to Philo."

"Yeah, but you don't have to wear what he creates. And it can be comfortable or excruciating, depending upon his mood." I laughed. "You just have to wear the despised money collar."

Kipp twisted his head as he thought of the confining collar. To say he despised it was not sufficient.

"Here are some other issues," I said. "And I'm really not being negative. I'm just giving you tips since you'll have to work up this pitch for the Twelve's approval." To make sure he heard me, I ran my hand down his furry back. "Peter and I would have to take a course in Old English. I was born after that time and in a different country with a different language. The French I can manage, but not the Old English." Kipp was watching me. "You'll need to find us an online course or something." My elbows were beginning to burn, so I sat up straight, brushing the dirt and grass clippings from my skin. "And we'd all have to extensively study the culture of the day, which will be vastly different from anything else we've experienced. Remember, dogs were not allowed in the king's forests, and those that were present had toes cut from their front paws so they couldn't chase deer." I tweaked his ear. "I wouldn't want you to come home with some trimmed toes."

Kipp shuddered. "What sort of barbarism was that?" He bared his teeth. "Anyone tries to trim my toes, better watch out." Kipp's nostrils flared as he considered the alternatives. "I'm not normally given to violence, you know, but I can't make any promises."

I laughed. "Not to change the subject too suddenly, but how's the supervisor gig going?"

Kipp had, in the past year, been promoted to a supervisory position as well as teaching ethics. And that was all good and fine, but now he was in the place he had to supervise Elani, who adored him, and not from afar. He became quiet, and I figured I'd touched a nerve. Sometimes Kipp had to be pushed, just a little bit. Then he sighed.

"I guess it is okay. I took it as a compliment when they promoted me, but it's hard work being fair with the lupines. They whine and complain a lot … you know how kids can be. And I'm trying to find a good fit for Fyre, but that hasn't worked out yet."

"How's Elani doing?" I asked, trying to be subtle.

"She is a good teacher with the lupines, but I think she needs to infuse a little more action into the day so that they don't get bored. I tried to tell her that, and she got angry with me."

I bit back a smile. "I've never wanted to supervise anyone, Kipp, so I commend your willingness to do so. Symbionts, as well as people, don't necessarily embrace criticism, even when they say they do."

"And?" he asked, knowing there was more.

"Kipp, we both know Elani has an immense crush on you. So, your approval means a lot to her on a personal basis. And, no, you can't help that," I said in a rush. "But you have to be aware of it and be sensitive."

"Maybe I'll just tell Philo to put me back where I was and get someone else to be in charge." He grunted and shrugged his shoulder, twisting his neck to relieve the tension.

"Well, you did just give me an idea. There needs to be a non-traveler who can back you up when you're gone. And Juno won't do it, because she subs in for Elani during time-shifts. How about considering Fyre?"

Kipp turned to look at me. His amber eyes had a distinctly honey-toned cast in the sunlight and almost glowed. "Petra, I don't give you credit enough for good ideas, but you just hatched one."

"Gee, thanks." Changing the subject, I asked, "So what did you think about Bruce Lee?" We'd watched a couple of his movies the previous night, much to the entertainment of Kipp and Juno.

"I still don't know how he managed to jump in the air high enough to kick out a ceiling fixture," Kipp replied, shaking his head. "But your point was well taken. He didn't use size or brute force to win a fight."

"You're welcome, wee grasshopper."

The sun was in the beginning phase of its daily arc, but I felt little motivation to move. Kipp and I watched, amused, as a gray squirrel cautiously moved close, looking for something he'd obviously hidden in the past. He'd dig furiously, then sit back on his haunches, bemused, before darting a foot to the right and trying again. Occasionally, he'd glance up at Kipp, not sure if Kipp was about to pounce. Finally, he bounded off, zig-zagging across the field until he found safety in a tree. Kipp's hulking presence was too much.

We made our way back home, a little more energized than usual. The front of my house, usually thought of as gently neglected, looked pretty good, and the whispered criticisms of my human neighbors had subsided. Fitzhugh had done a nice job of painting the door and the frame, and with help from Philo and Peter, the shrubs had been trimmed back, and the windows were at least visible now. As I gazed at it, I realized that the house was just a temporary possession. At some point, those of my kind were moved somewhere else. Our lack of obvious aging in a human world made us conspicuous. In ancient times, symbionts could easily be thought of as supernatural, and that just simply didn't bode well. As it was in contemporary life, we still stayed hidden from humans. As much as I like humans and have had close friendships and at least one serious love interest, they could not know of our capabilities. We could never be made to travel back in time to serve humanity in order to change history for a political or financial reason. The mere concept was contrary to our set of values and purpose. And, yes, there had been corrupt symbionts as we are just as imperfect as humans. But I would like to think we do try to stick to a code of ethics.

"Did you have a nice run?" Fitzhugh's voice met me as I opened the door, allowing Kipp to brush past my legs. The overhead fan was slowly turning; the room felt pleasantly cool, and a breeze that carried with it the scent of grass and flowers worked its way from the front of the house to the back, where it exited through the kitchen windows.

"Yes, very good." I took a seat at the dinette and waited, since he was preparing morning tea. "Hi, Juno," I greeted the elder symbiont. She wagged her tail as she found a nice spot on the floor. Odd, all the spots looked the same to me, but she seemed to have a decision tree at work as she circled and carefully eased herself down on the wooden plank flooring.

"Kipp and I were talking about the Robin Hood time-shift and tossing around ideas about how to approach it." I paused as Fitzhugh placed the teapot on the table to let the brew steep. I bit back a smile as he carefully set out the teacups, which were pretty, fragile things, and a pot of honey for me, since he knew I was a heathen and liked honey in my tea. From his point of view, one might add cream or sugar, or even a delicately sliced sliver of lemon in a pinch, but honey was for those of us who lacked in tradition.

"Well, from our research in the library, it would make sense to start with Ritson and conduct an interview," Fitzhugh said, after making a big production of fixing his tea to his perfecting standards.

"What if we travel back and Ritson won't speak with us? Or, we meet with him and it is a bunch of worthless information?" I poured my tea, adding a big spoonful of honey. The earthy bergamot scent from the Earl Grey became sweeter in my imagination and filled the air. "What then?"

"Well, you'd be in a position that other symbionts have shared in that the trip you envisioned evaporates." Fitzhugh shrugged his shoulders. "Nothing lost, nothing gained." He smiled. "There is one gain," he added. "Peter and Elani would get a little more experience under their belts." He laughed. "And Peter would have to wear knee pants and hose, and I can't think of anything more interesting than his reaction to that prospect."

I laughed. I'd lived through those times and recalled the fashions. The positive was that, for once, I would get off relatively light, as the women's clothes were fairly comfortable. As I thought back, I recalled an empire waist and flowing skirts with no hoops or nasty corsets. Yes, I wouldn't have to fuss and complain. And that might be a novel experience for everyone involved.

"Fitzhugh, you don't think this is a total waste of time, do you?" Kipp asked. He had chosen a spot near Juno and gazed up at us from the floor.

I was glad we respected and valued our elders. There seemed to be a growing trend amongst some human cultures to find elders to be nonessential. Instead of relying upon information shared down through the generations, things were easily found on computers and tablets, and the days of sitting around the circle of expertise to learn an important skill were gone. It was a sad trend, and I'm thankful we steered clear of it. My concern for humanity was that tossing traditions as easily as discarding a piece of trash would one day come back to haunt people. There was more to be lost than they conceived. And I say that as a very long-lived being, one who has seen a lot over the centuries.

"No, Kipp, I don't, and if I did, I would say so. I actually think it would be a fascinating trip, not only to pursue the myth of Robin Hood but also for you to experience the culture of the day. For Peter and Elani, this could be a critical, life-altering time-shift that helps them grow in experience and confidence." Fitzhugh sat back and his dark eyes met mine. A thin wisp of white hair had drifted over his forehead, and I leaned forward, taking the liberty to push it into place. He winked at me. "We ease our young ones into these difficult things nowadays. When you and I started," he nodded a Juno, "we just were thrown into the lion's cage. You, too, Petra."

My relationship with Fitzhugh was one of growth and accommodation for us both. Once, he'd been my most vocal critic, and I felt like a child under the supervision of a rigid taskmaster. Unfortunately, my tendency to oppose authority led to clashes that were unpleasantly memorable. But now we were comfortable with one another and sharing secrets that I didn't even take to Philo's doorstep. Fitzhugh enjoyed our intimacy, as did I. And it was not a romantic relationship, for the cynical who believe all close relationships must be so. Although I liked to think that he was once a pretty fine catch in the symbiont world—and still could be if he weren't so entrenched in his way of doing things -- Fitzhugh had spoken of a human woman he'd once loved, but that was many centuries in the past, and he seemed pretty much done after that. I didn't blame him. I felt the same post-William Harrow.

"Petra, are you listening to me?" Fitzhugh's query was a tad irritating since I'd been caught musing about other topics. No one likes to get caught.

"Yes, of course," I lied. Glancing at Juno, I saw she was smiling at me in the lupine manner, enjoying seeing me nabbed in an obvious awkward moment of untruths. I grinned back at her. "I do need some more tea," I said, pushing my cup towards Fitzhugh.

"Kipp, I'm happy to help you work up your application for the Twelve to review." Fitzhugh nodded at my partner. "I'll ask Victor to continue to review the archives for anything that might be helpful and bolster your claim that this is a worthwhile trip. And I think adding in the aspect that Peter and Elani could grow under an enhanced challenge, but do so under your and Petra's supervision, could be a good angle to include."

Kipp nodded, but I knew, from our long association, that he was still unsettled. So, I waited. He finally looked up at me. "Petra and I were talking about the toll that traveling takes on one's, uh, soul, and I think I'm finally understanding that after our *Titanic* shift, as well as the last one." He was referring to the assassination of Lincoln. Kipp sighed. "I know this would be a complicated time-shift due to the need to learn language and culture, and I don't want to do it unless everyone is completely on board."

I knew he was speaking of me but decided to let him be more

direct when he was ready. Fitzhugh raised his heavy eyebrows and glanced at me.

"Well, you know that Peter and Elani will be pushing to go because they are young and have no sense," Fitzhugh said, laughing. "All of us were like that once." He glanced at Kipp. "And you want to go, Kipp. That leaves Petra, so I think you need to ask her directly."

It took Kipp a full minute. "Petra, will you feel pushed to go knowing how I feel?"

"No, Kipp, I won't. I told you already that I'm still ready to travel and haven't hung up my valise yet." I smiled at him. "You'll be the first to know."

# FOUR

I was a little surprised that the Twelve seemed gung-ho over such a nebulous time-shift, but they were in constant competition with other collectives to do something that would blow the others out of the water, figuratively speaking. Such an ostentatious display was always a motivating factor. And that quality summed up one of the commonalities we share with humans. We, too, like to be successful and occasionally wear a feather in the cap. A very large feather.

Of course, the first step was to try and locate Joseph Ritson, and to do that, we had to shift to 1795 London and make our way to Gray's Inn and hope for an interview with the man. Since he apparently lost his reason and his sanity in 1796, it seemed reasonable to visit late in the year in December 1795. To be truthful, we were taking a chance we could connect with Ritson. And with that in mind, the four of us—Peter, Elani, Kipp and I—found ourselves in Karl's workroom being fitted for the first leg of our journey. Over the years, I'd spent many hours in that particular room, which smelled of old books, dust, piled-up fabric and machinery oil. It was with effort I restrained my sneezing.

Kipp and Elani always got by pretty easily, since they wore a money collar and had no other equipment needs. No reasonable person, we figured, would try and remove the collar from such massive lupines, and no one, to date, had made that attempt. As a matter of practicality as well as convenience, our furry companions carried our back-up currency in case we got in a bind. Peter had, up to that point, been fortunate in terms of clothing, which had entailed breeches, shirt, tie, coat and a hat of some type. About the worst complaint he had was about the hats, since he liked to say he didn't have a hat head, whatever that meant. I think he just didn't like to compress and conceal that wonderful pelt of dark hair that adorned his skull. And I, being female, had struggled due to the way that humans had decided to bind women's bodies and force the female form into contortions that were not designed by nature. I had actually lived through all the fashion reincarnations once and didn't care for repeating myself, but such was the life of a symbiont. My lips tightened at Peter's dismay as he realized that on the trip to 1795 England, he'd be the one who would suffer.

"Are you kidding me?" Peter asked, rolling his eyes at Karl.

"Do I look like I'm kidding?" Karl had taken over wardrobing and outfitting us for our time-shifts when the skilled Suzanne left our collective for love and adventure in Alpharetta, Georgia. Karl, I'd found, had no sense of humor, but his saving grace was that he was talented. He blinked his black eyes, which made me think of those of a reptile, and pursed his lips, a habit he displayed when annoyed. Almost without thought, Karl's hand drifted up to push the thin comb-over of hair to cover his balding spot. And all I can say is that I usually saw a lot of lip pursing, so I figured he was annoyed with me most of the time. I tried not to giggle at Peter and glanced at Elani, who studiously was staring at the wall. Kipp was no help, since his words kept echoing in my head. "Peter's wearing knee pants. Ha, ha, ha!"

"Well-dressed men in that time wore stockings on their legs and pants that went only to their knees. Now, if you want to dress like a street tough or chimney sweep, I can certainly create some tattered, well-used clothing that will make you look like a local worker." Karl put his hands on his hips and came close to sounding a mite petulant. "I thought the idea was that you wanted to play the part of a gentleman interviewing a gentleman."

"Yes, it is," Peter finally admitted, nodding his head. He seemed resigned to conceding defeat as his heavy forelock of dark hair fell over his eyes.

I, for once, was happy, since I would be free of some of the bizarre foundation garments that I'd had to wear in the past. However, I did have fond memories of a bustle I once wore that concealed within its basket a hidden cache of money. I called it my bustle bank, and it had been a clever creation of Suzanne. Karl was working on a soft woolen gown with an empire waist that left me breathing in freedom. For the times, all that was required was a chemise underneath, and women didn't wear actual underpants. However, due to my life spent in the twentieth century, I'd become accustomed to my drawers, had become appreciative of that tradition, and planned on wearing a pair anyway. How would anyone know unless someone peeked up my skirt? I figured I'd have to ditch them for the next leg of our journey, so why not indulge my need while I could manage it?

"Lighten up, Peter," Kipp finally said, after he mastered his humor. "You have really nice-looking legs, so you should be proud to show them off." He began to giggle again and stared at Elani, trying to provoke her to do the same. I saw her muzzle tremble, just a bit, as she clamped her teeth together firmly.

"Come on, Kipp," I said. "Let's go outside for a bit." As much fun as we were having with Peter, I didn't want it to go too far.

"And what's a cravat?" Kipp asked after we left the workroom.

"Something Peter won't like any more than the knee pants," I replied.

With Kipp at my side, we wound our way along the corridors of Technicorps until I found the familiar exit door that led to the garden out back. It had always been a favorite place of mine, and I'd spent many hours, collectively, on the lichen-covered bench situated beneath a towering tulip poplar. The groundskeepers kept the area groomed but with a natural appeal, and there were azaleas and large, bushy crepe myrtles that began to bloom after the blush of spring had faded. It felt cool beneath the trees, the sunlight only filtering through the leaves above to strike the earth in wavering strands of soft yellow. While I sat on the bench, Kipp conducted an instinctive survey of the area, using his infinitely more talented nose and ears to scan the ground and shrubs. A bird above was noisily scolding him, and I figured there was a nest nearby.

"Kipp, don't go near that azalea," I cautioned. "I think there is a brown thrasher nest, and the parents are agitated. Any closer and they will be dive bombing on your head."

"Okay," he replied, returning to me. After checking the ground for debris, he circled and plopped down in the mulch of old leaves and pine straw. "Although, why they would put a nest so close to the ground, I can't figure that reasoning. They're just asking for a predator to take advantage of an easy situation."

Because I enjoyed languages and being proficient was helpful to me in my part-time gig in the library where I translated old documents associated with past time-shifts, I'd gotten a jump start on Old English after Peter managed to find us an online course. The language was interesting to me, and with my background in other languages, it was easy to see the roots of how Old English began and even more, after the Normans invaded, the influence of French on the evolution of modern English. I don't like to brag, but I am fluent in French, Spanish, German, Icelandic, Russian, and Greek. Over my lifetime, I'd managed to perfect some regional dialects, too, which made me a favorite to by Fitzhugh when those of us struggling over some obsolete phrase would hit a snag.

There were steps behind me, soft against the ground, but I didn't have to turn to identify my visitor. I guess that is one advantage of telepathy as well as very close association with another symbiont over a number of years. It was Philo, who'd spied me from his office window. I glanced up and noted his shoulders were slightly slumped. Without reading my thoughts, he obviously knew what was on my mind and quickly corrected his posture to an almost military rigidity.

"You know I have to join you when I see you enjoying this nice weather," he said with a soft laugh. Without asking, he sat next to me, our shoulders lightly touching. "This is much better than being confined inside." His lips turned down for a second.

I often suspected others wondered if there might be a love match between the two of us one day, but that was impossible. I thought of him like a brother, and I knew his thoughts towards me never ran towards the romantic. And both of us were too smart to disrupt what we did have, and that was something good.

"How are things coming along in terms of preparing for the first phase of your adventure?" Philo asked, directing his inquiry to Kipp.

"Peter's being fitted for knee pants, panty-hose and something called a cravat, and Petra's trying to learn Old English," Kipp answered, cutting a glance at me.

Philo let his head drop back as he laughed. And it was good to see him like that. He'd struggled after his marriage collapsed, and in many ways, he lost his family, since he was estranged from his son, too. But moving out of his former house that contained too many memories and importing Vashti, as well as Peter and Elani, into his home, had not allowed him any time for sad reflections.

"I love spring," he remarked. "But I always look forward to autumn and getting to walk with you in Duke Forest," Philo said, his eyes meeting mine. Reaching forward, he pulled a blossom that had fallen from one of the trees and was snagged in my dark hair. The sound of a lawn mower buzzed, and I could smell the earthy, organic fragrance of fresh-cut grass. The leaves overhead rustled, disturbed by a persistent, nagging wind.

"Yeah, but if this trip goes as I suspect, we may not be here in the fall," I answered.

"There will be other falls," Philo responded. He stared off across the green lawn, which seemed even greener due to abundant rain that had fallen late the previous winter. I knew if I waited, there would be more. Philo and I had the conventional symbiont relationship in that I didn't just barge in on his private thoughts. And it finally came.

"I wonder if living with me is going to be enough for Vashti," he began, taking a deep breath. "She was accustomed to traveling, and now she is stuck with me in my boring, no adventure household."

"Well, it is pretty dull," I began before digging my elbow in his side. "What's making you wonder about her?"

"I don't know."

"My thoughts, in case you want to know, are that Vashti is very bright and assertive and will let you know what she wants to do." I paused to let him consider my words. "I don't think you need to spend a great deal of time trying to read her mind or anticipate her needs." I laughed softly. "And haven't you seen how she looks at Fyre? I think she's really happy right where she is for now."

"That's true, I suppose." He sighed again. "I don't want to hold her back, that's all." Philo was sounding a little defensive.

I knew something else was bothering him and decided to wait him out. He became quiet as we sat, side by side, gazing off at the landscape. Mama or daddy brown thrasher landed lightly on the ground a few feet away, seemingly oblivious to the large figure of Kipp, who lay unmoving, his russet muzzle pressed down into a clump of leaves. The big bird puffed out its spotted chest and began to flick debris aside with its bill in a search of a meal. I glanced at Philo and saw a smile pull at the corner of his mouth. He was enjoying the solitude and companionship simultaneously.

"I think I worry about you, Petra," Philo began, his words halting as he struggled to share his thoughts. "I realize I've never traveled, but the idea of the risks you take is troubling to me."

"Has it always been so?" I asked. Kipp caught my eye and, without being obvious to Philo, shot me a big, hovering question mark to lodge in my brain. He, too, wondered where the discussion was leading.

"More so now, I think," Philo responded.

I sat for a while, not certain how to proceed. Finally, I took a deep breath. "Do you think that the loss of Claire and Silas has anything to do with your feelings?"

He didn't answer for a minute, but I felt him stiffen next to me. I'd hit a nerve without trying.

"Why would that have anything to do with you?"

"Philo, you moved across the street. We've always been friends, but I think you have established a new family by the move, and it includes me, Kipp, Juno, Fitzhugh, Vashti, Peter, Elani, and even silly Lily." I paused. "I think you worry more about all of us now."

His lips compressed as he considered my words. Symbionts share another quality with humans. Sometimes, we don't enjoy the feeling of emotional vulnerability. And having a close friend slap you with such a notion could be difficult.

"Is he okay?" Kipp asked, speaking to me privately as was our habit.

"Yes. He just is taking care of emotional baggage, Kipp. But he'll be okay." I closed one eye at Kipp, who wagged his tail.

Philo caught the tail wag and turned to stare at me. "Are you guys talking about me?"

I widened my eyes. "Why no, Philo. That would be horribly rude." But then I began to laugh softly. "Of course, we are, you goof. We're worried about you."

"Yuk," he replied, rolling his eyes. "I don't want that. And you don't need to, and I'll tell you how things are. I'm actually happy right now. And I had not been happy for a long time. So, you two can relax your guard."

"Okay, boss," I replied, giving a mock salute. Deciding it was time to change the subject, I asked him something regarding our business. "Why on earth did the Twelve approve this time-shift?"

He shrugged his shoulders. "You know how it is. The Twelve want us to be the most progressive, edgy collective on earth." Philo's dark eyes darkened a bit more as he frowned. "They don't seem to mind that our traveling pairs are put at risk through such nonsense."

"What's wrong with you?" I asked, as he jerked his head around to stare at me. "Risk is what we do, by our very nature. And any symbiont pair has the right and responsibility to decline a time-shift that looks ill-advised."

Kipp spoke up. "That's the way I view it, Philo. Actually, I think the Twelve holds us back by being too cautious." His amber eyes were bright, as they usually were when he felt passionately about a subject.

Philo laughed softly. "Spoken from the mouth of a true adventurer, Kipp. I don't think there is anything from which you'd shy away."

"That may not be true," Kipp responded, "but I do think we have to follow our instincts and do what we do best."

"I'm talking like an old, way too cautious symbiont," Philo acknowledged. "Maybe I do just want to keep those I cherish close to me."

"Well, you know, we'll be back, all four of us." I pushed against his shoulder. "Snap out of it."

"You promise?"

"Yes, I do."

"Well, you better. I've just gotten Peter to agree to do half of the cleaning at home, and I don't want to lose that sweet deal."

It was only a few days later when we had a scheduled leaving party. That particular jump to 1795 was planned to be brief, targeted, and didn't require extensive planning. Kipp and Peter did the research on what was known about Ritson, and we'd been to London in the past, so that part was not a challenge. Kipp was unsurpassed in his ability to target a time and location better than any symbiont I'd known. I figured I would play a minor role in that part of our exploration since Peter would be the one seeking an interview. In other words, other than getting my clothing together, I relaxed.

Karl had supplied Peter and me with a main set of clothing as well as outerwear and a few articles to help freshen up the look if we were delayed a few days. I only hoped that if we arrived in London, Ritson wouldn't be on a journey to the continent or some such nonsense. Everyone involved knew this was a pretty wild try at something that hadn't been done before, so if we failed, I didn't think it would smudge our reputations. But no symbiont liked to have a failure tagged on his or her portfolio. All that was left was a small leaving party, and since we were hoping to only be gone a couple of days, then return home to plan further, hopefully, for Robin Hood, small seemed appropriate.

I'm not certain when the leaving party tradition began, but it basically was a lot of work for the traveler, who was compelled to entertain friends and family. The party was a nice send-off and probably had evolved due to worry over the departure into the unknown of the traveling pair. What we did was dangerous work, and the leaving party lightened the mood lest it become dark and somber.

I glared at Kipp, who lay on the kitchen floor, lounging, doing nothing. He wagged his tail and didn't even bother to offer his usual teasing comment about lacking thumbs. However, I'd enlisted the help of Peter, since he did have hands rather than paws. Glancing at Peter, I realized I'd developed a fondness for him from the time I'd first met him in Fitzhugh's library, where he toiled, unhappy with the tedium of the work. He'd seemed to be a bit of an unmotivated slacker, but it was only because he had not found his true vocation.

"What?" Peter asked, catching my eyes on him. Self-consciously, he pushed his heavy mop of dark hair off his forehead, where it lay, like the unruly forelock of a wild pony. He'd grown a nice beard again in anticipation of our time-shifts, and it made him look older than his fifty-plus years. In symbiont years, he was still just a kid. And where he could be impulsive and brash, Elani made the perfect counterbalance since she was, by nature, more deliberative.

"You've grown on me," I said, smiling.

"Do I take that as a compliment?" he replied, returning my smile.

"Oh, yes." I returned my attention to the crockpot of vegetable chili. I received no personal validation from cooking—which I saw as a necessary chore -- and applauded when the crockpot was invented. If it could be reasonably assembled in a crockpot, then I was a happy camper. Despite the collective groups of carnivores who outnumbered me, the chili was always popular, and there would be some left over for Fitzhugh. The kitchen carried the savory scent of the spices which drifted into the front room, which once upon a time might have been called a parlor. Fitzhugh was there, lighting a few candles, since our guests would arrive shortly. The idea of a leaving party also entailed a rather vigorous roast of the symbionts, and I'd been a target for quite some time. I could only hope all my bad and humiliating actions had been revealed and that I had no secrets left to expose.

Elani was resting on the floor near Kipp, her active mind at rest. She'd shown the most rapid evolution to traveler that I'd ever witnessed. And the best quality about her was that she was fearless to explore the boundaries of her lupine skills, having been motivated by the unusual qualities displayed by Kipp. She'd shown enough trust in us to reveal her inherited skill to learn about the qualities of a human by physical touch. And that was something even the talented Kipp could not manage. I thought it was interesting that of the four of us, two lupines and two humanoids, the ones with the broadest array of skills were the lupines. Peter and I could manage time-shifts and telepathy, but that was about it. Well, maybe not quite. I'd found I could manipulate dreams, too.

The front door opened; I could hear the voices of Philo, who'd brought Vashti, of course, as well as inviting Victor and Fyre. Considering the proposed brevity of this first hop back into the past, I could have forgone the party except that it was tradition. And a moment later, I felt the presence of Peter's mother, Evelyn, who'd surrendered her worry over her son's vocation. She made her way to the kitchen, where she gave a hug to an embarrassed Peter, who managed not to roll his brown eyes and say, "Oh, Mom."

Evelyn was a pretty, petite little thing, with the eyes and hair the color of a Carolina wren. She'd stopped badgering me to guard Peter like a Doberman, and she seemed to have decided there was nothing she could do to keep him safely at home. Nevertheless, I always assured her I'd do my best to keep an eye on him. This time, I merely winked at her, unseen by Peter, who was busy pouring the chili into a large serving container.

I lacked a dining table of any size, so we huddled in the front room as twilight overtook the lingering day. The windows were open, and a cooling breeze from the northwest kept us comfortable; outside, I could hear the barking of the neighborhood dogs, which appeared to have an enthusiastic chorus ongoing. The insects began their chirping, too, a sound I enjoyed. And as we ate and chatted, I waited for the inevitable roast, something acutely humiliating dragged up from the files of history. But it never came, and I was oddly disappointed. Fitzhugh glanced at me, his gray head tilted to one side.

"What?" he asked, his dark eyes twinkling.

"I was waiting for it," I replied.

He laughed. "We found something new and especially horrible, but I persuaded Philo to wait until you get back from this, uh, road trip, and we will pull it out for the next one, hopefully to chase Robin Hood through the forests of Sherwood."

"Okay, I guess," I said, forcing my shoulders down. What on earth had they uncovered?

We finished the evening early, since Peter and I were left with the chore of cleaning up, which was another obnoxious tradition. Philo, the last to leave, gave me his customary hug and kiss on the top of my head but stopped short of doing that with Peter. Instead, they exchanged manly handshakes. Fitzhugh lounged in the kitchen, watching Peter wash while I dried. Kipp, Elani and Juno were out back, enjoying the yard.

"I feel optimistic about this trip," Fitzhugh remarked. "In any case, it is good experience and is a targeted shift in terms of the time frame."

I can't explain the physics involved in time-shifting, but it was a fact that just shifting to a corresponding time of the year, relatively speaking, was simpler than an adjustment of the time as well as location. Kipp, since he designed this trip, would be the leader, and I knew without a doubt he could land perfectly, with us in tow. I had the distinct feeling Fitzhugh wanted to linger, but when Juno drifted in, tired and ready for bed, I shooed them to their room.

"Be careful," Fitzhugh said, his dark eyes resting on mine.

"Always," I replied, smiling, since he knew I'd often not been so. Age and experience had helped me to gain more patience and the care that came with that acquisition.

Fitzhugh leaned in and, taking a page from Philo's book, gave me a quick kiss on the top of my head and a squeeze of my shoulders. He didn't look back as he went into his room. Juno followed after a wink and nod at me.

Peter used the kitchen to dress while I went to my room to don my clothing. I was happy; an empire waist conceals many problem areas and my waist and bust weren't compressed and confined. With a nice linen chemise worn underneath, I was perfectly content in my gown. In my earlier days, I conducted extensive research on hair styles and all the other necessities, but I was feeling lazy and just pulled my hair back and wound it in a chignon which I pinned. I'd be wearing a hat, so what did I care for the niceties? Kipp was on the bed staring at my reflection in the mirror.

"I approached Philo and Fyre about his taking over a few of the management type issues, and both are on board." Kipp licked his forepaw, frowning at something on his foot.

"Toe jam?" I asked, laughing softly.

"No, and thank you very much. You tried to lop off my toenails with those garden shears you call nail clippers. I will take care of them myself," he said, breathing heavily.

I glanced at my mirrored face, studying, for a moment, my too-large nose, which made my face seem out of balance. Harrow had appreciated my nose and the resulting imperfection it caused. A pair of hazel eyes stared back at me, more prominent with my hair confined and not brushing the curves of my face.

"I'm glad it worked out okay with Fyre. I like him and wouldn't want him to feel lost," I said, meaning it. "How do I look?" I asked, doing a little spin and pretending I was on a catwalk, strutting.

"Beautiful," Kipp replied, wagging his tail.

Of course, Peter was horrified at his ensemble, even though he'd been fitted and knew how he'd look. I tried not to stare at his knee pants, the pale-colored hose on his legs, as well as the tight-fitting jacket.

"Kipp, remember this was your idea," Peter said, staring at my partner, his brows drawing together in a frown. Kipp, from my perspective, demonstrated admirable restraint and merely commented on how authentic Peter looked.

Kipp and I had both been to London on previous time-shifts. For this jump, he studied the maps again, localizing the area near Gray's Inn. And to manage landing us in the latter quarter of 1795 would be another stretch, but not a big one for his skill level. Kipp walked over to Elani and gently touched muzzles, a gesture I was a little surprised to see.

"Are we ready?" Kipp asked.

With that, the four of us sat on the floor. I crossed my legs beneath my body, and Kipp lay next to me, his large head resting across my lap. Peter and Elani copied our poses and after a few minutes of deep breathing and focus, I felt as if I were dropping off into the darkness, the sound of wind rushing in my ears. It was as simple as that, as I let Kipp guide us out of our contemporary home to land, hopefully, in a time long past.

# FIVE

The first memory I have of that day was that it was cold, very cold. A brisk wind whistled sharply as it struck the flesh of my face; instinctively, I reached for Kipp and found instant relief in the familiarity of his solid body next to mine. It was natural, now, that I would always reach for Kipp, seeking his strength during moments of uncertainty. There are always a few moments of disorientation upon landing from a time-shift, and I blinked my eyes as I tried to sort out our new reality. It was impossible to even hazard a guess at the time, and the darkened sky gave us no clue. The wicked bite of the cold air shook me from my stupor, and I felt much like a newborn animal that needs to gain its footing quickly, lest danger arrive. Glancing to my left, I was relieved to see Peter and Elani sitting next to me. The whole business of team time-shifting was unique to us, and I still think it was only due to Kipp's unusual set of skills that enabled us to do it with such precision. Kipp's moist nose nuzzled my face anxiously.

"Are you okay?" he asked.

"Yes, just freezing," I answered with a shaky laugh. "And grateful I'm not sitting in a puddle of water," I added. Damp clothes would not have improved my mood, I thought darkly.

It was necessary that time traveling symbionts assess the

situation and get moving in such a way as to blend into the immediate surroundings and do so without delay. Although our physiology somehow creates a bubble where we land in a free space and not in a crowd of people, I'd landed near people before and in doing so caused quite a bit of excitement. As I glanced around, we seemed to be in a small, urban park, with a few trees left untouched amidst buildings that seemed to crowd anxiously, hovering over the tiny bit of nature remaining; empty benches were scattered about for the convenience of the populace. Fortunately, I didn't see any humans—only a thin dog that ran away, pausing to glance over its shoulder at our unexpected arrival -- and stood, stretching a little to work out a kink in my right calf muscle as well as my back. Elani, as usual for her, was yawning, her eyes blinking sleepily as her ears flattened against her head. She always seemed bored by the process, while Peter was on the alert, his brown eyes wide as he scanned the area.

"I don't see anyone," he breathed with relief. Peter pulled his great coat closer about his body and tried not to complain about the cold. His dark hair had fallen into his eyes, and I reached up to smooth it back and correct the angle of his hat, which had scooted to the back of his head.

We both paused to unpack our reversible backpacks, which, when turned inside out, became carpet-bag-type valises. This was a staple of our trips, some type of carrying case that we could affix to our bodies during the time-shift. I figured for our Robin Hood trip, if it were to come to pass, the carpet bag would have to go since that object wouldn't have existed in early medieval times. I was relatively confident a conventional back-pack would cause suspicion amongst the people who lived in 1192. We heard the sound of hooves on the road and saw a man huddled over the reins of a duo of large draft horses, which were pulling a wagon heavily laden with wooden barrels.

"I beg your pardon," Peter called out as he rushed to the road. "Could you direct us to a place where we might find shelter? We are from out of town and became lost."

The man, whose reddened face was almost obscured by the heavy muffler he'd wound around his neck, pulled a pipe from his mouth and glanced to where I stood with the lupines, who were always attention-grabbing due to their size. "It's a bit harsh out here," he said, nodding. "There is a tavern just down that road a little ways, and they should still be open."

"What time is it?" Peter asked, glancing up at the sky once more, hoping it would give him a clue.

"It's getting on close to midnight," the man replied. "And I'd rather be in my bed than staring at the arses of these horses," he added before seeming to realize there was a lady present. "Beg pardon, miss."

He nudged the huge beasts into movement, the wheels of the wagon creaking against the backdrop of the forlorn park with its skeletal trees. I ran my hand along Kipp's back, enjoying his warmth beneath the palm of my glove. Elani flanked me on the other side as we joined Peter and began to walk in the direction the man had given. It was only two blocks, we found, and as we walked, we did encounter other people, usually men in pairs, either well-dressed or otherwise. It was difficult to judge our location based upon the diversity of clothing worn. We assumed it was London but couldn't be sure yet, but at least we knew the man driving the wagon spoke English. The sky overhead seemed to drop, so that the clouds hovered too close for comfort as a fog bank, opaquely dense with moisture, drifted through the streets. The air was thick with the smell of coal smoke from chimneys, mixed with something else that was vaguely unpleasant but indefinable.

The buildings we passed were constructed of stone, brick, wood and timber, so we still had no clue as to the time in which we found ourselves. The road was best described as macadam, with a well-defined curb; some trash littered the edges, but I think one could say that of any densely inhabited city. A crisping layer of snow that had partially melted and was refreezing lay across the curb, almost as if the leaves and debris had been bleached during the daylight hours. There were a few lit lanterns overhead but no gas lamps that I could see, so that was one promising observation, since there wouldn't have been gas street lamps in 1795. A quartet of men approached us, nicely clothed, and they nodded their heads, tipping their hats at me while trying not to stare at our furry companions.

"You'd think they've never seen a dog," Kipp snorted, as he shook his head in disapproval. "Their mothers might have told them it is rude to stare at somebody just minding his own business." Elani merely giggled at his indignation.

"But you're so lovely," I teased him, tweaking his ear.

Up ahead, we saw a building that had more visible lighting than the others, its windows framed with a welcoming amber glow in the otherwise stark harshness of the street. A sign overhead gently swung, caught by the insistent cold wind that burrowed its way through my long cloak to my bones, it seemed. As we drew closer, I could read the sign ... The Black Dog. Glancing down at Kipp, he smiled back at me, recalling our adventure to check out the ghostly tale of a spectral black dog that haunted parts of England.

"Black Shug," Elani remarked, catching our thoughts.

"I think you were scared that night," Peter said, poking me gently in the ribs. "At least I found you hanging on to me for dear life."

As I recalled, we grabbed one another that night—and I'm pretty certain Peter was as frightened as was I -- but I decided not to quibble. All I wanted was some warmth for a few minutes, and he could hang on to his false memory of bravado. We approached the large, scarred oak door, and it swung back unexpectedly as two men, more than slightly inebriated, fell out of the aperture into the road. Well, they didn't exactly fall, but it was close enough not to debate the point. Peter held the door for me, and we swept inside, happy to feel the almost immediate blaze of warmth from a large, stone hearth that consumed one side of the room. We were met by a heavy-set man who seemed to have a permanent scowl imprinted on his face. He wore a stained apron that stretched across his barrel chest, and it was questionable if that apron had ever been laundered. The man's nose was large, curved with a hook that caused the tip to almost meet his upper lip, giving him the appearance of a predatory bird. His sleeves were rolled back to expose a massive set of forearms. His physique made me wonder if this man was the premier arm wrestler in town.

"May I be of help?" he asked, looking at Peter before glancing at me and nodding. He was trying not to stare at the lupines, but it was difficult, and I saw his eyes taking covert, peeking glances. As it were, I saw a couple of other dogs resting at the feet of their humans, so the lupines were not a problem. It was just their size and appearance that caused people to take a second look.

"What magnificent dogs," the proprietor finally stammered.

"Why thank you, sir," Peter responded. "They are a fine set of Siberian Deerstalkers," he added, trying not to grin at me, his lips trembling slightly. Kipp's tail began to whip with enjoyment. Our journey was underway, and like actors in a role, we were digging into our parts. It was always exciting, challenging, often fun and sometimes terrifying.

After a couple of moments of polite chit-chat, the man led us to a table near the fire, since he astutely determined that I was about as frozen as a tv dinner. He assumed us to be upper middle class—or lower upper class, which would equate to about the same level, I suppose -- and was very deferential, since the majority of his clientele were more representative of the working class. His round chest threatened to get even rounder as he catered to our needs, bringing a steaming pot of hot tea to the table.

"Sir, I know this sounds a strange inquiry, but could you tell us exactly where we are and the date?" Peter smiled disarmingly. "We've been traveling and, well, you know how it is."

"You're near Charing Cross station," the man began, confirming that we were in London. I shared a glance with Kipp and nodded. "It's January third," the man added.

"And the year?" I asked, ignoring the man's raised eyebrows.

"Well, miss, it just became 1796," he replied, trying to ignore such an odd request.

Peter glanced sheepishly at the man and almost whispered, "Forgive her, sir; she has some problems with her memory."

Relief flooded over the man's face, along with pity. In an over-exaggerated way, he slowly closed one eye at Peter, glad he was in on the family secret, as it were. "I understand, sir." Then, as if he thought I, perhaps, was also hard of hearing, he repeated again loudly, "It's 1796, miss."

As he left, I leaned over to pet Kipp. "Good job," I said, getting a head start since I knew his perfectionist nature would be appalled that he'd missed his mark by a few days.

"But I overshot the time," he began.

"Kipp, trying to hone in on a particular date is not easy, as you know. There is an acceptable window, and you made it." I glanced around the room, which was surprisingly busy considering the time of night. It seemed to be a working-class establishment, and the people, most of whom were men, knew one another. There was a burst of raucous laughter from a corner of the room; on the far side of the dining hall, there was a spirited game of darts in play. A thick fog of tobacco smoke curdled in the air; I noted the interior walls were thoroughly stained from years of pipe smoke and a chimney that was not vented properly. The room smelled of old onions, over-ripened vegetables, grease, and more than one barely washed body, but the latter was probably the result of sweat born from honest labor, so I had no beef with it.

"I thought I'd try a pint of ale," Peter said, lowering his eyebrows as he stared at me across the table.

"No way," I answered with a laugh. "All I need is for you to get a snootful and start acting goofy."

I thought he was going to pout, but Elani adroitly intervened with her smooth and silken manner and diverted him into discussing our plan to meet Joseph Ritson, since we were depending upon Peter to take the lead. We paused in our deliberations as the proprietor arrived with a platter of meat, cheese, bread and pickles. He'd also chopped up some meat for the dogs, which he'd mixed with some potatoes and carrots in a couple of bowls.

"I thought your doggies would be hungry, too," he said, beaming, proud of his thoughtful gesture. Of course, he knew as well as we that there would be monetary compensation for his kindness.

Kipp cut a look at me. "I'm adding this guy to my favorites list."

"We also are in need of temporary accommodations," Peter began, tilting his head to the side and smiling at the man, who I thought would faint with excitement.

"I don't usually have guests, but my single tenant has left and there is one room upstairs," the man indicated with a gesture. His thoughts betrayed his notion that having us stay would edge his humble establishment another peg up the competitive ladder and help with business, which to my naïve eye seemed pretty robust. And, as history would be recorded, a couple of people from out of town, along with their Siberian Deerstalkers, stayed the night at The Black Dog public house, enjoying the comfort of a room and the hospitality of the proprietor.

An obviously drunk man wove his way amongst the tables to approach us. He clumsily pulled his cloth hat from his head in deference to my presence before addressing Peter. "Interested in a game of darts, young master?" he began, slurring his words. "We're taking wagers on the winners." Peter politely shooed him away. It was obvious the men had pegged Peter as no real challenge and greedily thought they could make a little coin off of the evening. Kipp glanced up at me, curious as always.

"Why would throwing an object at a board be so interesting?" he asked.

"There is a fair amount of skill involved," I replied, giving him a piece of cheese from my plate. I tried not to stare, considering the sensitivity of the subject, as Kipp and Elani were lying so close they almost were touching. They were stretched in front of the fireplace, the flickering blaze managing to highlight the fluid palate of colors in Elani's lovely fur. The lupines had bolted down their chow, while Peter was still chewing a piece of the rubbery meat on his plate. I smiled at his effort; he shrugged his shoulders good-naturedly. "Not the best cut of meat?" I asked.

Before Peter could respond, the tavern owner returned, smiling, since he figured he had good news. "I've had the lad prepare the room for you, and we are pleased to accommodate such fine people," he added, as if we would applaud his efforts. As he waited for our effusive thanks, he rocked back on his heels, massive arms crossed across the soiled apron that barely covered his chest.

The main room was still relatively busy, but I was tired, and we had a long day ahead of us if we were to pursue Ritson. I waited while Peter took the lupines out to the back alley for a covert break. A couple of the men began to glance at me, uncertain why I was left without an escort. From their perspective, only a certain type of woman would be sitting unaccompanied in a tavern after midnight. I tried not to yawn; centuries of lewd cat calls and waggling eyebrows leaves one relatively bored with such nonsense. Peter returned with the lupines and, using a lantern that left a trail of smelly smoke, the tavern owner's son, who couldn't have been more than ten years old, led us up a rickety staircase and along a narrow balcony that overlooked the main room. We passed a couple of closed doors that were obviously where the owner and his family lived. The boy, who looked tired and had no doubt labored since early that morning, pushed open a door and set the lantern on a low, beaten table with rickety legs that were splayed unevenly against the worn floor. I glanced around the room, which had white-washed walls on three sides and some ancient wallpaper on the fourth. Obviously, someone had once tried to brighten the grim surroundings, but now that small bit of decoration had faded to the point the design had melted into a shapeless gray mass. There was one straight-backed chair, and in the center of the small room was a bed with a sagging mattress suspended by a knotted web of rope. Oddly enough, the linens looked fairly clean, as did a heavy, down-stuffed coverlet.

"I put a pitcher of water on the table," the boy stuttered, glancing up at us shyly beneath a tangle of wheat-colored hair. "And the chamber pot is under the bed."

"Thank you, lad," Peter replied, handing the boy a coin. The child's face lightened briefly before he darted away.

"I'm tired and want to get some sleep. So, turn around," I said, waving my hand at Peter, who flushed. "There's no screen or privacy, so we'll just make due." He nodded, defeated, since there were no other options. As we began to undress, turning our backs to one another, I laughed.

"What?" Peter asked.

"When we first started this business of traveling together, I remember how careful we were to be private and how awkward we felt. Now, it's just like a typical routine."

"Like family," Elani said.

"I personally still think that we lupines get the best end of the deal," Kipp remarked, his thoughts sounding a little brusque after

Elani's thoughtful remark. "We don't have to take baths, wear clothes, or act all fancy like you guys do. We can stay, well, uh, natural."

"And hide your amazing talents under a bushel," I replied. "I envy you two, in case you didn't know it."

There was only the single bed, which featured a lumpy, straw-filled mattress. I stared at the bed, then at Peter, who was looking at the wallpaper, a corner of which was peeling away from the wall. Kipp was wagging his tail, enjoying the moment.

"I can take the floor," Peter began.

"Nonsense. We'll all pile in together," I replied briskly. "It's cold in here, and we can benefit from the shared warmth." I smiled wickedly at Kipp, who would have blushed if he could have managed such a feat. "There, buddy," I said to him privately. "You thought this was awkward, and now you and Elani will be cuddling, too. How do you like that, chuckles?" Kipp bared his teeth at me in response.

To say it was merely cold didn't seem sufficient. The thin chemise I wore did little to provide any warmth at all, and I watched, fascinated as my breath formed a silver fog in the air. There was no heat source except for our bodies. And I was the last to fall asleep, struggling to fight the numbness gathering in my toes and fingers. Kipp pushed closer, finally parking his large jaw heavily on my shoulder. My companions were actively dreaming while I was still awake, and even though I politely abstained from eavesdropping on the private cognitions of Peter and Elani, I felt buffeted by the emotional rollercoasters that rested on the other side of Kipp. Fortunately, his thoughts were quiescent, and before long, I too fell into a dreamless state.

Once I got warm, I'll admit it actually was a very pleasant night spent. Well, I suppose such things are graded on a continuum, and I have spent some rough, unpleasant nights over my lifetime. I clung to one edge of the mattress, Kipp lay between me and Peter, and then Elani was on Peter's other side. Very proper, of course, but I never planned on telling Peter's doting mother that I'd spent the night in the same bed as her little boy. She wouldn't have understood, and it could have made for difficult times spent in each other's company. Upon awakening, Peter and I dressed hurriedly, not due to convention but rather because of the frigid temperature in that bleak room.

We made our way downstairs to find our friendly tavern keeper had some breakfast waiting and was lingering anxiously to hear the report of our room and service evaluation. He was hoping to get a five-star rating, no doubt. I only nibbled at the fare, which included some dried beef with gravy sharing a plate with large hunks of bread and cheese. The only thing missing was the ubiquitous pickle as a delightful condiment. As our host brought out another steaming pot of tea, it was clear he wanted to demonstrate some, uh, "poshness" for us. At our request, he summoned a four-wheeler, and shortly we found ourselves outside again, where an unforgiving wind from the north chewed its way through my woolen cloak. I pulled the soft hood up over my head as Kipp pushed closer, trying to share his warmth, but I was still cold. Peter, likewise, flanked me, his shoulder brushing mine.

"It's a little brisk," he finally conceded, smiling at me, his cheeks red from exposure to the elements. Elani looked up at me, wagging her tail in support. She would have given me her ample coat if she could. Peter handed me into the four-wheeler, and after giving the driver instructions to take us to Gray's Inn, we began to thread our way through the city. I was actually grateful for the year, since there would be no possible way I'd run into Harrow or anyone else associated with him from Whitechapel. He'd not been born yet. But I would have given a great deal to see him as a young man in his knee pants, his face all dark with serious intent. He was rarely light-hearted, but there were times I like to think he was so when in my company. Perhaps that was cruel vanity playing tricks on my memory?

"No, it isn't," Kipp replied to my unspoken thoughts in our private way. "He loved you and still did to the end, I bet." He sighed and placed his big head on my lap. "I'm sure of it." Kipp was obviously in a thoughtful, sentimental mood. "Some have the capacity to love deeply and forever, and nothing can change that feeling for another." In his humble way, he didn't realize he was describing himself.

My fingers threaded their way through his dense pelt. I'd removed my gloves to blow on my hands and was now glad, since I could use Kipp as a personal heat source. Across the carriage, Elani was gazing at me, and I wondered if she and Peter had worked on achieving the intimacy Kipp and I shared. It had been her wish, and it could have been my imagination, but I thought they seemed more at ease and speaking less. That probably meant they were sharing more privately, just as did Kipp and I. Elani blinked her eyes once, and I realized she was confirming my notions in lupine Morse code. What a special girl, I thought. As I continued to watch, Peter's hand had rested on her back, and he stroked her gently, almost absent-mindedly, but I knew him better. Peter's active mind was rarely at rest and wasn't at that moment, despite the sleepy, vacant look in his eyes. The carriage jostled over a rough pothole and jarred us all out of our semi-dream state.

"Pardon," came the words from the driver in the box. "Bit of a hole there, sir."

I couldn't image how unpleasant the elements were for him. It had begun to snow again, and as I glanced out the window, the flakes began to fall faster, harder, and fatter. It was a moist snow, rapidly turning into a slushy cover on the roadways. We were passing some store fronts where people had set large containers that were essentially fire pits used as warming stations for the day workers. Clever entrepreneurs offered coffee, tea, and steaming pasties for sale and were doing a brisk business if the lines were any indication. Despite the harsh and desperate conditions, laughter rang out as we made our way through the streets of London.

Kipp's mind and the connection he had to my thoughts was often like an anvil, strong, insistent, unavoidable in its intensity. But as we rode along, it felt more like a feather drifting on a breeze, and I wondered if our association was maturing. We trusted each other's constancy in our lives, and maybe there was no reason to feel the partner's presence with such strength.

Peter began to fumble in his pocket, first one, then the other, before retrieving something. He grinned at me. "I was hoping I'd not lost my card," he said.

"I'm glad you didn't," I responded, lifting a dark brow.

Peter, like me, was working on expanding his knowledge of languages and was adequately fluent in French. Since I was, too, we decided to play the part of visitors from France, with Peter acting as a university history student in search of an interview. Since we didn't know Ritson, we wanted to avoid any issues in case he was not journalist-friendly. But who could turn away a bright-eyed student of history? Or at least we hoped that to be the case. Peter handed me the card.

"Charles Hugo," I read, smiling. "Obviously a nod to Victor Hugo, who's not yet been born."

Peter grinned at me across the close intimacy of the carriage. "I thought it clever."

I glanced out the window, and if I'd had any residual sleepiness, the cutting breeze that whipped at my face dissolved that bleary-eyed, lazy, unmotivated state. The sky felt too close to earth, the clouds seeming as if they would collapse and fall in on top of us at any moment. The snow was lessening but not so the wind, and the air felt thick with the promise of more inclement weather. We passed a street corner where a girl, who could have been no more than seven or eight years of age, pushed a cart filled with something I couldn't see, fighting against the snow and ice as she made her way. Young children had to work back then, and survival was a thing of grim desperation. My mood turned south, and Kipp pushed closer, distracting my thoughts to him.

"You're always easily touched by the struggles of humans," he observed.

"Maybe, but it is hard to watch children struggle so at an early age. And, yes, I know the deal because I lived through these times," I reminded him.

"You can't save everyone," Kipp began.

"And you're one to talk," I replied.

The carriage began to slow and finally rocked to a halt. We had arrived at Gray's Inn and would begin the next step of our quest.

# SIX

Gray's Inn was home to professionals, usually barristers, but others congregated there also, undoubtedly bending their heads in lofty consultations. Its inhabitants were of the upper crust, for the most part, and the spotless uniform of the servant who met us spoke volumes. The men who lived at Gray's Inn wanted to be respected, awed, and maybe viewed with the occasional spark of fear. The servant, a middle-aged man with dark hair swept back severely from a high forehead, stared at Peter's card before indicating we should wait in a small parlor. It had taken us a few moments to find the right block of rooms, since Gray's Inn fed a sprawling campus. The snow had subsided for a brief time but now returned with a vengeance as I stared outside through a window damp with condensation. The rippled glass caused the yard to appear blurred, a shadowy window pane of white flakes falling upon dormant grass. But the fireplace in the parlor was roaring, and I stood close to it, hoping the waves of heat would dry the hem of my gown, which had become soiled. We hadn't even met Ritson yet, and I was already a mess.

"It won't matter," Peter said, trying to soothe me. "Ritson will understand the inclement weather and long dresses that drag in the snow. I'm sure he's seen it before."

Kipp nodded his auburn head, tilting it slightly as he expanded his superior telepathy to beyond the room. I knew he was eavesdropping on anything possible. Elani stood next to me, allowing the warmth of the fire to dry her damp coat. The fellows didn't seem to care, but I, for one, wanted to look presentable. The servant returned, his soulful eyes on us, whatever personality he had contained by the livery he wore. I wondered if he ever let loose and just had some fun. It was hard to tell with his Buster Keaton flat expression and practiced self-control.

"Mr. Ritson will see you," he said, his voice appropriately tuned for the setting. There was none of the culturally stereotypical "The *guvnor* will see you now, mate," in play, and I was a little disappointed.

I glanced at Peter, who raised his eyebrows. It seemed pretty lucky that we'd hit gold on our first strike, but I wasn't complaining. I had occasional bursts of good luck over the years but also had my fair share of disasters.

"It's me and Elani," Kipp said, as we lined up behind the servant. "He told Ritson that a couple arrived accompanied by two very large dogs, and he's curious."

"Why?" I asked, letting my hand touch the top of his head, resting between his two upright ears. His fur was still slightly damp from our brief exposure to the falling snow during our journey.

"How would I know?" Kipp replied, sounding cross. He was obviously disappointed I wasn't just happy with the morsel he'd fed me.

After climbing a staircase that was made of carved oak and would have been considered an irreplaceable beauty in modern times, the servant led us to a door at the end of a narrow corridor. After clearing his throat, he tapped politely on the wood, and after waiting for a moment, he pushed the door open, ushering us inside.

The room was a mess, but a delightful mess, and if I'd had a year or two just to hang out and go through every book, paper, and nook and cranny, I'd have been happy. There was a stack of books resting on the floor, while on the table I noticed loose pages of what must have been a manuscript. There was an empty bird cage hanging from a verdigris-covered stand in the frost laced window, hinting that perhaps at one time, Ritson had shared his rooms with a companion of some sort. It was the room of an eccentric thinker, one who was filled with curiosity as well as certainty. It was the room of Joseph Ritson.

"I almost sent you away, but I like dogs, and Bellville said you had two nice dogs." His tone was rude, unpleasant, and unforgiving. Obviously, the rumors of his harshness were not exaggerated. Ritson didn't bother to stand and was sitting in a wing chair near a blazing hearth. He wore a muffler round his neck, his hair had not been combed, and his gray-flecked beard looked untrimmed, much like a patch of overgrown shrubbery. He seemed his age, fiftyish by then, with very direct eyes and an abrupt manner. Sir Walter Scott was almost the only man who could tolerate him. Ritson didn't suffer fools lightly, but he was about to suffer us.

"Mr. Ritson," Peter began, cranking up his French accent. "This is such a pleasure, and I beg your pardon for interrupting your morning."

Ritson stared back at him, his face difficult to read, but not his thoughts. They were not warm and fuzzy.

"May I present my sister, Mademoiselle," and then Peter stumbled. He'd not thought of the name by which he'd present me. To cover, he began to cough, politely, into a kerchief. "Excuse me, sir, the cold outside has irritated my throat." It was obvious that he'd gone completely blank and couldn't hatch a name for me.

"I'm Petra Hugo," I smoothly swept in, touching Peter's arm for good measure. "Are you alright, brother?" I smiled at Ritson, hoping I wasn't showing too many teeth in the process. Smiling convincingly was a finely balanced art, I'd discovered.

"Yes, thank you."

Ritson was still staring at us, not speaking, before his eyes flicked down to Elani first, then Kipp. He clapped his hands lightly together, and Elani and Kipp played like dogs, wagging their tails and walking forward, heads down, ready for attention. A faint smile tugged at the corner of Ritson's mouth, which was almost concealed by his untidy, overgrown mustache. He leaned forward and began to touch Elani's head, and when he did so, she began to gather her impressions of the man by way of that physical contact.

It was a unique skill, one possibly not ever documented—although Fitzhugh was still working on that bit of research—and one not possessed by Kipp. And I thought he could do everything. Instead, Kipp used his telepathy to do his deep dive into Ritson's memories that were not accessible to the rest of us. Come to think of it, we humanoids really relied upon our lupine partners. Many of the things we'd accomplished as a species had been done on their furry backs.

Finally, Ritson looked up at us. "I like dogs," he said. "I don't usually like people," he added, his dark brows pulling together to form a uniform, unpleasant line across his forehead. "But as you are allowing me the pleasure of your dogs' company, what is the purpose of your visit?" He glanced at the window. "The weather is hardly conducive to pleasant travel." His eyes flicked towards the soiled hem of my gown; I shifted uncomfortably beneath his gaze. He nodded, and we both sat, crowding together on a small lounge seat that faced Ritson.

"Mr. Ritson, I am a student of history and am researching England during the reign of Richard at the time of the Crusades. Of course, any review of that period brings into question the legend of Robin Hood, and with your publication of such definitive information about that subject, I wanted to meet you." Peter stumbled to a halt, and it wasn't his fault. Ritson had this unnerving stare that would render anyone almost speechless.

Of course, I stared back, trying to get a handle on the man. I'd seen pictures of a nicely dressed man, well-groomed and officious-appearing. But the man across the small room was dressed shabbily; I noticed his buttons didn't match the correct buttonholes, leaving gaps in his weskit. His hair had grown unfashionably long, and the grey locks appeared tangled and not particularly clean. His hands, which were large and expressive, were stained with black ink as well as the cuffs of his well-worn shirt, the neck of which gaped open. It was obvious he'd neglected to have his collar and cuffs turned for quite some time.

"He's on the downslide to whatever breakdown occurs this year," Kipp observed. "He's having trouble focusing his thoughts, and for a man who has had an amazing ability to concentrate and process large amounts of information, he's agitated over his deficits and angry at the world."

I knew Ritson to be a man who was barely tolerated by others even when on a good day. I couldn't imagine what would happen when he finally lost reason. Elani glanced around at me before resuming her pose, having sat before Ritson while resting her chin on his knee. Ritson allowed himself another brief, darting smile, as he finger-combed her thick coat of fur.

"What sort of dogs are these?" he asked, tilting his head to one side.

"Siberian Deerstalkers," Peter responded.

"Never heard of them," Ritson murmured.

I could tell he was drifting off from us, so I decided to push forward. "Mr. Ritson, how on earth could you pinpoint the place of Robin Hood's birth, as well as the date of his death? I know I am not the student of history as is my brother," I said, sweeping my hand at Peter, "but such a feat seems amazing to me." I widened my eyes. "I am very impressed." I glanced at Peter and saw that he had moisture beading on his forehead. It could have been stress, but the room was overheated, and I admit I felt a trickle of sweat that began between my shoulder blades and was rolling slowly down my spine. The lupines appeared relaxed, but I knew they must be suffering too and were just acting tough and nonchalant by not whining over something they couldn't control.

Ritson obviously didn't care for flattery, because the ominous line of dark eyebrows took up residence again across his broad forehead. He exhaled slowly, the sound loud in the room where the only other noise was the crackling of the fireplace. I noticed a clock on the mantle that had not been wound and had ground to a halt at some point. Time stood still in that crowded, desperate room. Yes, it felt of desperation and a man who was trying to hang on to his sanity.

"Mr. Ritson, if there is anything you can tell me about your research and study, I will be most grateful," Peter intoned, pulling out his earnest routine. Ritson didn't care for that either.

"Let me push him just a tiny bit," Kipp said. "His thoughts are pretty tangled up, and he is, uh, kind of suspicious of you. I don't think we'll get him to talk any other way."

"Can't you do your deep dive, Kipp, and just retrieve his memories?" I asked, hoping for another path. There was an issue with Kipp doing something that was marginally unethical by contemporary standards, and we only pulled it out of his toolkit when everything else failed. But maybe we were at that point since Ritson was difficult to crack. I started to give a definitive no, but the moment was becoming strained, and the man was obviously on the road to some type of mental collapse, which made managing his thoughts and feelings even more complicated. And from my telepathic survey of the man, I knew Kipp was right. Reluctantly, I nodded my head.

Kipp did what only Kipp can do, and that was to plant a soft suggestion in Ritson's mind that he might enjoy speaking with these two delightful young people. As Kipp began, I comforted myself that such a manipulation was just a tiny little nudge of sorts. And maybe Kipp wouldn't have to include it in his report back to the Twelve. I felt myself relax.

"Well, you know, young man, years of research go into compiling information as well as checking any possible references from the times that substantiate stories and lead one to believe there are factual underpinnings." Ritson laughed softly. "I had a young man about your age who was working with me, and I had to give him the heave-ho. He had no patience for tedious work."

Peter was nodding his head, brown eyes engaging, managing a pleasant but not too pleasant expression. I knew from the tone of Ritson's voice that something big was coming, if only we would remain patient and act obsequious.

"And then I had a visit from a man who brought artifacts he'd inherited ... or so he claimed. For all I know, they could have been stolen. But there were documents that specifically named the man we knew to become Robin Hood. They were mostly legal documents as well as letters." Ritson had allowed Elani finally to lie at his feet, where she kept her physical connection by resting her jaw on his foot. He stretched back into his chair, letting his head tilt back. "I had an expert on old documents examine what I was given, and he agreed that they could be dated to the appropriate time frame." Ritson closed his eyes as he concentrated. "It was a combination of the style of writing, the language used, and the types of parchments." Ritson opened his eyes to stare, his eyes first on Peter, then flicking briefly towards me.

"Do you still have those items?" Peter asked, holding his breath.

"No, young man. The visitor, who didn't tell me his real name, I suspect, took them with him." Ritson was starting to question his agreeability to talk with us as Kipp's magic potion began to wear off. His natural irritability began to flood the room again, making the area seem small and cramped with emotion.

"I would hope," I said, smiling like a silly fool, "that there was something from the famous Sheriff of Nottingham."

Ritson took my bait, unable to keep himself from showing off just a little bit. "Yes, there was, Mademoiselle Hugo. He exchanged letters with the Sheriff of York, and in those letters were discussions about the criminal behaviors of a man they named as Robin Hood and efforts to contain him and gain control of the king's forests." He paused a minute, his eyes flicking towards the window, where the snow was heavily falling, obscuring the view outside. "The letters were dated between 1191 and 1193."

"Kipp," I hissed privately to my partner, "see if you can get the date the man visited Ritson with the artifacts."

"Why would that be important?"

"Maybe it's not; it's just instinct," I replied.

"Okay," Kipp said and redoubled his concentration on Ritson's stored memories. "I think it would have been the first week of October 1793," he said, panting a little with effort, "and I get the impression of a Monday or Tuesday, maybe. I can't be more specific than that, but Ritson ties that visit with something else that occurred, and he has stored it in that way."

As the glow of Kipp's involvement faded, Ritson began to withdraw into his disturbed thoughts, and we became just props in his world. Finally, the moment became strained as he spoke less to us, and Peter tactfully chose an opening for us to depart. Ritson didn't stand or acknowledge our leaving. We started down the hallway, trying to find our way back to the front parlor of the building. Elani helped guide us by keeping her nose down, picking up our scent on the floor. I felt like I was trailing a bloodhound. Peter, his eyes glowing, grabbed my arm in excitement.

"Petra, I think that is enough for us to propose a time-shift. Kipp, since this was your idea in the first place, what do you think?" Peter, in his impulsive way, had not sorted out all the issues related to such a complicated trip. It was my job, as the experienced member of the team, to apply the brakes gently to the runaway mine car in which we sometimes found ourselves. Kipp, too, could get swept away with a notion without full consideration of possible consequences.

Kipp surprised me with his response. "I want to think about it," he replied. "I need to compare what he was telling us with what bits and pieces I could retrieve from his memories of the day the man brought him the artifacts." Kipp looked up at me. "But I can tell you that my first impression is that they matched up, and that might indicate there were actual, physical relics that substantiate the existence of Robin Hood in the 1190's."

Elani had little to say until I prompted her to share her impressions of Ritson. "He is a man who has a lot of anger," she offered. "But beneath that cloud of emotion, I found someone who feels insecure and wants respect but never quite gets what he thinks is owed to him. He felt, well, very sad." She was allowing his depression to affect her, so I briskly ran my hand down her back and smiled at her. She glanced back, wagging her tail a couple of times.

We continued to follow the carpeted runner that led us down the hallway and to the beautiful staircase that was recognizable as a reference point. We descended to find Bellville in the parlor, his mask-like face composed, expression shuttered as befitted a good gentleman's gentleman.

"Bellville," Peter said, "would it be possible for you to summon us a four-wheeler?"

"Yes, sir. It would be a pleasure."

How nice it was to be met with such an agreeable response after fighting with Ritson for any morsel and having to descend to lupine manipulation in order to get what we wanted. Bellville, however, was no fool, and the weather was fierce. So, he sent a young lad who worked as a servant, and we waited in the warmth of the parlor until the boy, who was crusted with snow on the top of his rag hat, returned. Peter gave the boy a large coin, probably the most money the boy had ever seen, as evidenced by the shocked look on the child's pale face. Peter took my arm and hurried me along the sidewalk, our feet crunching in the snow, and handed me up into the carriage; Kipp and Elani jumped in after us, their fur covered with white flakes. I began to brush some of the stuff from Kipp's face, since he had no room to shake it loose.

"We'll go back to the Black Dog tavern, retrieve our back-packs, and go home," I suggested. "There is no reason to stay." I glanced at Peter, and he was avoiding my gaze. "What's wrong?" I asked.

He exhaled forcefully, a loud noise of irritation. "I muffed the whole visit," he began.

I didn't reply, knowing he needed to talk.

"I didn't have a name for you, and that was a nice save, by the way. And then I couldn't get him going in the direction I wanted and ran out of steam." He looked up sheepishly. "I admit, he intimidated me."

"Well, he intimidated me too, so should I feel bad?" I asked. Leaning forward, I smiled and placed my hand on his arm. "The only thing I might critique is your not having a name ready for me. But other than that, you did fine. Ritson was tough."

Peter shrugged his shoulders and turned to gaze out the window at the passing snow-covered streets where people were hurrying along to get to their destinations without tarrying. It was clear Peter needed to feel a little sorry for himself and brood, and I had no issue with that. I could be like that at times too. I felt badly for the driver of the carriage who was sitting exposed to the elements, as well as having a nagging concern for the horse, which had steam coming off its large body in waves. The weather was raw, and I was looking forward to Kipp dropping me back down into a pleasant, sun-filled spring in the piedmont of North Carolina.

"Remember when we first met?" Kipp spoke to me privately.

Yes, how could I forget? Tula and I had been on a time-shift to study the language and culture of a prehistoric tribe. Tula put herself between me and danger and was killed, leaving me not only heartbroken but also stranded. Without her synergistic bond, I could not return home. Then the tribe, frightened by inexplicable climactic events, moved away, leaving me to a grim future. One day, as I sat looking out over the windswept valley as the days were growing cold and desolate, I felt a curious mind probing mine. I had no way of knowing it at the time, but that moment would usher in a new world for me as I finally met Kipp and embraced him as my new partner. There was one night when I huddled in the cave, cold and shivering, and Kipp used his heavy body to warm me. No, I'd not forgotten that moment or any since then. My hand found his head and we exchanged glances, his amber eyes on my face. Love, trust, and constancy were just a few of the words that crossed my mind.

# SEVEN

The library at Technicorps was an anomaly in a building that was purposefully neutral in its appearance. The interior was painted like the uninspiring but utilitarian interior of a battleship, with walls the color of putty. Fitzhugh, in his typically bossy, controlling way, had dictated the library be painted a deep, soothing color of green that reminded me of a study in some grand Victorian home. All we needed was a softly ticking grandfather clock and a wall covered in paintings of famous relatives to complete the picture. Our desks were wooden, not metal, and had been found in antique stores. Fitzhugh's was a treasured possession he'd brought from England back when such things were difficult to manage, and I can only imagine it was due to his sheer strength of will that it did happen. When one entered the library, I was located up front with Victor close by so we could collaborate with little expended energy. There was a cluster of overstuffed, comfortable chairs for reading, and often we gathered there to discuss difficult tangles in our work.

Although a traveler by profession, I needed a day job too. Symbionts have bills to pay, just as do humans. I'd been lobbying, along with some of the new, younger travelers we'd recently taken at our collective, for some type of hazard pay when traveling, but Philo and the Twelve remained unimpressed. To be honest, I was happy as things were, but it was difficult not to support my fellow travelers, who were fired with enthusiasm, so I kicked up a little dust … not much, but a little.

Fitzhugh was looming over my desk, frowning at ancient scribblings I was attempting to translate. Fitzhugh, Victor, and I were charged with translating old symbiont written accounts of time-shifts into modern English before those documents were scanned into a computer system. In doing so, we were documenting the history of our species. All collectives had similar activities, and periodically, everything was shared. In order to translate, one had to be proficient in languages, and that was one of my specialties. Peter had once labored here but was now occupied with Elani, and spent more time teaching young symbionts than in the library. And to be honest, he'd hated the translation business, thinking it was too slow for him. Occasionally, we were swamped, and he was pulled down to the basement, whether he liked it or not. He, too, had bills to pay.

"Petra, I think you are missing the entire meaning of this phrase," Fitzhugh remarked, pursing his lips. A lock of his long, gray hair fell over his shoulder.

In the past, such an uttering would have left me peevishly enraged, but our relationship had grown over time. Now I tried to listen to him while tamping down any irritation over his remarks. I'd found, when I bothered to listen, he had a lot of value to say.

"In what way?" I asked, looking up at him.

He stared back, an odd expression on his face, before laughing softly. Fitzhugh touched me lightly on the shoulder. "Once upon a time, you would have been insulted by my pointing out such a thing."

"Would you rather us fight?" I responded, smiling.

"Well, I admit occasionally I miss our spirited exchanges, but in general, no, I prefer a peaceful co-existence." Fitzhugh glanced over at Victor, who was trying to ignore our playfulness. "Tea?"

We both agreed, and Fitzhugh rambled off to the rear of the room where a small kitchenette was located. I decided to follow along and propped myself against the counter-top while he prepared a kettle of water.

"It seems the Twelve is very supportive of Kipp's proposed

Robin Hood time-shift," Fitzhugh began. His tone sounded unusually tentative.

"Yes, it seems so." I felt neutral and sounded that way.

"Are you not intrigued by the possibility?" Fitzhugh asked, as he spooned Earl Grey tea leaves from a decorative cannister.

"Yes, of course. There is just a lot to accomplish. Peter and I both need to continue to study the language as well as the customs. During that time, and for most of the medieval period, there was a great deal of suspicion of anything that fell outside of the norm. We must blend in seamlessly. And I wonder if Peter is ready yet."

"Why?"

"He became flustered when introducing me to Ritson and lost his focus and composure, and I had to introduce myself." I sighed, meeting Fitzhugh's dark eyes.

"And you've never, to use modern parlance, screwed up?" he asked.

"Oh, yes, I have and plenty of times, as you well know. It's just that I feel very responsible for him and his learning curve, and when things like that happen, I wonder if I am a competent teacher."

Fitzhugh shrugged his shoulders. "I think it is just something to chalk up to the business we do. It is inherently dangerous and entails a great deal of improvisation." Leaning forward, he tapped me on the shoulder. "Although, I would not refer to the lupines as Siberian Deerstalkers during this time-shift."

"Why?" I asked, feeling my mouth twist with humor.

"Don't you recall in your research that the toes of dogs living in the royal forests were clipped off to prevent them from hunting deer?" Fitzhugh peered at me, obviously wondering if I'd suddenly become stupid.

"Oh, I hadn't thought of that!" I exclaimed. "You're right," I conceded.

"And my point is that if you overlook something so glaring, then Peter will, too. If we were human, I'd say it's just being human, but since we're not, I'll say it's just being symbiont."

The kettle began to boil, and as Fitzhugh was pouring, I felt a comfortable, familiar nudge at the back of my brain. It was Kipp, a few floors above me, seeking me out for a love tap.

"What are you doing?" I asked Kipp privately, telepathically.

"Oh, just reviewing some performance evaluations of the new symbiont class," he replied.

"You sound just like a manager," I teased him. "Next, you'll need a suit, tie and briefcase, and you won't hang around with the likes of me anymore."

Kipp laughed in response, the sound of him echoing in my head, before he minimized his presence and returned to work.

"You were talking with Kipp, weren't you?" Fitzhugh asked. The scent of bergamot filled the small kitchenette.

"Yes. How did you know?"

"You get this far away expression on your face," he replied, pausing to look at me. "You always look a little lost, as if you are searching for something, and I always know when you've found it. It is Kipp." Fitzhugh smiled. "I recall that wonderful feeling I had with Lydea, and it was only a tiny bit of what you and Kipp share." He began to pour the tea into the delicate china cups. There were no mugs in use in Fitzhugh's world of tea time. "That sense of total understanding and acceptance. Humans, I believe, strive for such, but it will always be elusive, just out of reach, like a tempting fruit on a branch that doesn't hang low enough."

"You are very poetic today," I remarked, taking a seat at the small table that had been pushed to the corner of the rectangular room.

"I dreamt of Lydea last night and realized I missed her. Juno, who I adore, and I have a relationship like you and Philo. Friendly, trusted companion, but not a bonded symbiont. And of course, we were thrust together, and bonding was not our goal." He sighed, sitting across from me. "I think all this planning for such a major trip has left me feeling envious of you and your youthful team of adventurers."

"I'll trade places," I began playfully.

"And I'd go in a minute if I had a partner and if my legs could go the distance."

I gazed at him across the tiny expanse of table. He was very elderly for a symbiont, having lived more than a millennium. The two heart attacks were in the past, and his physician had pronounced him sound. But such a number of years to live was impressive by any standards, and he wouldn't have the ability to do some of the physical feats we might face. As I thought about it, I might not either.

"Oh, you'll be okay." Fitzhugh smiled.

"You are doing that more and more, you know." I sipped my tea while arching my eyebrows at him.

"What?"

"Playing like Kipp and just butting into my brain without knocking politely on my door."

"Do you object?"

"No." I smiled as his face relaxed. Yes, he was pushing some of our conventional rules, and why not, I thought? If the youngsters amongst humankind and the symbiont world could shake up the establishment from time to time, why couldn't an elder do likewise?

Victor walked through the threshold. "Hey, I thought you were making tea," he asked, frowning at us.

"And did you think I had to deliver it to you on a silver tray, complete with a biscuit and a watercress sandwich?" Fitzhugh was back, unsentimental and rude. I had to laugh as I rose to pour Victor a cup. Hastily, I sipped my tea since it was time for me to meet my companions in Karl's workroom.

Karl was excited about wardrobing us for our trip, and since word of the time-shift was making it around the collectives, it was an opportunity for him to showcase his talents. It was rare that such long-range trips were done, since so many of the really big events had been covered … and sometimes twice. Accordingly, he conducted research over a period of a few weeks as well as consulting with a fellow worker in another collective so that he could deliver perfection. Peter and I had one previous consultation since Karl had learned that despite his skills, it just worked out better if he involved the participants versus simply telling them what he was going to do and inferring that they better like it.

As Peter and I waited for Karl, who was in a meeting with Philo, I made myself at home at his work table and began to thumb through old wardrobe books. Peter, to amuse me, began to converse in Old English. I admit he was pretty good, but languages were my thing, and I was about five percent better, so I corrected him with abandon until he finally told me to stop.

"You know, Petra, I'm still learning, and you could be encouraging rather than just telling me everything I do wrong." He used his fingers to push his heavy mop of hair from his eyes so that he could glare at me with an unobstructed view.

I was embarrassed, since I'd been doing just that. Glancing at Kipp, I saw him shake his head from side to side and was waiting for it.

"Petra, Petra, Petra," Kipp sighed. "You don't teach others with that sort of technique."

"Okay, Professor, what should I do?" I decided to humor him.

"You have to bring youngsters along with a mild correction and guidance, but don't crush their aspirations." Kipp's eyes softened. "I'd have thought you knew that by now."

I rolled my eyes and shook my head. Of course, Kipp's discussion with me was unheard by Peter, so I finally glanced at Peter and told him I thought he was making great progress. The pleased flush on his cheeks was enough to tell me he needed my delayed validation. The door swung back and Karl swept in, and he looked neither relaxed nor excited. He seemed irritated as his dark eyes, which seemed to be all pupil with no iris, glared at me. I almost knocked down the chair as I sprang away from the work table.

"Philo tells me that I must operate within a tighter budget," Karl exploded. "How am I to make a realistic, quality product under that condition?" he asked, not really wanting an answer.

"I know, Karl," I remarked, my eyes wide while keeping my voice soothing. I felt a little like I was speaking to an agitated animal, trying to keep it from bolting away in panic. "Suzanne used to be forced to find mills to weave a certain fabric on order. Philo has never traveled and doesn't understand that you can't show up in 500 BC wearing polyester."

Peter, Elani and Kipp wisely stayed out of the dialog and allowed me to talk Karl down. Actually, although I had a purpose to my methods, I spoke truthfully. I'd been in the position where a minor detail, such as whether or not a button had been created yet, had caused quite a bit of trouble and some fast thinking on my part. And zippers! Don't let me get started on that topic.

Karl finally calmed down as Peter went to the counter and cranked up the Mr. Coffee. I wasn't sure Karl needed more caffeine, but he seemed to thrive on the stuff, so he relaxed as he sipped the triple octane brew, while Peter and I began to get fidgety, our hands slightly shaky as we grasped our mugs.

"Okay, let's review some of the needs," Karl finally said. Reaching up, he swept his dark hair back, carefully coving his balding spot in an instinctive way that needed no mirror to accomplish. "Your plan is to assume the role of the working class, not poverty-stricken, but a working villager type. And that is still the idea?"

"Yes," Peter replied, and I remained quiet while he explained. "We are hoping to integrate ourselves into a local village and be in a position to observe and listen."

"You realize that the villagers won't let you sit around and just observe and listen," Karl said, propping himself against his work table, shoving his hands in his pockets. "You'll have to work if you want to eat." His tone sounded a mite snarky.

"Yes," Peter replied, trying to keep the irritation from his voice. We'd both studied the times and realized we'd most likely be put to work in the fields. Peter, especially, might be forced into some pretty hard work and had been at the gym enhancing his upper body strength. Also, he and Elani had begun jogging with Kipp and me, something Kipp definitely enjoyed. I'd seen Peter without his shirt, and he was looking pretty buff. No six-pack, but definitely more toned. I couldn't say the same for me.

"For you, Peter, I've worked up a tunic, leggings, and a plain shirt that you pull over your head, with some laces at the neckline. There was a variety of footwear in use at the time, and I am looking at some low boots. Since you will be trying to blend in, I stuck with wool, since that was the primary fabric used by all classes, but especially the working class. Only wealthy people broke off and used cotton and even silk as fabrics." He opened a portfolio and pulled out a few pieces of translucent paper upon which he'd done sketches. Karl was actually quite a fine artist, much more so than

Suzanne had been. "There will be a mantle, of course, for you as well as one for Petra. Such overgarments were frequently worn and are functional to help protect from the elements."

"Petra, you will have a smock, which is otherwise called a body linen, and it is a plain garment that will fall to your ankles with a drawstring across your, uh, chest, to provide support." Karl's face turned red as Kipp began to giggle, enjoying the discussion of my need for some type of chest binder. I gave him a look that could turn the ordinary mortal to ice but not Kipp. Elani leaned over and gave Kipp a pretty significant nip on his shoulder.

"Ouch!" he exclaimed. "Why'd you do that?"

"Act like an adult," she huffed, glaring at him. "You're embarrassing her."

Kipp growled in response, garnering a withering stare by Karl. "If you will pay attention, please." With his forefinger, he delicately traced the drawings, pointing out some of the fine details he'd included. His face was slightly flushed, and I realized he was infused with pride over his work.

The pictures were just to set the stage, and Karl already had our garments ready for a fitting, so I retired to the dressing room and began to try on my outfit. First, I pulled the body linen, as Karl called it, over my head; it draped to my ankles as I pulled the drawstring beneath my bust to better fit the otherwise shapeless piece of fabric. The body linen was pale brown in color with loose sleeves that fell to my wrists. I sat on a bench and pulled on the woolen hose which came to my knees and were fastened with garters to keep them in place. Then I picked up the surcoat, which was sleeveless, and slipped the fabric over my head to fall to mid-calf. Karl had supplied a leather belt, which I secured at my waist. At least the woolen surcoat was a nice color of rich blue, and that lightened my mood until I stared at the coif Karl had created, sharing Peter's thoughts on the unattractive head-wear. We'd both wear the unattractive linen cap that tied beneath our chins. But since we would be looking for work, most likely to be found in the agricultural field, we also would have round caps made of straw with a small brim to shade our eyes from sunlight.

"Put on the hat," Kipp giggled from his position of comfort on some discarded fabrics he'd made into a soft nest upon the floor.

"One more word, Kipp," I warned. But I did have to get it over with, so I picked up the coif with distaste and pulled it over my head, securing the ties beneath my chin. More mature ladies, women of means, and widows usually wore a wimple, and the thought of having something covering my head and neck, too, made me feel as if I might suffocate. I couldn't wear underpants, and now that silly hat, I thought. And this whole trip was Kipp's idea. My mouth turned down in a frown. Reluctantly, I left the dressing room and stared at the others, my lips poked out just a little in defiance. But then I spied Peter, who was also miserable, wearing his linen coif, and upon seeing each other, we burst into laughter.

"I don't see what's so amusing," Karl whined, his lips pursing in disapproval.

No, he didn't and never would. Karl busied himself with retrieving our mantles, which were hooded and meant to wear as over garments. Peter, who had decided to become silly, pulled the edge of his mantle across his face and began to prance around the room as if he were some bandit. Elani's tail began to thump as she enjoyed the sight of her partner letting loose.

Since we couldn't deploy our usual reversable back packs, Karl designed a loose fabric sling that we could carry cross-body style. The sling would carry a few items, but very few, since we were travelers of little means. All of our coin, which would be silver, would be hidden in the lupines' money collars. Well, not quite all. Peter would carry a nominal amount in order to pay off bribes or give to greedy bandits. But we hoped we'd be left alone since we appeared to have nothing of value. Peter and I almost exclusively were conversing in Old English at that point in order to hone our skills. The times to which we'd travel were dangerous ones, and there could be no mistakes. Or so we hoped.

# EIGHT

I felt as if I were awakening from a long sleep during which my body had been twisted into a strained, unnatural position for an extended period. In other words, I ached ... and not just a little. My first small movement brought on a cascade of pain that was going to last until I could get mobile and work out the kinks acquired during the time-shift. After a quick moment of trying to regain my bearings, I recalled that Kipp, Peter, Elani, and I had traveled, and I was lying in a stand of tall grass. My first impression was that the earth beneath me was damp, and perhaps there had been a recent rainfall; the scent of rich soil, organic and dense, was thick in the air. Opening my eyes, I found there was an evolving sun that had just broken over the eastern horizon, and a gentle wind disturbed the grass, which made a soft, rustling sound as it waved in the breeze. Inhaling, I thought I caught a whiff of wood smoke, but it was just a faint impression. Instinctively, I reached for Kipp and found him close, his fur warm beneath my fingertips. That mere brush of my fingers against him was settling, and I felt reassured that all would be okay.

I'd tried to warn my companions that the really extensive time-shifts left one feeling a bit more bruised than those that were less complicated in terms of our body physics. It was as if the winds of time had battered our physical beings, and I was distinctly sore. Peter and Elani were near, hidden in the tall grass, and I thought I heard Peter moan.

"Are you okay?" I whispered, since we didn't know where we'd landed.

"I think so. But it feels like someone gave me a good whipping," he answered, keeping his reply equally soft.

We had a leaving party that was festive, and I don't know when I've had more fun at such an event since, for once, I was not the focus. The merry bunch of pranksters decided to roast Peter, and since he had little traveling history to reveal, his mother presented a verbal portfolio of embarrassing things he'd done since birth to present times. I must say, he took it all in good measure, and I laughed until my ribs ached. After the meal and general festivities, most of the guests drifted away to return to their homes, and Philo followed me out onto my narrow back porch as we watched the lupines prowl around the darkened back yard, pretending to be a wolf pack on the hunt. Who says that mature lupines can't have a little fun too?

"Do I need to tell you to be careful?" Philo began, putting his arm around my shoulder and pulling me close. I felt his warm breath graze my cheek. He was taller than I, and our height differences made it comfortable to tuck my head beneath his chin.

"Once, I needed to be told that all the time since I was much more careless. But I'm getting less interested in doing anything extreme," I replied, smiling up at him. "I'll be the one telling the other three to pull back and take care."

"I never thought we'd both get to the places we find ourselves," Philo said, choosing to sit on the concrete stoop. He stared into the darkness and became quiet for a moment as he listened to the soft sounds of the lupines panting as they walked through the grass, their heads down, taking in the smell of the earth. "I'm a manager, something I never thought I'd be, as well as a free-wheeling single guy." Philo laughed, and I couldn't tell if there was any bitterness there. If there was, he hid it well, and being a polite symbiont, I didn't pry. "And you are the deliberate and mature leader of a young team. You are the one telling the others to heed caution."

Philo bumped his shoulder against mine. "Who would have thunk it?"

We chatted about meaningless things, avoiding the issue of my leaving on a potentially dangerous trip. It was obvious that any time we traveled to a vastly different culture, inherent challenges were posed by our very presence. Finally, Vashti returned from the lupines' make-believe world and signaled she was ready to go home. Philo gave me a final hug and disappeared around the corner of my yard, swallowed up by the darkness. After Philo left, Peter and I returned to the kitchen to clean up the mess of the party, while Fitzhugh hung out at the dinette, turning one of the chairs so he could watch us work. His head was down at times, and he seemed more pensive than usual for him. As I was drying the crock pot, I glanced over and saw him trying to hide the fact he'd been staring at me.

"What?" I asked.

"Be careful," he replied.

Peter, for once, showed an unusual level of sensitivity, and after briskly clearing his throat, declared he was going to join Kipp and Elani out back.

I carefully folded my dish towel and sat down at the dinette across from Fitzhugh. "You know I will be, although that might not have once been the case." Smiling, I winked at him. "I've become the stolid old boring symbiont you needed me to be."

He laughed. "That could never be true. Just be careful."

Fitzhugh's words rang in my head as I sat up, peering over the tall grass, hoping there was not an army of suspicious men waiting across the field playing peek-a-boo with me. Kipp, meanwhile, was using his superior telepathy and confirmed that there were no humans close by, so I stood up slowly, trying to work the knots out of my neck and back. Kipp rose too, and stretched, first the front part of his body, then the rear, his ears flattened against his head. Peter was up, a grimace on his face, while Elani yawned. She, as always, was a relaxed traveler with an amazing ability to rebound quickly. Even more so than Kipp, I thought, shielding that notion from my partner since he might take offense.

"I smell woodsmoke too," Kipp remarked, confirming my

impression. "But it must be a fair distance away since I don't pick up on people." He lifted his nose to the sky. "This wind probably carries scents for a long way."

Walking slowly as I regained my equilibrium, I moved towards Peter, reaching out to touch his arm. "Take a few deep breaths," I advised. "These extended time-shifts are more difficult than the short hops." He nodded his dark head, leaning forward to place his hands on his knees. Turning, I smiled at Elani. "You amaze me, girl." She lifted her head and wagged her tail. "You are a natural, Elani." Her tail wagged harder.

We were in a grassy field bordered by a line of large trees, mostly oak and some birch, and scattered about were hornbeams as well as aspens. A breeze caressed the tops of the trees as the aspens turned silver against the backdrop of the sky. We'd aimed for a late summer landing, and the temperature was pleasant, not overly warm, but probably about right for the area. Of course, we'd have no idea of the time, place, or date until we found habitation and figured out some way to ask without seeming to be insane.

"Which way, guys?" I asked, looking at the pair of lupines. They were standing close, Kipp's vivid auburn coloring so different from Elani's softer tones, their heads up as they sampled the air with superior noses to Peter and me. Both lupines had a better sense of direction than did I, and I knew that for a fact.

"I'd say that way," Kipp replied, pointing with his nose.

That was good enough for me, and we began to walk across the field, the tall grass brushing against my legs as we made our way. From the position of the sun, we knew that it was morning, and the sun had burned off the low, thin veil of clouds that typically would usher in the day. Kipp had done his usual research of the area prior to our time-shift, so unless something had gone horribly wrong -- and with Kipp that would be a rarity -- we were hopefully in England, 1192. And if we had landed anywhere near Nottingham or Sherwood Forest, that would be a bonus. Peter was walking at my side, his head down, brooding, I thought. Although why he might feel anything less than successful was puzzling to me. After all, we'd made a lengthy time-shift, and he was typically the adventurous one who couldn't wait to see what was ahead.

"What's bothering you?" I finally asked.

"I'm not envious of Kipp," he began, "and I hope you believe that."

"Well of course I do," I replied, uncertain where he was going.

"I just wonder if I'll ever be able to travel with his accuracy," Peter replied, his cheeks flushed. He was obviously embarrassed to admit such a thought.

I touched his arm, and we stopped walking for a moment. "Peter, you are still learning this business. And as we've discussed, as a bonded team, you and Elani work together to create a whole. She lacks the ability to verbally communicate and build relationships with humans through speech. However, she can, through touch, learn much there is to discover about a person. She seems to have some superior ability to guide travel, just as does Kipp." I leaned down to ruffle the fur on Kipp's broad head. "I've led time-shifts back when I was with Tula, but I acknowledge Kipp is better at doing that than am I. Would I be foolish to insist upon taking control of something that he does so well?"

Peter's face flushed a deeper hue of pink. "You're right, of course. I guess I'm in a hurry to learn things."

"Peter, we live very long lives. You've got plenty of time. I'm still learning, by the way."

He smiled and looked at Elani, whose brush-like tail began to wag. I think we all need a little encouragement and hand-holding from time to time. We resumed our pace, and by the time we came to what was obviously a road or at least a frequently traveled place, the sun was directly overhead, and I could feel the sweat rolling down my back. There were ruts in the packed dirt where wagon wheels had moved. It seemed reasonable to follow such an obvious trail, and we began to walk, uncertain of anything at that point. After about two hours or so of constant walking, we came upon a stream of clear water that bubbled over a bed of smooth, polished rocks. There was a grove of large trees taking advantage of the natural water source, and my feet hurt, so it seemed a good place to rest for a few moments. I picked a place in the shadows cast by the trees. It was not hot weather, but the constant walking in the glare of the sun made it seem so. Kipp went to stand in the stream, letting the cool water soothe his paws. He glanced around at me and wagged his tail, smiling as do lupines.

"This is great!" he exclaimed, not meaning the water. Kipp sought adventure and never was one to complain about the physical exertions involved. Suddenly, his head twisted; his body became stiff, taut with apprehension. "Someone's coming," he breathed. Elani's head went up too, and her nostrils quivered as she tested the air, gathering scents lost to Peter and me.

Peter, who'd been exploring the creek, returned to my side. Humans approaching could either be good or very dangerous for us. Reaching out, he gently clasped my forearm. "Here we go," he said, darting a quick smile at me. He was nervous, but did an admirable job of hiding it.

We saw, first, a couple of riders visible when they came around a curve in the road, the rest of the party hidden by trees. Then, following closely, were more riders, as well as a large wagon pulled effortlessly by a pair of oxen. The wagon was tented, providing cover to whatever contents or passengers were within. The two front riders obviously saw us and urged their horses to approach. Their thoughts betrayed the fact they were paid as guides and protection for the rest of the party. The two men stopped, and one dismounted, approaching us, while his mounted companion looked warily from side to side, frowning as his eyes grazed the tree line. It was clear they were concerned about bandits and outlaws and had experienced a situation where a seemingly innocent traveler was actually a bait, while the rest of the bandits remained concealed until ready to attack. They were not wearing armor but were not dressed like peasants either, and both were armed with swords. The man who approached us was young, considering that the life span was not what it would be in contemporary times.

"Greetings, friends," he called out, and although his words were pleasant, he was nervous and worried, and I almost applauded since he was speaking in Old English. We obviously were in the correct country, and at least the man was using language that fit the times. The man's blue eyes stared at first Peter, then me, lingering for a moment, before the anxiety left his face. At that point, his instinct told him we were of no potential harm to his party. As would be fitting for a woman of the times, I'd covered my head with a length of very light, soft wool, wrapping it to make a modified wimple. My new head gear was the result of both Peter and my having told Karl that the coifs were a no-go. We needed straw hats anyway, for field work, and that was perfectly acceptable. Karl insisted we bring the coifs with us, and to keep down any arguments, they were stowed in our travel packs.

"I am Peter of Winchester, and this is my sister, Petra." Peter's Old English was good, quite good by then, and the man to whom he spoke didn't flinch, so I figured we were on the right course. "We are traveling in hopes of finding a village in need of some laborers for the harvest. Eventually, we hope to make our way to Nottingham." Peter had specifically picked a home location that was distant, we hoped, from wherever we'd landed.

"And what's in Nottingham for you?" the man asked bluntly, thinking he had a right to know such things.

"I hope to apprentice to a smith," Peter smiled easily. As he conversed with the man, I realized he really needed to give himself more credit for his skills of convincing conversation as well as lying with a straight face. He needed to worry less about Elani's talents and appreciate his own.

The man's eyes flicked towards the lupines, who were trying to look stupid and bored. Kipp even began to scratch at a nonexistent flea, his lolling tongue making him look dull and unconcerned. The man turned and looked back at the waiting party before beckoning them forward. The oxen, which had enjoyed a brief rest, were pushed into action, and the wagon creaked forward, swaying slightly as the wheels caught in the rutted road. In a minute, they drew to our location and stopped again. A well-dressed man, obviously with some wealth to his name as evidenced by his fine garments featuring a richly embroidered surcoat, was riding a palfrey, which pawed the packed ground restlessly, obviously eager to keep moving. I noted the distinctive headwear he wore and recognized it to be the customary head covering of a Jewish man. Before he could speak, a voice from within the tented area of the wagon called out, and the well-dressed man said something to one of the outriders. As we watched, the outrider dismounted and went to the rear of the wagon; a moment later, he assisted an elderly man to climb down the steps. The old man glanced at us, a smile tugging at the corner of his mouth, before he began to walk, picking his way carefully across the broken ground.

"I am Joseph of York," the elderly man said. His face was almost lost in the white beard that cascaded down to mid-chest. The flesh of his face was deeply furrowed with wrinkles, making his face look a little like a piece of fruit left out too long. I always thought of wrinkles as a type of road map, from one's birth to the end of life, a badge of honor that one had finally made it, and I never understood the need of humans to fight them off so aggressively. "I am happy for you to join our party as we travel towards Nottingham. There are villages between here and the city, and perhaps you will find one in need of laborers for the fields. The villages are preparing for harvest, after all."

Kipp was staring at Joseph as he talked, almost blocking me due to his focus on the thoughts of the elderly man. "Joseph has left York. Although it is safer now than previously, he is fearful there could be another riot such as happened in the past when many of his faith were killed by a mob."

I was half-listening to Kipp. The encouraging news was that we had landed in the correct vicinity, or at least one of the rumored haunts of Robin Hood. We were in a time period following 1190, since that was when the massacre of Jews in York occurred. I caught Elani's eye, who imperceptibly nodded her head.

"And you are welcome to rest from your travels in the back of my wagon, if you wish," Joseph continued, smiling and gesturing with his hands.

"But, Father," the man with the distinctive headdress began, before Joseph held up one hand. He obviously commanded respect because the younger man immediately stopped speaking.

"We are called upon to serve the weary pilgrim, are we not, my son?" Joseph smiled again.

We found ourselves invited into the confines of his wagon, where there were benches on either side of a center area, with crates stored at the front. Joseph, because he had a soft spot for the beasts of the earth, invited Kipp and Elani to rest, too.

"This is very kind of you, sir," I began, before Joseph shook away my gratitude.

"It is a little matter," he replied, shrugging his shoulders. From the weathered planes of his face, a pair of very clear brown eyes gazed at me; his glance was perceptive, acutely so, and I guessed nothing was easily missed by him. I noticed his clothing was not as fine as that of his son, but it was well made and of good fabric and definitely not that of the peasant class. "And I will enjoy the company, since I have no one with whom I may talk." As telepaths, we could determine his true intentions, and they were just as he'd spoken. He was being kind to weary travelers and enjoyed meeting new people. It was refreshing not to have to unravel intrigue. Elani was itching to have him touch her so she could explore his persona, but he didn't reach out to her. Joseph didn't dislike dogs, but he lacked some humans' need to touch and caress them in an almost instinctive manner. Elani was smart enough not to push her large body too close.

"He trades in spices," Kipp began, his thoughts active in the back of that swaying wagon.

I could smell the sweat rolling off the oxen as well as the earthy odors from the palfreys and the men who were guides and protection against outlaws. Daily baths were not part of the culture, so we all would have to desensitize our noses just a bit.

"He trades in something called saffron, as well as ginger, nutmeg, sugar, and cinnamon." Kipp glanced at me, needing an explanation.

"Many spices were just about as valuable as gold," I replied, keeping my remarks telepathic and private. "People used spices in cooking then, just as in modern times. Many things were grown in local gardens, such as basil, sage, marjoram, rosemary, and thyme. But other things, much more exotic, had to be imported from other parts of the world."

"Oh," Kipp mouthed.

"And why, young man, are you traveling?" Joseph asked, obviously not having heard the explanation Peter had given earlier.

"I hope to apprentice to a smith in Nottingham. But first, my sister and I had planned to find work at a village close by and earn enough to help with lodging and food." Peter leaned forward and nodded his thanks, taking a ripe plum held out to him by Joseph.

"It sounds like a difficult road," Joseph remarked. "But an honest one. And a good smith is worth much to a master, so I wish good fortune to you. There is a town near here, and I believe the reeve is a fair man, or at least as fair as can be found. I might suggest that you begin your search there."

"Thank you," Peter replied, bowing his head. As he bit into the plum, juice rolled down his chin, disappearing into his dark beard.

As we rocked along the uneven road, the four of us managed to keep up a lively private discourse while Peter continued to speak with Joseph. If we were accepted in a village to help as traveling workers, there would still be a learning curve. Much would depend upon whether or not the reeve, who was one of the locals holding administrative responsibilities to make certain the village met its goals in terms of production of crops, would allow us to stay there and work.

"The name of the village is Ashland near Trent, and the reeve, who I have met, is named Johnson. I will be glad to speak with him, if you will permit, since he knows I am a man of my word and it may influence him." Joseph nodded his head in a modest manner. "I would advise you to keep your dogs close, however."

"Why would that be?" I asked, knowing the answer.

"You don't want them going near the royal forests," Joseph replied. "They will either be maimed, or you will not see them again."

I met Kipp's amber gaze; the expression in his eyes was steady and confident. Yes, we were in a different culture and would need to be careful. More so than ever before.

# NINE

"Help me remember again the pecking order of these folks." Peter made a rare admission of having either forgotten an important piece of information or a lack of preparedness. I could either be irritated at him or glad he admitted to it before he made a big boo-boo. I decided to be glad.

"There will be a lord, who owns the land on which the village is situated. He uses the toil of the villagers to manufacture income, and they, in turn, get to keep some portion—albeit small—for themselves." Kipp replied patiently. "The lord could be a knight, an earl, an abbot—someone of means and influence—who has manors scattered over a large area. Then, there is a steward, sometimes called a seneschal, who is the lord's deputy and occasionally shows up in the village to make sure everything is being done correctly. The reeve will be the on-site administrator but is a member of the working class and is a resident of the village itself."

We were on our way again, having spent an evening with the kindly Joseph. His son obviously objected to having strangers in his camp, but it was also apparent that Joseph had lost none of his authority as he aged, and his son, Judah, would not openly defy his father. As we sat around a blazing campfire, Joseph entertained us with stories about his travels through Europe and how he landed in England.

"We felt forced to leave York," he said, his dark eyes meeting mine over the crackling fire. "The people decided that we were not acceptable, and there was a mass killing of many of my relatives and associates." His face crumpled with the tragic memory. "Although the danger is less now, the memories haunted me, and I could not remain there." Joseph's voice broke.

"How long ago did this happen?" Peter asked, trying to get a more solid idea of the year in which we landed.

"Almost two years have passed," Joseph murmured.

My eyes met Peter's. We were in the right time, and it should be 1192! Kipp, amazing lupine traveler, had done it again to perfection.

"I am so sorry for what happened," I said, my voice earnest. "I don't understand why a world this large can't accommodate all sorts of people of different backgrounds and beliefs."

"Because you have a kind heart," Joseph replied, smiling. He leaned back to rest against a small pile of blankets arranged for his comfort. He ignored his son's glance, although I knew Judah was wondering how his father could know such a thing about a stranger. "It is a gift of mine to quickly and correctly assess people I meet." Joseph's thoughts became troubled as he added, "One must learn such skills to survive in a harsh and unforgiving world."

"Father, please, it is time to get some sleep," Judah said softly. I glanced at him. He was a handsome man, with full, dark hair that swept to his shoulders and brown eyes filled with intelligence. However, the riot where so many Jews were killed in York had left him bitter. I felt he was essentially a good man and hoped that bitterness would not change him. Judah did like dogs, and Elani had managed to insinuate her way next to him, and he enjoyed running his fingers through her pelt. Elani looked at me, slowly closing one eye to indicate she agreed with my assessment of the man.

Out of respect for Judah, I turned on my back, hoping Joseph would try to disengage and rest. Looking up, I could see the black sky from between gaps in the canopy of trees that overshadowed our camp. It was a starry night with a quarter moon glowing softly silver hovering overhead. Kipp pushed close to me, acting like a security blanket as well as a heater.

"I think things are going well so far, don't you?" he asked. There was a tinge of anxiety in his query, since he knew he'd arranged this time-shift, and even though he wasn't responsible for the choices of the rest of us, he would feel so if we faced hardships. It was just being Kipp.

"Yes, and we lucked out to meet Joseph," I replied, my hand touching the top of Kipp's head for a scratch.

From a distance, we could hear howling, and it took me a minute to recall that there were wolves in England during that period; Kipp huddled closer. The horses, which were secured nearby with tethers, moved restlessly, a couple whinnying softly as their feet shuffled in the dead leaves and debris. Judah rose and went over to speak to the man who was taking guard. Joseph had fallen asleep, the sound of his soft snores filling the air. I was glad he was already sleeping so he'd not have the stress of worrying about predators nearby.

"Don't worry, I'll keep an eye out," Kipp murmured, nuzzling the side of my face.

"My hero," I replied affectionately, although I didn't think wolves would attack a camp the size of ours.

"I'll watch out, too," Elani said. Peter had already fallen asleep, and the drama was lost to him.

Sleep, however, came slowly for me, and I lay there reflecting upon my life and the current state of my existence. Kipp was close, his thoughts mingled with mine, occasionally retreating politely to give me some space but never going too far away. Neither he nor I would want such at that point in our relationship. I came to the conclusion that life was good. I was able to follow my natural abilities as a symbiont and traveler, and the state of my relationship with Kipp was beyond description, since it seemed perfect. My home was filled with elderly treasures who helped me become a better symbiont, I hoped. And just across the street was my oldest friend, who cohabited with my new traveling buddies. I'd noticed humans were always seeking an elusive path to happiness when the obvious stared them in the face. My obvious was staring at me, and

I felt oddly content. Finally, I felt sleep overtake me as I blinked my eyes shut, yawning as I squirmed down into the bedding I'd carried, along with my few other items, in a sling across my back. The thoughtful Joseph had supplemented our thin bedding with a heavier blanket, and I felt blissful and unexpectedly comfortable.

Because I'd spent half the night staring at the sky, when dawn broke and the camp began to stir, I felt as if I'd been hit over the head with something heavy. Kipp licked the side of my face, his tongue hot against my flesh. "Get up, lazy bones," he murmured. I glanced up to see Peter smiling, looking down at me. He leaned forward to give me a hand and pulled me to my feet. I'd not slept on the ground in a while and tried not to groan, since every muscle felt as if it had been exposed to some sort of extreme sport activity. I recalled once feeling almost that bad after an aggressive game of racquetball superimposed upon a body that was not quite up to the challenge.

"Is there anything that doesn't hurt?" Peter asked, grinning.

"Maybe the top of my head," I replied as I pushed my hair into some semblance of order.

Judah walked towards us, bowing his head politely. "Ashland near Trent is perhaps five miles distant," he said, his dark eyes glancing at first Peter, then me. He was trying not to stare at my tangled hair and sleep-swollen face.

"Oh, we can most certainly walk that distance," Peter said. "We are so grateful for your hospitality."

"My father insists we take you and that he introduces you to Johnson, the reeve." Judah's face darkened a little. "My father has a good heart and finds pleasure in helping those in need." He glanced over his shoulder at his father, who was washing his face in a basin of water. "I take a more cautious view of the world than does he."

"And maybe it is good for all of us to balance the two," I replied, smiling. "There is room for kindness but also to be wary of possible dangers."

Judah stared at me, not long enough to be impolite, but he was busy thinking. There was a part of him that agreed with my comments, but the York riot still weighed so heavily on him that it was difficult to move beyond that horror. Finally, he nodded. "I bow to your wise words," he said. Elani took that opportunity to edge up to Judah, and he reached down to gently run his hand over her soft fur. "She is a sweet dog," he remarked as the rare smile crossed his serious face.

We broke a cold camp after eating some crusty bread dipped in oil. There was also dried meat, yellow cheese, and fruit. Joseph made certain the lupines had a share of the food and was rewarded with wagging tails. I decided to walk for a while, following behind the creaking wagon, Peter at my side. I was still so stiff from a night spent on the ground that I needed to limber up before we arrived at Ashland and tried to act as if we could be farm laborers. There were dark clouds building on the western sky, looking like a roll of gray waves upon an otherwise placid ocean, and it was apparent there could be a threat of rain later in the day. Hopefully, we would be safe in some type of lodging by that time. The lupines decided to free wheel and were busy canvassing the countryside, their sleek bodies racing side by side as they sniffed out the land.

"Here is where the wolves passed," Kipp announced excitedly, his thoughts crossing over a small hillock to find me as his busy nose explored a track of ground. "Oooh, one of them left his business here, and I almost stuck my nose in it!"

I couldn't help myself, and I began to laugh and not softly. Judah pulled his horse back and stared down at me. Peter put his arm around my shoulder and shook his head at Judah. "She was thinking of something funny that happened to us during our travels. Petra can be a silly woman at times."

Judah smiled and guided his horse back to the lead position. I punched Peter in the side with my elbow. "Silly, am I? You try keeping a straight face when Kipp is sending all these crazy notions into your brain."

As we walked, we began to notice worked fields on either side of the road. As I swallowed, it seemed I could almost taste the fertile soil in the back of my throat. I quickly identified wheat, the golden stalks shimmering against the rolling landscape, moving in waves when caught by the wind. Since I had more agricultural history than Peter, I knew the field to be a healthy-appearing one, planted with care and calculation. It was clear that Johnson, the reeve of

Ashland near Trent, knew his business. Overhead, the sky blackened as a large flock of birds soared, their direction vaguely northwest. Kipp and Elani came back into view, their sides heaving with the effort of their run. I knew such to be good for them, as their physiology differed from ours, and their muscles needed extreme stress from time to time. Elani's jaw dropped in a smile as she drew to my side.

"Kipp found the trail of the wolves but got scared," she said, her tone a little smug.

"Was not!" Kipp replied, affronted by her accusation.

"I wanted to go after them, but he said not to." Elani snorted a little.

"Okay, you guys, just can it. We are getting close to the village and need to focus." Peter mildly chastised them.

The village appeared in a clearing ahead, and I began to assess it using my telepathy as well as a visual appraisement. It appeared moderate in size, with dwellings grouped around a center clearing. There was a circular stone edifice that probably contained the well where water was drawn. Off to the left was the largest building, and I was pretty certain that was where grains were stored after harvest. The homes, some no more than hovels, ranged from single-level cottages to two-level dwellings. They appeared to be made of timber and daub and wattle, the main building materials of the times. Thatch, thick and stained from weather exposure and green with thickened patches of moss and silvery lichens, served as roofs. From most of the dwellings, a thin line of smoke rose from a center opening in the thatch, since actual chimneys were yet to be invented. As we got closer, I could smell large animals, such as horses and cattle, as well as the distinctive odor of swine. Most of the people were already at work, and in one field, we saw a line of people walking, their bodies outlined against the land.

"If they are planting winter wheat, then we have arrived in late summer, maybe September," Peter murmured.

I glanced at him. His brown eyes were bright with excitement; a smoke-scented drifting breeze caught in his thick hair, and for a moment, he reminded me of the lupines with his energy and the brashness of youth. I'd once viewed all new adventures similarly, but age and experience had tempered that exuberance, and now I looked for potential dangers and was more risk aversive than I'd once been.

Our small party ground to a halt, and one of the riders moved to the wagon to assist Joseph. It occurred to me that Joseph might have looked much older than in reality, since the harshness of life during the times aged people prematurely. Or else he was one of the anomalies, a human who aged despite all factors to the contrary. Joseph, his white hair forming the illusion of a halo around his head when caught in the sunlight, smiled at me and nodded his head. From the village, a man approached, waving his hand at our party.

"Master Joseph," the man said, smiling, revealing a broken front tooth.

"Reeve Johnson," Joseph replied, reaching out to grasp Johnson's forearm in a greeting that was familiar yet restrained.

Johnson looked at us with curiosity, his gaze lingering on the lupines, a slight frown worrying at his face. He was a large man, especially so considering the times and the fact height and longevity of humans increased over the ages with improved nutrition and medical care. Johnson wore a straw hat, the indispensable tool of a land worker. His shirt was stained with sweat; his tunic had been discarded in the heat of sun exposure. If we'd indeed arrived in the correct time period, and Joseph's story of why he left York was our indicator, then baths were perhaps done weekly, if that. And Johnson smelled of honest toil … several days' worth.

Kipp's nose crinkled. But before he could say anything, I glared at him. "Kipp, you came from prehistoric times. I know you've been around people who don't bathe frequently. So, let's not dwell on the subject, okay?"

"Hey, boss, don't get cranky with me. You're the one who has to take a bath every day. I'm fine with this, doesn't bother me a bit." Kipp glanced up at me, his amber eyes meeting mine. "I don't want to hear from you if you get stinky."

"Let's all remember we are here to observe and record history. The customs of the day are just as important as other facts." Elani glared at Kipp, challenging him to say anything more. Wisely, he kept his muzzle clamped. It was nice to have another gal on my side.

During our private dialog, Joseph was making introductions of us to Johnson, who had folded his forearms across his chest. His blue eyes made an appraising evaluation of Peter, who was young and strong, so he would make a good field worker. He glanced at me and realized that I, too, could work in the fields, although a name popped up in his head as he connected me to a woman villager named Anne. He immediately thought I'd be of use to her. But then his gaze drifted to the lupines, who were sitting politely, their eyes blinking lazily in the sunlight. A deepening crease appeared between Johnson's dark brows.

"Them dogs can be trouble," Johnson began, pointing at the lupines. "If they get loose in the king's forest, we'll all be in for it."

"But, sir," Peter began before Johnson held up his hand.

"I'm called Reeve Johnson," the man corrected him, his face stern.

"Reeve Johnson, our dogs are good watch dogs, and they can herd on command. They were raised with other animals and do not hunt unless we allow it." Peter's voice was earnest.

"I'm not sure," Johnson began. He glanced at Joseph, almost apologetically.

"Will you let me demonstrate their usefulness?" Peter persisted.

Johnson didn't reply but also didn't say no, so Peter took Elani and Kipp aside. Turning, Peter squinted off into the distance, where he saw a small flock of sheep being prodded along on a dusty path by a boy carrying a staff. They were headed our way, so Peter made a display of making commands that were nonsensical. Kipp and Elani took off like rockets, veering at the last minute to circle the sheep, which were rather alarmed and, as sheep do, clustered tighter together, bawling as they allowed themselves to be driven by the lupines until they were nicely tucked away in a small corral.

"Kipp, Elani, return here!" Peter called, sweeping his arm out in a gesture that looked so silly I almost laughed out loud.

The lupines hadn't broken a sweat and returned to his side, both plopping their bottoms in the dust so sharply I feared a hip bone might have been fractured. Johnson removed his straw hat and scratched at his balding head. The smile came, reluctantly, Johnson's broken tooth exposed in the process.

"I figure you all can stay through harvest, but you need to keep your dogs from running in the forest. If it's heard that they are a threat to the deer or boar, his lordship will have their toes clipped and hobble them." His thoughts were clear on that, although he couldn't say so. Johnson actually liked dogs and strongly disapproved of the maiming of dogs. But he was a small fish with no ability to change that law, and his position as reeve was important to his survival. Like the other peasants, he would keep his mouth shut and do as told. "Be a shame to damage such nice dogs," he added under his breath. He looked over his shoulder, and I followed his gaze to a long, low cottage, built in the old style, that was located on the fringe of the village. An older appearing woman had just walked outside, her body stooped and appearing stiff with probable arthritis. Her head lifted with interest as she looked towards us, long gray locks escaping from her coif to drift over her thin shoulders.

"Let's go and meet Anne," Reeve Johnson said.

# TEN

Over the course of many years as a traveler, I have met humans who would become more than casual acquaintances. On occasions, I still dream of Perdy, a woman I'd met during my first time-shift with Kipp. Through the years, she remained a model of a fine human, strong, courageous, and loyal. And I know the love I feel for William Harrow will not fade. If I am fortunate enough to live the naturally long life-span of a symbiont, I will carry that special feeling with me until my last day. Later, I would add the simple name of Anne to my book of cherished memories. I'm sure humans have had the experience that they meet someone new and realize, immediately, there is something special in that encounter that will evolve into a meaningful relationship. It is almost a sense of familiarity not often felt with a stranger. That was my experience with Anne.

She looked older than she was, the result of a hard life of endless toil. A goodness of heart resonated from her; her face was open, happy, and welcoming as her gray eyes gazed at my face. As my mind searched hers, I realized she had a simple way of viewing the world but had managed to do this through the discipline of an acutely intelligent mind. No, she was not educated in any conventional manner but had wisdom acquired through a lifetime of experiences. Anne had the rare human gift of listening carefully to others and observing, taking in the thoughts of others to expand herself. Despite a harsh life, she lacked bitterness and radiated contentment and curiosity. Her eyes shifted to Peter, then the lupines, who were trying their best to fade into nothingness, a difficult task due to their remarkable appearance.

"Hello," Anne said. She lifted a thin hand discolored by sun exposure and brushed back a wisp of graying hair that had fallen across her face. I noticed her nails were short and ragged, the nails and hands of someone who worked the soil.

"Anne, these two people are going to stay with us and help with harvest," Johnson began. "I know you have a place in your cottage and maybe could accommodate them." He added, "They seem to be strong and willing and can be helpmates to you as well as the village."

I wasn't sure why he thought we'd be such sterling additions— since for all he knew, we might be terrible slackers -- but figured Joseph's recommendation had lent a lot to the moment.

Anne smiled, not hesitating. "Why, yes, since Sam and his family left, my home has seemed empty." Her gray eyes flicked to me again. "And I could use help with my gathering."

Kipp was watching her, his head tilted slightly towards the side. "She works, too, but not in the fields. She goes into the woods looking for things that are a part of the bounty of this village." He paused before continuing. "Sam was her son, who has traveled to another village where he hopes to become reeve one day." Kipp looked at me. "He's trying to move up in the world."

It was tough, in those times, to move out of the spot to which one had been born. There were the desperately poor, the peasants, and then there was the ruling class and its layers of complexity.

"Come with me," Anne said, turning. She had the beginnings of a dowager's hump in her back, and in her hand was a long walking stick made smooth from years of use. Despite the toll time had taken on her body, her mind was clear, her thoughts quick and lively. Somehow, the harshness of her life had added to her in a way that was wonderful to view. She'd leave the world one day, her soul unencumbered by darkness.

We followed her into what I recognized to be an earlier style of housing that lingered at the end of the century. One might think of it as a primitive ranch, since it was one long, low level. It had originally housed the livestock at one end, with a dung trench carved in the middle, separating the animals from where the people lived. There were open windows, but these were small so that they could be covered, if needed, in cold weather. In the center of the main room, there was a fire pit smoldering, and the interior of the cottage was smoky and dark. Lanterns had not yet been created, and light came from candles made of tallow. A class distinction was apparent with something as simple as a candle. The poor and peasant class used tallow, while the wealthy and church hierarchy burned candles made of beeswax. When the tallow was burned, those candles added to the general stink in the air. But instead of the stench I expected, I was almost overwhelmed by a multitude of scents, pleasant, floral, herbal and uplifting. I tried not to grin but couldn't stop myself.

"It's nice, isn't it?" Anne smiled, revealing a complete set of teeth.

On the right side of the cottage where the animals would have once resided, there were rows of drying racks, and from every conceivable place, flowers, roots, and herbs were air drying. We'd lucked out in that the atmosphere would keep down the usual pests that were common in those times. Although fleas weren't attracted to the lupines' body chemistry, they could be hungry enough to bite them or us. Anne's combination of drying substances would drive away fleas, lice, and rats. The strength of the odors created a natural, organic pest repellant.

"It's lovely," I replied, my eyes meeting hers.

"I go into the woods and find these things," she said, moving forward to show me, as I followed like a puppy in her orbit. "I have lavender, and here, you see, is some lady's bedstraw, which is good when making one's water is difficult. The roots and flowers make colorful dyes, too. Yarrow and meadowsweet are needed by the barbers and doctors who treat the ill and injured." She paused, squinting a little in the dimly-lit area before pointing to another bunched herb. "Verbain, too, is needed by the doctors, although some mothers use it in their homes to keep away evil spirits, although I don't believe in such things." Anne pursed her lips and shook her head from side to side, placing an emphasis on her opinion of such superstition. She led me to the wall where a series of shelves held clay pottery jars filled with the results of her labor.

Elani trailed behind her, her head cocked to the side as she listened closely. She was hoping Anne would stop and pet her, wanting that contact. Maybe it was something in her attitude of longing that compelled Anne to turn and look down at her.

"You're a pretty girl, aren't you?" Anne remarked, stretching out her hand to Elani, who took that moment to sidle next to the woman.

I'd learned how to identify the change that came over Elani when she made the physical connection that allowed her to divine the intention of a human without our typical telepathic intrusion. It was a combination of total relaxation with an "aha" realization, which would seem to be an impossible mixture but was not.

Peter caught my eye, and in our private way of communication, he said, "Petra, this is very fortunate. We really couldn't have fashioned a better situation if we'd tried."

Personally, I was happy since I'd had my share of sleeping on the ground, in hovels and racing from danger. The idea of this village with people who, so far, seemed nice, as well as a decent place to sleep, worked for me.

"Don't forget, however," Kipp bored into my happy zone, "there will be a lot of difficult physical labor while we are here."

"Gee, thanks." I frowned at him.

Anne finished the brief tour of her artistry, and we wandered back to the habited side of the byre house. Looking down, I noticed the rushes on the floor, which must have been recently laid, because they smelled clean, of sunshine and meadows. Cottages such as that had few furnishings, and Anne's was no exception. A battered small table was angled near the doorway, with two benches on either side. Pegs on the wall held a cloak as well as Anne's few items of clothing. A few pewter plates and cups rested on a roughly constructed shelf along with a pot for cooking. There were two beds at either end of the room where straw-filled mattresses were hung on ropes that crisscrossed wooden frames. In the corner was a low table with a large pottery bowl. My experience told me this was where we would take our bird baths.

"My son and his wife slept there," Anne mentioned, pointing to the slightly larger bed frame. "I hope that will be comfortable for you."

It was clear that she meant Peter and I would share the bed, and such a thing was not uncommon amongst peasants of the day. People were crammed together and shared small spaces. This time, Peter took the lead.

"This is more than we could have expected," he replied graciously.

Kipp began to giggle softly until Elani hushed him. I personally figured we'd all be so tired that it wouldn't matter, and I could probably sleep propped up in a corner. Peter hadn't done that type of hard work before, but I had. He was in for a rare treat.

There was a shadow at the door ... it was Reeve Johnson, who nodded his head politely. "Anne, I thought I'd take the young man with me to the fields and show him what work is to be done."

Peter smiled, hoping he looked eager, although I could feel the anxiety creep up his shoulders. He'd never handled a scythe before, and it took some skill. But I figured, after a couple of hours or so, he'd be an old pro. A sore old pro, but one nonetheless. After a quick glance at me, he put on his straw hat and was out the door. Elani, after touching noses with Kipp, followed Peter. They wouldn't be in the woods, so she should not be in any danger.

Anne looked at me, her gray eyes as soft as still lake water. "And you are with me ..." she stumbled as she realized she didn't know my name.

"I'm Petra, and my brother is Peter of Winchester," I said, smiling.

"Petra. What an unusual and lovely name." Anne looked at Kipp. "And his name is?"

"Kipp," I replied, laughing.

Her face sobered for a moment. "We will be going in the woods in search of some things, and Kipp can't run loose." She walked over to a peg on the wall near the door and pulled a coil of rope.

"You will have to keep him secured, or else the gamekeeper could have him clipped if he is spotted running."

I glanced at Kipp, waiting for him to whine and complain, but, instead, he meekly stood still and let me tie the rope to his collar. "I'm sorry," I whispered, feeling bad, not liking the idea I was treating him as something less than my equal.

"It's okay," he replied, his amber eyes meeting mine. "It's just part of this age and part of the role we play."

Anne watched our exchange, and for a moment, I half wondered if she knew what I was thinking. Her gray eyes seemed unusually perceptive and wise. I'd taken note of her lack of belief in a common superstition of the day. With few words, she led Kipp and me from her home, her long stick picking out the way as we walked past one of the houses located farthest from the central hub. With her stick, Anne pointed roughly northwest.

"The manor house where his lordship lives is over that hill," she said. "But he's rarely there since he has many homes." She laughed. "I don't think this one is his favorite, but when one is given something by the king, one graciously accepts."

I shared a glance with Kipp. After the Normans won the battle of Hastings, the king basically took land from the Saxon noblemen and parceled it out as favors to those who had served him. It would take centuries for the bad feelings lingering from that takeover to subside. But human culture was full of stories of conquest and defeat; it seemed to be the one constant.

Anne handed me a large basket she carried, and it was only a few minutes later that we were swallowed up by the green forest that formed a natural barrier at the outer edges of the village. I didn't have to ask but figured we were in Sherwood Forest, the territory of outlaws who sought to escape the wrath and punishment of the Normans. Anne found a narrow path that I would have missed, but even with that defined passage, the ferns and underbrush grabbed at my clothing. The tree branches met overhead, curving to create natural arches through which the sun could barely be seen. Occasionally, I'd hear the crash of some creature in the underbrush, startling me since I knew one of the citizens of this world was the dangerous wild boar. And a male deer in search of female companionship could also be pretty unpleasant. Kipp pressed close against me, his telepathy throwing out nets to keep us both safe.

"I gather items, as you have seen. A certain amount goes to pay his lordship, another goes to the church, and what little remains I get to keep." She shrugged her narrow, thin shoulders. "It is the way of things, but I can't complain." Turning, she smiled at me. "My house is warm in the winter, and I have enough to eat. What else is there to worry over?"

I didn't answer but smiled in return. "And what are we in search of today?" I asked.

"There is great demand for betony," she replied. Lifting a thin, gray brow, she added, "Both from the doctors and barbers as well as the abbots and monks." Shaking her head, Anne said, "The churches often have betony planted nearby to ward off witches and evil things. So, when I can find a good root plant and recover it to be replanted, it is a good day."

"And what use does the doctor have?" I asked. Kipp had stopped to sniff at a large snail that was leaving a moist trail along a piece of fallen tree limb, and I paused, since we were attached by the rope I carried.

"Oh, for wounds and boils and such," Anne replied. "I've used it myself on my boy when he was injured." Her gray eyes clouded for a moment. "That was a long time ago, and the boy is now a man." Anne's eyes met mine, and a smile brightened her face. "But such is life, is it not? We are born, we age, we grow old, if we are fortunate, and those we love leave us or we leave them."

I glanced down at Kipp; his amber eyes were bright as he returned my gaze. Even though lupines could not shed tears, his emotions were intense at that moment, as he registered his love for me. After all, he'd left his remote, primitive home to take a chance with an unknown partner. Leaning over, I ran my hand along his back.

"You're attached to your doggie, aren't you?" Anne observed. "I grew up loving animals, seeing them more as friends and companions than beasts to be used." She laughed, the sound light in the thickness of the forest. "My father would be so angry at me, agitated that I'd not want him to slaughter a sheep or make an ox work in the fields until exhaustion. Of course, my father was working until exhaustion, too, and he was never cruel. He was practical."

Anne gave a little soft cry of excitement. "Look at that!" She moved, sure of herself, weaving through some underbrush until she found a grouping of dark, glistening bunched plants sitting low to the ground next to a clear stream that curved through the forest floor. The narrow sliver of water formed a sinuous, silver path, rippling over worn, smooth rocks as it turned and moved out of my field of vision. Bending, Anne pulled her knife from its sheath at her waist and began to carefully dig down into the soil to remove the plants, roots as well as stems and leaves.

"This woad is in high demand," she grunted with satisfaction. "The blue dye will color many a fine lady's cloak," Anne laughed softly.

I knelt next to her, my knees sinking into the earth made soft and pliable by so much rotting vegetation from fallen leaves. Glancing around, I realized one could functionally disappear in a place such as this and live undetected for years. No wonder the authorities of the day struggled to clear the forests of outlaws.

"People could live hidden here, Anne. How would they ever be found if they were being searched for?"

"It is difficult for the sheriff to rid the forests of what he thinks to be criminals," she agreed, nodding her head. "Perhaps it is more luck than skill."

"Are there criminals here?" I asked, pretending to be a little alarmed, although all I wanted was to obtain information from the woman.

"Perhaps, although most of them are just people who refused to be taxed and fled." Anne shrugged. "Some of us make the best of the world while others fight back. Isn't that true of people in general?"

I smiled at her. "Yes, I think so, too."

Kipp was close to me, his body brushing mine, and I realized he had his nose in the air, canvassing the area.

"I smell woodsmoke again, but that could be from Anne's village," he remarked. Tilting his head back, he closed his eyes to concentrate. "I keep getting the impression of something hovering on the edge of my radar, but I'm not quite there yet," Kipp added, panting as he struggled to expand his abilities to their maximum. He then became very still, and my connection to him enabled me to feel his alarm.

"There is something large coming this way and moving fast." Kipp looked off to the north, his eyes straining, ears pitched forward. "It's an animal of some kind, but all I can feel is its aggression. Whatever it is, it's fiercely territorial, and it can sense we are here."

My mind raced as I took in his words. He would have recognized a wolf since he'd had experience with them. Perhaps a stag in rut, since the season was right? Then I felt my mouth go dry. What if it was a wild boar? To call them dangerous was an understatement. I stood from my crouching position and began to stare, hoping my eyes could pierce the dense underbrush for movement.

Anne looked up at me as she placed the last bit of woad in the basket. "What is it, Petra?"

"We need to go," I whispered. "There is something out there coming this way."

Anne had spent her life in the country and knew the forest and surrounding lands better than most. She also knew the dangers, but her senses were not giving off an alarm. I had to prod her.

"Kipp, begin to growl," I privately nudged my partner. We needed to get Anne suitably concerned.

Kipp, at my request, began a low, rumbling growl, even showing his teeth a few times. Anne knew the senses of what she thought to be a dog would surpass hers, and she glanced at me as I took the basket from her. Without running and trying to be as quiet as possible, we began our retreat. I ushered Anne in front of me, hurrying her as much as I could considering her gait was not quite as fleet as mine, while glancing over my shoulder occasionally to view the area we departed. Despite the laws, Kipp needed to be agile, and I stopped to untie the rope from his collar. He took up position behind us, lingering a few times to lift his head and flare his nostrils as he tried to take in the scent of whatever pursued us. And pursue was the right word, because now Anne and I could hear the trampling of the underbrush as something heavy and quick moved in our direction. The rank stench of the hidden creature filled the air, and I glanced at Anne only to see she'd turned pale.

"A wild boar," she whispered.

Kipp had arrived at the same conclusion simultaneously. He turned, bracing himself, putting his body between us and the charging animal.

"Kipp, no!" I cried, torn between leaving Anne and going to Kipp. Anne stumbled, falling to her knees as I huddled at her side.

It was then the beast burst through the underbrush, the musky smell of it filling the small clearing where we made our stand. Its body was covered in stiff bristles; the eyes were small and red as it turned its head to stare at us. The animal paused, and I saw the glistening white of an enormous tusk in its mouth. Boar were notoriously ill-tempered and unpredictable as well as dangerous. I'd had past experiences with just such a beast and had developed, as a result, a very healthy respect for wild boar.

I grabbed a large stick and started towards Kipp, who began a frenzied barking interspersed with growls that echoed amongst the trees. He'd planted his feet; the muscles in his shoulders began to flex, and he was clearly prepared to move. It was simply not in the symbiont make up to leave one's bonded partner behind to face danger alone. And my love for Kipp magnified that code even more so.

"Don't move!" Kipp's words sounded like a shout in my head. "I'm concentrating on him, trying to make him change his mind."

Kipp could influence many beasts, and it was possible he could make the boar rethink its need to attack us. I stopped but didn't drop my large stick—although I didn't think such a feeble weapon would be useful against the boar—and waited, holding my breath as I followed Kipp's thoughts. He was planting a notion in the boar's brain that Kipp was a big threat, one to be avoided at all costs. As I watched, the boar stopped its forward movement and began to twist its massive head from one side to the other in agitation. The beast's instinctual driving force was struggling against its need to deliberate an action based upon life experiences. I was a little amazed to find I was able, through Kipp, to follow the thoughts of the boar. As Kipp focused on the animal, it began to consider the fact that attacking Kipp might be ill-advised. After a few tense seconds, the animal wheeled and retreated, the underbrush swallowing him up as he disappeared from sight.

My knees felt weak, and I almost collapsed from both stress and relief. Until that moment, I hadn't been aware of the beating of my heart, which was pounding against the wall of my chest. Turning, I glanced at Anne, who was kneeling in a patch of ferns, her face beginning to regain some color as evidenced by bright spots of red high up on her cheekbones.

"What happened?" she whispered, almost as if speaking in a normal tone would conjure up the boar again.

"I'm not sure, but I'm glad it did," I replied. Reaching up with a trembling hand, I realized my face was damp with cold sweat.

"Your dog, your Kipp, he, well, he managed to ..." Anne broke off as she stared at Kipp. "The old boar that knows its way will charge the solitary dog but not your Kipp," she said, a smile beginning to show as she realized the danger was truly past.

Kipp returned to me, and I knelt next to him, putting my arms around his neck. As I pulled him into me, I smelled the wildness that was always a part of him, no matter how connected he was to me. And I wondered, for a moment, if I could ever touch that wildness.

"You have," Kipp replied, his tongue grazing my cheek in a sloppy kiss.

# ELEVEN

The story of Kipp's bravery spread amongst the villagers within a few minutes following our arrival. And in the manner of the chain of gossip, the tale had grown in proportion as it moved, and by the time it returned to us, it was vastly enhanced. And to Kipp's advantage.

"By gosh, I heard that old Kipp over there, well he stood down three male boar who were charging at poor Anne. He managed to chase them off, and last heard, them boar were still running for the hills. That old Kipp, now he's one good dog, I say!"

I overheard the villager who made that comment and watched him walk away, rubbing the stubble on his chin in amazement. Glancing down, I stared at the top of Kipp's head until he tilted it back to gaze at me with eyes half-closed.

"What?" he asked.

"You're enjoying this, aren't you?"

"What do you mean?"

"You're a new super hero, kind of like Superman. Except you are Super Kipp, lupine extraordinaire." Of course, I was teasing him. He actually had saved me and Anne from an attack and was pretty darn heroic, but I didn't want him to get a big head.

"Why do you always worry about the size of my head?" Kipp asked, taking my thoughts literally.

I threw back my head and laughed, partly from his response and also because I'd had a definite scare in those woods, and it was good to feel safe again. Looking up, I saw Peter running from the field, Elani at his side, and a flood of anxiety and worry preceded them, like a wave rolling across the surface of the ocean.

"Are you both okay?" Peter gasped, his face covered in sweat and fine flakes of dried wheat that had adhered to his flesh like glue.

I felt a stab of guilt. There I was merrily traipsing through the woods with Anne, the dense canopy of leaves above our heads keeping me sheltered and rather comfortable, while Peter was learning to use a scythe under the harsh, unforgiving sun. Of course, there was the incident with the boar, so my day had not been without incident, but at least I'd not been swinging a scythe in a field of golden wheat until my arms were like limp pasta and my back throbbed.

"Yes," I replied. "Thanks to Kipp."

Elani's eyes, always a wonderful soft, dark brown, much like melted chocolate, melted a little more as she gazed at her love interest. I realized if I felt a lightning bolt of love hit at that second, so did Peter and Kipp. It made for an awkward moment for all of us. Kipp actually pawed the ground, unsure what to say. Fortunately, we were spared because Reeve Johnson arrived, a wide smile on his face.

"That Kipp, he's one fine dog," Johnson said, leaning over to thump Kipp's sides so hard Kipp's teeth almost chattered. "No dog like him in all the country, I bet." He grinned, the broken tooth in his mouth resembling a damaged piece of picket fence.

The reeve went on to tell a humorous tale of his having been accosted by a boar when he was just a young lad, to hear him tell it. He'd been working with two dogs to track that particular boar which was tearing up crops, and permission had been received from the royal gamekeepers that the boar could be, well, dispatched. The boar, which during the story took on mythical proportions, arrived, and the two dogs took off, headed for home, their tails between their legs. Johnson shinnied up a tree and was stuck there for hours until the boar became bored and wandered off in search of some grubs and roots.

"But old Kipp, he'd not run off, I bet." Johnson thumped Kipp again.

"What is with the thumping, and why does everyone call me old?" Kipp's bottom lip poked out a little. "I'm not old."

"It's just part of being a hero, Kipp," I replied. "Enjoy it, is my advice. Such things never last forever, and eventually, you'll be back in the dog house." Smirking, I enjoyed my little clever remark. Kipp glared at me, pulling back his lips to show at least one canine incisor.

The villagers, although pleasant enough, tended to view outsiders with a cautious eye, since we could be thieves or scoundrels and were definitely not of their tribe. But Kipp's heroism had brushed away all concerns, and we found ourselves treated well pretty much from day one. It also helped, we found, to be a friend of Anne, and that particular fact carried a significant cachet. The villagers pooled their scraps of meat to honor Kipp, who shared his bounty with Elani. As time passed, we seemed to blend into the general flow of activity. Peter, after a few weeks of hard labor, became an expert swinging a scythe, and I admit I admired the fact he never complained once. For the most part, I worked with Anne, scouring the forest floor for her cherished plants and roots. And when not doing that, I was put to the fields to pull peas, which had matured after a spring planting. I quickly discovered that pulling peas was not friendly towards one's back. On more than one occasion, I would glare at Kipp, who'd be lying in a fragrant patch of clover to the side of the field, dozing lazily, as a few lingering honey bees buzzed around his ruddy head. The fact he lacked the ability to pull peas didn't make me feel any better. The weather wasn't particularly warm, but hours spent in an open field, bending over, took a toll, but since Peter wasn't griping, I wasn't sure how I could get away with doing so.

Anne, since she lived alone, shared cooking duties with some of the women who had smaller households to feed. As I returned to Anne's cottage after a twelve-hour span of pulling peas—and who would have thought there were so many peas to be pulled -- I nodded my head as Joanna, one of the younger women, was leaving. She was a pretty little thing, married and obviously pregnant, her belly jutting out beneath a too-large smock. Her blue eyes met mine, then quickly darted away, and I'd found capturing her glance for more than a nano second was as elusive as finding bigfoot.

"I brought some pottage," she said, a smile appearing before she ducked her head.

"Oh boy," I muttered privately to Kipp. "More pottage."

"But you said that Joanna's is the best," he observed. "And I must say I find it rather tasty."

Actually, hers was one of the better pottages to be had since it was full of barley, peas—probably some I'd picked were staring back at me from my bowl—onions, cabbage, leeks, and sweetened by cooked apples and pears. It was hearty, and typically it was accompanied by the thick, homestyle bread that was full of grains. I found I missed my morning tea or coffee—living in contemporary times had spoiled me to such niceties -- but such a thing did not exist in 1192 England. The ale was home brew and often bitter, and I found I had developed a taste for the sweetened barley water that was a byproduct of pottage creation. Pottage was meant for the peasants, the working class. The ruling class, from what I knew, would be chowing down on freshly cooked meats.

Anne met me at the door. "How has your day been?" she asked, smiling.

"Oh, I think I pulled a lot of peas," I replied with a laugh.

"That is good," Anne said, taking my effort literally since it benefited the village and helped to meet the quota set by the steward, who was notoriously rigid about such things.

While I'd been pulling peas, Anne and another village woman had been working on laundry. I was glad to see my smock, as well as Peter's shirt and breeches, were drying in the lazy, late afternoon sun. Laundry was something done infrequently at best, and some degree of body odor was taken for granted as a part of everyday life. If you didn't stink, you obviously weren't working hard enough.

Kipp stared at me. "It was a lot of work," he remarked. "Not like your just throwing stuff in a washing machine and turning it on."

"And your point is?" I asked.

"Nothing," he replied archly. "But they had to put the clothes in a trough with wood ash and soda, then pound it with wooden pestles, rinse it, etcetera. You might act a little more grateful."

I stared at him until he looked away from me. He seemed to have forgotten, momentarily, that I was born in the 1600's myself and had pounded many clothes on rocks as well as using a washboard until my knuckles bled. I was no babe in the woods. Was it my fault the conveniences of the future had spoiled me?

"Tomorrow, we will venture into the woods again," Anne said. "Reeve Johnson wants you to go with me as before, along with Kipp." She paused, her expression mildly distressed. "I don't care for having to tie him up, but there is nothing else we can do to keep him safe." She glanced at Kipp and reached down so that her hand grazed the sun-warmed top of his auburn head. He twisted his head up, his eyes meeting hers, his tail wagging. "I'd not like seeing such a sweet boy maimed."

That night, Anne fell into a deep, restful sleep, her soft snores rumbling across the narrow space to where Peter and I lay with the lupines. I had the idle thought that many contemporary issues with poor sleep would be solved by hours of physical labor daily. I'd not run across any of the villagers who lay awake at night fretting over something silly, such as their cable being out or not having a good signal for the cell phone.

"Reeve Johnson was telling the other men that he's concerned some of the forest outlaws will make an appearance," Peter said. He turned, leaning on an elbow to look at me, the outline of his face barely visible in the darkened room. "He has no issue with the outlaws, who don't steal from the villagers but usually come to obtain things in trade."

"Why is he worried then, if they don't steal from the village?" Kipp asked. Kipp was stretched along my back, his jaw propped on my shoulder. As he exhaled, his warm breath tickled my ear and the side of my face. Elani was spooned between me and Peter. It was a lot of symbionts packed into one small bed with a lot of heat generated.

"When the outlaws come, it gets the attention of the bailiff, who tells the steward, who alerts the lord, who notifies the sheriff, and then the villagers get more inspection than they desire." Peter sighed deeply. "There is always the suspicion of the ruling class that the peasants are in cahoots with the criminals." He paused before adding, "It is considered a punishable offense to collaborate with the outlaws on any level."

The room was dark, with the exception of one guttering tallow candle that was trying, but not succeeding, to overwhelm the pleasant fragrance of the flowers and herbs in Anne's collection with its own nasty funk. Peter's face looked oddly pale against the black backdrop, although I knew his skin had darkened and his muscles had hardened due to his labor in the fields. It occurred to me that he might be the superior traveler since his lack of whining was notable. I couldn't recall any time-shift in my life where I'd not complained about something. I lifted my hand and gently ran my fingers through the fur on Elani's head, my fingertips finding the funny little bump on her skull between her upright ears; her tail gently thumped the unyielding mattress upon which we lay.

"Well, I'm ready to get the show on the road," Kipp said, exhaling loudly through his nose.

"And what show is that?" I asked.

"We made this trip to look for Robin Hood, or at least to make an attempt to discover any facts behind the legend." He gave a lupine sigh. "So far, all we've done is look for plants, pull peas, and cut wheat."

Elani stirred, and I could feel her agitation without accessing her thoughts. "Kipp, that's not true. We've accomplished a great deal in that we have established ourselves into an insular culture. I think you are too impatient."

Peter began to grumble too, along the same lines of Kipp, and I finally stepped in. "Guys, I've had trips where I remained for a couple of years in human time. Other symbionts have remained longer, if you review the records of past trips. Patience is critical here, and realizing that becoming invisible is just as important as achieving the final goal."

Kipp pushed closer, digging his muzzle into my shoulder, his way of letting me know all was okay between us despite the minor friction. "Okay, I bow to the wisdom of the old symbiont in the room," he teased.

"Old?" Reaching back, I lightly tickled Kipp's belly, causing him to squirm. "I'll show you old tomorrow."

Peter's day of hard labor helped quicken his pace towards the land of nod, and he was asleep within just a few minutes; his dreams would have buffeted me, except I blocked them from my awareness. In the distance, thunder rumbled, and as I lay there in the darkness, I could hear the sounds of a storm coming closer and closer until the rain began to fall, softly at first, then with more energy. The thatch roof held but became infused with moisture, and the interior of the byre house became heavy and thick with humidity. Restless, I rose and walked to one of the tiny openings that served as a window. Outside, a flash of lightening flared, illuminating the other homes in the village. I felt something brush my leg and glanced down. Elani had joined me, and I'd been so preoccupied I'd not noticed her until then.

"Why can't you sleep?" she asked. Her dark eyes caught a spark from the lightening that flashed in the tiny sliver of the window as she gazed up at me.

"No particular reason. Sometimes my mind is just racing, and I was too busy thinking and couldn't rest."

Elani nodded. "Yes, that happens to me, too. Peter will be deeply sleeping, and I'm left, my mind vacant, a little lost without him."

"I've noticed a change in the two of you," I said. I'd been tentative about asking how their relationship was progressing, but I felt she'd given me tacit permission to be a busy body.

"We're not to where you and Kipp are in terms of completeness, but we've made a lot of advances, and I think we are much closer. I know we have fewer blocks, and the reflexive habit we've all been taught to gain permission before entering into another symbiont's thoughts is less and less an obstacle." She sighed softly.

I felt something else was on her mind but didn't want to push. It seemed prudent to wait as I tried to remind myself about counseling my young companions the value of patience. Outside, the rain seemed to fall harder, and I could see the vague outlines of pools of water forming in the ground. This would probably delay the cutting of wheat until the crop had dried.

"Petra, can I ask you something?" Elani's voice was soft, tentative.

"Of course."

"When you love someone and they don't love you back, how long does it take not to hurt?" The interior of the byre seemed to close in on us.

I quickly assessed Peter and Kipp, who both were still asleep. In fact, Kipp was caught up in an energetic dream that smacked of humor. "Elani, I think you are making assumptions not based in fact." I decided to be direct. "Kipp may not say anything to you, but that is not a gauge of his feelings. And, no, I don't know what they are, and he hasn't told me."

"Oh, Petra, I didn't expect you'd violate any privacy of his," Elani breathed.

"I know that, sweetheart. All I'm saying is you need give things more time. And that's from one female to another."

She grunted softly and pushed a little closer to my leg. Although the weather was not cold yet, I felt chilled and shivered in the thin shift I wore at night. With a light scratch of my fingers on the top of her furry head, I signaled it was time for us to go to bed. Somehow, we managed to squeeze back into our symbiont sandwich without awakening the boys. And at some point, we both fell asleep, which was good, since the days began before the sun broke the eastern horizon. Such was the life of rural farming people. And both Peter and I had a long day of labor ahead.

We were awakened to the sound of Anne rambling quietly around the small cottage as she lit a couple of tallow candles and began to breathe life into the smoldering fire pit, which quickly filled the length of the byre house with thin wisps of smoke. As the lupines ducked outside for their morning constitutional, Peter following, heading toward the privy in the stable yard, I took the large basin out to the well and began the process of drawing water. I figured at the rate I was going, my muscles would be better defined upon my return home. Looking around, I could see the dimly-lit narrow windows of the nearby houses, accompanied by the occasional sound of a human voice. Others were wakening, no doubt preparing for another long day in the fields. But no one complained. It was, after all, just a way of life, and there was really no benefit to be had by making it more unpleasant by fussing and moaning. Peter joined me, taking the large basin that we used to do our modified bathing.

"Hey, Petra," Peter began, pausing awkwardly as if he wasn't certain how to continue. "I'm sorry about my attitude last night. I mean, the impatience. It is one of my flaws, as Elani likes to remind me. I know we have to work slowly and wait for things to unfold," he concluded with a rush of words and reddened cheeks.

"No problem," I said, smiling at him. He was doing just fine, in my opinion.

After taking turns dashing water in our faces and drying off with a stiff piece of wool fabric, we sat down at the small table, Peter and I squeezing together on one of the little benches. Anne had placed some bread and cheese on the table, along with some dried fruit. She'd already given Kipp and Elani some pottage left from the previous night, along with a few scraps of dried fish.

Kipp saw me glancing at the meager fare that had been set in front of him. "You know we can hunt if needed, despite what the rules might be."

Elani nodded, her enthusiasm apparent. "I am enjoying it, Petra. The pottage is growing on me."

It was an adaptation of our kind that we have naturally vigorous constitutions, and we can survive extended periods of deprivation in terms of food with no long-lasting harm to our bodies. The hearty pottage supplemented with some occasional meat protein was more than sufficient for the lupines, although they'd both become accustomed to better fare. I personally would have killed for a Pop-Tart, so I guess we all had to suffer just a little.

It was then we heard a loud scream, the sound definitely female, from nearby. Peter and I just about fell over one another as we ran to the door, followed in a flash by Kipp and Elani. Kipp's ears were pricked forward as he zeroed in on the location and began to run, followed by the three of us. Dawn was just breaking, and the glow of the sun on the edge of the horizon gave soft illumination to the village, just enough that we didn't trip over one another.

"A mother in distress," Kipp said, glancing over his shoulder at me.

In a few seconds, we were at the bank of a small flowing tributary to the larger river Trent that lay out of sight beyond the tree line. As result of the previous night of rainfall, the water was dark, swollen and flowing rapidly. One of the villagers, a woman named Alice, was at the edge of the water, her hands held to her face in horror. As other villagers began to crowd close by, I saw a head bobbing in the dark water, arms flailing in the air. It was a child, Alice's son!

As a group, we began running down the bank, trying to keep up with the child. His head disappeared a couple of times before he popped up again, riding the current. I could see part of his buoyancy was due to a large tree limb to which he clung. But I couldn't think that would last because the flow of the water against his body was too great. At some point, he would tire, and his grasp would fail. Kipp and Elani ran ahead of us, and before I could say anything to Kipp, I saw him angle his body and accelerate, leaving Elani behind, and without pausing, he launched himself in the air, landing in the blackness of the rushing water, his body submerging for a moment before his ruddy head broke the water and he began to paddle. He'd timed his jump, having gotten downstream ahead of the boy, and he began to move to intercept the child.

Peter grasped my arm as we continued to run. What Kipp was doing was dangerous, and even if he got to the child, what were the chances the boy, in his panic, would grab Kipp and disable his ability to swim to safety? Oh, Kipp, I thought to myself, as I began to pray softly. I saw Elani's muscles bunch, and I realized she was about to follow Kipp.

"Elani, don't!" I shouted at her in my mind. There was no way she could help Kipp, and she didn't need to put herself in danger, too. "Let him handle it," I added, my thoughts a little softer. She turned, her eyes locked with mine, but did as I asked. Her mind quickly assessed that her presence might interfere with Kipp and cause him to fail.

Kipp had managed to intercept the child, who let go of the piece of tree limb and clutched a handful of fur on Kipp's back. Even at my distance from him, I felt Kipp wince in pain. Kipp allowed the current to keep moving them, wisely not fighting against it, since fatigue would have overwhelmed him quickly. But slowly, he began to angle towards the shore, using his legs to paddle them towards safety. The men, who'd figured out Kipp's plan, went farther downstream and formed a human chain to help retrieve the boy. Reeve Johnson was the one who grabbed the boy, and that was fitting since the child was his grandson. Kipp followed, his head hanging with exhaustion. He staggered up the bank and sank down into the grass, his fur wet and tangled.

"Oh, Kipp!" I cried, falling to my knees and pulling him to me. I ran my fingers through his wet, matted fur. His eyes met mine before he let me tuck his head beneath my chin as I rocked him slightly. "Why would you take such a risk?"

"Wouldn't you?"

# TWELVE

I was grateful to be back in the forest with Anne. Her presence was calming, always inspiring, and following the paths of her thoughts was such a pleasure that it left me feeling warm and comforted. It was rare I met a human whose memories weren't shaded with some degree of darkness, even if very minimal and fleeting, but such was absent in Anne. Kipp was at our side after again being proclaimed a hero by the cheering villagers. For the locals, he was fast approaching the popularity of a rock star. Reeve Johnson, in particular, was beholden to us. There was little question that without the quick response of Kipp, his grandson would not have survived.

Drops from the previous night's rain fell on our heads with little soft plops as Anne led me on a different path than we'd taken before. The morning was cool, and a fine, damp mist covered the floor of the forest, causing my mind to take a whimsical turn and think of fairies and other creatures of myth and mystery. As we passed through stands of leafy underbrush, the wool fabric of my gown was brushed with moisture, leaving dark fingerprints upon the garment. After locating a nice selection of plants that were on Anne's bucket list, we stopped for a brief rest on the bank of a narrow stream that was no more than a thread of water that had opportunistically formed in a crease in the soil. I'd found a lichen-covered boulder that served as an admirable woodland throne, listening to the sound of the water as it flowed, wondering why something such as water made a sound at all. It was both cheerful and soothing, and I felt any residual tension from the earlier activities of the day receding as my shoulders relaxed. Kipp's actions, although understandable, had terrified me. I wasn't afraid of being left stranded in 1192; it was being left without Kipp that was so frightening. Even more so than Tula, he was my other half, and in perhaps the way symbionts were meant to be, together we formed the whole of an organism. I was no longer certain of who I would be without him. Anne had taken up residence nearby and was rubbing the calf muscle in her right leg. On our last trip out, she'd stumbled and strained her leg, which had not quite healed. But there was no time for rest in the eyes of the peasants who worked for his lordship.

We'd brought some fruit and cheese, along with a crust of the thick brown bread that was a staple, carried in a cloth sack, and took a few minutes to enjoy our lunch. I gave Kipp pieces of cheese along with some sliced apple, using the knife I carried on my belt in the style of all the villagers. The knife was utilitarian in purpose, used for everyday tasks as well as being the indispensable dinner knife for mealtime. As Kipp chewed a piece of the apple, some juice dripped down on his paws. He stopped eating to meticulously groom the tops of his feet, doing so until the fur gleamed. My attachment was such to him that I almost could taste the sweetness of the apple juice he savored.

"You didn't need to worry so much," he remarked, glancing at a point just over my left shoulder. There was a brightly colored bird that had landed on a branch behind me, and I was happy to note I could appreciate its colors through Kipp's mind without having to turn my head. "I was being careful."

"I know, Kipp," I replied.

Anne was watching us, and once again, I had the odd impression that she knew more than she let on. Her thoughts didn't indicate this, but it seemed to be more pure instinct on her part. She smiled as she caught my eye. "Your doggie is very brave," she remarked.

"Yes, he acts without stopping to be fearful," I replied. "He's saved my life, too."

"Maybe that explains your bond of trust."

I looked over at Kipp and saw his body tense; his thoughts of alarm quickly followed.

"I'm getting something on the edge of my senses," he murmured, his amber eyes locking with mine for a second. "I hope it's not another boar."

"I hope not either," I replied. He wasn't one to complain, that not being a quality of his, but I knew the morning rescue swim had tired him. Kipp wouldn't be up for a tango with a boar.

He turned his head to the left, then the right. I saw his nostrils flare as a softly-driven breeze rippled through the tree branches above, causing the leaves to flutter. The canopy was still thick and darkly green, although there were hints of change in the leaves, some of which had tips that were beginning to flash flames of yellow and orange. The mist, which had been ushered in on a tantalizing burst of cool morning air, was beginning to dissipate. The vanishing vapor was a prelude of autumn, which hovered expectantly just beyond our view.

"It's a group of men," Kipp said. His eyes flew open, startled, before he twisted around to gaze at me. "One of them is a symbiont!"

I registered what he said with a considerable amount of dismay. Finding another symbiont could pose issues, since we were duty-bound not to share any of our knowledge of the future. Even an inadvertent slip could lead to altering a timeline. As my mind raced, I, too, felt the touch of a curious, politely probing mind. Indeed, there was a symbiont traveling with a small group of humans, unless I'd lost my touch. Since we weren't certain yet the origin or purpose of the group, I looped the loose tether by which I attached myself to Kipp around my hand.

"Kipp, remember, we can't share any knowledge with this symbiont." I nodded at him.

"I'll follow your lead," he replied simply.

Of course, our telepathic exchanges were lost to Anne, who was sharing a sweet story about her son, Sam, who had moved away. There was a poignancy to her tale, which spoke of her loss while embracing his need to provide adequately for his family. But as the hidden group moved close enough that their soft footsteps were clearly audible, she became silent, her gray eyes darting over the dense underbrush, searching. A moment later, the leaves parted, and a tall figure stepped forward, dressed in the Lincoln green tunic of a woodsman. His hair was blonde, falling to his shoulders in waves, with a face handsome enough to grace the cover of a torrid romance book. Beneath eyebrows that were surprisingly dark considering the pale crown of hair, a pair of eyes the color of his green tunic met mine. His body was very lean, with the type of hardened muscles that were the result of regular daily exertion, not built from a gymnasium, but from running and constant movement.

"Well, hello!" he called out, motioning with his hands for the rest of his party to come forward. "I was making my way to the village in hopes of finding Anne, and here she is."

"Master Robin," Anne cried, struggling to her feet with my light assist. "It's been too long."

I glanced at Kipp. We were looking at what had seemed to be a man but was not. And we were looking at someone called Robin. Could it be? Or rather, could he be? Quickly I mentally nudged Kipp, needing some private dialog that would exclude this new symbiont player. "Don't tell him that we are here in search of Robin Hood. Let's play our cards close for the time being," I cautioned.

And to this day, I'm not sure why I was so cautious, but my instinct told me to proceed with care and deliberation. I took a moment to evaluate him further. He was carrying a bow in his hand, the long bow made of yew wood that was the hallmark of a marksman and hunter. Although his appearance was pleasing, it was clear neither he nor his men had been near habitation in the recent past. They were exceedingly travel-worn, and their tunics were soiled from sleeping on the forest floor. Robin spoke to Anne, registering her introduction of me before doing what symbionts do best, and that is communicating telepathically with a fellow symbiont while simultaneously engaging in a verbal exchange with a human. In fact, we do that sort of thing effortlessly and quite well.

"I haven't run into one of my own kind for years," Robin said, smiling at me, his thoughts for me and Kipp alone. "What are you and your partner doing here, of all places?" He frowned slightly. "Or are you travelers?"

"Yes, we are," I replied simply. "And all I can say is that we are linguistic experts and are here to study the merging of Old English and French."

Robin smiled again, nodding his head. "Ah, a mystery," he said. He tilted his golden head to the side. "But it might be fun to share secrets and gossip a little, don't you think?"

I turned my head away from him, hazarding a quick peek at his companions. They appeared to range from teenager to middle-aged men. They carried bows and all, even the youngest, seemed hardened to their life in the forest.

"Are you also known as Robin Hood, outlaw?" I asked, turning my eyes back on him.

"Some may call me that, while others call me friend," he replied cryptically. "Certainly, the sheriff of Nottingham and others would like to see me in their hands."

I broke off from him for a moment to focus on Anne, who was speaking to Robin.

"Master Robin, you said you were coming to look for me. How can I help you?" she asked. Anne moved forward and stretched out one of her thin hands to clasp Robin's arm. He gently placed his hand over hers in an affectionate manner.

"One of my men is ill, and I hope I can persuade you to give me the appropriate medicine to nurse him back to health." Robin glanced at me. "And I also am planning to convince Reeve Johnson to let us trade currency for items."

Anne's eyes darkened. "It is risky for him, Robin," she said. "If the sheriff learns you have been at the village and that the reeve helps you in any way, he could be considered a conspirator to your activities."

I caught Robin's eye again and resumed my telepathic discourse. "And what are your activities?" I asked.

Kipp was very quiet, and I felt him leave my mind for a moment. I suspected he was engaging in a gentle probe of Robin, and he fully had the capability to do so without Robin's knowledge. I didn't like doing that to a fellow symbiont since it clearly was pushing the bounds of ethics, but reason told me that some investigation was necessary since we'd fallen into a totally unexpected situation. Kipp knew the rules, after all, and it was up to me to trust his judgment, which I did. So, what was my problem?

"I thought you knew, since you referred to me as an outlaw," he replied easily. When he smiled, a dimple appeared in his cheek, making him comelier than ever. It was easy to see why people fell under his spell as he was clearly charismatic, a quality I lacked.

"No, that was what I heard, not what I know to be a fact."

"My men and I are not outlaws, but we do take money from those bloated with riches that they've stolen from the poor. We return those riches by modest trade." Robin shrugged his shoulders. "A simple story."

"So, you are a thief but justify it by doing good deeds?" I asked.

He wanted to laugh, but since our dialog was not heard by the others, it would have been misplaced to do so. Instead, he smiled again, and I saw another flash of that elusive dimple.

"If you say so," he replied simply.

I was trying to goad him to see how he responded, and he was thwarting me every time with good humor and even replies. I didn't want to admit it, but I liked that about him. For a moment, I privately wondered if my caution was misplaced. After all, Robin was one of our own kind. I would continue to ponder that question for years. Symbionts interface with humans in order to travel to the past and discover facts. But symbionts also build bonds with humans to ensure survival. Robin appeared to be isolated with no partner. What else was he to do?

His men, a ragged bunch, crowded closer and huddled near the stream where they paused to fill the water bladders they carried. I caught the eye of one who could have been no more than a boy, albeit a tall boy. How had he fallen into becoming a companion to a group of alleged outlaws?

"That's Timothy," Robin said, his voice audible for all to hear, as he caught my curious gaze. "His parents died, and the sheriff had him tossed from his home." Robin ducked his eyes for a moment to study the smooth wood of his bow, running a lean hand along the shaft of the bow. "He's with us now."

The boy named Timothy glanced at me, his dark eyes shy and evasive, and I felt like I was trying to make contact with something wild. His face was covered in grime, and his hair, which had escaped a leather thong to contain it at the nape of his neck, hung in limp strands around his face.

"And who is your companion?" Robin asked, nodding at Kipp, resuming our private form of telepathy. "I notice he is very closed about his thoughts and has not introduced himself yet."

Kipp, from where he lay amongst the fallen leaves and ferns that grew in bunches along the bank of the stream, raised his massive head, his amber eyes meeting Robin's green ones. They appeared to engage in a staring contest, and I was interested to note that Robin looked away first, so Kipp won.

"I'm Kipp." And that was all he said before Kipp closed his mind again.

"You're not very friendly, Kipp," Robin replied, his manner superficially easy.

Kipp ignored him, licking his paw. He was following what I'd told him, and that was to be very cautious about what we shared until we had a better sense of Robin.

"He's kind of shy and retiring," I lied. "It takes him a while to warm up to strangers."

Robin's mouth tightened as he lifted his eyebrows, clearly skeptical of my explanation. Robin glanced at Anne, enjoying her beaming smile in his direction. Yes, he had charisma. But as a symbiont, he should not have taken on a leadership role of a group of humans; whether or not they were outlaws was beside the point. He was altering their timeline, and maybe he didn't know it yet, but he was laying down a historical tract that would last for hundreds of years. Perhaps in his isolation from others of his kind, he'd lost track of some of our most important tenets. Or maybe he'd never been taught them to begin with? Was he an orphan, like Kipp, without a teacher?

"I know you are curious," he opined. "And without your saying so, I realize you disapprove of me. I think I can explain myself, Petra," he said, using my name for the first time.

"We'll see."

It was clear that Anne was returning to the village with Robin and his band of not-so-merry men in tow, so we began to thread our way through the narrow pathways, ducking branches and skipping over rocks, moving in single file, like a procession of orderly children. Robin led the way, his hand holding Anne's elbow like a courtier, his manners impeccable. I followed, allowing my mind to quickly brush over those of the men who were behind me. My main impressions were that of stress and concern, since any time they approached habitation, there was a risk for the group. Young Timothy was behind me, and as I stumbled on a thick root, he leaped forward to grab my arm as an assist.

"Thank you," I gasped, regaining my balance.

He nodded shyly, not speaking, his eyes meeting mine for a second before retreating again beneath the fall of his dirty hair.

We were almost at the village when I suddenly remembered Peter and Elani. They, too, could not reveal our purpose to Robin. Yes, he was one of our kind, but he was a stranger to us, and we would need to know a great deal more about him before letting down our guard.

"Kipp," I nudged my partner privately, "run ahead and tell Peter and Elani the situation. Make sure they know to play dumb."

I released him from the tether, and he bounded forward without a word, his auburn coat flashing amongst the deep greens of the underbrush before he was lost from sight. Robin turned to glance at me, a smile on his perfect face.

"Where's he off to?" he asked, resuming our telepathic dialog.

"We have other friends, and I thought he could go fetch them to meet you." A little off the truth but not by much, I thought smugly. And at least Robin did behave as a courteous telepath and not intrude in my thoughts without permission. It appeared someone had taught him some basic manners of how to get along and play nice.

Robin's green eyes were unblinking for a moment before he

looked away. "Petra, we will need to speak further about this situation," Robin said. "Your disapproval of me is obvious, but I've really done nothing wrong."

"I don't disapprove," I replied. "I just need to hear more."

"And you will."

# THIRTEEN

Robin led us to the edge of the village, approaching warily. His fair head was up, making me think of an animal testing the scents in the air for danger. At one point, his green eyes met mine, and I thought I was greeted with a tinge of humor, but his thoughts were guarded. He, like us, was playing a role, and no matter how hard he tried, he'd not be a true member of the group of men with whom he traveled. Robin, for all his comely appearance, was not human and never would be. And that was always the elephant in the room.

The outlaws never stayed long since there was always the risk one of the villagers might sneak away to warn the authorities. After all, there were rewards for information, and life was hard. The rewards posted for information leading to the capture of Robin Hood could change the path for an entire family for several generations. Reeve Johnson approached to meet the outlaws, clasping Robin's forearm in the traditional greeting between men, but his anxiety was palpable to us. He liked Robin and trusted him, but his worry was more about some informer within his midst. He understood the struggles of the people and how that could motivate someone to turn against the others. Loyalty, in difficult times, was a fragile thing.

Peter and Elani arrived, accompanied by Kipp, who'd given them the warning of avoiding divulging our purpose to Robin. Yes, I might have been being overly cautious, but my instincts were guiding my decision-making. Since we couldn't read the tea leaves of the future, we had to be equally careful not to alter Robin's timeline, something he set in motion years earlier when he joined humanity and left the association of his own kind. Robin's fair head nodded in interest at finding two more symbionts in his neighborhood. His privately conveyed thoughts were clear as he indicated he'd find some way to have some time with us without the distraction of human minds. As he turned to walk away with the reeve, Peter came close, making certain Robin wasn't focused on our thoughts.

"What happened?" Peter asked, his sun-darkened face close to mine.

"I was as shocked as you are to find a symbiont in our midst. But I want us to be careful, Peter," I said, glancing at him first, then Elani. "We don't know his intentions, and we also can't reveal that what he is doing here has lasted in legend for centuries. If we do that, he will have a glimpse of the future, and it could cause him to inadvertently change a timeline."

"But isn't he already doing that through his presence here?" Elani asked, tilting her head to the side.

"Yes, but that has already occurred. Let's not compound the issue."

It made for some awkwardness, but I knew of no other way to proceed. The other villagers began to complete their day of work and straggled home in pairs and small groups. There were still chores to be done, and after the livestock was fed and secured, it was time for a gathering around an open fire, where the women brought food for Robin and his small group. As outsiders, we hovered at the edge of the festivities, listening as Robin told some amusing tales of life in the forest.

"And how are your men?" Johnson asked, passing a tankard of bitter ale to Robin, who nodded his head.

"Well, for the most part, although I need to procure some medicine from Anne. A couple seem to suffer from bad humors and their breathing is not good. Friar Thomas, who will join us in the morning, has done his best, but there are some things we lack." He shrugged his shoulders. "But it is all we can do." Robin glanced up at Reeve Johnson and a frown crossed his even features. "You seem ill at ease," he remarked easily.

The reeve's face flushed with color as he hesitated for a moment, pausing to choose his words. "Master Robin, it is difficult for us. You are well-liked and welcomed, but if word gets to his lordship, we could be punished by the sheriff." Johnson began to stutter, uncertain how to continue.

"I know, and I don't wish to bring any hardship to you," Robin said, reaching out to touch the man's shoulder. "You have been good to me and my men." He stood, stretching his arms over his head. "And now you've given us a feast," he added smiling. "So, we will find rest and concealment in the forest and perhaps just send Friar Thomas in the morning to fetch the herbs and plants we need from Anne."

The reeve stood, too, and appeared more anxious than before, obviously concerned he was potentially alienating an ally. Robin, just like us, could read the man's thoughts.

"Not to worry, Johnson. We are friends and that won't change." With a nonverbal signal, the small band of outlaws began to trail towards the darkened tree line, melting into the green underbrush within seconds. Robin glanced over his shoulder, his eyes catching mine. His thoughts crossed the distance. He wanted us to meet him later on that evening.

Anne was tired after our busy day and fell asleep quickly, her breathing deep and regular. She slept like one unbothered by worries or bad memories. We waited another half hour or so and then quietly crept from the byre house. Outside, there was only a pale sliver of moon hanging in the black sky, which was fortunate, since it would make us less visible to any nosy neighbors. We worked our way around the back of the house, clinging to the exterior so that our movements would be difficult to follow. Kipp lifted his head before glancing at me and nodding. He didn't pick up on thoughts of alarm, so we seemed in the clear. At least for the moment. Within a few minutes, we, too, vanished into the thick woodland, and for a second, I had the fanciful notion that I was a creature of the night, my eyes able to pierce the darkness. But I realized I was, due to my attachment to Kipp, seeing the world through his eyes with his superior ability to sense and process the natural world. With ease, I followed him. Once, I glanced over my shoulder at Peter and Elani and realized they were doing the same as us. The atmosphere and prospects were exciting; my mouth went dry as I could feel my heart thudding against my chest wall.

The touch of another symbiont mind felt as soft and fleeting as a feather upon mine. Robin was close by, having left his men to meet us. He was curiously tentative, but I wondered if perhaps that was due to the isolative nature of his existence. The lack of a full moon, as well as a thick, overhanging canopy of leaves, left us in almost complete darkness. We were locating each other through our telepathy; the setting felt elemental, primitive. And suddenly, Robin was there, and I could make out the faint outline of his fair hair.

"Let's sit for a while," Robin offered, as courteously as if we were guests in his manor home. I half expected him to summon Jeeves to bring some tea and watercress sandwiches, the crusts cut away, the tasty morsels sliced on the diagonal.

We found a downed oak, which made for a relatively comfortable bench, and sat while the lupines circled briefly before plopping to the forest floor. Kipp, as before, had quietly left my mind, and I didn't ask him what he was doing. I wasn't sure I wanted to know.

"I realize you have questions, and I am prepared to answer," Robin began. "I was born about two hundred years ago, and I've always lived in this country, although it is only in the last fifty that I have been in Nottinghamshire as well as Yorkshire from time to time."

He paused, and I rushed in. "Where is your family, your community?"

"I'm getting to that," he replied patiently. "I, like you, had parents, of course, but sadly no siblings. We were part of a small collective of symbionts and time came to relocate, as I know you understand that need." Robin glanced at me, his eyes glittering despite the blackness of the woods. Without having been told, he recognized me as the unofficial leader of our small group, in deference to my age and experience.

"Yes, I've had to relocate many times," I remarked.

"I had no interest in bonding with a lupine for traveling because I'd fallen in love with another symbiont in our collective. However, her health was fragile, and she wouldn't have been able to engage in the rigors of relocation, since the plan involved leaving England for the continent. So, we stayed behind, and I appealed to all the healers to try and help her become stronger." His voice broke. "They failed, I failed, and she died."

"I'm sorry for your loss, Robin," I murmured.

"Thank you," he replied simply.

"But that doesn't explain why you stayed here and became leader of a band of outlaws," Kipp said, his tone blunt and no-nonsense.

Robin laughed softly. "I took you to be the one who was all about business, Kipp, and I see I'm not mistaken. But no offense taken." Robin sighed and tilted his head back, gazing upward at the trees that loomed overhead. There was the narrowest of gaps in the branches above us where the silver disk of the moon peeked back at our upturned faces.

"The collective did not approve of our love and union, including my own family. I guess I lost my need for their communion and sought it elsewhere. I found a quite nice association was to be had with humans, and over time I became a trusted gamekeeper for a prosperous Norman lord in Lincolnshire." Robin took a deep breath, and I could sense he was flexing his muscles as he tried to relax. "But you know how it is ... I had to move on since my lack of aging made me rather conspicuous. After a series of makeovers, I found myself here in Nottinghamshire. Inadvertently, I drew the attention of the man who was serving as the sheriff at that time, and to call him intolerant and rigid would be an understatement. I was branded a criminal when I hadn't even got started. After fleeing into Sherwood for concealment, I stumbled upon a ragged band of refugees, and that is what you see now. A group of poor men, who committed no great crimes except to perhaps kill a deer so they wouldn't starve."

His tone had become dark, cynical, and harsh. Isolated from his kind and still reeling from their rejection of him and the loss of the symbiont he loved, he must have gravitated towards some type of family, and that was a band of desperate humans in need of a leader. Our leadership warned against such things since no matter how close our ties might be, we are not human. Even as I considered Robin's actions, I became aware of my foibles over the many years I'd lived. And then, unbidden, William Harrow's face appeared, even as I tried to convince myself that I was different from Robin and had taken the virtual high road. Was I a hypocrite? I'd even considered staying with Harrow, despite all else. Only Kipp knew of my internal struggles. And Fitzhugh, but to a lesser degree.

"Petra, it's not the same at all," Kipp murmured, his thoughts only for me to hear. "You quietly loved Harrow, returning his feelings for you. He never married, so if you'd stayed with him or not, he would have had no offspring and there would be no appreciable change to the timeline."

"But maybe he didn't marry because he was waiting for me?" As I said it, I wondered if such musings made me sound as if I thought I was such a spectacular catch that a human male would pine for me the remainder of his mortal life. But Kipp knew my heart, and that wasn't exactly it.

"I understand, Petra, that you know how fragile is the human timeline, and it takes only the tiniest push to set it off-kilter." Kipp spoke the words I needed to hear. "I believe you tried and are still trying to do the right thing by everyone."

I realized Robin was waiting for us, for me, to address him. As I sat organizing my thoughts, the seconds seemed to stretch into uncomfortable minutes. We were quiet, even telepathically, and I focused on the sounds of a pair of owls, who were calling to one another in a woodland romance. The wind had picked up, and the massive limb of one of the towering oaks was scraping against that of a neighbor, making a loud, moaning sound that sounded more than a little human.

"I wish I could tell you more about us, Robin, but I can't. As we've moved into the future as a species, some of our tenets have become even more rigid due to our caution not to negatively affect the human species." I glanced towards his shadowy figure. "And I appreciate you haven't pushed or prodded for information." I think he nodded at my affirmation but wasn't quite certain. "I can assure you that we intend not to affect you or any of your activities or that of your confederates." I paused. "We are here only to observe and learn." Privately, I wasn't quite sure yet what course of action would be best for me and my companions, but it was always wise to keep doors open.

Robin cleared his throat. "And I would expect nothing less, Petra. We are a curious lot, are we not?"

"I do have a question for you," Kipp spoke up. "Have you ever, in your guise as an outlaw, brought harm to a human?"

"Why do you ask?"

"Wouldn't that be the ultimate in altering the timeline of another species?"

Robin became quiet for a moment. "I have fought back in self-defense, but to my knowledge, I have not killed a human. I may have wounded a human but never have I killed one."

Kipp grunted softly.

"I do have the right to live, you know, Kipp."

Robin's tone was becoming defensive, and the last thing we needed was for him to become alienated from us. He was, after all, the expert in the culture and time period, and we needed him. He definitely had no need of us.

"Kipp," I hissed privately to my partner, "let's back off a little."

I could feel Kipp's irritation, but he did as I bade him. Robin stood, his tall, lean body visible to us, since our eyes had become acclimated to the darkness. His body language signaled it was time to end our meeting.

"Before you go, Robin, would it be possible to see where and how you live?" Peter rushed in, having been silent for the entire time. "We're visitors to this culture, here to learn the language and times, and I can't think of anything more fascinating than to see how you make do living in the forest."

Robin laughed softly. "It may sound romantic and such, but the life is very hard. Except for the times we can trade with some of the local villages for food items, we are left to fish, hunt the king's beloved deer and boar and ..."

Robin didn't get to finish, because Kipp broke in again. "Rob people and take their money and valuables."

I rolled my eyes. Obviously, Kipp couldn't stop himself. Of course, I was neither his mama nor his supervisor, so he could express his opinions as freely as the rest of us. And, perhaps, pushing Robin to a place of discomfort served a purpose.

Robin took a deep, measured breath and exhaled slowly as he counted to ten. Finally, he turned to Kipp. "It is clear you have an issue with me. Would you prefer to continue this aggressive questioning or would you like to be even more direct?"

Peter, Elani and I waited for the next exchange. Asking Kipp to be direct was a loaded question.

"I really don't have an issue with you. I just prefer factual information and like to lay everything out on the table." Kipp settled back on his haunches. "I understand that you have become isolated here, without the support and counsel of other symbionts. Believe it or not, Robin, I really understand that particular situation since I found myself in identical circumstances a long time ago. I realize how easy it is to interface with humans in ways not intended. So, of everyone here, I do understand. But I don't want to gloss over the situation and make it appear like everything is all goodness and light."

Robin may have smiled, but it was difficult to tell. "Kipp, I just decided I don't have an issue with you, either. It has been a long time since I've been around my own kind, and the thought that I have been on the edge of misbehavior, even more than on the edge, is something I need to consider. Again, I appreciate your candor."

Robin's words smacked of honesty, and it seemed he and Kipp had done a manly chest bump after laying everything out on the line. Robin's ability to take a direct assault on his ethics and life choices and respond in such a manner was an admirable quality and took a fair amount of introspection and strength of character. I realized I'd been holding my breath for the entire time and released it before I became dizzy from lack of oxygen.

"And, yes, Peter, you are welcome to come to our camp." Our

eyes were acclimated to the darkness, and I could just make out the movement of Robin's head. "Why don't you discuss it amongst yourself and have Friar Thomas bring back word to me during his visit tomorrow? That way, you can make a decision in private." He paused for a moment before adding, somewhat awkwardly, "There are no women in our group, so Petra might be the odd one out. But we can make accommodations."

I couldn't see his grin but knew it was there. We parted then, thankfully, and Peter and I allowed the lupines to thread a path back through the forest towards the slumbering village, acting as our guides. No one spoke for several minutes until Elani finally marshalled her thoughts.

"Kipp, I wasn't sure where you were going, but I think it was helpful. Robin needed some pushing for us to see how he would respond. Initially, there was some understandable defensiveness, but then he seemed to hear your concerns and recognize your intent." Elani spoke from her head and not from her infatuation with the amazing and unpredictable Kipp.

Peter was next to Elani, his hand resting on her massive shoulders, fingers lightly tangled in her fur. Even so, he occasionally stumbled on a root or fallen branch. Our way was not easy. He was being very quiet, that is, for Peter.

"I really would like to see their, uh, hideout," he said. "The opportunity to view the shelters they constructed, how the community survives, how decisions are made within a group of men who have been outlawed from their homes …" Peter's head turned towards me. "I can't think of a more fascinating study."

I was getting concerned. The guidance for a group of young, relatively inexperienced travelers was supposed to come from me, as the one with the most traveling history under my belt. First, there was Kipp, who was rude and confrontational to a fellow telepath. There is no need to consider how badly that could go. And then Peter, all full of spunk and energy as well as curiosity, wanted to visit a hideout of criminals so that he could make a sociological study of the group. Not to mention the fact that group was constantly on the run from the authorities. No, nothing to see there, I thought grimly. As my thoughts churned, I realized I might need to check myself.

How does one supply wise leadership without squelching enthusiasm and hampering learning?

"Petra, what do you think?" Elani asked. For once, she was more tuned into me than Kipp, who had retreated into his grumpy shell.

"You realize we've met the goal of this time-shift," I replied. "Our job was to see if there was a historical basis for Robin Hood, and we have managed to stumble upon him quite accidentally." I had suddenly stopped walking; Peter and Elani almost crashed into me. "We could return home now and be done with all this."

"But, Petra, think of the opportunity ..." Peter began.

"I didn't say no, Peter, and after all it is a group decision, correct?" I was feeling pressured. Our destiny was not all carried by me. The need to protect my friends from potential danger pressed on me, I'll admit. "I'm simply pointing out that we have choices."

"But, Petra ..." Peter said.

"I need to sleep on it," I replied, cutting him off. "I recommend you all do the same."

# FOURTEEN

I'm not certain how we efficiently bypassed the villager's dogs, which usually barked a chorus of welcomes and warnings, but we did. We managed to sneak back into Anne's byre house without disturbing human or beast, and after we climbed into the bed, the four of us engaged in a vigorous debate. It was clear it would be a sleepless night. And it was equally clear I took the position of the one with an alternate point of view, which seemed to happen with some frequency. Kipp, Elani and Peter all voted to remain, at least for a short period of time, and make at least one foray into the forest to observe Robin's activities. Since Robin had not mentioned any women in his gathering, it would probably be odd for me to turn up since doing so would be disruptive. After all, the men would have to make accommodations for someone of a different sex.

"We are at the close of the season," Peter said, carefully keeping his tone reasonable. "What if I tell Reeve Johnson that I need to go on to Nottingham to pursue my apprenticeship, and after I get established, you will join me? In the meantime, you can keep working with Anne."

"I guess that is as good as any reason," I replied, my tone even and noncommittal.

Peter was quiet for a while; the silence dragged on for longer than necessary. "You know you can trust me, Petra."

"Of course, Peter," I replied. "I do trust you," I added, honestly.

"I've had some screw-ups, but I will be on guard with Robin and not reveal anything that should be kept from him." Peter turned towards me, playing peekaboo over the large form of Kipp, who served as our modesty barrier.

"You realize, Elani will be at risk, since a canine living in the king's forest is a target for gamekeepers." I spoke truthfully, as the safety of the lupines was a constant concern for me.

Elani peered over Peter's shoulder at me. "I want to go," she said, her tone emphatic. "There is no way I'd stay here and not be a part of this. I feel as strongly as Peter that this observation is important."

Kipp left my thoughts at that moment, and I realized he didn't want me to be aware that he was worried about Elani. My hand found his fur, and I gently stroked his back. He gave a deep, lupine sigh that shuddered his entire body.

"Kipp, what do you think?" Elani asked.

"Do you want to know what I think or what I feel?" he responded somewhat cryptically.

"Both."

"I think, from a purely intellectual point of view, that not to spend at least some time in study of Robin's activities would be a waste. We actually don't know how he is with his men, how decisions are made, what type of leadership he provides. Those are key to his interface with humanity and perhaps will give us a better perspective to take back to be recorded. I believe it's not just that we found him, but to discover who we found." Kipp adjusted his position a little, trying to get a too-large body comfortable in a too-small bed. "In terms of my feelings, I don't want you to take the risk. You are important to us as a team, and, well, you're important to me personally. It's hard to put into words, but I'd feel a void in my life without you." He rushed on. "It's more than friendship to me. You're, well, special." Kipp skidded to a halt, and if he'd been humanoid, his face would have turned a lovely shade of deep pink.

He'd come as close to an admission of love as we'd see anytime soon.

"Thank you, Kipp," Elani replied simply. She was smart enough to not glom onto his words and become all sentimental, recognizing he'd quickly retreat to a safe place. "I'll be especially careful." Elani cleverly changed the subject without seeming too obvious. "What did you get from Robin, Kipp?"

"What do you mean?"

"Kipp, we all know you probably made a dive into what makes Robin tick, since you can do that without him knowing and we can't. And you were very quiet during all our exchanges." Elani spoke what Peter and I had been thinking but had not said.

"I felt it was necessary," Kipp began before I cut him off.

"And I'm glad you did."

"He is exactly who he says he is," Kipp said. "I don't pick up any thoughts that would make me think he has ill intentions. I think he was lonely and found companionship with humans. And due to his natural charisma, he effortlessly fell into a leadership role."

"I feel better knowing that," Peter opined. "Especially if I want to spend some time with him."

"Petra," Elani posed, waiting.

"Yes?"

"If you don't mind me saying, I understand your caution. You are supposed to be careful and evaluate these trips from a different perspective than can any of us due to your years of experience."

I wasn't old by any means but felt it at that moment. Was I the aged codger who dampened the enthusiasm of the youngsters?

"And you need to keep doing that, I think. You've seen things that we've not and have learned from mistakes." Elani's thoughts trailed off for a moment as she gathered them. "I don't want you to feel left out or not in step with the rest of us."

I smiled to myself. Elani brought a wonderful and needed sensitivity to our tiny quartet. "And I don't, Elani, I promise you. I just don't want to be a drag when I point out caution is needed. I believe in democratic rule, and if the majority wish to push on, I'm fine with that. I actually see the need to remain here, but I wanted to point out the alternative, too." It felt good to have some resolution.

Since the loop of dialog had closed, it was safe to sleep. But I could feel Kipp forcing himself to stay awake, and after Peter and Elani drifted off, his mind touched mine. "Petra, I think I've figured something out."

"What?"

"I think some of your reluctance to do anything risky has to do with me." He paused, and I could feel his embarrassment. "Not that I am arrogant or anything like that. I mean, you lost Tula, and I think you fear losing me. That fear makes you overly cautious. I know from your history you have been a trailblazer, taking on difficult time-shifts without batting an eyelash. This cautious attitude is not characteristic of you."

I knew he was right. In that moment, he'd summed up the foundation of some of my recent negativity. And I wasn't sure how I felt about being caught. Pushing closer to him, I put my cheek on his warm, furry shoulder. Kipp had become integral to my life and experiences, and our bond was unique. It was hurtful to think of existence without him. Would there be any life without Kipp?

"Thank you, Kipp," I breathed. "Thank you for understanding," I said simply.

I'm not sure how any of us managed to sleep after the evening we'd spent, capped off by Kipp's unexpectedly honest revelations as well as Elani's gentle probing of me, but we did. I think I was the last to fall asleep, watching my companions begin to breathe in the patterns of deep sleep. Turning, I gazed at the guttering embers in the fire pit, allowing myself to be hypnotized by the winking of a few lingering little soldiers, unwilling to die.

---

Friar Thomas looked to be no more than a teenager, with a pleasantly round face set incongruously upon a thin, angular body. But he probably was in his late twenties, so he was getting on in years for the times. His hair, which would have been a lovely, lustrous brown, was cut in the unattractive tonsure required of his profession. What a shame, I thought. I liked him upon first glance, my feelings a combination of instinct mixed with telepathy. It was a fact we symbionts had an unfair advantage over humans in that we could tap into their unspoken thoughts. And I was very curious to learn how he'd taken up with a notorious band of outlaws. It seemed he had not yet been brought to the attention of the authorities and could move seamlessly between the forest dwellers as well as the civilized communities. At some point, that concealment and duality would probably not last, and he was on borrowed time before he, too, would have to disappear and avoid notice due to a bounty on his round, partially-shaved head.

He was obviously popular with the villagers and brought his knowledge of healing to the poor workers who relied on Anne. I was at Anne's side when she brought one of her concoctions of betony tincture meant to help suppress infections. Friar Thomas was using a heated sharp piece of metal to burst a boil that had appeared like Mount Vesuvius on the shoulder of one of the villagers. I was pretty impressed that Thomas knew to heat the metal, since people in that time would have had no knowledge of bacteria. But I found it had more to do with cauterizing the area, from Thomas's point of view, and there was no magical insight into the fundamentals of a staph infection. As Thomas worked, a small circle of curious onlookers had gathered; I caught the eye of a small girl who was hiding behind her mother's gown, her dirty fingers clutching at the woolen fabric. She ducked away, shy, not wanting me to catch her looking. She was a pretty little thing, with hair the color of a spring daffodil. I tried not to speculate about the difficulties of her life, shutting my mind from such concerns.

As the villager tried not to yell when the boil was opened—and I bet that stung—Friar Thomas's eyes met mine. "You don't flinch when seeing these types of things, do you?"

"No, I don't," I replied. "Although it is not pleasant."

"No, I agree. But necessary."

Thomas grunted with satisfaction when the boil finally drained. I guess his instinct told him to use some water to cleanse the area, since the knowledge of so much that had to do with medicine was lurking in the distant future. He then began applying the tincture of Anne's healing potion to the area. There was no way to cover the wound, so hopefully, it would just begin to heal. Since Thomas had been dealing with probable staph, I was happy to see him wash his hands. Following his thoughts, I realized he was just fastidious by nature, and as he found the drainage to be yucky, he wanted it off his skin. Some things just have simple explanations. As Anne returned her kit of potions to her byre home, and the villager wandered off, rubbing his shoulder and muttering, I had an opportunity to speak with Thomas alone.

"Friar Thomas, Robin told us that my brother, Peter, could return with you to the woods."

Thomas's eyes moved back and forth for a moment, making certain there was no one close by to hear our discussion. Then, they rested on my face. His eyes were a light brown, a rather unusual shade, and arresting. Set in an otherwise unremarkable face, they spoke of a quick intelligence.

"Yes, Robin has told me that. And your brother is aware of the danger of moving between two such different worlds?"

"You make that journey," I remarked, smiling.

"And it is increasingly difficult." He sighed, the sound seeming much too old for a man of his relative youth. But as I reminded myself, late-twenties were older than they seemed in comparison to contemporary times. "At some point, I, too, will lose that ability and will be confined to the forest."

"Do you mind?"

"Service is service, my lady, and I will go wherever there are people who yearn for knowledge."

"So, you teach?"

"I have the benefit of some education, I confess, and am teaching some of the men how to read and write. That, I believe, is the first step needed to make any changes in one's society. It is difficult for the ignorant man to fight back against injustice without a broader view of the world."

Kipp nudged my leg with his nose. "I'm liking this Friar Thomas. His motives are clear, and he has a good heart."

My hand dropped as I gently tousled the fur on top of Kipp's broad head. His fur gleamed in the sunlight, the rays coaxing the ruddiness from his coat.

"You are fond of your companion, who, I hear, is quite the hero." Thomas smiled.

"Yes, I can't imagine life without my Kipp."

After darting another quick look around the area, Thomas said, "In two days, your brother needs to travel down the road as if he is headed towards Nottingham. He needs to pause where the river forks, and I will tell Robin to meet him there." He hesitated, just for a moment, before adding, "I will do my best to keep him safe."

I reached out and gently touched his arm with a fingertip. "Thank you. I trust you."

Our discourse was interrupted by a flurry of activity as a man on horseback, accompanied by a small party, arrived at the outer edge of the village in a rush of loud voices and clouds of dust. I noticed that the villagers made an almost comical attempt to quietly disappear while not appearing deliberate in their actions.

"The seneschal," Thomas breathed. "Not a man to be trifled with," he added, lifting his eyebrows as he glanced at me.

Once again, my instincts were in motion, and after saying a hasty goodbye to Thomas, I slipped back behind the hedge of a nearby byre house before easing around the far corner, Kipp at my side. I peeked out and saw Thomas staring after me, a flash of confusion on his face before he nodded and walked out to where Reeve Johnson was meeting the seneschal. Following Thomas's thoughts, I realized he wondered if perhaps I was a criminal of some sorts, fearful of being seen by the seneschal. But he felt no judgment, one way or the other.

"Hello, master," Johnson said, pulling out his most subservient tone. If he'd tugged at his forelock of hair and fell to his knees, I would not have been surprised.

I heard Kipp growl softly and glanced down to see the strip of hair on his back raised from neck to tail. He looked up at me, and I saw the gleam of exposed teeth.

"What's wrong?" I asked.

"The seneschal—Sir Donald—is a brutish man. I can feel his enjoyment of the fear he inspires in the villagers. He's a bully who likes to terrorize others." He glanced at me. "And why are we hiding, may I ask?"

"Instinct, Kipp, purely instinct." I had no better answer. Somewhere in the back of my mind, it occurred to me that the less visible we were to different groups of people, the better off we might be in the future. At that moment in our experience, we were only associated with the villagers, and that was enough for the time being. "I think we need to keep a very low profile," I added, in way of explanation.

I watched as Donald dismounted and began to walk towards the barn where all the fruits of the villagers' labor were stored. He was short and walked with a bow-legged swagger. It was obvious he was not concerned with cleanliness, and his body odor was detectable even to me where I remained concealed.

"Whew!" Kipp said, exhaling. "Somebody needs to tell Sir Stinky to take a bath."

"Oh, Kipp, please," I moaned, trying not to start laughing.

After a few minutes, the seneschal returned, with Johnson rushing after him; the reeve's anxiety was apparent as he almost wrung his hands.

"We will make the quota, Sir Donald. You have my word."

"You better, or we will find someone who can inspire these peasants to work. This is his lordship's land, and I expect you to fulfill your obligations, Johnson."

A poor hapless chicken happened to be in Donald's way, and he kicked at it in his agitation. The bird squawked and ran, dragging a wing for a moment until it seemed to recover and dashed to shelter.

"Son of a gun," Kipp muttered. "Takes out his anger on a poor, helpless animal. I'd like to get hold of him."

"Kipp, please," I said. "Remember, we are here to observe."

"You might observe me taking a chunk out of Sir Stinky's hide." Kipp exhaled forcefully.

# FIFTEEN

I walked with Peter down the road, the surface of which was deeply rutted due to a recent rain, but now the ground had dried to an unyielding hardness under a bright sun. It did not make for easy walking, and one had to take care not to twist an ankle. To either side, large trees crowded close, their leaves bright and brittle with the autumnal transition to orange, amber, yellow, and red. The air was thick with the smell of the dying leaves and the chill of a coming winter season. We didn't talk amongst the four of us. I noticed, but discreetly did not mention, that Kipp was walking next to Elani, his ruddy shoulder almost brushing against her lovely coat. Their heads were down, ears flattened; their thoughts were still as the surface of a highland pond on a brisk, winter morning. As we rounded a curve, I began to feel the tingle of another symbiont mind which signaled the approach of Robin. I stopped, pulling Peter to a halt next to me.

"You know I really do trust you, Peter," I said, needing to tell him. In the past, it had not been so, but things had changed. Things must change for us to grow and experience the world as evolved, questing symbionts.

He smiled, and although much of his face was hidden behind the heavy beard he'd grown, I could see a flash of teeth. "Thanks,

Petra. I know there've been times I've not done much to earn your trust, but I hope I've gotten a little smarter than the day we began working together."

Impulsively, I reached up and hugged him, first A-frame style, then with a tight bear hug. It was nice to feel him return the gesture with equal ferocity and affection.

"Be careful," I whispered, giving him a quick kiss on his fuzzy cheek.

Robin broke through the dense forest at that moment, the sun finding the top of his golden head. A chilling breeze, which was winding through the trees and causing the crisping leaves to rattle, became caught up in the shoulder-length locks of his pale hair. For a moment, he had the appearance of a wild creature, head up, his nostrils flared for the scent of danger that would be carried upon the wind.

Smiling easily, he asked, "Who's with me?"

Peter stepped forward, as did Elani.

"And you've decided to stay behind?" Robin asked, his vivid green eyes glancing at me, then dropping to include Kipp.

"It seems the best course of action, at least for now," I replied. "I have no wish to disrupt the balance in your party of men."

Robin laughed. "And I have no doubt you'd do just that since they are not used to a pretty face."

I smiled, enjoying the compliment as well as his easy-going manner. So far, none of us had found anything of issue to be had with him. He was just doing his best to survive and decided not to travel a lonely path. Neither symbionts nor humans enjoy total isolation as it becomes difficult to nurture one's heart and soul in a void. We are both, to some degree, social creatures.

"I think the best course of action would be to, perhaps, plan on meeting us back here in say three weeks," Robin opined. He glanced up at the sky. "I think you might like to leave before the weather becomes harsh." When we didn't answer, he continued. "At least, you could move to a climate more pleasant to continue your studies."

I glanced at Peter, who nodded in agreement. "Three weeks it is."

Peter's eyes glanced towards Elani, who was standing some distance away, her head still down, next to Kipp. "And what about those two?" he whispered to me.

"A mystery yet to unfold," I answered.

"Time for us to disappear," Robin said, his eyes scanning the immediate area. Of course, his telepathy, just like ours, gave him an advantage in eluding possible pursuers, but at the same time, when his men were near, it could make for confusing signals. He had to keep a constant vigilance, which must have been tiring.

"Sounds good." I tried not to make my response sound too tight, but I was finding it hard to speak.

"They'll be okay, Petra," Robin said. "I promise to look after them as if they are my family." His words were unexpectedly sentimental and warm.

His men remained concealed in the woods, but I could feel their curious minds. It was unusual that Robin would invite outsiders, since it could put the group at risk. But they trusted Robin completely and had deeded the leadership role to him. That ended any concern. Timothy was there, as his thoughts were known to me. He was a desperate child thrown into the midst of a savage world. One wondered what his path might have been if the circumstances had been different. Reluctantly, I turned away and began to return the way I'd come. Kipp joined me, and I could feel him forcing himself not to keep staring over his shoulder at Elani.

"It's tough, isn't it?" I asked.

"Well, saying goodbye is always tough," he replied.

"More so now, I think."

"What do you mean?" he asked, his tone getting slightly defensive.

"Your feelings for Elani have changed, Kipp." Before he could say anything, I added, "You realize this is not my first rodeo, and I happen to know all about love, since I've been there myself."

He became quiet as we walked, closing his mind to me for a few minutes. The wind, which had ruffled Robin's yellow hair, continued to blow at our backs, causing me to pull my mantle closer for warmth. Reaching up, I pulled free my coif—and yes, I'd finally surrendered to wear it since it did keep my hair confined and was, therefore, a functional item—and deftly braided my hair so that the loose strands would stop whipping around my face. Kipp looked up at me, wagging his tail to indicate his amusement at my surrender over the hated coif. As quickly as he felt humor, his mood became serious once again.

"Why does it feel so strange, then?" he asked. "I love you, but it doesn't feel like this."

"How does it feel, Kipp?"

"I feel like there is a lump in my stomach. My heart seems like it is beating too fast, and I'm anxious when she is apart from me."

I laughed, not in mirth but in commiseration. "Oh, yes, that's how it feels."

"But it feels like I'm sick or something."

"That's just about right," I said. "You'll make it, Kipp. I promise." Reaching down, I let my hand run the length of his broad back. "Millions of humans and symbionts have survived."

He hesitated, and I knew there was more, but it was prudent to wait. "I worry, Petra."

"About what?"

"If --and it is a big if -- Elani and I ever decided to be a pair and form a union to raise a family, how would that impact you and me?"

"Well, that remains to be seen. Traditionally, when one of us pairs up with another symbiont, it becomes pretty impossible to maintain the old bond that travelers keep. You would want to cohabit with her, raise a family with her, and your life goals would be different than they are when you travel with me."

"But what if I want it all?"

I sighed. "Don't we all. But you'd quickly find it would become impossible, Kipp, and you'd have to choose."

We walked along in silence for a while until a flock of crows, who were cawing loudly, passed overhead, casting a brief shadow across the road. Kipp gazed up at the darkened gathering, watching until they disappeared behind a grove of old oaks, and then he suddenly stopped walking.

"I now understand why it was so hard for you to leave Harrow," he said. "But you chose life with me." He looked at me, the sun caught in the amber of his eyes. "You made a sacrifice, Petra."

I laughed. "I'm not that noble. But I realized that I couldn't do both at that time, and I was unwilling to push you into an unknown. It was too much to ask of anyone. And it was especially too much to ask considering the unpredictable outcome of the situation." Yes, that was the issue for me. Would a human man be able to comprehend that I, although I looked very human, was not, and would his feelings be the same? Kipp had assured me they would, but that was probably just Kipp telling me what I wanted to hear. He began to walk again, and I hurried to catch up with him. "Kipp?"

"I understand life and relationships more than I did before. They are just not easy."

"Never."

---

I was put into service with three other women, our job being to gather up the cut wheat to bind and stack it. Reeve Johnson, for a big, tough guy, had almost seemed apologetic as he asked me to take to the fields consistently. His intuition had told him, despite my gameness, that the hard work required was not something that I'd been doing regularly. Of course, his gentle attitude towards my work had more to do with Kipp than me. After all, Kipp had saved his grandson and Anne, and as "mistress" to Kipp, Johnson felt beholden to me. Ordinarily, I don't care for people feeling obligated to me, but if I could benefit a little in this harsh world, I wasn't going to complain. As I bent over to gather some wheat for binding, my hand went to my lower back, which had decided to throw a fit of muscle spasms. As I rubbed my back, I realized my main job with Anne had been pretty cushy. Perhaps it's true that you really don't appreciate something until it is gone. I glanced down at the palms of my hands, which had been almost raw but were improving. Anne had taken one of her healing salves made of lanolin from the wool of the sheep and coated the abraded flesh before binding my hands with strips of wool. Unfortunately, I'd lost the strips of wool hours earlier, since my hands had been put to hard work.

"We'll miss your brother, Petra," Johnson had told me. His dark eyes seemed sad and preoccupied, and indeed he was, since the visit from Sir Donald had left him worried and unsettled. "He's a good lad with a cheerful heart, and the other men liked working at his side." Johnson's eyes fixed on mine. "But we need all the help we can get."

I assured him that although I might lack Peter's strength and probably endurance, I'd do my best. And the gathering of wheat for binding and stacking might not sound like hard work, but it was, and I was grateful to be on Mary's team. She was over six feet tall, with arms like a heavyweight prize fighter. The women were willing laborers, and I usually found we were either laughing at some ribald commentary on the men or singing a song. Mary had just finished a tale about her husband's lack of proficiency in terms of their marital bliss—a story he might not have cared for being shared as we toiled—when she lifted her head. With her great height, she served as our herds' lead giraffe.

"Sir Donald is back," she intoned, her heavy brows drawing together to form a line across her forehead. "He's a right nasty fellow, is that one." She knew, as did the others, that the best defense was a good offense and bent to her work, pretending not to see the seneschal as he turned his palfrey towards our field.

"Kipp, time to beat it," I said, my thoughts finding my partner who was on the edge of the field, basking in the sunlight. As soon as the thought left my mind, Kipp got up slowly, so as not to draw attention to his large body, and skulked into the underbrush. I still thought it prudent to keep a very low profile, since while traveling, one never knows what circumstances might arrive. I pulled my straw work hat down over my face and turned so that my back was to Sir Donald and his small retinue. Mary saw my movement, even though I'd tried to be subtle, and with a nod at the other women, they closed in around me, forming a shield of workers. It said much about Mary that she didn't question me, and whatever motives I had for trying to hide from the seneschal, she really didn't care. We were one as a group, and it felt good, a moment for me to privately celebrate.

Sir Donald pulled his palfrey to a halt; he was close enough I could smell the stench rolling off his unclean body. I thought of

Kipp referring to him as Sir Stinky and almost giggled. Yes, we all had some degree of body odor due to hard work in the fields, but Sir Donald ramped it up several unbearable notches. He must have decided that the yearly bath was his route to cleanliness. He and his horse cast a shadow that fell across our group.

"Johnson," he said. "Your women seem to work harder than your men." Donald laughed loudly and went on to make a coarse joke about Mary due to her size.

Mary turned her head slightly and her eyes met mine. Sir Donald couldn't see, but she rolled her eyes disrespectfully and stuck her tongue out for good measure. I wanted to laugh in agreement but just closed one eye as we exchanged winks.

"We will make the quota, Sir Donald," Johnson said. "You have my oath."

"You better, or there will be payment due."

Fortunately, Sir Stinky took his party and headed north; their destination was Nottingham from my following of his thoughts. Kipp ducked back from his hiding place in the underbrush, shaking brambles free of his coat as he did so.

"Well, that's interesting," Kipp remarked. "The king's brother, Sir John, will be visiting soon, and all the well-placed figures are meeting to make certain everything is in preparation. Donald is worried about not making a good show for him." Sitting in the grass, Kipp yawned sleepily, the sun having made him lazy. "I might suggest he take a bath so that Sir John doesn't faint once he gets a whiff of him."

"The Count of Mortain," I said, taking a deep breath. "From all accounts, he could be a nasty customer. Perhaps we won't fall under his review."

Darkness was falling, and finally, our work day was put to rest. I walked back to Anne's dwelling, trying not to stagger. I was dirty, exhausted, and curiously empty. It became clear, quickly, that I missed the presence of Peter and Elani, and although I tried to put such thoughts out of my mind, I was worried about them. But the three weeks had passed, and I had plans to meet the next day. As the thought crossed my mind, I felt my heart leap in excitement. It would be good to be reunited, and I never thought I'd harbor such feelings of eager anticipation. As I entered the byre house, I was met by Anne, smiling and content as usual. But she had a surprise for me that particular evening, perhaps sensing my worry over Peter and Elani. From her perspective, I was missing my brother and had natural sadness and grief over the loss.

"I had one of the other women help me, and we have prepared a hot bath for you, thinking you would enjoy it." Anne stepped back so that I could see the wooden tub on the floor; steam was coming off the surface of the water. True, the tub was so small that it would be all I could do to get my backside down into the water, but it was a wonderful gesture and was the result of hard work, as were all such things. Anne helped me take off my gown, which I'd worn all week in the fields. She was used to such and didn't bother to wrinkle her nose at the odor. "I know you plan to journey to Nottingham tomorrow to meet your brother, and I thought it would be nice to feel clean and presentable." She added, "We did laundry today, and your other shift is clean, Petra."

I felt humbled. While I'd thought I'd had it rough working the fields, Anne had worked on laundry, which was no easy task, as well as toting in water to heat over the fire pit for my hot tub. She never would have said as much, but she knew that I was not accustomed to the work-flow and admired that I joined the others without complaint.

"Let's clean your hair first," Anne suggested.

Taking a clay jar, she shook out her concoction of what I would think of as soap flakes, or shaved pieces from a block of the noxious stuff that passed for soap. But Anne, in her clever way, mixed hers with rose petals and dried lavender to create something that was rather nice. She used a hollowed gourd as a scoop and began to pour the hot water over my hair before working the soap flakes into the strands.

"Mmmm," I murmured. "That feels good."

I glanced at Kipp, who was lying nearby, his muzzle on his forepaws. "I know I tease you about needing a bath, Petra, but I bet that does feel good." He paused before saying, "My connection with you is so close that I can almost feel your physical exhaustion." He closed his eyes for a moment. "I wish I could have helped more."

"Don't worry about it, Kipp." I closed my eyes as Anne's fingers worked the soap into my hair.

"Yeah, but this was my idea, and I get to lie in patches of clover daydreaming while you work your hands raw." Kipp exhaled, the sound loud in the small room. Suddenly, his head lifted, his nostrils flaring. "Elani's near, needing to meet with me." He hopped up and walked to the door, glancing at Anne, who let him pass. "I'll be back soon."

It was an odd sensation as he left my mind, although just before he did, I felt his excitement over meeting Elani. And he didn't return until I'd finished my bath and was wearing my clean body linen for the evening. My hair smelled of roses and sunshine, and I almost felt like laughing with joy. It was good to be clean again.

I helped Anne dispose of the bath water, and we sat together at her small table, enjoying a meal. It was the usual pottage, but this time she had some fresh fish for which she'd traded in the village's system of agreeable barter, and although I liked to keep to my vegetarian self, there was no way I could not eat some of the fish she'd so carefully prepared. I'd done this before and would again since travelers must meld into the time in which they are thrust. I recall eating a lot of meat—in fact, mostly meat—during my prehistoric days when I met Kipp. Somewhere, there were the remains of a mammoth with my name on it.

There was a soft scratching at the door; I rose, and Kipp entered. He nosed up to the table, interested, as always, in food. Anne nodded, and I shared a piece of the fish along with some pottage and a crust of the brown bread. He took a minute to sate his appetite, as his jaws crunched at the fare. When he finished, he looked up at Anne, wagging his tail to indicate his pleasure.

"He's a good boy," Anne remarked. She reached out her hand, and Kipp walked close so she could gently stroke his head and neck. "And so handsome," she added with a smile.

She was tired, as was I, and she lay down just before me. The small center fire pit had died down, the smokiness of the interior of the byre house fading as darkness fell. I sat on the side of the bed, waiting for Kipp. Reaching to my shoulder, I pulled a tendril of my clean hair to my face, inhaling the sweet scent of roses. Kipp glanced at me, his eyes bright.

"You must feel better. I know you smell better."

"Yes, to both," I answered smiling. "What did Elani have to say?"

"She said that Peter will meet us tomorrow before midday, at the place where we met Robin at the juncture in the road."

"And how has their, uh, study progressed?"

Kipp climbed into bed, assuming his usual posture of relaxing next to me with his jaw pressed upon my chest. Now that we had the small bed to ourselves, we could actually stretch out a little.

"She said it has been a wonderful study, and that she and Peter will have a lot to report back to the Twelve in terms of the life of the men who were considered outlaws." He laughed. "For once, she said, Peter won't mind recording his impressions and actually can't wait to get home."

"That is a change," I commented. "I hated to have to tell the reeve I was leaving, since he's become a little attached to us and appreciates the work ethic, too." I sighed, and turned my head over to glance at Anne, who lay sleeping. "I will truly miss Anne."

"Me, too. It feels a little like leaving Purdy again, doesn't it?"

"Yes, the pain is similar."

"But it is what we do." Kipp pushed his jaw closer until it almost caused pain. "And it is what we will always do, Petra."

I wasn't sure if his remark had to do with the discussions about Elani and his need to reassure me he wasn't going anywhere. And I could have asked, but I wasn't ready for the answer.

# SIXTEEN

As much as I try not to emotionally engage with humans, I've never mastered that particular symbiont art. I willed myself not to look over my shoulder as I left Anne's humble, memorable byre home. I was filled with a sense of loss as I turned towards the north in search of Peter and Elani and our path home. Kipp nudged me softly with his pointed nose, keeping my feet moving forward. I'm not sure that symbionts are any more immune to shedding tears than are some humans, but I definitely fell into the category that I could cry with abandon when the mood struck me just right. I could not help but know Anne's thoughts, of course, and they were filled with emotion. Her memories, as much as she tried to prevent active recollection, went to the time her son left her home, and the feelings combined all her past losses with my departure. In a short period of time, she'd become attached, and in the way we shared the intimacy of her small home, she regarded me as family. Kipp gazed up at me anxiously, knowing my heart.

"She'll be okay, Petra. Anne isn't alone, you know. The other villagers love her, and she is constantly surrounded by gentle, good people."

I knew he spoke the truth and not just words to soothe me. My hand drifted up to pull a lock of my hair free from its braid so that I could get a whiff of the lavender that Anne had used to clean my hair. What a generous thing she'd done, helping me get prepared to leave her with clean clothes and a clean body. In hard times such as those, a tub bath was a true labor of love when gifted from one in the world of the peasant to another. I glanced down at Kipp and smiled.

"I know, Kipp. This happens sometimes. We love humans, they love us, and we must always leave." My tone changed. "Our relationship with them is not based upon honesty, and maybe that's why it bothers me so."

"Now you are thinking of Harrow," Kipp reminded me, as if I needed such a thing.

"Yes." My hand went automatically to my throat without stopping to remember that I'd left his cherished gift of pearls at home. A peasant working in the fields had no need for pearls or any other adornment. My neck felt oddly barren, and it added to the sadness I felt.

We stopped talking at that point. I'd deliberately left early, before the sun actually broke the eastern horizon, just so that I'd not have to tell people goodbye. Maybe that was a cowardly act? I'd already told the reeve that I'd be leaving, and he took the news good-naturedly. His thoughts betrayed what he'd never have told me: I was a clumsy, if willing, worker. I'd managed to damage too many otherwise good peas by getting my skirt tangled up and losing sight of the small targets; my hands had grown soft in a contemporary world, and the soreness of my fingers and palms made it difficult for me to grip much of anything. Odd, a big tough guy like Johnson never thought to correct me or even look perturbed. He was genuinely thankful to have workers, even relatively pitiful ones such as me. Now, Kipp, that was another matter. Kipp had faced the charging boar as well as saving Johnson's grandson, so he was honestly sad to see Kipp's furry body disappearing around the curve in the road.

Since I knew I'd be going home, I'd "accidentally" left behind my small cloth sling in which my extra gown and shift were carried, knowing one of the other women in the village could use the items. I wore the blue mantle Karl had made for me since there was a definite and persistent chill in the air. Although I wouldn't be around to experience it, I felt there would be an early winter that year. Looking up, I pulled the hood of the mantle close around my face as I watched the sun began its ascent, taking a deep breath as the last leg of our journey began. As soon as Peter and Elani could get free of Robin and his men, we would travel home. And after a reasonable period of readjustment, Peter and Elani would take time to chronicle their experiences. For a business as risky as ours could be, I was thankful that other than the boar and Kipp's river experience, we'd been in safe quarters with little excitement. Smiling, I glanced at Kipp, who wagged his plumed tail.

"Just think, we'll soon be home with Fitzhugh, and he can prepare a pot of Earl Grey for you." Kipp laughed in the lupine manner I knew so well.

"I've missed tea and coffee," I replied, my tone wistful. "And it will be nice to become reacquainted with honey, since that delicacy is not offered to the peasants." My mouth almost watered as I thought of a cup of hot tea made perfect with just the correct dollop of honey. Fitzhugh had learned to tamper his frown, since he was more of a purist where tea was concerned. Recently, I actually thought I caught a glimpse of a smile as he watched the blissful expression cross my face when the taste of the honey registered on the back of my tongue.

The road was empty, save for us and the flocks of birds, which seemed mildly disturbed by the cooling weather and brisk winds, but I realized as we drew closer to Nottingham that the byways would see more traffic. I only hoped that our rendezvous with Robin would take place in a desolate stretch.

"I'm looking forward to being at home, too," Kipp said. "It will be interesting to see how Fyre has handled the administrative tasks in my absence." He paused before continuing. "I've given some thought to giving that up if he enjoys the work and all went well."

I stopped, surprised since Kipp had concealed such notions from me. "Kipp, but you've only just started!"

"Yes, but Fyre is older, has more experience, you know." He shrugged, not meeting my eyes.

"And that is not a good reason. Philo wouldn't have offered the job if he didn't think you were qualified."

"But I don't like having to do evaluations," Kipp began, poking out his bottom lip just a little.

I laughed and began to walk again. Glancing up, I noticed that the sky, which had begun the day as an unbroken wash of pure blue, was beginning to show clouds, the underside of which were darkening as they moved towards our location. I'd like to leave before the rain began, I thought, glancing at Kipp, who agreed. The back of my neck began to tingle, and shortly following, I felt the light touch of a distant symbiont mind. It was Peter, who, due to his connection to me, had sought me out and now could easily find me, using his telepathy to ping my location. Elani followed, her gentle mind brushing mine as softly as a feather. Of course, she touched Kipp, too, and I couldn't help but notice his head lifted, and he began to move with more purpose and excitement to his steps.

We passed a fork in the road, and my instinct told me we were still heading towards Nottingham. The trees suddenly began to crowd either side of the hardened, rutted surface of the road, and I knew Robin had picked a place of superior concealment. It was only a few minutes later that I followed the signals given and left the roadway, following an almost invisible game trail that led down a gentle slope to a shallow valley. The center of the area was relatively clear, with a surrounding border of old-growth trees of various species. Robin, accompanied by Peter and Elani, was just breaking free of the tree line, Peter throwing up his hand in greeting as he saw us. Elani's tail began to wag, and she didn't bother to conceal her bold glances at Kipp, although she was generous enough to include me, just for a moment.

"I told you I'd bring them back safely," Robin said, pushing back the hood that covered his pale hair. The sun, for an instant, broke through the thickening layer of clouds and found Robin's gilded head.

"Where are your men?" I asked, although I could locate them myself. Indeed, several humans were hidden in the underbrush at the base of the large trees.

"Oh, they are a shy bunch," Robin laughed.

Peter looked as if he'd grown another few inches in height, the beard on his face thicker than ever, but it didn't conceal the grin on his dirty skin. No, he'd not bathed, I don't think, since he'd left me.

"It appears you really lived life on the land," I remarked, the corner of my mouth twitching. It was difficult not to remark upon his lack of hygiene, but I kept my thoughts to myself. Well, Kipp knew, but that is a constant with me.

"Yes, I have, Petra." Peter reached out to give me a hug and truly subject me to his stinky self.

But it was so good to see him that I didn't mind. "Robin," I said, turning to him, "thank you for your hospitality and the care you showed our family." Odd, even as I said it, I realized I thought of Peter and Elani as family.

"It was interesting and good for me to have two of my own kind present for a change," Robin said. "I'd forgotten the simple pleasure of telepathy. It is actually a lot of effort to have to continuously say what I think and how I feel. Peter and Elani just knew." It was clear he'd developed fondness for the pair in just a short period of time.

It was then I saw Kipp's head go up; a moment later, his body tensed. Elani followed, then Robin, perhaps because his senses were better attuned to the environment than either Peter's or mine. But then I felt it, too … the sense we were being crowded in, with unfamiliar human thoughts just arriving from the distance. Robin's eyes opened wide, and his anxiety hit us all like a blast of chilled air.

"We are being surrounded," he said, before turning towards where his men were hidden. With a sharp whistle, he made a motion with his hand, and the hidden outlaws began to creep away, melting into the woods. Robin's eyes met mine. "You four will need to find concealment and time-shift quickly," he said, "before you are found." As a gesture of farewell, he grasped my arm, nodding.

My throat constricted as I felt my heart beat accelerate. Peter's dark eyes met mine, but oddly, I felt no such anxiety in him. He seemed to have mastered the situation better than I. Without speaking, Peter grabbed my hand and began running towards a copse of trees behind which, he hoped, we could find the hiding place we needed. Kipp and Elani raced at our sides; of course, they could have left us behind since they could move much faster, but the thought didn't enter their minds.

We'd only gone a short distance when I heard the sound of horses … not one, but several, galloping, with men's voices echoing across the shallow bowl of ground across which we raced. Indeed, there were more men to the right and left of us and undoubtedly ahead, concealed by the woods. The whistle of an arrow sounded, almost clipping the top of Peter's head; he ducked and clenched my hand tighter.

"Let go," I urged. "We need to split up! We're too big a target."

Peter immediately released my hand, and he veered slightly right with Elani while Kipp and I went left. My thought was to circle back to the trees and make our escape from there. However, one of those moments occurred, unpredicted, unwanted and desperate in its nature. Another arrow was loosed from a man on horseback. I didn't have to follow its trajectory but heard its target as Elani gave out a surprised yelp of pain. When it hit her, she and Peter had reached the underbrush, and it was probably pure luck on the part of the archer, since she'd just left his line of sight.

"Elani!" Kipp shouted, stricken. He and I likewise had found the tree line and paused for a moment, as we telepathically searched for our friends. Kipp flattened his ears out and closed his eyes. "She's alive, but injured, Petra! What do we do?"

I knew then what was needed, but it would be difficult to persuade Kipp. "Kipp, we need a diversion." He glanced at me, hope sparking in his amber eyes. "I'm going to create, uh, something, while you go to Elani."

"No, I can't leave you," he began before I roughly cut him off.

"Kipp, I don't have time to argue, and you must do this thing. Elani and Peter need help now, and I am the only one who perhaps can slow down these men for a few minutes." I glanced up at the line of horsemen who were advancing. They looked dark, menacing, and full of dangerous purpose. "You will find me later, I promise."

And before he could say anything, I ran out of our place of concealment, moving towards the Norman soldiers, waving my hand and shouting. I've said before that symbionts must be able to think quickly in desperate situations, and I'd had that flash of intuition which card to play in my limited deck.

"Help me!" I called, speaking French since I was addressing Norman soldiers, and I wanted them to think I was on their team. "I was being taken captive by that man," I cried, pointing vaguely towards the dark woods. I could feel Kipp's anguish at being left behind, but he knew he had to do as I'd bade him. Glancing back once over my shoulder, I saw Kipp melting into the woods, disappearing in less than a couple of seconds.

Since I was running directly at the line of charging horses—and I'm no hero, so I'll admit I was terrified—they had no option but to slow a little, lest they run me down. I suppose they weren't in the mood to trample a solitary woman, so they did pull up, giving my friends and Robin's men the time they needed. And to make the moment even more dramatic, I pretended to fall into a faint, throwing my arms in the air and collapsing to the ground. I think I added a little more zing to the moment by making certain my mantle swirled in a flash of blue, the hood concealing my face as I hit the ground. If it weren't for the issue with Elani, my acting might have seemed humorous, if not a bit overplayed, to any observant symbiont onlooker.

Two men dismounted, while the others crowded around me. I kept my eyes closed, listening to their heavy steps as their boots struck the ground. They were wearing heavy garments made of thick leather to help protect them from weapons used by an enemy, so as they walked, I heard the steady creaking of the leather as they moved. Opening an eye just a slit, I glanced at a pair of boots resting a foot from my nose. The men's thoughts betrayed their consternation, not sure what to do with this unexpected occurrence. As they pondered, I heard another horse approach, and there was an exchange of thoughts between the men that revealed their anxiety. A new player was in town, an authority figure, and they feared his disapproval that their chase had been interrupted.

"Why are you not pursuing the outlaws?" the new arrival asked, his irritation clear, although his voice remained even-toned and level, lacking harshness. It seemed he knew he didn't have to be stern to get his point across and motivate his men.

"My lord, this woman ran from the woods, and we could not trample her," one of the men answered, hoping his feeble explanation would not earn him disapprobation.

I heard another creak of a saddle and then another pair of feet appeared, inches from my nose. The boots were well-made and a definite notch above the others that crowded close to my face. I guessed it was time to go into action, so I fluttered my eyelids and began to murmur in French.

"Help me," I whimpered, holding out my hand to the man who towered over me as I lay in the wind-blown grass of the meadow. As I glanced up, I was surprised to see a handsome man with almost black hair and brown eyes that were more golden than chocolate. He seemed equally surprised to find a woman, speaking French, who, though dressed in simple clothes, appeared to be a gentlewoman. He reached down and, clasping my hand and elbow, helped me to my feet.

"That man," I said, making tears appear in my eyes, "he waylaid me and was taking me to the forest outlaws to be held for ransom." Turning, I pointed off into the woods, my gesture vague.

The man, who was tall, lean and attired in a fine tunic with an embroidered surcoat that fell past his waist, looked at me with curiosity, since I was an anomaly. I spoke with the language of a Norman, but I was dressed as a common woman of England.

"I am Petra Hugo," I said, working quickly on my story as my mind churned. "My husband was the younger brother of Sir Randall Hugo, who has holdings in southeast Wessex. After my husband's death, I was traveling to Nottingham." The man continued to stare at me, not speaking, giving me a moment to work on my embellishments to the tale. I continued, "I was persuaded to dress as a peasant, so as not to be a target of the outlaws who travel the countryside. But the men who were my guides stole my money and were taking me to others who would hold me for ransom, hoping my brother-in-law, Sir Randall, would pay them money for my return." I began to cry with earnest. "They betrayed my trust!"

There, I'd committed myself to a story, and as the man considered my words, I began to mentally create the rest of my fake life, since I would be living a lie, once again. And my survey of the man who stood before me was that he had a very bright, agile and quick mind. I'd have to keep my story straight, or he'd easily catch me as my fabrication unraveled.

"I am Sir William Wendenal," he finally said, nodding his head over my hand, which he still held. "You will come with me." He lifted his head, gazing at the darkened line of trees, resignation on his face that the catch of the day had missed his net. "I am the Sheriff of Nottingham."

# SEVENTEEN

W ho would have thought that we would not only meet up with Robin Hood, as we did, but also, I'd managed to run smack dab into his nemesis, the Sheriff of Nottingham? Was there some type of greater purpose at work, I wondered, just set into motion to make the situation more complicated and fraught with danger? I searched my memories for the information I'd studied about this man, since I'd run across his name while planning for this time-shift. Odd, as much as was recorded of many of the notables, little was known about William Wendenal. His origins, whether noble or obscure, were not known. But he was apparently given the legal duties over a large swath of England to administer the law while King Richard was absent from the country and was considered to be a man of some importance. I recalled that in 1194, he basically disappeared from history, and his duties were assumed by another noble. Although I'd not planned on being in the hands of the sheriff, at least I could try to solve a little side mystery as I waited to be reunited with my team.

My team! The thought filled me with anxiety! What had happened to Elani? The sound of her cry of pain kept echoing in my head; her safety was my primary concern. And, Kipp? When would I see him again? He had been such a constant, never leaving my side, that I felt grief well up in my heart. Managing without him took me back to when Tula died, and I was a solitary symbiont for a long time until Kipp arrived. This absence of Kipp was just what he'd said he thought I feared the most, and here it was, staring me in the face.

"My lady," Sir William said. "You look distressed," he observed, his voice cool and controlled.

I glanced at his face, glad that Anne had given me such a magnificent bath the previous evening. The fact I wore clean clothes and smelled nice helped my story seem a tad more plausible. Eventually, I knew, I'd have to flesh out the rest of it, but for now, I could get by with letting my situation keep the sheriff from interrogating me. His thoughts were of curiosity, concern and some irritation that I'd made such a stupid decision. If only I'd allowed a man to help me, perhaps a kinsman, then I wouldn't be in such a predicament.

"Yes, Sir William," I answered. "I realize the folly of my choice and now am in an unfamiliar place with no means." I tried to look a little vulnerable without being so obvious as to bat my eyelashes at him or cry. "I have no family here to call on for help, you see."

"But certainly, your brother-in-law," he began, turning his head to the side slightly as he spoke. His face was lean, all hardened planes, with a nicely groomed beard in the style of the day. The almost black fall of hair came to his shoulders in a fashionable quasi pageboy style. He, perhaps, had a little vanity about him, but not much.

"Oh, no, Sir William. There are hard feelings and are the reason why I left." My eyes met his; he found me quite attractive, despite my large nose, which threw my face out of balance. I decided to leave the rest of the story hanging, an enticing piece of fruit full of mystery. Of course, I had a good reason at the time—I'd not fleshed out the rest of my story. However, the time of reckoning would come and soon. At my words, his mind became filled with curiosity, and he would question me later, when he felt there was an opportune moment. I knew, instinctively, that he would not let me be vague the next time we spoke of my origins.

Turning to one of the men, he issued a command for the soldier to go to Ashland near Trent and secure a cart and horse. The man took off at a gallop and would probably return in just a short time, considering the pace of his horse, which was large and had a ground-eating gait. But that short time meant the sheriff had ample opportunity to further interrogate me. In the meantime, the sheriff commanded the men remaining to search the nearby forest on the off chance any fleeing outlaws remained.

"This was a dangerous choice you made, my lady," he said, returning his curious eyes to my face. "There are desperate men all over England, men we've yet to make conform to the laws and expectations of the citizenry. And women should not travel alone, just accompanied by a paid guide." William smiled, keeping his tone deliberately gentle. "Surely you see the error of your choice." It was a statement, not a question.

I nodded my head, letting him gently chastise me as would be expected in a patriarchal society. We'd moved beneath the limbs of an old-growth oak, where the massive branches twisted and turned towards the sky. The leaves were a brilliant yellow, perhaps a week past their prime. Glancing upward, I could see the hovering cover of gray clouds was thickening and looked as if someone had dipped a brush in water and feathered the paints used in a delicate watercolor, as the gray tones melted into softer hues of lavender.

A familiar mind touched mine. Kipp was back! My knees almost went weak, and William, though he didn't know the reason, saw me almost stumble and took my elbow in concern. He was a highly-attuned man to the condition of others, it seemed.

"Petra," Kipp called out, his telepathic touch reaching me from his hiding place in the dense underbrush. "Elani and Peter are secure, back with Robin and his men."

"And Elani?"

"She is badly hurt," he answered, and there was a catch in his mental voice. "The arrow pierced her, and she has lost a lot of blood. Robin has sent for Friar Thomas to see if he can heal her." Kipp's voice in my mind was strained. "I feel helpless," he added, "and I don't know what to do."

I tried to keep calm as I continued to respond to the sheriff, but inside, my heart was beating faster; my throat felt constricted with anxiety. It was up to me to direct Kipp, whose thoughts were spinning aimlessly.

"Kipp, you need to return to Peter and Elani for now." He started to interrupt me, but I shushed him. "It is the only thing to do. You can help Elani with her healing, simply because of the connection the two of you share."

"She and I don't have the bond that you and I have when we tried such things," he replied, haltingly. He wanted to believe what I was telling him; that much was clear.

"Kipp, you have the bond of love and friendship. Let yourself reach out to Elani, and I promise you that your presence will help her summon the strength she needs."

"But you, Petra, what will happen to you?" Kipp sounded anguished and more than a little torn.

"This man is the Sheriff of Nottingham, Kipp. He will take me back with him, and I think I will be kept safely, uh, somewhere." Kipp started to interrupt again. "Kipp, listen to me. This is the only thing to do. I will tell the sheriff that my precious companion dog was frightened away during my abduction. At whatever point Elani is stable, you need to come to Nottingham and search for me. I will make up some reason for us to accidentally meet, so I can be reunited with my lost dog."

"It sounds pretty shaky," he replied.

"It is shaky, but it's the play we're going with, Kipp."

Kipp fell quiet, his usually disciplined mind taking control again, as he pushed his anxiety over Elani's condition to the back, just for a moment. He clearly didn't like my proposal, but the sense of it was obvious. If Elani didn't recover, Peter couldn't time-shift home. He'd be stranded in 1192 England. And Kipp and I couldn't leave him behind, so we'd be staying, too. Elani had to make it, and not only for the needs of the team, but just because she was precious and loved, and I would not have it any other way.

"Okay, Petra. I don't like it, but you're right. Listen for me in the days to come. I promise I'll come for you."

The sound of his voice in my head became soft and finally diminished altogether as I realized I was alone. My anxiety and worry over Elani, as well as Peter, coupled with the loss of Kipp, felt overwhelming, and without meaning to, I began to cry. Sir William's face softened, since he didn't understand the context, and he reached out to gently touch my arm.

"My lady," he said, "I will see you to safety." He had a naturally chivalrous attitude towards women, it seemed, and the fact he considered me pretty and probably of some quality birth didn't hurt things one bit. In his world, if my brother-in-law was a noble, then I was too, at least by association. And the brother of a noble would have taken care to marry in the same social class. In the sheriff's world, I was one of his kind.

I knew my story would need more details, and then there was the issue of my missing dog. So, without trying to seem overly dramatic, I lifted my head and began to look around. "Kipp!" I cried out.

"And who is Kipp?" The sheriff frowned slightly, turning his head to look at the dense line of forest.

"My dog. He became afraid when your men rushed in. I don't know where he went."

"If he is in the forest, there is little likelihood we can locate him." William was just being practical. He also had no interest in searching the dense woods for a dog, especially when a storm threatened. As he considered the situation, his eyes drifted upwards towards the sky, which was becoming ominously overcast. "The dog will show up at some point, my lady." The words were meaningless, just an attempt to soothe me.

"You think so?" I asked, my eyes wide.

"Yes, of course," he lied.

I was relieved to see the soldier returning, driving the cart, his horse tied behind. The break from the constant attention of the sheriff would give me time to organize my thoughts. Lying may come easy to symbionts, but keeping one's story straight is a true art. The sheriff gently handed me up to the cart's bench seat, and after reassembling his men, we made our way back to the road where I was jostled all the way to Nottingham as the wheels of the cart fell in and out of the deep ruts carved in the road.

The journey was not long, and I was a little surprised at how close we'd been to all this historical action just by our habitation at

Ashland near Trent. Chalk one up for luck. The castle at Nottingham was situated on the top of a hill, providing the inhabitants with a commanding view of the countryside. It had, of course, like most structures, evolved over the years, from a primitive earthen fortification to the heavily reinforced wood and stone construction that stretched in front of my eyes. The natural promontory upon which it sat was the perfect setting, easily defended from any attackers.

Our party, which had grown as some of the other members of the sheriff's strike team rejoined us, made its way through Old Castle Square, which had existed as a Saxon gathering place long before the modern castle was built. The peasants glanced up at our group with more than one curious eye darting my way, since a woman in the company of the sheriff and his soldiers was unusual, to say the least. A short time later, we entered the town of Nottingham, which was a Norman town, populated by both Normans and Saxons. The air was filled with the scents of wood fires combined with the stench of animal fat being cooked down and rendered for its many uses, which included the almost unbearable tallow candle. The smoke got in my eyes, and I tried to suppress a coughing fit since everyone else seemed immune to it. Most of the people were of the working class, with skilled tradesmen making up most of the population.

The sheriff eased his heavy horse next to the cart in which I rode. "My lady," he said, nodding his head pleasantly. "I plan to take you to the castle and provide you with refuge there." His golden-brown eyes glanced at the people we passed. "A gentlewoman cannot be left to the devices of these peasants."

I thanked him while realizing he was bursting with curiosity at my decision to leave my fabricated home and travel to a distant, unfamiliar town. He, of course, had been privy to many situations over his lifetime which exposed him to the underside of humanity. With that background, his thoughts ran to extreme speculation. What if my brother-in-law, following the death of my husband, had made untoward advances towards me? After all, in the sheriff's eyes, I was comely. Or what, and his thoughts darkened, if I were some type of conniving wench who had managed to get myself booted from the family residence? Just as soon as he considered the latter possibility, he discarded it because he did not wish to think such a thing of me. He wanted me to be the innocent victim; that much was clear. And that attitude definitely worked to my advantage.

The cart passed the front gates, which were open with tradesmen going in and out. It was a place of busy activity, purposeful, and there was no apparent sloth. Life, in general, was full of movement that supported basic survival. I saw one peasant leading in a young bullock that was bawling and struggling against the rope that tightened up around its neck, and I knew, unfortunately for the creature, it was about to become dinner. Preserving meat was usually done by salting or smoking, but for the wealthy people, the meat was often brought to the kitchen, killed and prepared as a fresh dish. I looked away from the animal, since it seemed kind of lost and anxious, having been separated from its herd. I couldn't change the culture, nor was it my desire. But I did feel for that poor bullock.

I gazed at my surroundings as the cart moved through the bailey. I could see the kitchen, stables, a garden, fruit trees, and other outbuildings that made up the basis of what was an enclosed and relatively self-sustaining system. A cool wind whistled through the courtyard, carrying with it the scents from the kitchen. Inhaling, I realized I was hungry, as I'd not broken my fast that morning before leaving Ashland near Trent. The cart rocked to a halt before a towering stone keep. The sheriff dismounted from his horse; I noticed he ran his hand gently along the creature's neck.

"Make certain you cool him down and walk him slowly before feeding him," Sir William ordered, his golden eyes looking catlike as the man who took the horse murmured something in response.

It was clear the sheriff picked the war horse, although he had smaller palfreys in his stable, as an act of intimidation against Robin and his men. The horse was massive and somewhat ill-tempered as it tried to take a nip out of the peasant's arm. The man was too afraid of the sheriff to complain and retreated, leading the horse and rubbing his arm, his eyes downcast. I noticed the servant didn't make eye contact with the sheriff as I reminded myself of the definite class distinctions in 1192 England. Not only was there an insurmountable barrier between the peasants and the nobles, but also there was the cultural divide resulting from the Normans having conquered the previous Saxon rulers.

Sir William walked toward the cart and glanced up at me, smiling. I noticed he had all his teeth, which seemed in good repair. Of course, he would have the best of everything. For a moment, I indulged myself to think of Kipp, wishing he were with me to do a deep dive into the memories of the sheriff. It was odd that, for a very notable character who apparently was well thought of by the king, he completely disappeared from history around 1194. Nothing was known about his origins or his life after another man assumed the mantle of the sheriff. And from my reading, that guy who succeeded Wendenal was no one with whom to trifle. He administered justice—if one could call it that—with a heavy hand. I sighed, trying to push the thoughts of Kipp from my mind. Without his constant presence in my head, I felt more alone than I'd ever felt in my life. I was curiously empty, lacking even the minor motivation to reach out and learn what I could about the humans in whose company I now found myself. I almost visibly shook myself; it was time to get a grip. This was the job, after all, and no one promised an easy ride. And Elani's return to health was the primary concern since all else relied upon that. I would not entertain any other consideration.

"My lady," Sir William said, "may I assist you?"

He held up his hand, which I took, feeling the warmth of his flesh against mine despite the coolness of the air. Interestingly, he'd removed his gloves just before taking my hand, and as my mind followed his thoughts, I realized he did it out of courtesy. His golden eyes glanced down at my hand, and I almost felt a wash of panic if he were to see how worn my palms had become from labor. It would be in direct conflict with what I'd told him of my life as a lady. Luck was not on my side, and his eyes narrowed as he took in the condition of my hands; it was time to be proactive.

"Sir William, I dislike having to ask, but is it possible I could be provided with some healing balm for my hands?" His eyes met mine. "My gloves were lost during my journey, and you can see what happened to my flesh as a result." I smiled, trying to make the gesture somewhat bittersweet. "I fear I am not accustomed to a harsh life."

I felt him immediately relax, and the now-familiar smile returned. I wondered if that smile sprang into action frequently—although I had my doubts -- or if he'd brought it out of hiding to charm me? And I couldn't tell, despite my telepathy. I know I was unable to detect deceit in the man at that moment.

"I will have a servant see to it, my lady," he replied.

And with that, he took my arm and assisted me down from the cart. My descent put me into close proximity to him; he did not step back immediately, but almost reluctantly did so a moment later.

"Let me show you inside," he said, his manners impeccable.

For a moment, I had a fear that if I went into that looming keep, I'd never be allowed to leave again. It took all my strength not to glance over my shoulder at freedom. My mind took flight, and I pretended that Peter and Elani were there, and Kipp was at my side, and we were time-shifting home. But my fantasy was short-lived as William led me up the stairs to the second-floor entrance, his hand firmly on my elbow. The heavy door swung open as a servant greeted the sheriff, the man's eyes glancing at me in surprise. He knew, as did the others, that the sheriff had gone hunting for Robin Hood and a gang of outlaws. Instead, he returned with an unfamiliar woman who could be a lady or perhaps something else. The sheriff's hand tightened on my flesh as he ushered me past the threshold. Not able to resist, I turned my head to watch the massive door of oak and iron swing closed behind me. There was a sound of finality as it shut.

# EIGHTEEN

"Papa!"

The sound of a young girl's voice echoed from a gallery above the great hall in which I stood. In the center of the room was an enormous fire pit, which was well-tended; the blaze radiated waves of heat as I felt my face flush. Craning my neck, I looked up and found the louvered vent in the ceiling that allowed the smoke to exit the hall. Despite that ventilation, wisps of smoke drifted through the air, causing the atmosphere to seem congested. Fireplaces and chimneys were on the cusp of creation in terms of advancements in civilization. A small gathering of servants stood, waiting, expecting a command at any moment. Such was their life of anticipation of orders. Since an arched ceiling -- and the engineering required to create such a thing -- was still a clever notion yet to be invented, the main ceiling was supported by evenly spaced massive pillars of wood. At one end of the room was a dais where a long table stretched the length of the platform. The wall behind the platform was covered in faded tapestries that hung almost from the ceiling to the floor. Ornate metal cornices held candles, but the light did little to cast any illumination; there were no windows or openings, and the flickering candlelight seemed too minimal for such a large area. The room smelled of the accumulation of the reeds that made up the floor covering, dogs that roamed about at will, and human bodies in various stages of cleanliness or lack thereof. In other words, it was just about right for the times, a rich bouquet of pleasant and not so pleasant fragrances. A couple of huge wolfhounds rose from nests they'd created in the rushes, their eyes gazing first at me and then at the sheriff; as their tails began to wag, I realized that being a friend of the sheriff was probably not so bad.

"Papa!" the girl shouted again as she leaped at Sir William, who willingly hoisted her up in his arms.

"Lisette," he responded, his tone mock stern, but there was an unmistakable fondness in his eyes. "I have told you the proper way to greet me, and here you are once again, launching yourself at me in a most unladylike manner."

She was a pretty child, with hair an unusual shade of titian gold and eyes that matched her father's gold-brown ones. I could see some of his features in her pixie face and wondered where her mother might be. He released her to the ground gently, and she grasped his hand. She glanced at me, tilting her lovely head to the side. There was little doubt she would be breathtakingly beautiful as a grown woman. I, of course, was following Lisette's thoughts and realized she was attempting to demonstrate good manners and not interrogate me as to my purpose. The only sign of her overwhelming curiosity was a slight tremor of her lips as if she was holding back the flood.

"Lisette," William said, "this is Madame Hugo, and she will be staying here with us for a period of time." He waited, amused, watching the flow of expressions cross Lisette's little face. It did not require telepathy for me to recognize she was itching to ask questions but knew better. "Would you like to show her your room?" he asked, knowing she did.

"Please, Madame," she said, reaching up her hand to link with mine, her fingers feeling warm against my flesh.

"There," Sir William laughed. "I have delivered you safely." His eyes met mine. "I have some pressing business and will speak with you later. In the meantime, I will ask Lisette to see to your comfort."

His last words pleased Lisette greatly, as she was being treated as an adult by him, given such a grave responsibility.

I watched him greet his seneschal, a tall, muscular man called Sir Gilbert. The man's dark eyes flicked towards me with curiosity, but he was well-trained enough not to question the sheriff. As the two men walked away, I thought it interesting that Sir William would just assume he could order me around and map out my life. In fact, that is what he was doing, and maybe that tendency came with the responsibility of his office. It was clear he thought he had a good intuition about me and wanted to expose Lisette to a woman who seemed to comport herself well. I guess I'd made a good impression so far.

Lisette, with the open mind of a child, was easy to read. I could feel her aching for a female companion and followed the thoughts that hesitantly touched on the loss of her mother. It seemed Sir William had been married, and his wife, the mother of Lisette, had died at some time in the past. One of the hounds, a smaller version of the large wolfhounds that lurked in the great hall, took up at our side, and I reached down to pat his head, smiling as he gazed up at me with a pair of enormous brown canine eyes that had that perpetual expression of begging that some dogs seemed to master.

"He is called Jester," Lisette said. "I can tell he likes you, and that is important if you are to be my friend."

"Am I to be your friend?" I asked, smiling.

"Why, of course, Madame. We will be best friends," she said, sounding more than a little like her father could when he was touching on the imperious. Bossiness ran in the family; that was apparent.

She guided me up a series of steps that led to a landing along which rooms were located. There was no extended hallway but rather rooms situated like the spokes of a wheel. This would be where the family lived and perhaps entertained special guests, I thought. Some of the servants lived outside of the main keep, while other of the lesser staff members might reside in the first level beneath the great hall, if this castle was designed like many others characteristic of the period. For the moment, there was no one on the landing save for me and Lisette, and I wondered why the sheriff would have released his daughter to the care of a stranger. I had not really focused on his thoughts at the time, but decided he knew I had no opportunity for mischief while in his house, and Lisette was old enough and sufficiently precocious to speak up if she felt I was not doing what was expected of me. Jester padded along next to us, his heavy panting almost as loud as our passage itself.

Lisette pushed open a door and, still holding my hand, pulled me into what served as her room. The walls were made of wood, whitewashed, and covered in pretty tapestries that featured animals and forest scenes. The hand that had created them was no doubt talented. I walked forward to look at one that caught my eye.

"My mama made that for me," Lisette said, her voice sounding both proud and sad. "She made all of these for me."

I glanced at her little face with its delicately upturned nose and lips the color of a new rosebud. "And where is your mama?" I asked.

"She has gone to live with the angels," Lisette replied. Her lips trembled a little. "Papa tells me I must always think of it like that and not be sad." Her head twisted to the side as she looked at me, her expression wistful. "Is that right, Madame?"

I reached out my hand and cupped her chin; my heart squeezed at the expression on her face, one which revealed how much she'd been affected by the loss of her mother. "I'm sure your father wants you to have good thoughts," I replied, not knowing what else to say. She had a tender heart, and despite her elevated position in the society of the day, she was unspoiled.

Lisette seemed to shake off her sadness—having probably been told to do that many times—and gave me the quick tour. She was especially proud of her bed, which was canopied so that the fabric panels could be shut at night to keep out the cool drafts that were endemic in a stone and wood building with no central heat. I did spy an iron brazier that was probably filled with hot brands at night to give off some heat in the room.

"Papa lets Jester stay with me and keep me warm," Lisette said, giggling.

"What a clever idea!" I replied, lifting my brows as if amazed at the thought.

"Shall I find a dog to sleep with you and keep you warm, Madame?" she asked.

Of course, her words were so innocent and thoughtful, but immediately I thought of Kipp. He would be the one to keep me warm, and who knew where he was at the moment? Hiding in the woods, helping Elani and Peter, eluding capture … my thoughts grew anxious as I struggled for control. Lisette, like her father, was very perceptive.

"Madame, what is it? Did I say something wrong?"

"Oh, no, my child," I replied, trying to smile. "I had a dog named Kipp, and he disappeared into the forest. I miss him." I touched her cheek with the palm of my hand.

Lisette drew close, her pixie face compressed into a frown. "Oh, Madame, I'm so sorry. But I will make sure you have a dog to keep you warm, even if he isn't your Kipp. And maybe he will come back?" She sounded hopeful with the optimism of a child.

"Maybe," I replied.

"Let me show you Papa's bird," she said in a transparent attempt to distract me. Without waiting for my response, she grabbed my hand and began to pull me from her room, out into the corridor and to a closed door. Giggling, she put her ear to the door before tentatively pushing it open, sticking her head through the crack.

"Good!" she announced.

Well, of course, I knew better than to go into a man's bed-chamber without proper invitation, as it was an overt invasion of privacy, but I was so curious to see the sheriff's room that I didn't launch any objection to the child. I tried to pretend innocence and followed behind, allowing my eyes to take in as much as possible before a discreet retreat. The room was larger than Lisette's, naturally, but oddly more spartan in decoration. I might have thought there would be opulent wall hangings and such, but the walls were bare. All that I saw was the large bed with the linen curtains similar to those in Lisette's room, a desk that appeared to have parchments and ink ready for inscriptions, as well as a large round table piled with rolled parchments and books. Books, for the times, were a valuable and rare commodity, and most were produced in monasteries, although learned men were beginning to take some control of the flow of information and access. Opening one, I saw it was written in Latin.

"Here she is!" Lisette announced with her musical, lilting voice.

On an ornate brass stand, a falcon perched, hooded and motionless except to turn her head to the direction of Lisette's voice. Despite the fact she was quiet and seemingly at ease, the bird projected a sense of power and intelligence. I had the odd sensation she could see me quite clearly behind the fabric of the hood.

"She is the best hunter of the flock," Lisette boasted, "and I named her Jehanne."

I walked closer, fascinated, as I'd never been close to a captive falcon. The beauty of her markings and the fine, soft, downy feathers on her chest barely disguised the musculature of her lithe body. The little hooded head tilted my way as she heard my footsteps.

"Hello?"

I jumped, guilt written all over my face. The sheriff had arrived, his hands on his belt as if he was preparing to disrobe and change clothing. Lisette seemed not bothered a bit and skipped towards him, smiling.

"I wanted to show Madame your beautiful Jehanne," she said. "Jehanne is the best hunter in all the country, the world," she boasted, her face beaming.

"Lisette, you should not enter another person's room without permission," William began, but it was clear his heart wasn't into chastising her too severely. "Next time, please ask."

"Don't be mad at Madame," Lisette said. "I brought her here."

"Oh, I have no doubt of that," he replied, smiling at me. "What do you think of Jehanne?" he asked me, although the question was just a filler. He was being polite, enjoying talking with me for the moment.

"Oh, she is quite beautiful," I replied honestly. It felt awkward, standing in his private quarters, but I could think of no way to excuse myself since I was there by invitation of Lisette.

"She provides company, a quiet strength that is comforting," he replied. "And then there are my books."

I was glad to leap at that invitation. Smiling, I walked to the table and glanced down at the one that was written in Latin. Easily, I translated the Latin to French, thinking it might serve me well to demonstrate some talents in case he decided I was a worthless burden. And, no, I wasn't just showing off.

"Ah, you are educated, I see, and can read Latin." Without waiting for my response, he asked, "I assume you can both read and write French and Latin?"

"Why, yes, I can. My father had me learn when I was young. His eyesight was failing, and I read to him," I lied, thinking quickly.

Sir William became quiet, but his mind was working, and I was following his train of thoughts like a terrier after a rat. Lisette, in his way of thinking, needed some education since she would be in the upper tier of society and would have to compete with other young women one day for suitable marriages. The ability to read and write French and Latin would be a feather in her cap. He kept thinking. I, from his standpoint, had to be feeling pretty desperate since I claimed there was no family to help me and was a poor widow at that point who'd been robbed of my funds. He was feeling confident and rather smug and more than a little sure of himself. There was no doubt I would accept his offer to stay at the castle, at least for a while, and teach Lisette. He could not validate all of my story, but I appeared to be a lady, educated, and well-mannered, and Lisette already enjoyed my company. And to make the deal even sweeter, he felt I was obligated to him since he'd dramatically rescued me from the outlaw horde.

"My lady," he began, the now familiar smile on his face, "I would consider it a personal favor if you would stay with us, at least for a time, and instruct Lisette in the proper use of French and Latin as well as the written word."

"Oh, please, Madame!" Lisette was about to begin to whine and plead; that was clear. Her loneliness was obvious.

"I am grateful, Sir William," I began, meeting his golden eyes, which seemed to be a little darker than before. "For the time I am here until I make other arrangements, it would be my pleasure to teach Lisette what I know."

He expressed his gratitude, but his words were false. He knew before I responded what my answer would be. And even if he'd misjudged me, he could simply tell me that he could not, in good conscience, allow a vulnerable woman to exercise poor judgment and leave the safety of his abode. I knew all that, obviously, and decided to play along with the game. After a short period of time, he'd relax his vigilance, and I could slip away to hopefully melt back into the countryside and be reunited with my team. I figured my best chance was to gain his trust.

As he spoke to Lisette and his attention was off of me for the moment, I could really focus on his thought patterns and feelings. He genuinely loved his daughter; that much was clear. But in terms of the rest of us, there was a subtle deviousness about the man, not necessarily in a wicked sort of way but in a manipulative one. William Wendenal had learned to manage people with the use of a steel hand concealed within a velvet glove. But as he glanced at me with those gold-brown eyes, I realized something else. He'd also loved his wife, and for some reason, I reminded him of her. That, in many ways, explained his need to take over my life and control me. Suddenly, I didn't know what to do with my hands, which seemed to be hanging awkwardly.

"I have to meet with my subordinates," he said, nodding at me politely. "But I have made arrangements for you to join me for dinner so that we might better become acquainted." He smiled at Lisette. "Lisette, would you please show Madame Hugo to the room next to yours?"

Oh, great, I thought, trying not to moan aloud. What I didn't want was any alone time where he'd have the opportunity to pick apart my fragile tale. But I made myself smile and murmur how delightful sharing dinner with him would be. Taking Lisette's hand, I gently pulled her from his room so we could make our exit. We passed the door to her room, and she opened the door to a smaller chamber while tugging on my hand, laughing.

"Here is your room, Madame," she said.

Lisette managed a graceful pirouette across the floor as I followed her inside. The chamber was little more than a cell, but that actually was a benefit in a drafty, unheated castle. Smaller rooms were warmer in winter.

"Are you pleased, Madame?" Lisette asked, tilting her head to the side. A tiny frown marred her smooth complexion.

"Yes, Lisette. And you are to call me Petra." I reached out to gently touch a ringlet of golden hair that hung over her shoulder. "It will be much simpler."

"Papa says I am to address old people with their title as a way of showing respect." Lisette looked up at me, clearly confused about the rules.

"Well, perhaps I'm not that old," I remarked. "And I will tell your father that I prefer a simple name rather than a title."

"If you insist," she hesitated, thinking of my name and how it would sound rolling off her tongue. "Petra." Lisette seemed pleased with herself. "It is a strange name, but I like it," she remarked with a child's unguarded bluntness.

We were interrupted by a servant, a woman who probably was no more than thirty but looked as if she could be twice that age. She was pleasant enough, but her eyes lacked any spark of happiness, and deep within her was a resentment of serving the Normans. She was Saxon, after all. I disliked being one of the people she despised, but there was nothing to do about it. In that environment, one chose sides, and I was committed. Kipp had last seen me in the company of the sheriff, and he would look for me in that same company.

"My lord, the sheriff, has told me to find you some suitable clothing, my lady," the woman said, after taking a quick peek at me. She was sizing me up, although given the way clothing fit in those times, she could miss my measurements by quite a bit, and the garments would still work. The indispensable belt worked to pull everything together.

As the servant disappeared down the gloomy passageway—and there were no open windows, just occasional slits through which the sun could build a pattern upon the floor if the day was clear -- we heard the rumble of thunder. The storm that had chased us to Nottingham had arrived; a crack of lightning was visible through the narrow peep.

"Jester does not like that sound," Lisette said. Her eyes followed the dog, which began to skulk along the passage until he got to her room. She followed and opened the door. "Come in, Petra, and we will keep him company until the storm passes."

As she opened the door, the dog ran quickly inside and managed to nose his way past the linen drapes that concealed the bed. Giggling, Lisette ran after him and pushed back the fabric. "Come on, let's hide," she invited, reverting to her child persona.

Laughing, I climbed on the end of the bed, enjoying the feel of a thick woolen blanket beneath me. It seemed I'd not rested for hours—and I hadn't—and it was good to relax. Glancing at Jester, I had a moment of sadness as I thought of Elani and Kipp. But it probably was only a minute or two later when I fell asleep.

# NINETEEN

Sir Gilbert's hooded eyes were dark, secretive, despite their deceptive resemblance to those of a spaniel ... soulful, depthless and exquisitely sad. It was difficult to determine his emotions from his facial expressions, and I was grateful for my skills as a telepath. His shoulders were broad and heavily built, straining against the fabric of his tunic. No doubt, he was a physically powerful man, just the right sort to enforce the more unpopular of the sheriff's notions. As the sheriff's seneschal, I was aware that he was just beneath Sir William in the food chain and probably made sure he kept his position by doing whatever was necessary. His stability in the job made me realize I should view him with caution despite his puppy dog eyes. His thoughts, as I followed them, were calculating. He was infinitely curious about my origins and planned on being the inquisitor to Sir William's pleasant, engaging host.

"How did you find the fish?" Sir William asked, tilting his head at me. The dim lighting in the room cast elusive shadows; as the shadowed areas shifted and moved, the solid planes of his face appeared distorted and slightly unreal. An invisible air current must have disturbed one of the candles, which began to flicker, causing light to dance across the darkened walls. If it had been just the two of us, the setting could have taken a romantic twist. I was glad for the presence of Sir Gilbert, despite his malignant nature. He could put a damper on just about any occasion.

"Very good," I responded. What else was I to say?

We'd moved on to the second course, which consisted of soup served in little individual two-handled pot-bellied bowls. One drank the broth then used the spoon to dig out the onions, leeks, and whatever else might be lurking at the bottom of the crock. I found I missed the sweet beverage that was a byproduct of the preparation of pottage, but now I was treated to wine. Fermented beverages were not something I'd had of late, and I planned on keeping my sobriety intact and my head clear. In other words, I sipped it sparingly. In any case, it was unpleasantly bitter, and the taste lingered on the back of my tongue.

"My lady, if you will permit my curiosity, could you tell us how it is you left your husband's home?" Sir Gilbert almost purred; his voice was quiet and persuasive.

I glanced at him, trying not to appear to be evaluating his appearance. His clothing was certainly several notches above the ordinary but not the quality of that of the sheriff, who wore an embroidered tunic made of fine wool that had been dyed a rich cobalt blue color. Like everyone else, Gilbert had his head covered and wore a brimless cap. I'd been given a gorget made of linen and a small round cap to wear upon my head which anchored the fabric drape. I was grateful when I first met Sir William that I'd remembered to wear my modified wimple made of a piece of thin wool wrapped around my head and neck. Only, uh, loose women appeared in public with their hair uncovered. In a casual setting between close associates, family members, and intimates, the rules were different and laxer, but since we were dining as a trio and Sir Gilbert was being introduced to me, the head coverings remained.

Sir Gilbert was doing the dirty work for the sheriff, who wanted to seem all goodness and light in my eyes. But I really couldn't blame them. How was it a woman, who could read and write in French and Latin, just popped out of the sky and land near their castle? Sir Gilbert, by nature, was a cautious and suspicious man, much more so—and surprisingly so—than the sheriff.

"Why, Gilbert, surely we don't need to interrogate Madame

Hugo," the sheriff said, laughing softly. But his thoughts were just the opposite. He was frankly curious.

"And I would greatly prefer if you would call me Petra," I said, smiling at the sheriff. "It makes things so much easier without formalities." After he nodded, I continued. "It is not a pretty story, my friends. My husband and I were married in France." I ducked my head for effect, trying to appear as if I was struggling to control my emotions with the onset of sweet and tender memories. "Our parents were close associates, and that is how we came to be betrothed. Peter's brother came here to support the king and as such was rewarded with lands and a title. Peter and I came later as guests." I tried to look sad and successfully managed to conjure up tear-filled eyes, although I couldn't force a teardrop to fall down my cheek, as I felt my nose become red and congested with the strain of trying. "Peter's health prevented him from being a warrior, like his brother, and we lived with him as family, as the brothers were very close.

"As often happens, jealousies occur. My sister-in-law did not care for me and quite frankly resented the fact I could read and write and she could not." I shrugged my shoulders. "I even offered to teach her, and her resentment only worsened. So, when Peter died, she did all she could to fuel the notion that I should leave and make it on my own. In order to keep a peaceful home, my brother-in-law conceded, and I was asked to leave." I glanced up at the two men who were staring at me. Gilbert's eyes were unreadable, while William's seemed filled with concern and compassion. Gilbert's thoughts mirrored the expression in his eyes … he was still deliberating and wasn't ready to root for team Petra.

"In fairness, my brother-in-law did give me a generous amount of currency so that I could have some comforts while I made my way in the world." I paused, waiting.

"Why Nottingham?" Gilbert asked the obvious question.

"I met travelers who had been here, and they claimed it was a growing town with moral leadership. They convinced me it would be safer here for a solitary woman than many other places I might choose." I felt the little compliment towards the men who were sharing a meal with me might go a long way.

"What you say is true, Petra," William said. He was clearly pleased over my words, and I'd said everything he wanted to hear. "Nottingham is safe ... Gilbert and I have worked diligently to make it so. But there are still dangers out there, as you found when the men you trusted turned out to be scoundrels."

I dropped my chin, trying to look suitably chastised. My understanding of William was that he enjoyed being the dominant male, and I needed to let him think I accepted his guidance and wisdom. In fairness, he was only doing what was culturally appropriate for the times, so I took no offense to his thinking I was helpless without his strong leadership.

"Your words ring true, Sir William."

"If we are to call you Petra, then I am William and this is Gilbert," he responded with a grand wave of his hand.

We became quiet for a moment as two servants appeared to remove the soup bowls and deliver trenchers made of thick bread filled with freshly cooked meat. The dogs, which were gathered in the hall, recognized they were in line to profit from the meal as they were accustomed to grabbing the bits and pieces that might be dropped or even thrown if a human was in a cheerful mood. One particularly large, shaggy fellow with a brindled coat sidled next to me, flicking his eyes tentatively towards my face, having learned to be judicious in his begging. It was a fine art for the dogs. Too much boldness could earn one a swift kick. Too humble, and one would miss out on a choice bit of something. Glancing down at the food that had been set before me, I realized I was looking at what remained of the bullock, the one that had protested being led to the slaughter. Typically, I'm pretty talented at concealing my emotions, but something obviously peeked past my mask, because William's facial expression changed immediately.

"Is the meat not to your liking?" he asked, frowning.

"Oh, it looks very fine," I replied. "It is just I'm not accustomed to eating so much, and the fish and soup were a feast in my eyes." Looking up, I saw the frown, which could appear like an unexpected thundercloud, disappear as the smile reappeared.

"Ah, you must forgive us," William said, glancing at Gilbert.

"We men have hearty appetites and enjoy our food. Perhaps we have demonstrated poor manners?"

"Oh, no, not at all," I said, rushing my words. "Please, continue." If the wolfhound continued to hang out at my elbow, he might benefit big time.

Gilbert was not finished with me. "If I understand, Madame Hugo, it would seem your husband's family here has abandoned you." Without waiting for an answer, he added, "Have you considered returning to France and seeking the shelter and safety of your own family?"

"Yes, I would like that one day." I tried not to glance at the trencher full of steaming beef that still lay on the table before me. A perceptive servant arrived, his steps as silent as those of a cat, and removed the wooden tray. The wolfhound who'd staked out my trencher sensed he'd missed a golden opportunity and followed the servant like a great, lumbering shadow. Almost immediately, I felt my stomach, which had begun to turn, settle. Internally, I chastised myself for getting way too soft.

William glanced at me; the expression in his gold-brown eyes was hidden, but I had the advantage of telepathy. At that moment, he felt more than a little like a big spider, one which was spinning a web to keep me contained. He liked me and already had decided that given enough time, he might like me even more. And Lisette liked me, too. So, for William, this was a win-win situation. I needed help, and he appreciated the fact I would be beholden to his generosity. But it was more than just that, and I wished I had Kipp with me to do his unique dive into William's deeply stored memories that I lacked the ability to access. Despite my limitations, I could perceive the grief that still haunted William and realized the death of his wife had left a void. It was obvious he'd loved her greatly. It was either fortunate for me—or perhaps, unfortunate—that I reminded him of her, and that memory fueled his need to be protective and possessive of me. Beneath the fine trappings of his office, he was a lonely man.

The candles, which were made of the coveted beeswax available to men of wealth and power, flickered again as one of the servants returned to the room. It was interesting to live in such a dark world where it seemed mystery and suspense lurked in every corner. There were no large windows, as castles were built for defense and security. It felt little better than a large cave. I looked at William, watching how the movement of the minimal light played across his face. He caught me watching him and smiled in response. I felt my face flush and was glad the room was sufficiently shadowed to conceal the stain on my cheeks. The meal was drawing to a close, and I confess I was fatigued from playing a game of mental dodge ball all evening. I needed to be alone for a while to recover; that much was clear. It is a truth for symbionts that too much time spent with humans is simply exhausting.

"I hope you will not find me ill-mannered, but I am tired and would like to go to my chambers to rest."

William immediately responded, asking to accompany me, an offer I politely declined.

"No, please, finish your meal," I said.

Both men stood as I exited, and I removed myself from their thoughts, cutting off my telepathy, depleted, not wanting to follow them any longer. The female servant I'd met earlier met me on the landing, her head dipped, her expression masked. Once we arrived at my small room, she opened the door and ushered me inside.

"I have brought you clothes," she said, her tone flat and neutral. She, of course, was speaking Old English and had learned, in her position of servitude, to conceal her emotions while in the presence of Norman nobility.

"What is your name?" I asked, smiling, changing from French to her language.

"Margaret," she replied, her eyes meeting mine for a flash. She saw my smile, something that was rare in her world when coming from a Norman. "Folks call me Peg."

"I appreciate your kindness," I said.

Her eyes made a quick survey of my face. She was unaccustomed to being told such things, and something such as gratitude for having done her expected job was unheard of. She flashed a smile before swiftly ducking her head.

"Where did you get these clothes?" I asked, looking at a chest, the lid of which was opened. Peering inside, I could see shifts, tunics and other various articles, all made of fine fabric and some with exquisite embroidery.

"They belonged to the sheriff's wife," Peg responded.

Oh, my, I thought to myself. I had no wish to play dress up in the deceased wife's clothing, but what was I to do?

"When did she die?" I asked, taking a seat on the narrow bench at the foot of my bed.

"Oh, it was last year, about this time," Peg answered. "She was a good woman, very kind and lovely." Peg paused to look around, obviously wanting to make certain no one else might be lurking to overhear her gossip. "The sheriff was very much in love with her and has not been the same since."

"I feel odd, wearing her clothes…" I began, tentatively.

"Oh, don't you mind that, my lady. The sheriff is a practical man. He can't give her clothes to any of us, since they would be too fine. And he can't give used clothes to ladies, since they would take it as an insult."

I tried not to smile. "Thank you, Peg." I guess her evaluation was that I fell somewhere between a lady and a servant, which made me rather unique.

She'd filled the brazier with some hot coals from the fire pit, and even though the radiated warmth would not last long, it was enough to make the small chamber bearable.

"The sheriff said I'm to look after you most particular," she said, nodding her head.

Peg had also brought a basin of water and lingered, since she was accustomed to helping her "lady" with all elements of life. To make her happy and feel she'd done her job and not get in trouble with the sheriff, I let her help me remove my tunic down to my shift, and then I washed my face with the water, patting my skin dry with a piece of woolen fabric. It quickly became apparent that Peg enjoyed bossing her ladies as she sat me down on the wooden bench at the end of the bed, pulled out a comb, and began to work it through my hair. I'm not certain why, but it always feels better when someone else does that. Anyway, she braided the mass carefully and made certain I knew where the garderobe was when I needed a potty visit. I assured her that Lisette had already given me the grand tour.

"Well, if you'll not be needing anything else," she said as she left.

I climbed into the bed, pulling the linen drapes shut to help with the heat conservation. Stretching out, I tried to review the day and plan my next moves. But it was difficult to concentrate. Thoughts of Elani filled my mind. Was she alive? Somehow, I felt I would know empathically, despite the physical distance, if she were dead. And next, the anguish of missing Kipp filled my heart and mind, and I began to cry. With effort, I made myself stop. Getting emotional would not change the situation, and the build-up of feelings would only cloud my judgment when it was critical I maintain my focus.

It was then I heard the door to my room creak softly as someone opened it. Holding my breath, I reached out with my mind. Thank goodness, it was not Sir William! I definitely didn't want to play tag with him! It was Peg, instead. A moment later, I heard a snuffling sound, then a panting and a large, furry body parted the linen curtains and pushed its way past to join me. It was one of the wolfhounds, the massive dog that lingered at my elbow during dinner and might have been rather terrifying in other circumstances. It seemed Lisette had made true her promise to find me a bed warmer. The dog was actually quite a pussycat, despite his intimidating presence, and after sniffing my feet, he curled up, half covering my legs, muttering and making funny noises as he got comfortable. And yes, although he was no Kipp, he made for a nice sleeping buddy.

---

"Are you awake, Madame?"

Lisette's high-pitched voice startled me out of a dreamless sleep.

"Yes," I lied, struggling to sit up.

She parted the linen drapes farther and climbed into my bed, laughing as she spied the wolfhound, who had rolled on his back and was lounging, his considerable bulk resting upon my legs, which had gone numb from his weight.

"You like him?" Lisette asked.

"Yes, thank you. He kept me very warm last night."

"His name is Hero," she said, reaching out to run her small hand along his coarse fur. "When he was a young dog, Papa took him out on a hunt, and he showed such bravery that his name was changed." Lisette made herself comfortable, crossing her legs in a most unladylike fashion, as she continued to finger comb Hero's brindled, wiry coat. "Some of the others have bad tempers, but Hero is gentle. That's why I knew you'd like him."

She began to hum a pretty tune before breaking out in song. I tried not to laugh as she crooned for me, since she was all seriousness. But the situation struck me as funny—and I'm not entirely sure I knew why.

"What will we do today, Madame?"

"First, call me Petra." At her look of alarm, I continued. "It will be okay with your father when I tell him I asked you to use my name."

"If you say I must," she replied, pretending humility while inwardly feeling excitement she was being encouraged to violate the rules she'd been taught by her exacting father.

"We will begin your lessons," I said, expecting the usual response of a child to such words but finding myself pleasantly surprised that she smiled and even clapped her hands. Lisette, it seemed, liked the challenge of learning.

"Papa sent you some of my mama's clothes," she said. "He told me I should understand that you had none, and you are a lady, and you need to be dressed well. He did not want me to be upset if I saw you wearing her clothes." Lisette's pretty little face dropped as her hands began to worry with the woolen blanket on my bed.

"If it bothers you, Lisette, I would never think to wear them."

"Oh, no, Petra. It will make me happy, I think."

The wound of losing her mother was still fresh. I realized she was going to use me, unconsciously, to fill that gap, and internally it rocked me. Once reunited with my team, I would return to my home. Lisette would be left behind, again. It would be necessary for me to tell her, often, that my stay at the castle was temporary. Even with that, her immaturity would make her tend to believe what she wanted to think and not the reality.

"I probably won't be here very long," I said, reaching out to touch a lock of titian curls. "But it is very generous of you and your father to help me feel welcome."

She glanced at me with her father's gold-brown eyes, her expression guarded. "I hope you stay, Petra."

"I have family in France," I replied. "And one day I'll need to go home, just as this is your home, Lisette. But in the meantime, we will have great fun together, and I will teach you how to read and write, that is, if you are a good student."

"I am the best," she replied, her tone a little defiant. That was her father speaking, I realized.

"We will see," I said, arching my brows.

I rushed her from my room, having her remove the reluctant Hero, who had decided he liked me, too. I'd never been so popular, I thought wryly. Using the basin of water, I managed a bird bath and had finished pulling a fresh shift over my head when Peg appeared.

"Let me find you something for the day," she offered, beginning to rummage through the trunk. Finally, she pulled out a purple long-sleeved tunic of soft wool and helped me tug it over my head. She next selected a surcoat of a different shade of purple that had embroidery on the front and back. The belt made the unfitted garments appear attractive once a waist was created.

Peg pulled out the comb, which seemed to be in perpetual residence in one of her large pockets, and carefully combed and braided my hair before draping the gorget around my neck to loop it up where she topped my head with the round cap. Have mercy, I thought. This was way too much work for a symbiont accustomed to sweat pants and a bandana to keep the hair off my face. I'd learned to enjoy the slovenly attitude and demeanor afforded me in the contemporary world.

"Thank you," I told her.

"The sheriff has left for the day," she said, making conversation.

"Oh," I replied, wanting to ask but not wishing to appear overly curious as to his business.

"He's going back to that place where he found you and try to roust out the outlaws again. He especially wants to find the men that stole from you." Her pale blue eyes were huge in her thin face. "I'd hate to be them if he manages to nab them."

I silently agreed with her assessment. The sheriff had a relentless nature and would not easily give up Robin or his followers.

Lisette, who seemed to have no compunction against going into people's rooms uninvited, pushed back the door and skipped to my side. She brought with her the sweet scent of flowers, and I thought her hair might have been washed in rosewater. A fetching little tunic almost touched the floor; she wore a long surcoat that was embroidered in a flower motif. The long ringlets of titian hair cascaded over her shoulders. She seemed to have the same disdain for head coverings as did I.

"Petra, I want to show you our gardens today," she announced, her lips pursing in a charming little bow.

As we left the keep and I allowed her to guide me throughout the other buildings and areas that comprised the castle proper, I could not help but notice there were two armed men trailing us. When I turned to gaze at them, they almost comically tried to act nonchalant. It was clear the sheriff had guards, if not for me, then for Lisette. She caught my glance.

"I heard Papa tell Sir Gilbert that you were to be watched at all times. I think he fears for your safety." She glanced up at me, her face as innocent as her thoughts.

My notion that the sheriff was a spider only too happy to keep me in his web was not far from the truth. Leaving this place would be difficult.

# TWENTY

"My lady, I am very happy to meet you," Friar Thomas said, tilting his tonsured head slightly as a token of respect. "And I am so distressed to hear you were the victim of mischief in our lands." He proved to be the consummate actor because when his eyes met mine, they were remarkably empty of any hint of recognition of me. Robin had sent him as a messenger, and he was eager to have a moment alone to share. The only thing I could read was his need to find an opportunity to speak with me without the sheriff or a servant hovering within earshot.

"We always welcome Friar Thomas to our community," the Sheriff of Nottingham said, smiling. He was playing the engaging, gracious host, always hoping to cultivate approbation in me.

We were in the great hall; with no windows to allow light, the room was filled with moving shadows. Uncounted days had passed since my arrival in Nottingham, and outside, a late autumn storm raged, bending the trees and stripping them of what few leaves remained. One could only speculate the fury of the storm signified the arrival of much colder weather. Friar Thomas was standing next to the fire pit to dry his long tunic and mantle, which were sodden with the rainwater. Unlike some modern-day humans who might fret over such things, people were accustomed to exposure to the elements, and a little water was no big matter. The odor of damp wool, which was more than a little soiled, filled the immediate space as I tried not to sneeze. A servant had been sent to fetch hot beverages, and after the dogs had settled -- since there was typically a fair amount of barking and uproar as unexpected guests arrived -- the sheriff led us to an alcove where the servants had placed refreshments.

What I needed was for the hovering sheriff to leave, at least momentarily, so that I could speak with Thomas alone. If Kipp had been there, he could have planted a suggestion to compel the sheriff to do as he wished; inwardly, I chafed at my lack of some of the more archaic symbiont skills which could have been useful. But fate was good to me that day, and a servant arrived, bending to whisper something to the sheriff. I, of course, couldn't help but listen in, and it seemed a messenger had been sent from Prince John. The sheriff mastered his facial expressions, but inwardly there was a dash of anxiety. After begging our pardon, the sheriff left.

"My lady, we only have a moment," Thomas said, keeping his voice low. His dark eyes darted around the alcove, searching for any eavesdroppers. "Your brother is well; his dog, Elani, was gravely wounded, but she is stable, and I think, with time, she will recover." He saw the tears flood my eyes and reached forward to pat my forearm. "Do not worry, my lady. She is only weak, like a newborn kitten. Her constitution is vigorous." A shadow of a smile touched his rather plain face.

"And Kipp?" I asked, my voice breaking.

"He is naturally protective, and he stays by Elani's side all time. He seems, well, attached to her." Thomas smiled. "I had to be convinced by Peter that your Kipp wouldn't bite me if I were to bring discomfort or pain to Elani during my attempts to treat her wound." He glanced around again, forcing his hunched shoulders to relax. "Robin wanted me to tell you that as soon as he thinks your brother can travel again, he will make arrangements to send for you." Somewhat emboldened by my emotions, the friar reached out and gently touched my hand, his fingers just a whisper touch against my flesh.

Of course, Thomas had no idea what the word "travel" meant

for us, but I did, and so did Robin, since he'd used it purposefully. The bottom line was I needed to stay put for the time being. Logically, if I tried to leave now and reunite with my team, the sheriff would search for me, and in doing so, put all of Robin's men in danger. Thomas became silent as we heard the voice of the sheriff as he returned.

"All shall need to be in order by the time of his arrival," William said, his tone brusque and no-nonsense. As he came into view, his expression changed, chameleon-like, as he assumed the mask of the face he chose to wear for me. "Prince John is arriving at the end of the month from Leicester, and all must be made ready for his visit."

I felt my heart leap in my chest. And as I considered the sheriff's words, I had very mixed feelings. My primary role was to serve as a historian, an investigator of truths, and meeting the brother of the absent king would be fascinating. But that meeting would thrust me into a higher profile than I wished, and it was already way too high for my liking. It would only take one peasant from Ashland near Trent or, perhaps, Sir Donald, to recognize me as a poor, traveling farmworker and blow my fragile cover. I could only hope I'd been successful in concealing my appearance from Sir Donald during his two visits to the village. Maybe I could feign illness? Or just be indisposed? But my instinct told me no since William would want to show me off like a new pet or a pretty bauble.

"William, would it be very impolite for me to request a few moments with the friar for prayers and meditation?" I tried to sound very humble and needy.

"Why, of course not. I will retire and give you privacy." William said the only thing he could, but he was not particularly happy with my request, since he wanted to be privy to all that impacted me.

After he left, I leaned toward Thomas. "You must get a message to Robin," I whispered, throwing out my telepathic net to make certain there was no one within earshot. "He must divert Prince John to York." I tried not to smile as Thomas's eyes grew large. "And I know this will not make sense to you, and please don't ask me to explain, but tell him that Kipp will know how to make it happen."

"My lady," Thomas began, trying to control the expression on his face. He clearly thought the strain of my position had left me unhinged.

"Thomas, you must promise me to use those words when you speak with Robin. I realize you think I'm probably deranged, but I am fully in control of my senses. Kipp must know that Prince John is leaving Leicester to come to Nottingham."

"I promise," he finally said, taking a deep breath. "It makes no sense to me, but I will do as you ask."

"Well, the world can be confusing, and many things seem odd at times," I replied, my expression grave.

We heard the high-pitched voice of Lisette as she broke into an unexpected song, the sound of which drifted down from the level above to our secluded alcove. The expression on my face must have reflected my feelings about the girl.

"You have become attached here," Thomas said, his voice neutral and noncommittal. Inwardly, he hoped I was not getting too comfortable.

"No, Thomas, I have not. I must be careful in my position, which is precarious, as you can clearly understand. But I have no animus towards a child, and she is a sweet-natured girl who has become fond of me. I see no need to be churlish with her."

He ducked his head, and when he raised his face to me again, I could make out faint patches of color on his cheeks.

"I beg your pardon, my lady. It was wrong of me to question your motives."

Leaning forward, I gently touched his hand. Looking down, I could see his fingernails were ragged and torn, his cuticles overgrown and dirt-encrusted. In another age, such things as manicures might be imperative, but not in 1192. Survival was king.

"It is of no matter," I replied, reassuring him and noting the smile that reappeared. "In this day and time of political intrigue, it is probably wise to question everyone's motives."

"Except Robin's." His dark eyes met mine with a look of certainty. "He is a man of his word who has done much to help the poor."

"What all has he done?"

"He educates the men, and, my lady, we know that the ability to read and write as well as think from a broader perspective is the key to freedom of the soul. Even if one has few earthly rewards, one's heart and mind can soar." Thomas looked down at his mantle. "I have only what I wear on my back, and I feel I am a free man." He shrugged his shoulders. "What else is needed?"

"You speak wisely," I replied. "But a more equitable society would surely be an improvement?"

"And that begins with education, my lady."

He was clearly going to say more, but a servant appeared, asking as to our comfort and needs. As we turned him away, the sheriff arrived. He practically vibrated with a current of irritation and wished to peel me away from the side of the friar.

"Friar Thomas, do you wish me to arrange accommodations for you?" William's voice was pleasant, but his thoughts were hoping Thomas would decline. From William's point of view, I enjoyed speaking privately with Thomas, a fact that made him less than comfortable and affected his usually charitable thoughts towards the friar.

"No, thank you, Sir William. I have to go see the abbot, and from there, I know not where I will travel."

Of course, that was a lie, and I marveled at how well he managed to convey innocence and truth. Thomas was planning on hot-footing it back to Robin's side. I had the advantage of knowing his thoughts, and as crazy as had been my request for him to get a message to Kipp for me, I knew he would simply because he'd given his word.

William shifted from one foot to the other, impatient for Thomas to leave. In fact, he escorted him personally to the front door of the hall. I went as far as the fire pit where I stood close to the flames, having become chilled in the dim alcove where I'd met with the friar. William returned to me and noticed I was rubbing my arms with my hands.

"Petra, you are cold," he observed. With a snap of his fingers, he had a servant bring two chairs that were placed at a comfortable distance from the fire. "Let's sit for a moment until you are warmed."

I didn't want to, but what could I say? Instead, I murmured a soft thank you.

Fortunately, any intimacy promised in that fireside chat was broken when Lisette arrived, bringing her sweet scent of roses and, perhaps, lavender. Her fragrance disrupted the otherwise cloying smells of wet dogs, damp rushes that were more than a little moldy, and the ever-present smoke. She pulled close to me, putting her arm around my waist. William was always happy to see her but privately had wished for a few moments alone with me. I had, to that moment, managed to have Lisette, Peg, any of the other servants, or even Sir Gilbert present at almost all times to dilute the intensity of having to manage William's growing interest in me.

"And how are your studies progressing, Lisette?" William asked as she transferred her attention from me to him as she crossed over to climb onto his knee.

"Quite well, Papa," she replied. Her eyelids shuttered the expression in her eyes, her long eyelashes resting like feathers against her pale, delicate flesh. She peeked one covert glance at me, her gold-brown eyes catching a spark from the flickering flames of the fire pit. Lisette was waiting to see what type of report card I would give her father.

"And, my lady, what do you say?" William asked, smiling at me.

It was easier to deal with him when he was genuine and relaxed as he was at that moment. Something about his connection with Lisette disconnected all the other parts of him that could be filled with intrigue and manipulation. Maybe that was the one part of his life that was real. And, as I considered it, much of his nature was probably formed by the politics of the day. There were a lot of sharp elbows being thrown and one had to learn how to climb the hierarchical ladder to success. It was how advancement was accomplished. Privately, I wondered if much had changed in the contemporary world in which I lived.

"Oh, she is an excellent student," I replied. There was a stirring at my arm as I realized Hero, who'd also become attached to me, was nuzzling for some attention. He looked formidable but was really a big softie. But I have to admit he was a nice buddy to have made, since the coming winter made the unheated bed chambers uncomfortable, to say the least. Laughing, I ran my hand along the top of his head, tugging gently at his floppy ears. Bathing a dog was not in the mix in medieval times, so he carried with him a rich, cultivated bouquet of stink. Yeah, he'd been working on that odor for a long time and was proud of it.

"Well, I am glad to hear this," William said. "We are to have a very important visitor at the end of the month." He laughed as Lisette's eyes grew impossibly round and large. "Sir John, the Count of Mortain, is to be our guest."

He might have wanted us to think he was happy and looking forward to the visit, but inwardly he was anxious. Sir John's political aspirations were known to all. He had no loyalty to his brother, Richard, who was absent from the country. John's hope was that Richard would never return, and he could ascend to become king of England. John was ruthless and busy pulling together a coalition of Norman nobles to back him as he cast his net of influence wider and wider. William had been given his current responsibilities by Richard, with whom his true loyalties rested. But he had to play nice with John, or else his survival was not assured. As William glanced at the top of Lisette's titian head, he closed his eyes and inhaled, catching the scent of her clean hair with its fragrance of rosewater. He loved her deeply and wanted to keep her safe. I remembered, in that moment, what it was like to breathe in the scent of my baby George when he was fresh from his bath. That type of love was something I understood and appreciated in the man who sat across from me.

"The Count of Mortain!" I said, trying to sound impressed, since I knew William had dropped an enormous teaser and expected a response. "How exciting for you, William!"

He laughed softly. "Yes, exciting, but there are many preparations to make." The sheriff added, "We really don't have adequate niceties here for the prince, so one of our local nobles will house him and his contingent." He tried to look disappointed, but inwardly he was quite happy. William held no wish for Prince John to be sticking his royal nose in the management of the shire. "I am arranging a day of competitions for his entertainment." He glanced at me, the firelight dancing in his golden eyes. "I hope, Petra, you will attend some of the games as I believe you might find them amusing."

I wasn't being asked, of course; I was being told. So, I did the only thing I could do. I nodded and smiled.

At that moment, Sir Gilbert approached, his dark eyes resting on me for a long moment. He didn't like the fact the sheriff felt a growing affection for me, and although not exactly suspicious of me, since I appeared to be a well-bred lady from his point of view, he worried my presence might soften William's resolve. The sheriff was known as a no-nonsense guy and had become even more so after the death of his wife. From Sir Gilbert's perspective, William was easily made malleable by the influence of a soft-hearted woman, since he needed to look good in the eyes of his partner. Gilbert had no such compunctions nor weaknesses. His dark eyes met mine, and for a second it was as if we completely understood one another. I smiled up at him.

"Sir Gilbert, you have just come in from the cold rain. Will you share the fire with us?"

He was forced to respond to me. "Thank you, my lady, but I have matters which require my attention. I fear I will need to take the sheriff from you."

I focused on his thoughts and realized he had information about Robin Hood! As the two men left to go to William's rooms to talk, I worked on some reason to follow so that I could telepathically eavesdrop from a safe distance.

"Lisette, return to your room, please. I will be there shortly, and we will begin work on your penmanship."

Fortunately, the headstrong little girl didn't fuss and happily skipped through the great hall before scampering up the stairs to the landing to her room. After giving her a minute, I followed, walking slowly, trying not to draw the attention of any of the servants. I climbed the stairs and glanced up and down the corridor; no one was lurking, so I tip-toed down the hall, hoping to get close enough to eavesdrop clearly without the interference of other human minds busy at work. It was then I could follow what Gilbert was telling William. Leaning against the wall, I focused in on the thoughts of the two only to learn that a man, who'd once been a part of Robin's company, was, in exchange for payment, giving information about the gang of men, their usual whereabouts, and methods of remaining hidden so effectively. From Gilbert's perspective, the information could help in terms of narrowing any search of the vast forests of Sherwood.

I heard a floorboard creak and glanced around to see Peg, who stared back at me, her blue eyes wide. But before I could move, the door to William's room was flung open, and Gilbert stood there, his bulk filling the doorway, his dark eyes narrowed with suspicion.

"What are you doing?" he asked, his tone agitated. William crowded behind him; his brows pulled together in a frown.

"I have lost a stone from my brooch," I said, thinking fast and glad I didn't have the brooch pinned at my throat. Fortunately, it was one I used to help keep my mantle in place. I could feel my heart pounding in my chest as my throat tightened. Desperately, I glanced at Peg, who paused for only a second.

"My lady, I think I found it!" she cried. Leaning forward, she pretended to pick up something and cradle it in the palm of her hand. "I can reset it for you."

William's face relaxed as he smiled at me. "Perhaps we need to get you a new brooch," he said.

"Oh, that is so kind of you, but I am very content," I replied. "My mother gave it to me, so it has great meaning," I added shamelessly, working in a sentimental element for extra pizazz. My eyes darted to meet the dark ones of Gilbert. He remained concerned about my presence, but his thoughts didn't link me to Robin Hood. If anything, his mind entertained the notion that I was some sort of mole sent by Sir John to investigate the inner workings of the sheriff's domain. Gilbert had no loyalty to the prince; his loyalty was to William, and it ended there. He understood palace intrigue and all that accompanied it, but he no aspirations other than to serve as seneschal. Maybe that made him a little unique for the times?

Not wanting to linger, since I'd had about as close a shave as I'd had in quite a while, I turned and joined Peg, pretending to look at the palm of her hand. Together we went to my room, shutting the door behind us.

"Thank you, Peg, first of all," I breathed. "But why did you do that?"

Her blue eyes met mine frankly. "I like to listen at doors, too, and have had to think of quick explanations in the past." She smiled. "I'm quite good at it."

"But aren't you concerned that I was listening at the sheriff's door?"

"No, because that's how you learn what's going on. And if I were you, I'd be listening, too. Sir Gilbert doesn't care for you, and he might be talking about your business to the sheriff." She nodded her expression one of sage wisdom. "You need to be hearing all that."

"And why would that be?" I asked, wanting her assessment of the situation.

"The sheriff is clearly taken with you, my lady. One only has to look at his face to see how he feels. Sir Gilbert wants to be able to influence the sheriff, and anyone who gets in the way of that is a threat to him." Her eyes searched my face. "Don't you understand?" Although she tried to modify her tone, it was clear she thought I was a dunderhead.

Yes, I understood political machinations. I'd been through various reincarnations of it many times before. And while I tried to steer clear of being a major player in such nonsense, I appeared to be caught smack dab in the middle this time. There was no doubt that what Peg said was largely true. She had experience with the two men, and I did not, so her opinion mattered.

"In any case, I am beholden to you, Peg. Thank you for what you did," I replied simply. Reaching out, I took her hand in mine. "I call you friend."

Her face colored, making what had seemed plain rather lovely, as the pink flush rushed over her thin cheeks. She wasn't accustomed to kindness from the ruling class.

"Oh, it's nothing, my lady."

But it was something to me.

# TWENTY-ONE

It seemed the weeks passed simultaneously slowly and quickly, if that is possible. The agony of being without Kipp and my concern for the fate of Elani was oppressive; I felt out of balance, lost, and without direction. But I tried to fill my days with teaching Lisette, which was a joy. And the other side of life in Nottingham was minimizing, when I could, time spent with William. Doing so became more and more difficult as he purposely sought me out. It was clear he liked having a sounding board, and there were times he used me for that purpose rather than Sir Gilbert. That fact did nothing to improve my status with the seneschal, whose dislike of me increased exponentially.

The days preceding the expected arrival of Prince John were filled with a rush of activity. William was preoccupied since he wanted Nottingham to be prepared; he desired to show off his territory as being well-managed and productive in terms of the many villages and the peasants who worked the land. His future was largely dependent upon the opinion of John. I, while not speaking of my thoughts, wished fervently that Kipp had received my message and could, using his arts, divert the prince.

William found a few moments to speak with me between meetings with Sir Gilbert and other advisors, as well as the numerous sycophants just trying to score points that could enhance their livelihoods. "As I had mentioned, I am arranging a tournament and games for the entertainment of Prince John. I expect you to attend," he said, the filtered sunlight reflected in the gold of his eyes.

How was I to answer? I realized he would not let me stay behind and miss out on the revelry and excitement. Kipp, where are you, I wondered, feeling the pressure of my precarious position escalate.

William and I were walking through the orchard that was a part of the castle grounds. There were only a few brown, crisp leaves left clinging to the branches of the fruit trees; a savage, biting wind rattled the leaves as more detached, carried by the breeze. The dead leaves, which had fallen to the earth, crunched beneath my feet as I walked, a physical reminder of the harshness of winter to come. Despite my mantle, which I pulled closer about my body, I felt chilled to the bone. I hoped to be rid of this place by the time snow might fall. William, with his radar on me at all times, noticed my movement and drew closer. He was close enough that his body grazed mine. When I didn't draw away, he took that as tacit permission and gently took my arm. I glanced at him from the corner of my eyes. He was, indeed, a handsome man. But I'd already fallen in love with one human man, and that was enough for one lifetime. Besides, I felt no such romantic inclinations towards William, despite his attractive exterior. All I wanted was to be reunited with Kipp, Peter, and Elani and return home. I tried not to smile as I thought of Fitzhugh and Juno—and even the silly Lily cat —waiting for our return. The picture of Lily stalking Kipp through the house, occasionally grabbing on to one of his legs and allowing herself to be dragged across the floor, filled my thoughts. I was clearly homesick.

"My lady, how thoughtless of me!" William exclaimed. "It is too cold for your comfort. Let's return to the warmth of the fire."

As we made our way back to the keep, I followed William's unspoken worries. He'd arranged an archery tournament, as well as wrestling matches, horse races, and acrobats who were arriving from different parts of the countryside. And though it wasn't actually fencing in the modern sense, there was some type of swordplay also on the docket. I figured the fact the weather had turned cold was of no consequence, since the inhabitants of England at that time were accustomed to working and playing despite the variations in the temperature. As I aggressively sifted through William's thoughts, I was relieved to find there would be no jousting, since that particular, uh, sport held a horror in my heart. I privately envisioned men falling beneath wounded chargers, while the cries of the distressed horses filled the air. It was then I felt a stirring, a familiarity of thoughts. It was Kipp! He had returned to me! The force of the moment caused me to stumble, and William grasped my arm more firmly.

"Petra, may I help you?" he asked, the words dull, coming as if from a great distance to my ears. All I could think of was Kipp, who was running, racing, to get to me.

It was then I heard a bark, and I turned to see my beloved Kipp running across the courtyard, being pursued by a poorly motivated servant who was shouting at his fleeing body.

"Kipp!" I cried, grasping at William's hand. "It is my Kipp!" Pulling free of the sheriff, I darted forward and knelt on the ground, which had been made hard by the chill in the air. Kipp almost knocked me down in his fervor to be with me, as I once again could run my fingers through his ruddy coat. I buried my face in his fur, which smelled of the woodlands, fallen leaves, fire smoke, and wilderness. "Oh, Kipp," I cried, feeling the tears on my cheeks.

"It's okay, Petra," Kipp responded. "I'm okay; we're all okay." He pushed as close as possible as I felt his warmth through my woolen mantle.

"Elani?" I asked.

"She's getting better, much better."

I exhaled and said a prayer of thanks.

"And this must be the long-lost Kipp." William's voice sounded above me. "I'm glad he has returned since he seems to bring you such happiness."

"Yes, thank you, William." I smiled up at him, making a poor effort to wipe the tears from my face.

"Let's return to the hall," William commanded, impatient to herd me like a lost lamb. He liked dogs but didn't understand my emotional response to Kipp. But then, I was a female, and such excessive displays of feelings were expected, he thought with amused tolerance.

I stood, Kipp at my side once again, as we made our way inside. The gang of wolfhounds began to bark, their fur bristling with agitation at the newcomer in their midst. As always happened with dogs, they quickly determined that Kipp was not a member of their team and quietened in confusion, settling uneasily back in their nests carved out of the rushes on the floor. William guided me to a chair near the fire pit while he sent a servant to fetch hot mead. As William began to expand upon the upcoming games to be held, Kipp and I kept to our private conversation.

"Tell me more about Elani," I begged.

"The arrow pierced her deeply but didn't strike a vital organ. The main issue was blood loss and trying to prevent an infection. The friar obtained items from Anne that have seemed to work, so far. Elani is getting stronger and should be able to travel again." Kipp's voice broke slightly.

"I'm sorry, Kipp. I know this has been traumatic for both you and Peter."

He glanced at me, his amber eyes full of emotion. "Being separated from you has made it much harder. All I could do was worry about you." Kipp paused, looking away for a moment. "I was afraid."

"I know, Kipp. Me, too."

"So, what is it with this guy?" Kipp asked, tipping his long nose in the direction of the sheriff, who was continuing to speak about archery. "He seems, well, taken with you."

I tried to suppress a facial grimace, since William, who was watching my expressions, would see and ask. "Yes, apparently, I am so full of charm that he just can't do without me."

"You're just a magnet for human men, it seems," Kipp replied dryly.

"I wish I weren't for this particular man," I replied. "He is uncomfortably possessive and has transferred many of the feelings he had for his wife to me." Pausing, I searched for an explanation. "He still grieves her loss."

Kipp closed me off for a few minutes as he conducted his deep dive into the layered memories of William. After a while, he glanced at me and nodded his head. "He is very grief-stricken, as you say. When he's with you, he has some excitement and feels his life is less empty." Kipp tilted his head slightly to the side, like an attentive dog that spies a rabbit lurking in a field of clover. "He also loses some of his, uh, harshness, when he is with you."

At that moment, Sir Gilbert entered the hall, bringing with him a flow of frigid air as the flames in the fire pit brightened suddenly before subsiding, fed by the fresh air. His dark eyes observed Kipp as he moved closer.

"I see you found your lost dog," he remarked, glancing at me, his voice carefully neutral.

Kipp pretended to ignore him but focused his telepathy on the seneschal. "What did you do to him?" Kipp asked me. "He really doesn't like you one little bit."

"He resents what he thinks is my softening influence on the sheriff," I replied.

"And he thinks your story about losing your dog was made up," Kipp added. "He's surprised to see me here."

It was clear, due to Gilbert's hovering presence, that he wished to speak with the sheriff without an audience. I stood, excusing myself, aware that both men's eyes remained on me until I vanished from sight on the landing. Since I was supposed to be teaching Lisette, I went to her room, Kipp at my side. With her love of animals, she threw her arms around Kipp's massive neck, squeezing him tightly enough that he widened his eyes and glanced helplessly at me.

"Oh, Petra, he is beautiful!" she exclaimed, smiling as she playfully tugged on one of his ears.

Kipp, tolerant soul that he was, sat politely and permitted her examination of him. She stood back at one point, her head tipped to the side, her pretty face puckered in a frown of contemplation.

"He needs combing," she remarked. "I see twigs and leaves in his fur."

"Petra, I've been living on the land," Kipp began, looking at me. "I can't help the way I look."

Ignoring him, I walked to the table where Lisette had

parchment and ink and began to examine her penmanship. With a critical eye, I perused her work and began to gently give feedback until I realized she was ignoring me. The little girl had retrieved a comb and plopped down next to Kipp, who sprawled on the floor. He'd been running for a long time and was understandably fatigued. With care, Lisette began to pull the brambles and twigs from his coat and used the comb to work out some of the tangles in his fur.

"Ah," Kipp said, closing his eyes. "I could go to sleep right here." He opened one amber eye to glance at Lisette, who'd begun to croon a childish song to him. "She's a sweet girl," he observed. "Innocent, thoughtful, and kind. I like her."

"I like her, too," I replied. "It will be difficult to leave here, and I think my doing so will hurt her, for which I'm sorry." Glancing at him, I smiled. I'd not felt this optimistic for quite some time. Elani, per Kipp's report, was stable and improving. And I was reunited with my Kipp. Maybe we symbionts are a little like humans in that we take the given things in our lives for granted until they are gone. Kipp was critical to my existence now. Even more so than Tula, I had a special bond with him that was unique. We finished the thoughts of the other, and Kipp's mind was the one place I knew I was completely safe. How many humans or symbionts can make such a claim? I almost shook myself to rid my mind of such sentimental notions. It was time to buckle down and get to work.

"Kipp, how on earth did you manage to divert Prince John? Or did you?"

"Oh, please, Petra. Child's play!" Kipp rolled his expressive eyes at me. "Well, I exaggerate just a little. It was a bit more difficult than I let on."

"Details, please!"

"Robin and I went to Leicester and remained hidden there until the prince's party was ready to depart for Nottingham. I used my telepathic influence to encourage John to believe diverting to York would be in his best interest." Kipp licked his paws, unconcerned with the world.

Although he tried to sound nonchalant, I knew the effort expended must have been considerable. The ability to manipulate the thoughts and notions of a human was difficult as it were, but to do so at a physical distance was even more taxing, if not downright amazing. As I watched Lisette continue to croon her little girl songs and pluck debris from Kipp's coat, I wondered at what point in our collective history had his skill to manipulate others through telepathic suggestion become extinct. The records did show some evidence of the use of such talents, but it had been generations in the past.

Kipp looked up at me, following my thoughts as usual. He was modest about his advanced skill sets, but there was no doubt about it that he was just a special kind of guy. His tail wagged briefly.

"Just think, Petra," Lisette's high-pitched voice interrupted my thoughts. "Tonight, you will be extra warm. Not only do you have Hero, but now you have Kipp."

Kipp's eyes widened. "Who is this Hero?" He followed my thoughts as I felt my face flush. "So, I disappear for just a few days, and you already have found someone new to take my place!"

Of course, he was just playing with me, happy to be back at my side. Arranging my long shift, I managed to huddle on the floor next to him and Lisette. Together we continued to groom and tidy up my Kipp. It was later, after we'd resumed our lessons, when there was a polite tap on the door before it swung open. Sir Gilbert stood there, glowering, a massive presence almost blocking the doorway.

"The sheriff would like to see you, my lady," he growled, his eyes unreadable beneath a dark line of heavy brows. He was clearly agitated, and it took no telepathy to see that.

I stood, Kipp springing to his feet at my side, ready for whatever might come.

"Dog stays here," Gilbert said, staring at Kipp, who managed to return that stare and then some. Most humans blinked at Kipp's unnerving stare since instinct told them there was intelligence and force of will packed into that canine-appearing package. But Gilbert didn't turn away. Not a bit.

"My Kipp goes with me, or I don't go, Sir Gilbert," I replied tartly. I knew he didn't care for me, but his attitude was growing a bit thin. It seemed way past time to establish myself. In the background, I heard Lisette giggle, which didn't help things at all. Sir Gilbert didn't appreciate being made to look a fool.

The seneschal managed to keep his expression guarded, but inwardly my words angered him. He was unaccustomed to people, and especially female people, not following his directives. "As you wish .... my lady," he responded, pausing more than was polite to add the "my lady".

Yes, we knew where we stood with one another. Peg arrived as if she'd been summoned by magic to help me dust off the back of my shift, since the floor was not particularly clean, and arrange my head covering, which I'd removed while in the privacy of Lisette's room. The wimple was a little hard to bear, and I felt as if I were suffocating with all that fabric around my neck and head.

"But it looks kind of cute on you, Petra," Kipp observed, trying to needle me.

"We'll see if they can arrange one for you, Kipp," I replied, tweaking his ear. "Maybe something in a pretty turquoise blue." It was good to be together again.

I followed Sir Gilbert to one of the anterooms on the main level of the great hall. William was seated at a table, his head bent forward in concentration as he stared at a pile of parchments. When he glanced up at me, the worry seemed to leave his face as he smiled. He ignored Kipp since he was accustomed to having dogs constantly underfoot and sprawling in a tangle wherever they chose to lay. Gilbert was just being nasty to me about the presence of Kipp, wanting to deprive me of something I enjoyed.

"Petra, I have just been notified that Prince John is not coming to Nottingham as earlier planned. It seems he felt a trip to York to be more pressing at this time." William's voice remained neutral, but his thoughts were mixed. Part of him was intensely aggravated that he'd gone to great trouble and expense to set up a day of games and tournaments just for the prince's amusement. But the other part was relieved, since John was a well-established schemer, and it took a great deal of mental energy to joust with him for days on end.

"But the tournaments will go on," William continued. "And this evening, many of the nobles who were joining the entertainment I had planned for Prince John will come here for a feast." He paused, uncharacteristically hesitant for him. "I would like you at my side, in attendance." As if he feared I might decline, he bobbed his head. "It would mean much to me." That was about as humble as he could get.

Kipp pressed close to me. I was sitting across the table from William and could feel Kipp retreat into his examination of the man. Of course, what could I say to William but yes and watch his face relax? While he and Gilbert talked about the preparations for the feast and tournaments, I eased my vigilance and let Kipp channel his findings to me.

"He was not born a noble," Kipp began. "William was the son of a blacksmith who worked for a noble. His master saw promise in him early and educated him alongside his own sons." Kipp strained a little, since the memories were so deeply embedded. "He eventually became a squire and fought at the side of his master with such skill that the king rewarded him with lands and titles."

"A man of humble beginnings," I remarked to Kipp.

"But Sir Gilbert is something else," he said. "He was born to a noble family and came by his title as a matter of his birth. He recognizes William is not the son of a noble, although he doesn't know all the background. Even though he is very loyal, there is a current of resentment that a man who was common is his master."

"Interesting," I said.

"Perhaps all our talk of preparations is not suitable for you, Petra," William remarked, his eyes on me. "I forget myself and have become tedious, I fear."

"Oh, no, not at all. I was just remembering something having to do with Lisette," I replied lamely. Looking at him, I smiled, watching the anxiety melt from his face as I did so. "Her lessons are important to me and not something I take lightly."

"And nor do I," he replied.

# TWENTY-TWO

"You look beautiful, Madame," Lisette breathed, her soft little chin resting on my shoulder as she glanced at the polished piece of metal that served as a primitive looking glass.

I glanced at my reflection, which was faded and distorted; my face looked too wide, my head strangely elongated, and despite the fact I felt I was looking in a carnival fun-house mirror, I could get the general impression. As it were, I would have to rely upon Peg and Lisette to be my guides. Turning my head, I glanced at Kipp, who blinked his eyes lazily.

"Is that the best you've got?" I asked, needling him.

"William will approve," he replied sassily, ignoring my frown.

Peg, from the depths of the trunk of clothing, pulled a soft blue long-sleeved tunic of very fine wool. I was grateful for the fabric, since the great hall was unpleasantly cool, relying upon the fire pit in the center of the room to supply central heating that was woefully inadequate. After laying out several garments and looking at them with a critical eye, Peg chose a pale gray surcoat with intricate embroidery in a color matching the blue in the tunic. Once she had me outfitted, she began to dress my hair, tut-tutting over the strands which were never easy to tame.

"I wish I were old enough to come to the feast," Lisette said, her voice a little plaintive. "But Papa says I must wait until I come of age to attend." She moved so she was in front of me, watching Peg's fingers manipulate my hair. "What does that mean, Petra?"

Her small dog, Jester, was sprawled on the floor, his sides rising and falling with the easy, deep breathing of a sleeping hound. I'd followed enough of Lisette's thoughts to realize she'd picked him specifically to give him some cover from the other dogs which, with their need to enforce pack hierarchy, tended to pick on poor Jester. At Lisette's side, he had a human advocate and was treated like a canine prince. I felt my heart warm towards the child.

"It means, my lovely girl, that one day you will become a woman. When that happens, your father will look for a suitable man for you to marry. And then you will become a mother and teach your children all you have learned in life."

Her face twisted into a frown as she walked over to where Kipp lay and plopped on the floor next to him, her legs crossed in a most unladylike pose. With gentle fingers, she began to comb through Kipp's thick fur; if he'd been a cat, he would have purred.

"What if I don't want to get married or have children?" she asked, leaning towards me, her face filled with earnestness.

I wasn't sure how to answer that question. She would have no say so in her life's choices. It was the way of the world, and as a woman of importance, her father would seek out a union that would enhance his power and authority as well as ensure her survival. She could only hope there might be some love in the marriage.

"Well, my sweet, I think you are much too young to worry about such things," I replied.

"You'll be smart, young mistress, to do as your father tells you," Peg chimed in when I thought I'd put an end to Lisette's worries. "He is a wise man and will know what is best for you."

I was fascinated by their ease of communication with one another. Peg spoke Old English but had, in her work in the castle, picked up some French phrases and was beginning to add them to her lexicon. The same had happened with Lisette—in the reverse -- and I knew I was an observer of how a new language, which would evolve into modern English, was being born.

Lisette didn't reply, but I'm pretty sure I saw that bottom lip poke out just a little. Her command of Old English was limited, but she had learned enough that she caught the drift of what Peg was saying. William might find he has his hands full with her one day. Yes, she was sweet-natured, but she was intelligent enough not to meekly accept everything expected of her. But those thoughts made me wonder what happened to William and Lisette. William, for a man of great importance, would disappear from history in a short time. That seemed odd and without a solid explanation. All that I'd been able to determine during my research was that when King Richard returned to England in 1194, another man took over the responsibilities held by William, and William de Wendenal vanished from the records. That in itself was a fine mystery to solve, but I knew I wouldn't be around to do it.

"When do you think Elani will be well enough to travel home?" I asked Kipp, as I managed to speak with him telepathically while simultaneously dealing with Lisette's worries over childbirth, which she'd heard could be painful. Really, I needed to divert her to something else if I could get Peg to change the tone of the conversation.

"I think within the next week or two if she continues to heal at the pace she was when I left her." Kipp rolled on his side, allowing Lisette to lay her head upon his shoulder as she continued to fret and argue with Peg.

It was a fact our lupine brothers and sisters had an advantage in their ability to recover from severe trauma at a rate superior to our own. Hearing his words gave me optimism that we could be back at home before the snow would fall. I'm not sure why I'd set that particular climactic event as a marker, but I suppose I had to start somewhere.

"There, my lady. You look very lovely," Peg breathed with satisfaction. In her world, she shared in my accomplishment since she'd helped create the product.

I knew it was time to join William in the hall; anxiety hung over me like a cloud. It was improbable I would be recognized, since the only quasi-noble person I'd seen before coming to Nottingham was Sir Stinky—make that Sir Donald -- but he'd not managed to get a good look at me. At least I hoped not. With a final adjustment to my wimple, draping it so that as much of my face was covered as possible without me actually wearing a mask, I began to make my way to the hall, where I could hear loud voices joined in laughter. Kipp was with me, of course, ears forward, attuned to all the thoughts swirling in the air. Personally, I had to focus and limit some of the onslaught of human thoughts since too many at one time could be overwhelming.

"Ah, Petra," William greeted me in the hallway outside his room, taking both of my hands in his. His eyes held a glow of warmth, much too heated for my comfort, I admit. "You look quite beautiful."

I knew that wasn't true, although I probably looked fairly okay. William didn't seem bothered by the size of my nose, which had never been thought of as pert or petite. In any case, he tucked my hand up in the crook of his elbow and proceeded to make a grand entrance as we swept down the stairs to the great hall. I was horrified to see the room teeming with people since I'd hoped for a more intimate gathering. And not only were there men present, but also, they seemed to have brought their better halves along, as I spied a number of finely-dressed women in the hall. I guess it had been advertised as a couples' dinner. The next hour was spent in what I would call circulating in the room. Since it was crowded, Kipp staked out a place amongst the hounds, after there was a little dispute about territory, which was solved quickly. While I was being introduced to all the guests, Kipp kept up a running commentary to me about his observations.

"Gee, Petra, this dog that keeps growling at me is starting to get on my nerves. I could tell him that he stinks, needs a bath, and his breath is bad, too, but I am just lying here, quietly, minding my own business." He paused before adding, "I'm sure I could take him."

"You are doing great, Kipp," I replied. "Please don't start a dog fight. You are managing to blend in, and don't think I'm not envious. I feel like there is a spotlight on me."

"That woman you just met, the one in the nifty red outfit, she is saying something nasty about you to the other woman. I think she has a little crush on William and is jealous."

"Yes, Kipp, I'm aware that she just referred to me in a most uncomplimentary way."

"Well, I don't like her," Kipp huffed. "Oh, no, here comes Sir Stinky!"

That was the moment I'd been dreading. What if he had caught a glimpse of my face while I was working that day with the women in the fields? My cover would be blown, and I'd have to do some quick thinking to manage a response. And even worse, Sir Donald was in the company of Gilbert, who already had a grudge against me. Gilbert would just love to hear any suspicions about me.

"Ah, my lady," William said, since he'd dropped being familiar with my name in the presence of others; in fact, he was referring to me as Lady Hugo, which seemed a bit farfetched, but it was his call. "May I introduce you to Sir Donald, who is the seneschal overseeing the lands of one of our nobles."

As Donald acknowledged me, I got a whiff of his body, and it seemed it had grown a new layer of funk since I'd last seen him; I tried not to cross my eyes. But his fragrance didn't appear to bother anyone else, so what was my problem?

"Whew, I didn't know it was possible, telepathically, but I felt that jolt you just took from him as you inhaled," Kipp whispered. "Can an odor be transmitted telepathically? We must ask Fitzhugh to research the topic."

"Are you trying to make me lose my poise, Kipp? Now stop it!" I replied, trying not to laugh.

"How nice you are visiting our beautiful countryside," Sir Donald was saying. He kept peering at my face, what little was visible considering the drape of the wimple. Thankfully, there was no echo of recognition, and he was just curious, period. He knew William had been without a consort for a year and was wondering who I might be and if a marriage was in the wings.

William continued to tow me around the room, never leaving me to my own devices. And as I focused on his thoughts, I realized he was actually being kind to me. He was sensitive enough to recognize I was ill at ease amongst so many strangers, and he chose not to leave me to flounder, trying to create dialog and conversation when I knew no one except him and Gilbert. Finally, we made our way to the large table, which was set on the platform overlooking the room, and I took my seat.

A series of medieval entertainments took place as we ate, beginning with some jugglers who were fascinating to watch. Next was a series of singers, all of whom crooned pretty ballads. Last was a jester, who managed to insult almost everyone in the room, to the great delight of the crowd. As I watched him perform, thinking what a risky proposition it was to do his type of work, I wondered if modern-day insult comics got their start in ancient halls doing the work of the jester. There was another roar of laughter as the jester made another ribald commentary that was sharply on target.

The servants, who I noticed kept their mouths shut but were quietly observant, served the guests, dealing with rudeness, casual disregard, and overt unkindness. Why I wondered, would a conquering class of people act so in regards to the inhabitants of the territory they had absorbed? It seemed ahoer-sighted, and it was obvious to me the advantages of building alliances rather than creating divides. But who was I but an observer of the human condition for several hundred years?

After the meal, which seemed to stretch for hours, William ordered the floor to be cleared and musicians were ushered in. Reading his thoughts, I realized with dismay that there was about to be a dance party, which meant none of this was ending any time soon. I was even more horrified when William took my hand and led me out to initiate the first dance. Glancing at Kipp, I saw his head lift with interest from his lazy nest in the rushes. One of the wolfhound bitches had cozied up to him and had her large head resting along his shoulder.

"I see you've made friends," I noted wryly, addressing Kipp.

"Yes, she seems to like me despite our apparent differences." He laughed softly. "And now your friend is going to show you off to the crowd."

Kipp knew that I was not a particularly accomplished dancer and tended to trod upon the feet of my partner. As a consequence, I tried to avoid it as much as possible. But William was not about to let me sit meekly.

"Sir William," I whispered, "I have not danced in a very long time and am unfamiliar with the steps and patterns."

"William," he replied. "I've asked you to call me William. And I am a very good leader and will show you."

I peeked at Kipp again, noting his eyes were bright and alert. Even though he'd been kidding with me about William's attentions, he felt sympathy for my position of possible humiliation in a crowd of people. I didn't know the dances popular in 1192, and a potential disaster loomed. I'd lived long enough to survive the waltz, polka, square dancing, the Charleston, the twist, the bump and even the funky chicken. Surely, I could make it through whatever was going to be thrown my way.

"Petra, I will show you," William repeated his words, a smile tugging at the corner of his mouth.

And that's what happened. He actually managed to do it in such a way that I could follow him and repeat what he demonstrated, and although a few of the people in the crowd snickered unkindly, most of the others were happy it wasn't them having to get up and dance in front of a room full of people. It seemed no one particularly enjoyed showing off dance skills—or the lack thereof—before a crowd. I managed not to stomp on his toes, which was an accomplishment for me. But on the other hand, William was dancing very close, which made me uncomfortable, his eyes on my face at all times. His thoughts revealed the intensity of his attraction for me, and I was like a little meteor caught in the gravity of a large planet. The pull was inexorable, taking me with it, despite my attempts to stay clear. Finally, at William's invitation, others took to the dance floor, and that helped diminish some of the intensity. I was surprised when Sir Gilbert asked for permission to take my hand. William released me with a laugh, and I waited for Sir Gilbert to make the first move.

"You dance well, my lady," he said.

"No, I don't, but thank you, Sir Gilbert," I replied softly.

"The sheriff is quite taken with you."

"And I will be leaving here at some point, hopefully, to return to my home in France." I hoped to resolve his resentment about me.

"Ah, the sheriff will not be happy about that, my lady. He wishes the companionship of a wife and a mother for Lisette. And for reasons of the heart, he thinks you can be that person." Gilbert looked down at my face, noting the flush on my cheeks. His thoughts were still conflicted towards me, but he was smart enough to realize that he would only oppose the sheriff in regards to me at his peril. He realized I would win that battle, figuratively speaking.

"And what about you, Sir Gilbert?" I looked up at him. He was a huge man, and I felt like a child next to his hulking figure. "Have you no wish for a wife, a companion, and a family?"

He laughed softly. "All things in good time, my lady." Then his expression changed. "But first, we must stabilize England, and that begins with a rightful king at the helm as well as dealing with the Saxons who wish to foment destruction of what we've built."

He was speaking of people like Robin Hood, of course. His thoughts went on a quick mental review of what had been done. And in response to his thoughts, his feelings and emotions became dark and tangled. To say there was hatred and frustration in the man was an understatement.

"We cannot allow brigands and outlaws to control the countryside," he continued. "I only have to mention what happened to you as a sample of what is wrought when evil people are not controlled or eliminated."

Ah, we were back to me again, and his suspicions returned. He was not at ease with my story nor my presence. I was relieved when William reclaimed me.

"My lady, you seem fatigued," William noted, his perceptive eyes peering at my face with concern.

"Yes, William, I have not slept well and would beg your pardon to return to my room and rest."

"Why, of course," he replied. "I forget that you are from the country and maybe are not as accustomed to large gatherings and festivities such as we have here in Nottingham." He was trying to politely give me an out, even though he was disappointed.

"Not at all, William. It has been very pleasant, and I've enjoyed the evening," I lied.

We managed to speak of meaningless things for a few more moments before I was pardoned and allowed to return to my room, exhausted, where Peg waited. Kipp, also, was glad to leave the nests of the quarrelsome wolfhounds.

"How did you find the entertainment, my lady?" Peg asked.

"Peg, I wish I could have stayed here in my room with Kipp, just resting." At the expression on her face, I added, "I'm not one for large gatherings. And I can't dance."

"Oh, you did quite respectable, my lady," she replied diplomatically. Despite her kind words, I knew she'd been watching me covertly from the landing and found my dancing skills to be below par. She helped me remove the wool tunic, and when I was down to my shift, which I wore to bed, she withdrew to fetch some hot coals for the brazier, leaving just Kipp and me.

"I'm sorry I was teasing you, Petra," Kipp said, sitting at my feet, looking up at my face. His thoughts registered acknowledgment of the shadows of fatigue beneath my eyes. "I was all comfortable with my new friend curled up next to me, keeping me warm, while you were being paraded in front of a room full of strangers. It had to be difficult."

"It was. And, Kipp, you know I can't dance, so that didn't help things at all." Reaching forward, I tousled the fur on the top of his head between his ears. "It's not your fault," I added, trying to diminish his worry. "And I'm sure I looked funny trying to follow unfamiliar dance patterns."

"Well, I wasn't going to say anything," he replied kindly.

After Peg brought the coals and fixed the brazier so there might be a few minutes of warmth in the small room, I retired to my bed, pulling the linen drapes so that the space felt like a safe cocoon. Kipp circled a few times, trying to figure out his footing on the surface of the mattress, before plopping down next to me, his jaw on my chest as was customary for us. I rested my arm along his back. It was odd; it seemed we'd never been apart, although it had been weeks. Sighing, I tried to pull him closer, my thoughts curiously blank and at ease. It was then I heard the door to my room creak open, and a moment later, the drapes parted to reveal Hero, who'd become my sleep buddy in the absence of Kipp.

"So, is this the guy who took my place?" Kipp asked, his eyes widening as Hero tried to figure out the new dynamics posed to his nightly routine.

"Yes, and he is warm," I replied, laughing.

"Is there going to be enough room for all three of us?" Kipp asked, his thoughts slightly alarmed as Hero went through his circling routine, making little muttering sounds as he tried to build a nest in the bed coverings.

Finally, Hero was satisfied and dropped like a big rock, landing half upon my legs, the muscles of which began to spasm under the weight. He opened one brown eye to gaze at Kipp, then me, his shaggy dog eyebrows working as he checked out the competition to his bed as well as the situation in general.

"All we need is your new girlfriend to show up, and you and I will have to find a new bed," I remarked with a smile.

"Well, I'm not used to sharing you, but we are, after all, called upon to make sacrifices," he replied archly.

"Go to sleep, Kipp," I murmured. "It's been a long day, and tomorrow might be even longer."

"That's an illogical statement, Petra, since all days are twenty-four hours, but we'll go with it."

Kipp was back in all his glory. I felt my heart sing.

# TWENTY-THREE

F ortunately for the spectators as well as participants, the competitions that had been planned took place under a bright sun and clear skies. The wind, which in the previous days accompanied a bone-chilling cold, had diminished, and the countryside was still. As I glanced off at the gently rolling hills, which had been crisped by the change in seasons, I took note of the beauty of the land. Although the air was cool, the lack of wind made the day much more tolerable. And I was grateful, since I'd been given no opportunity to decline. Even Lisette was allowed to attend, since there was no bloodshed planned. Although most children were exposed to violence at a young age, since such was considered to be a part of everyday life, William was oddly protective of Lisette. He was not of the camp who believed one needed to toughen up children. Or more correctly, he didn't want to apply that rule to his child. I glanced down at her titian head; the rays of sunshine were caught in her hair, making it seem like the strands were made of spun gold. Eventually, she would view things which would harden her; such was inevitable. But it was due to William's soft heart towards her that she remained insulated from some of the more horrible things in the world.

The sheriff, in anticipation of Prince John's attendance, had what would be called in contemporary times stadium seating constructed of wood. The nobles would get the prime seating, while peasants could view the activities from, uh, the infield. I guess things hadn't changed much over the passage of centuries. Rich and notables tend to get the best seating and goodies in present times, too. Since there were peasants who would attend, I was mildly concerned that I would be noticed and could only hope my friends from Ashland near Trent had better things to do rather than fritter away their time with questionable entertainment. Since Kipp was such an attention-getter due to his size and color, we'd jointly decided that he would hide out beneath the seating, where some long cloth banners draped close to the ground, creating a snug cave for him. I didn't like his not being at my side, but our position was precarious.

"Are you comfortable, my lady?" William asked. He was on one side of me, Lisette on the other.

I was snug, my woolen mantle tucked around my body. Nodding my head, I tried to avoid his gaze. Being a telepath was useful, of course, but it gave me an unfair advantage over the human man who was at my side. He was planning on asking me to marry him; that thought was clear. I needed to be gone before he actually summed up the courage to pop the question. Once he asked, my life at Nottingham would become more complicated if I delayed a response. If we'd been in another day and age, I could claim an appropriate period of mourning, but such didn't exist in 1192 England. People just moved on with their lives as quickly as possible. Death, due to illness, was so frequent that people were not allowed to prolong inaction as a result.

The horse races had just finished, and the winning rider presented himself to the dais to be awarded the prize, which was a pouch of silver coins. As several very large men began to pair off for wrestling, Kipp knocked on the door of my thoughts. "Petra, I think we may have a little problem," he said. "Reeve Johnson has come specifically to watch the wrestling matches. He has some of the other men from Ashland near Trent with him."

Trying not to draw too much attention to myself, I pulled my hood over my head and lightly draped part of my wimple over my lower face. William, of course, noticed and turned towards me.

"You seem bothered by the weather," he observed. He tilted his head back slightly to gaze at the unblemished sky. "It is such a lovely day," he added.

"I fear I am cold-natured," I replied. "But my mantle is enough, my lord."

I could only hope that with my hair covered, Kipp not in sight, and the lower part of my face concealed, I would not be obvious to Reeve Johnson and his companions. After all, they would not be expecting to see me at the side of the Sheriff of Nottingham. My mind searched for that of Reeve Johnson, and was relieved to note that after only a cursory examination of the nobles seated in the stands, he focused on the wrestling, since a friend of his was one of the contestants. I hadn't realized until that moment that I'd broken out in a cold sweat.

"Papa," Lisette began in her lilting voice, "may I go to see some of the merchants' stalls?" Enterprising businessmen and women had set up displays close by and were selling food, drink, fabrics, pottery, and numerous other items. It was clear that watching large men grapple with one another held little interest for her.

"Lisette, it would be ill-mannered for me to leave right now," William replied, mildly chastising her.

"Would it be inappropriate for me to take her?" I asked, hoping to be able to leave my spot where I risked being so visible.

William stared at me for a moment, not wanting me to leave but also realizing Lisette had become restless due to her age.

"I'm actually thirsty," I added, hoping that would tip him over the edge.

"Yes, my lady, that would be very kind of you." He said the only thing he could.

There were stairs at the back of the raised platform, so it was relatively easy to sneak away. I linked my fingers with Lisette's, since she was bouncing up and down with excitement.

"Kipp, help me watch out for the reeve," I said.

"No problem, Petra. He is still watching the wrestling matches. I think he's going to go get some beer and nachos," Kipp added, trying to help me to relax with some humor.

Lisette and I walked a short distance from the gathering and began to examine the different goods displayed by the various vendors. Lisette picked up a piece of soft fabric that appeared to be silk; the man who was smiling at us knew that only the noble class had money to purchase such a rare and costly item. Lisette's little mouth was open in an "O" of astonishment as the man showed her other fabrics that were popular amongst the wealthy.

"Oh, this is so soft," she breathed, looking at me with her father's eyes.

Smiling at her, I finally managed to pull her away, and we continued to walk. The stalls were decorated with banners, and some creative vendors had employed musicians to draw people to their goods like the Pied Piper. Everything was colorful, filled with movement and gaiety. From behind us, I heard the crowds roar, which could only mean one of the wrestlers had won.

"Oh, what is that?" Lisette darted forward.

Fearing she could get lost or, even worse, abducted, I dashed after her. She stopped, abruptly, in front of a stall, and even from a few feet behind her, I could smell the fragrances of things being peddled there.

"Welcome, young mistress," a man said, addressing Lisette.

I walked up and was shocked to see Judah, the son of Joseph of York. He glanced up and his dark eyes betrayed the immediate recognition as he saw my face. But he was smart enough to say nothing and, instead, nodded his head.

"Petra, what are these?" she asked, glancing up at me, delight on her face.

"Spices, my child," Judah answered. He turned to me. "And you, my lady, are you interested in rare spices?"

Kipp chimed in at that moment, from his cave beneath the seats. "Oops!" he exclaimed with chagrin. "I missed Judah!"

"Obviously," I replied. "Let's see what he does."

To make matters worse, at that moment William arrived, since there had been a break in the activities.

"Judah, it is good to see you here with your goods," William said, his voice polite and measured. "May I introduce you to Lady Hugo," he said. Turning to me, he explained, "Judah is the son of one of our local merchants, Joseph of York."

Normally, a vendor would not receive such courtesy from a Norman lord, but Joseph was well thought of and wealthy in his own right, and William had been glad to welcome him to Nottingham when he fled York. As I searched William's thoughts, it was interesting to find that he had few biases in terms of religion and was more focused on people contributing to the common good, despite differences in backgrounds. Even as I realized that, I knew he would go along with whatever the current craze might be in order to keep himself and Lisette safe. Judah's eyes met mine as I read his thoughts of confusion. He must have seen some mute appeal in mine, because he decided to go along with the ruse and pretend as if he'd never met me.

"It is an honor, my lady," he said, tilting his head respectfully.

I have to give it to him. He was smooth and gave absolutely nothing away. His thoughts ran the gamut, quickly, before deciding I was some type of spy sent by someone, although he couldn't quite figure out who. But since he and his father were not political, he had no allegiance to William, and as long as he was left unharmed, he would not interfere in the politics of the day. I felt my heartbeat begin to slow.

To amuse Lisette, William purchased some small pouches of spices from Judah, as well as allowing Lisette to tow him back to the merchant who had the piece of silk she had so admired. I lingered just a moment.

"Thank you for saying nothing," I said, nodding to Judah. "I can't explain myself, but circumstances have brought me to this place. I mean no harm to anyone," I added, "and hope to leave soon."

Judah's handsome face remained stoic and composed as he listened. "It is not my place to question a Norman lady," he replied. "If that is what you truly are."

"No, I'm not," I said, my eyes on him.

"And if the sheriff finds out you are not who he thinks ..."

"It will not go well for me."

I could feel Kipp in my mind, holding his breath in anticipation, wondering what Judah might do next.

"I did not see you, my lady," Judah said. "I am only a spice merchant, after all, not nobility. I see many people in my travels and it is easy to forget faces, since there are so many over the course of time."

"Petra!" Lisette was calling me.

"Thank you, again," I breathed, turning away to find Lisette was holding up the piece of silk she'd admired.

"Kipp, maybe I'm safer back in the stands," I said, feeling the cold sweat of anxiety roll down between my shoulder blades.

"I think so, too."

I was relieved to see that the small contingent from Ashland near Trent had departed, happily congratulating the winner of the wrestling bout, as I took my seat back on the dais. A couple of the Norman ladies who'd gossiped cruelly about me the previous evening nodded coolly as I passed them. Despite my fine garments, they were just not impressed.

William leaned towards me, his face close enough I could feel his warm breath caress my cheek. "My lady, you will enjoy the archery," he said.

It was then I felt Kipp's attention focus, mine following just a second later. Robin was there, one of many men who were planning on taking place in the archery demonstration! While most, including Robin, were dressed in the garb of a commoner, a few of William's men also planned to compete. Robin had the hood of his tunic pulled up so that his golden hair was covered and his face was cast in shadow. As the competitors began to line up, since they were all striking at targets set at a measured distance, Robin's mind reached out to me and Kipp.

"I'm here to create a diversion," he said. The sly humor that would have infected his spoken words was present in his thoughts. "Elani and Peter are ready to travel, and you two need to head south, towards the forest, so you can join them."

The knowledge that Elani was fully healed filled me with joy, and I felt Kipp's heart sing along with mine. If Elani and Peter were fully evolved in their role as travelers, I would have just told Robin to return to the forest and tell them to go home, and we'd do the same. But I wasn't quite certain they were ready to solo time-shift. What if they ended up in the wrong place?

"I don't think so, either, Petra," Kipp said, his thoughts mingling with mine from his hidey-hole beneath the bleachers. "Elani could do it, but the fact she is recovering from a severe injury that debilitated her concerns me. I think we need to be there to make certain everything goes as it should."

"I agree, Kipp." I glanced out at the line of men; Robin's tall figure stood out just a little since his height and build were not typical of the times. He was dressed in the green tunic that was common. "Robin, you are taking a terrible risk being here," I said, my thoughts reaching out to him.

"I'm responsible for your predicament," he replied.

"Not really," I began before he interrupted me.

"I feel I am. And, besides, I've become very attached to Peter and Elani and want to see them return home before anything else bad happens to either them or you and Kipp. This is my land, my time, and I am your host. Let me do what I must."

I let it go at that point since I knew he needed to concentrate. Instead, I focused on the thoughts of the people around me, most specifically on William. He was not suspicious of any of the archers, and his mind was relaxed. He glanced at me, smiling.

"This is always enjoyable to watch," he remarked.

The sound of loosened arrows began to fill the air with a whistling noise as the men began their competition. It didn't take long to whittle down the number of competitors to a handful. It was then I began to get a nagging worry, something tickling the back of my mind, like an insect buzzing around, insistent and elusive, avoiding the brush of my hand to swat it away. Kipp's ability to concentrate beat me to the mark, as usual. It was Sir Gilbert! He, for reasons perhaps best attributed to instinct, had become suspicious of Robin. There had been no actual plan to have an archery contest to entice him since Robin Hood was considered too clever to be drawn in by such a ploy, but Gilbert knew of no one locally that could approach the accuracy of the tall man in green who had made it to the final pair.

"Robin!" I called out to him with my mind. "You're in danger. Leave now!"

I saw his hooded head move slightly to the right, then the left. Gilbert's men were quietly circling the field. Slowly, Robin began to aim at the target, which had been moved to an impossible distance for most archers. He was ignoring me and didn't respond. I realized, then, he was sacrificing himself so that Kipp and I could flee during the activity following his capture.

"Robin!" I was shouting at him, telepathically.

"When they take me, Petra, it is time for you and Kipp to leave. You'll only have a moment when the sheriff is focused more on me than you." Robin paused before adding, "Tell Peter and Elani I'll miss them."

He loosed the arrow, which found a perfect mark, and as soon as his posture relaxed, Gilbert's men surrounded him. Robin's tall, strong body showed resignation in its posture; there was no escaping so many men. He didn't bother to give any resistance at all.

"Petra, what do we do?" Kipp asked.

"Kipp, I can't in good conscience leave here knowing he will be locked up and probably executed. Surely we can find another way to get rid of this place."

It was then something happened that cemented my resolve. Two of Gilbert's soldiers walked towards the huddle of men, dragging between them the struggling form of young Timothy, who'd been caught lurking on the fringe of the crowd of peasants.

William left the dais, excited since this was the moment he'd been anxiously waiting for a very long time. As he left, I saw Robin's head, revealed now that his hood had been yanked back, turn to look towards me.

"Now, Petra, you are free of him."

"Robin, they have Timothy! You may be willing to sacrifice yourself, but are you willing to sacrifice a boy, too?"

I'm not noble and desperately wanted to leave that place and go home. But I wouldn't have two lives left hanging in the balance to secure my release. Kipp remained silent, taking my lead. But I knew his heart and his resolve matched mine. Lisette dashed after her father, so naturally, I chased after her, finally grabbing her hand as she stopped, just outside the circle of men, to stare up at Robin. It was hard not to look at him, since he held that magical quality of charisma. Kipp left his spot and raced up behind us, his body pressing against my leg.

William was gloating as he slowly circled Robin before stopping to face him. "Am I addressing Robin of Sherwood Forest?" he asked, knowing he was, but enjoying the moment.

"Yes, you are. And am I addressing the Sheriff of Nottingham?" Robin replied, his tone playful and hinting at disrespect on the cusp of his next words.

"Yes, you are." William was staring at him, unblinking. "You have many charges against you as well as a death warrant which will be served promptly, in case you worried you might linger in confinement."

"Oh, well, I'm certainly relieved to find I won't linger long," Robin replied easily.

"How about your friend?" William asked, his eyes shifting to take in Timothy. "Does he, too, wish not to linger?"

"Sir William," Robin began, "Timothy is just a boy, a young lad, and has committed no crime. I have only seen to it that he has food to eat."

"And he is a member of your band and will suffer the same fate that you suffer." William's voice became harsh. "Take them to the stockade!"

Robin's thoughts met mine. "Petra, there is nothing more for you to do. Don't make my sacrifice meaningless."

I felt furious. "I didn't ask you to sacrifice anything, so don't lay a guilt trip on me, Robin. If you want to die, so be it. Timothy, now that's another thing."

Kipp pushed harder against my leg. "Calm down, Petra. Robin, we will think through this carefully and find some way to get Timothy and you free. And we will get home, eventually."

I tried to calm my breathing, knowing my face was flushed with anger. And such emotions in me would appear inexplicable to the humans who were present. Lisette glanced up at me with her perceptive eyes and clever mind.

"Petra, are you alright?" she asked.

Of course, her query drew William's sharp attention. I replied quickly, "I just became flustered with so much activity."

As Kipp and I watched helplessly, Robin and Timothy were roughly taken back to the castle as the remainder of the day's activities continued. Kipp returned to his spot beneath the seating, and I took up my place at the side of William, whose excitement was almost uncontained. The capture of Robin Hood was a big feather in his cap.

"Don't worry, Petra. We'll set them free." Kipp's thoughts floated up to where I sat, my hands clenched nervously in my lap.

"How, Kipp? They will be under guard."

"I'll figure something out." Kipp's words sounded filled with confidence.

I only hoped we could fulfill his promise.

# TWENTY-FOUR

The short trek back to the castle was difficult since my mind was roiling with worry over how we would help Robin and Timothy escape their confinement. Lisette kept tugging at my hand and peeking at my face; her instinct told her something was amiss with me despite my protests that all was well. Fortunately, William was busy with some of the nobles who had sought an audience with him and lagged behind. I already had my hands full with Lisette, who was almost as perceptive as her father. Really, she would be a handful when grown with the experiences of a lifetime to sharpen her intuition. What might be a tiny splinter now would be a dagger later in life. And I bore her no ill feelings about such an evolution since such was necessary for her to survive and thrive in a difficult world.

The day had been long, and I begged to return to my quarters to rest, leaving Peg to manage Lisette. Thankfully, I shut the door behind me, leaning my weight against it as I stared at Kipp. Despite his calm attitude, I knew he was concerned, as was I. The room seemed smaller than in actuality, as if the walls were collapsing around me. My throat felt tight; it was difficult to swallow.

"Kipp, there are things we could do—or rather you could do -- to distract any guards so that Robin and Timothy can escape." I bit my lower lip, almost until it hurt. Disgusted, I shook my head. "But if we somehow tamper with the guards, they will be held responsible for the escape of their prisoners and could face harsh punishment."

"You're right," Kipp conceded reluctantly. "We have to remember that the guards are simply following the instructions of the sheriff, and their personal feelings in the matter are of no consequence to him or anyone else. For all we know, there could be a guard who is sympathetic to the cause of the Saxons and Robin Hood." He paused and took a deep breath. "No, we will have to come up with a scheme that doesn't put anyone else in danger."

"Like what?" I almost whined.

"Let me think!" Kipp exclaimed, unexpectedly impatient and irritated at me. That was something that was rare between the two of us but spoke to our joint feelings of guilt and responsibility, especially for poor Timothy, who was truly innocent.

There was a soft tap on the door before it swung open at my invitation. It was Peg, whose thoughts revealed her concern about Robin. Her worry for Timothy was greater since he was such a young boy. It was clear the word of the arrest of such a notorious criminal as Robin Hood had quickly circulated through the keep. Peg didn't know if he was a good man or a bad one, but he was most likely a Saxon, and due to that fact, she felt some allegiance towards him.

"My lady, Sir William is asking if you will join him in the main hall." Her eyes met mine. "I tried to tell him that you seemed, well, fatigued, but he was most insistent."

"Thank you, Peg," I replied, clenching my fists. I was a little amazed I kept my tone even and measured. Peg might have some positive notions towards me, despite the fact she thought I was a noble and a Norman, but it would not help my cause to tip my hand in front of her.

Kipp stood, wagging his tail to signify that we were okay; his brief rush of irritation towards me was forgotten.

The sheriff was waiting in one of the cozy anterooms off of the great hall; a servant had filled a brazier with hot brands, and the room was small enough that the tiny bit of warmth spread, making it tolerable. When I entered, William stood, smiling, holding out his hand to me; I smiled in return, not wanting him to be agitated, but did not take his hand. The candle flames danced as I passed; the smell of beeswax drifted through the air, temporarily overwhelming the earthy mustiness from the rushes that covered the floor.

"Petra," William began. "I beg your forgiveness for having disturbed you, but there is something I need to discuss."

"Uh oh," Kipp whispered in the back of my mind. "Here it comes."

Kipp's telepathy was so advanced that he'd determined what William was about to say before the thoughts had fully coalesced into words. I didn't share Kipp's level of skills, but my intuition and years of playing a role in the human world told me what was next.

I nodded my head and took a seat across from William, deliberately putting a little distance between us. He'd changed into a fresh tunic that was covered in intricate embroidery that was the result of a skilled hand. I idly wondered if his wife had done the lovely needlework, just as she'd fashioned so many similar pieces for Lisette.

"Petra, I hope you know how much your being here has been a great comfort to Lisette." He glanced at me before lapsing into an awkward silence. His hands, which lay on the table between us, seemed restless as his right forefinger gently tapped out his last spoken words. William's face was shrouded in shadow, his expression guarded.

"She is a precious child," I replied, filling the gap by mentioning the obvious fact.

"It was difficult for her to lose her mother," William said, "and as much as I might try, I cannot take the place of a mother in her life."

"Of course," I murmured. I folded my hands in my lap, desperately wishing to be anywhere else other than that small, intimate room. "I'm certain you've done your best," I added hopefully.

"I, too, have been lonely since the passing of my wife." William looked at me, his eyes bright in the dimly-lit room. "And then you came into our lives, and it was if spring had arrived; with new life everywhere, the land becomes green with growth and promise."

239

His words reflected his true feelings, and I recognized how vulnerable he'd left himself with such a poetic declaration, which he'd composed on the fly. Odd that such a taciturn man thought in those terms, ones I might have attributed to the likes of a Robert Browning. And I knew I'd have to be very, very careful in my response. William, for all his attraction to me, was a powerful man accustomed to getting what he wanted. There was a ruthless side to him that was tempered by his experiences as a spouse and father. But the side of him that believed incarcerating a boy such as Timothy was a just and appropriate action formed the dual part of his nature. Sweet words he would speak to me, and then, in the next moment, he would be willing to execute harsh punishment on a mere child. I glanced at Kipp, who had backed quietly out of my thoughts. He couldn't help me with this situation. Kipp blinked his amber eyes once; it was a gesture of trust.

"Your words, Sir William, are very kind." Before he could speak, I rushed along and added, "And I am so happy that Lisette has allowed me to be a part of her life."

He frowned. It was obvious in my response that I didn't include him in my happy place.

"I was hoping you would also be pleased to be a part of my life, Petra," he responded, his tone sounding a little hurt and confused.

My mind raced. How could I get him to back off while still allowing me to do all that might be needed to release Robin? Would his feelings for me go far enough that I could compel him to willingly release Timothy? My instinct told me not to push it that far.

"William, you must forgive my inadequate words. I have always been reserved in matters of the heart, and it is difficult for me to express my feelings."

"That's good, Petra, keep doing that!" Kipp whispered in my head. "He's interested in your choice of words and likes that you seem vulnerable and meek."

"My first marriage was arranged, as I believe I told you, and I've never been allowed the opportunity to choose a partner." I tried to smile at him. "It leaves me feeling awkward and unsure of myself." It might have been helpful if I could have made my voice sound tremulous, but I just couldn't manage it. And yes, that behavior was shamelessly manipulative, but symbionts must do certain things to, well, fit into what is expected by humans. When I have tinges of guilt press upon my soul, I remind myself that I play a role when traveling. Humans are not dealing with the real article.

William laughed softly. Kipp was correct in that he liked what I was saying.

"Petra, my dear, you simply need a strong husband to guide you. Most women are lacking in confidence and such a lack is a charming quality."

"So, he thinks being a wimp is a good thing for a woman," Kipp growled. "I don't care for some of the attitudes around here. He should see you when you have a full head of steam and are ready to fight for a good cause." Kipp snorted softly, his nostrils flaring with agitation.

I ignored Kipp, who always was my champion, and willed myself not to break out in a cold sweat. Fortunately, a servant glided in, silent as a gentle wind current, bringing a tray with wine for us to share. William poured me a serving, which looked like way too much for my liking. There was no way around it, and I took a sip, noting the sour bite of the wine.

"I'd stay away from that wine," Kipp advised, almost making me laugh. "If you get tipsy, then who knows what will happen." After a second, he added, "Petra, you need to keep your thoughts clear and focused."

"I've got this, Kipp," I hissed back, narrowing my eyes as I glanced at him.

"Petra, I would like for you to become my wife and mother to Lisette," William said, as I almost spit out my mouthful of the bitter drink.

I paused, not certain what to say. And then it was if the clouds parted, a brilliant sun peeked past the darkness, and I knew how to delay him. I was only sorry there wasn't a horn section in the orchestra of life to trumpet out a triumphant "ta-da".

"William, your words are well received by me," I said while thinking how stunted and formal I sounded. Maybe I should have added a "my lord" for good measure just to earn brownie points?

"My family in France would like to know of any plans I might have, especially if marriage is involved." I tried to smile, feeling my lips quiver as I scrambled for something else to say. "They are very, uh, traditional, and would like to believe they help guide my destiny. Before any announcements are made, I would like to be permitted to send a message to my family and request they travel here to meet you and Lisette." I stumbled for a minute, honestly unable to recall what I'd told him about my family of origin, and I knew he'd remember everything. It was best to keep it vague. And I'm the first one to confess that my clumsiness was not a good quality for a symbiont who needs to keep all stories in line. I'd allowed myself to get sloppy. Kipp, however, wagged his tail again. He recognized it was not as simple as it seemed, especially when one was laboring under constant stress. I felt my lips tighten as I tried not to look silly, smiling at what seemed to be my dog.

William wasn't exactly happy that I didn't fall into his arms with a resounding "yes", but at the same time, he recognized my request was not out of bounds and was what he might expect of a noble lady. The wheels began to turn in his mind. What if my family was wealthy? There might be a sizeable dowry involved. And although he was not exactly in need of more money, would it hurt to benefit financially from such an arrangement?

"Wonder if he'd feel the same if he thought you were poor?" Kipp asked.

"Probably, since he did ask not knowing how much money I might have in the bank. But now I've given him another reason to delay pressuring me." The taste of the wine lingered bitterly in my mouth, and I longed for some fresh water to rid myself of the flavor.

William resumed our dialog with one another. "Petra, whatever makes you happy brings me pleasure. And if you need time to contact your family, that is what you shall have."

I stood, abruptly, feeling my face flush as I did so. Maybe it was the wine, but I'd only had a sip. The situation was very stressful, and I longed to be free of the place. But first, Kipp and I had to develop a scheme to free Robin and Timothy.

"I am very tired," I began, "if you will pardon me, my lord." I backed away quickly, not wanting to share the closeness of that room with the sheriff.

William appreciated my polite and deferential manner and was drawn to what he thought was a gentle-hearted woman. I tried not to smile as I wondered what he'd think of me if he really knew what and who I was. It would be the biggest surprise he'd ever had in his life! Thankfully, he released me, and as I rushed through the great hall, I noticed Sir Gilbert lurking near the central fire pit, watching me with intense interest.

"He knows that William was proposing to you. And he still doesn't like or trust you," Kipp observed helpfully.

The pile of wolfhounds had learned to ignore Kipp, but as we passed, Hero's large, grizzled head lifted with interest. With a groan and sigh, he stood and began lumbering after us, eager to join us in bed. I'd miss the big old dog -- at least I hoped that I was not premature with my feelings -- upon return to my contemporary home. As it were, I was stuck in 1192.

I returned to my quarters where Peg awaited. Her blue eyes were enormous, taking quick, darting glances at my face as she assisted me with removing my clothing. After I washed my face, she made me sit and began to comb my hair. I glanced at the bed where Kipp and Hero were jockeying for the best position. There were a couple of good-natured growls from the pair before Kipp, always a gentleman, allowed Hero to choose first.

"So, my lady," Peg began. "Did you have a nice visit with the sheriff?"

I had no wish to give her gossip to spread, so I nodded my head. And so as not to be a total liar, I added, "I've asked him to allow me to contact my family in France. Hopefully, they can come to Nottingham and meet the sheriff and Lisette." It wasn't exactly the truth but also was not a complete fabrication. I just omitted the proposal part.

"And how would it be for you to be married again, my lady? Is it something that gave you pleasure before?"

Peg was obviously quite intuitive since, despite my not filling in the blanks, she recognized what had happened. I knew she was trying to find out about my past life; Peg was as curious as everyone else as to what made me tick and the events that led to my improbable appearance. She'd given up thinking I was, perhaps, a spy and was leaning towards the theory I was basically looking for security, wealth, and position. And what better place to find it than at the side of the Sheriff of Nottingham? To give her credit, she didn't fault me for such enterprising notions. It was a harsh world—especially for women—and if I could score an advantageous spot where I'd have nice clothes and plenty of food, she was rooting for my success. Since I treated her with kindness and respect, she felt she might not do as well with some of the other women who were chasing after the eligible sheriff. Especially that hussy who wore the red dress at the dance party.

As I chatted with Peg, I was aware that Kipp had retreated from my mind. I knew or thought I knew what he was doing. He was busy calculating a way to free Robin and Timothy. And I was willing to let him take the lead. He was brighter than was I, and I trusted his logical approach to problem-solving.

"There, my lady," Peg said with satisfaction. She'd combed my hair until it was shiny and somewhat tamed before braiding it for sleep.

"Thank you, Peg," I said, genuinely appreciative of all she did for me. I recognized she served without being given an option not to serve, and it would have been my preference not to have her at my beck and call. But it was part of the world at that time, and I was forced to fit into the general milieu. True, she could be working the land in one of the villages instead of doing things to bring me comfort, but in any case, she would have a life of toil and poverty versus that of so many of the vapid, wealthy women who were part of the nobility. I'd met some of those women recently and preferred time spent with Peg, for what it was worth.

After she left, I managed to squeeze into bed, ignoring Hero's grunts and mutterings as I disturbed his rest. He was large, intimidating, and rather frightening until one became aware that he was a big softie, a meek animal despite his appearance. Laughing softly, I scratched his head, speaking nonsense to him until his brown eyes closed and he drifted off to sleep.

"Are you done playing with that dog?" Kipp asked, his tone

impatient. "You know, I've been waiting to talk with you for quite some time."

"Yes, Kipp. I'm all yours. What have you worked out?"

"Well, here is how I see it, Petra." He scooted up just a little so his head would be at the perfect angle to rest upon my breastbone. "We obviously can't just leave here and not address the incarceration of Robin and Timothy. I need to try and get down to the area where they are being held so that I can see what options there might be. Since we don't want to implicate any of the staff, we need to work out a way for Robin to release himself."

"What?" Kipp's words didn't make any sense to me. "How do we do that?"

"Try and keep up, Petra," Kipp replied, his tone a mite sharp. "We obviously will have to obtain the key, since I suspect there will be an actual lock. If there is, we will use the key to release him but leave behind something -- a tool, a piece of wire or metal -- and that will lead William to believe Robin picked the lock himself."

"Won't that depend upon how the door is constructed?"

"Yes, which is why I need to take a little trip to the jail, or dungeon, or whatever you call it." Kipp stopped for a moment, his mind working furiously. "Tomorrow, while you are spending time with Lisette and William, I'm going on a little field trip. Since the dogs here roam everywhere, I should blend in."

"Why don't you just find Robin, telepathically, and let him clue you in?" I asked. As it were, I could feel the presence of Robin but couldn't tease out his thoughts well enough to have a fluid dialog with him remotely. Kipp could, of course.

"I have tried to speak with him, but he is being remarkably stubborn, insisting we leave. It's hard to continue when he won't cooperate," Kipp replied. "I think I need to see the corridors, what type of security there is, and what would be the quickest exit. Robin, from his vantage point, might not be able to give me all those details." Kipp became quiet, but his mind was still churning with ideas.

"How are we going to get the key?" I asked. "And why do you think there is even a key?"

"Well, that's the bad news, and I haven't worked out all the details. I do know there is one and where it is kept."

I started to ask how he knew such a thing before I remembered I was dealing with Kipp, who had the ability to divine notions from the heavens, it seemed.

"And?" I asked.

"Sir Gilbert keeps it, either on his person or in his room."

"You've got to be joking, Kipp! How on earth will we snatch the key from him without his knowing?" I tried not to let the frustration control my thoughts but failed.

"I'm working on it, Petra," Kipp replied patiently.

I was getting tired and Kipp's planning, which seemed convoluted, was making me feel as if we were caught in a maze, tangled, confused, and unclear of our exit. It was cozy in the room, despite the cold in the air. Between the cover on the bed and the heat generated from Kipp and Hero, I was as snug as I'd been in a long time. But none of that counted for much, since my goal was still beyond my reach. Somewhere, Elani and Peter were hiding in Sherwood Forest, waiting for our return. And in confinement, Robin and Timothy languished, waiting for certain punishment. The little bit I'd gathered from the thoughts of the sheriff, when he wasn't focused on me, indicated that Robin faced execution. He'd put himself in danger to allow Kipp and me an opportunity to escape. I couldn't leave him behind. And it had nothing to do with his being a symbiont, either. It was just the right thing to do.

"I know you are, Kipp." My hand reached out so that my fingers could weave a pattern in his thick fur. The touch of my hand against him was comforting to us both. "I trust you completely, as always."

"Well, ditto," he replied gruffly. "But thanks for that, Petra."

He fell asleep before I did, and I lay there listening to his easy breathing; his mind was clear of worry, no dreams to plague his thoughts. With great effort, I turned off my own worry and paced my breathing with Kipp's. Eventually, I, too, joined him and Hero in a place of rest.

# TWENTY-FIVE

"Thank you, Abbot James," I said, trying to force a smile on my face, fearful the expression would appear stiff and not genuine.

The man before me commanded much authority in the community, and I realized a small word from him whispered into the ear of the sheriff counted for much. Probably much more than would my small words, despite William's affection for me. William had arranged for the abbot, with his many connections, to see that my letter to my fake family made its way to France where it would be handed from abbot to monk to friar, eventually to find its way to the countryside in the southernmost part of the country. I figured a few more miles wouldn't hurt and had picked a location as remote as possible. And by the time word got back to William that there was no family, Kipp and I would be long gone. Or at least I hoped so.

I glanced at the abbot's face, which was pleasantly round. It was clear that he benefited from the best that society could offer, from beeswax candles to the finest food. Even his clothing was exceptional. His robe was woolen since the weather was cool, but the scarf draped around his neck and shoulders was of silk, a fabric only affordable to the wealthiest people. With effort, I hid my feelings of distaste. Friar Thomas, with his humble dedication, was infinitely preferable. I realized when the peasants toiled the land, a significant portion of their earnings went to support the abbot and his causes as well as helping him amass personal wealth. I didn't approve of James using the church to extort money from a subjugated people. It was one thing to give to the church of one's free will but another to be forced to suffer under tyrannical rule.

Abbot James was a short man, his eyes about on a level with mine. His eyes were small and pale-colored, almost lost in the folds of flesh that surrounded them. There was no gentle scent of invitation or kindness; instead, they appeared hardened and cold, glittering as they caught the light in the great hall.

"Tell me, my dear, how do you think your family will receive the glorious news that you are to be wed to Sir William," he asked, tilting his tonsured head to the side as he watched my expressions. Before I could answer, he added, "I'm certain you realize you are the most fortunate of women to be chosen by such a fine man."

Following his thoughts, I recognized he was a calculating man. Anything that impacted William would have an effect on him, too, since he depended upon William's ability to keep the peace as well as collect and distribute taxes. I try to remain neutral towards humans since my job is to study and gather information, but I didn't like Abbot James. And in a tit-for-tat world, his thoughts betrayed the fact he didn't like me, either. He worried I could have a softening influence on William, as had William's first wife. It benefited the abbot for the sheriff to remain hard and unrelenting.

"Oh, I'm certain they will be very happy that I will be so well taken care of," I lied, saying what was expected even though it grated on my nerves.

"Hold it together, Petra," Kipp intoned, his thoughts hovering on the edges of my brain. "And while you entertain the abbot, I'm going to reconnoiter the jail where Robin is kept."

"Reconnoiter?" I asked.

"I'm adding to my vocabulary," Kipp replied airily.

With that he was gone, his auburn body sliding away unnoticed, as a servant brought a tray of snacks as well as wine for the ever-hungry abbot. And while he and I chatted about marriage and the responsibilities of such a commitment—although he'd never been married and I had, but that seemed to be a superfluous argument—Kipp kept up a running commentary in my head.

"I've gone beneath the second level of the keep, and there are numerous rooms, some almost like a dormitory, for servants." Kipp paused, and I could almost see through his eyes as he scanned the dimly-lit area. "There is a passageway at the side that I think will lead to the cells."

I glanced up as William approached, Lisette at his side, her little hand clasped in his. Yes, he was a doting father. But his love for his child didn't seem to expand to have consideration for other parents who loved their children, too, but suffered under the tight-fisted rule and hierarchy of the day. Lisette nestled up to me as she sampled a few of the sweet treats on the table. I kept my dialog with them rolling along as I continued to communicate with Kipp.

"It's not really what I'd call a dungeon," he began. "At least it's not like what you see in the movies." His excitement mounted. "There are no torture rooms or anything I might have expected. Whew, it's pretty close in here," he intoned. "It feels like there is no air circulation at all, and it's kind of difficult to breathe. I've connected with Robin and am using that link to try and locate him. I've just entered a dark, narrow passage, but I see some lantern light at the end. Odd, there are no guards or anyone at all."

"Maybe they feel there is no need," I opined. "Anyone would have to enter the front of the castle past the guards that are posted there, then enter the keep and pass numerous servants to get to a locked door."

"Yes, there were several people I passed," Kipp remarked. "They ignored me, of course, since I'm just a dog."

It was at that moment he found Robin, who was locked in a cell with Timothy. And through the magic of Kipp, we had a three-way conversation.

"Petra, I don't think there is anything you can do here," Robin said. "It's best for you and Kipp to leave when you have the opportunity and reunite with Peter and Elani and go home."

I took a deep breath, not wanting to argue, but a point needed to be made. "Robin, you, by trying to help us, are influencing the timeline of yourself as well as Timothy. It's not just sentimentality

on my part. We have to restore the natural timeline as best we can."
Before he could reply, I added, "And Timothy is an innocent who
doesn't deserve to be sacrificed for us."

There was no reply from Robin, who knew that what I said was
valid. He loved Timothy, as did the men in the company, and felt
compassion for the boy, who, through no fault of his own, had a
rough path in life.

Kipp continued to nose around, excited there were no posted
guards since that would make our task a little easier. "Petra, I think
our scheme to obtain the key from Sir Gilbert and leave behind a
piece of metal, like a wire, in the lock to the cell, will work. It will
appear to the sheriff that Robin was able to pick the lock and free
himself as well as Timothy."

I could almost taste Kipp's satisfaction at the arrangement. But
there was one nagging problem. How on earth would we get the key
from Sir Gilbert?

"We'll work it out," Kipp replied confidently.

"I hope so," I said reluctantly.

"There is one issue," Kipp said. "Uh, Robin says that the sheriff
has arranged for his execution, as well as that of Timothy, by the
end of the week. That gives us two days to figure something out."

"Great, Kipp. Nothing like a little pressure." I forced my
shoulders down since they'd crept up to about the level of my ears.

"My lady, do you anticipate members of your family will travel
here to celebrate your marriage?" The Abbott's voice snapped me
back to attention. His pale eyes were on my face as if he knew my
focus had wandered.

"Undoubtedly," I lied, making myself smile. All the while, I was
thinking that Kipp and I had to figure out a way to get the key to
Robin's cell from Sir Gilbert. I was glad when Kipp rejoined us, his
massive presence blending in due to all the dogs that milled around
at will in the keep. The abbot's eyes flicked over at Kipp,
unconcerned, just another big dog to ignore. The abbot didn't like
dogs, but he wasn't fearful of them.

Lisette had crowded onto my lap at that point, her slender arm
around my neck. Of all that would occur, leaving her abruptly was
the most tragic. She'd become attached, in the fashion of a child,

immediately, trusting and with no concerns. I was about to betray her trust and hated myself for it. But Robin and Timothy's lives hung in the balance, and no matter what, I was not a human and could not linger in 1192. I could only hope she would forgive me one day.

Kipp sidled up next to me, his head on the other side of my lap. Idly, I let my fingers find the top of his head, the fur warm and vital beneath my flesh. He, of course, knew my heart and the sorrow I felt about Lisette.

"I hate it, too, Petra. But you didn't seek out these circumstances. It was all accidental. There is nothing else to do."

"She lost her mother and has attached her affections to me, Kipp. I just didn't want to hurt her." I glanced down at him to find his amber eyes on my face. They were filled with sadness evolved from his naturally compassionate nature as well as his love for me.

"I know," he said, sighing deeply while pushing a little closer.

I almost visibly shook myself. "We need to find that key," I said, my thoughts resolute. "We are running out of time."

That evening, Gilbert returned from the countryside. He'd been sent by the sheriff to motivate a reeve who was lagging in his responsibilities. I was sitting in the great hall, working on a piece of embroidery—and, yes, I knew how to do such a thing although it brought me no pleasure and I was just trying to fit in—as the fire by which I was seated cracked and popped as a servant added more wood. William and Lisette had taken a trip to the home of a local noble, who'd invited them for dinner. I begged off, saying I felt unwell. William wisely figured it was a "woman's ailment" of some sort and didn't ask for details. Gilbert paused, glancing down at me, his eyes briefly flicking to include Kipp, who lay curled at my feet. The seneschal smelled of horses, decaying leaves, and faintly of wood smoke. A smile grazed his lips.

"Good evening, my lady," he said. The sneering tone had disappeared.

I realized he had given into the inevitable and decided that it was better to join in the fun than be seen by William to be obstructive to the marriage. Gilbert was a smart man, wise and savvy, and he had a solid grasp on politics.

"Would you like to join me and share the warmth of the fire?" I invited, hoping to get some time alone with him so Kipp could decide about the key.

Gilbert hesitated, not wanting to sit with me but also thinking he needed to garner some cachet with me since I was William's chosen one.

"Thank you, my lady. It has been a long ride, and the wind was cold." He nodded his head and sat.

"Was your journey fruitful, Sir Gilbert?" I asked. Telepathically I told Kipp to get to work.

"Yes, I believe so. On occasions, the reeves become much too sympathetic to the peasants, who, after all, are supposed to toil. I have a way of motivating people." Gilbert smiled at me.

I bet you do, I thought privately.

"You seem very comfortable here," Gilbert observed, his dark eyes resting on my face.

"Oh, yes, the fire is warm," I replied, deliberately misunderstanding him.

"I am glad for your comfort," he said. "I think you are comfortable, also, that you will marry the sheriff. When that happens, you will be in a position to influence him through his affection for you as well as Lisette." He smiled, the expression not making it to his eyes. "You will become a lady of great power."

"I don't seek such a thing," I replied. Covertly, I glanced around the great hall. The servants had melted into the shadows when Gilbert arrived. They weren't gone but just hiding where they could easily eavesdrop on the conversation. I took a deep breath, waiting.

"All people seek such, my lady." Gilbert said. "I think it is disingenuous of you to say otherwise."

"So, you think I am lying to you?" I'd grown tired of his verbal wordplay and was frankly irritated at him. Maybe he would enjoy a little more directness in our discourse?

"Of course not, my lady," Gilbert said, his eyes opening wide with pretend surprise at my remark. "I think you are just modest," he lied.

"Keep him talking," Kipp said to me privately. "I need more time."

A servant arrived with a carafe of wine. After pouring a goblet for Sir Gilbert, the man silently slid away into the darkness; I could detect his anxiety as he disappeared. Gilbert commanded respect with the servants, but it was based upon their fear of the man. Gilbert tilted the goblet to his mouth and took a long draw of the wine, smiling in satisfaction. The day had been long, and his thirst was great.

"I can only hope we become friends, Sir Gilbert, as you realize I will do nothing to disrupt the functioning of this place." I smiled, trying to look earnest and hopeful.

He clearly felt very threatened by me, and my sweet words would do nothing to change that. But what did I care? We needed to get the key, free Robin and Timothy, and hotfoot it back to the forest where Peter and Elani waited. Gilbert could nurse his private victory at my departure privately or publicly for all I cared. The fire was beginning to wane, and that was my signal to leave. I rose, noticing that Sir Gilbert did, too, strictly as a matter of courtesy. He was smart enough to know he could only push his sassy line with me so far at his peril. In a contest between us for the sheriff's affection, I won.

After begging his pardon, I began the climb up the stairs towards my room. Kipp followed, as did the loyal Hero, who was looking forward to a night of slumber with his new best friends. I felt a pang of sadness for Hero. Once we left, he'd be relegated to the floor of the great hall, jostling for supremacy with the other members of the pack. He was one of the elder hounds in the group and had lost much of the ability to assert any dominance with the younger and more savage ones. I wished I could have taken him home with us to join my crowded household, but that was impossible.

"No, Hero is not coming home with us," Kipp said. "I'm tired of him taking over the bed, in case you wondered. He's enormous, stinks, and has bad breath. I have to smell him all night long while you are sleeping." After a pause, Kipp added, "He's an open-mouth breather."

I laughed in reply. Kipp was being silly since he knew the physics of time travel, and Hero was staying put. Peg met us, and after she helped divest me of my clothing down to the shift I wore at night, I climbed into bed, grateful for both Hero and Kipp, since the room was exceedingly cold.

"What is your conclusion, Kipp?" I began. "And what do we do about the key?"

"Gilbert keeps the key to the cell along with other keys to the keep on his person, which means he only removes them from his custody at night when he sleeps." Kipp pushed closer. "We will have to sneak into his room, get the key, go down to Robin, let him out, and then return the key."

I began to feel the anxiety well up in my throat. Things that sounded so simple were usually fraught with peril. I tried to move a little since one of my legs was trapped beneath Hero. He growled, good-naturedly, before moving just a tad. Wiggling my toes, I was relieved to feel some sensation return.

"Robin and Timothy have their mantles and can cover their heads and bodies sufficiently to blend in. And in any case, I don't think any of the peasants will be highly motivated to sound an alarm since they are fellow Saxons. There will be a degree of loyalty and, uh, turning a blind eye to their escape." Kipp paused while he considered the plan. "I'll need a piece of metal or wire, something thin, that we can leave behind in the lock so it will appear Robin picked it. That way, no one will be held in suspicion about his escape." Although it was dark in the room, Kipp's eyes glittered as he turned his head towards me, the fur on his face brushing my cheek. "I think that's the best we can do, Petra."

I pulled him closer, enjoying his warmth as well as that of the slumbering Hero. For a moment, I envied the big old dog, since he had none of the worries that Kipp and I shared. His main concern was a warm place to sleep and something to eat. Yes, he'd still compete with the younger dogs during the hunt, but he was falling farther and farther behind. But even with that, he didn't worry about it. His concerns were in the moment, not about his future.

"I can pry the metal clasp off the large brooch I use on my mantle, and we can use that for the piece of metal." I tried not to sound too worried as I went on. "And I guess I'll have to sneak into

Sir Gilbert's room and get the key." No, nothing much to be concerned about. If he caught me, the gig was definitely up.

Kipp sat up in bed abruptly, and it was as if a lightbulb flashed inside his big head. "I've got an idea!"

"Good, because I'm tapped out."

Hero gave a start, growling, since Kipp's sudden movement disturbed him, and there was a moment of bared teeth before the two managed to make up and decide they were friends after all.

"If you and Hero are like peas and carrots again, Kipp, please tell me your brainstorm."

"You'll ask Peg to bring you something for sleep and then you will manage to put it in Sir Gilbert's beverage tonight. When he is sleeping soundly, you can sneak in his room, get the key, and we will free Robin and Timothy."

I stared at him, disappointed, thinking he really had something for a moment. He waited, clearly pleased with himself.

"Kipp, there are too many if's in that calculation. We have no idea if I will have access to anything Gilbert might drink. And since he and no doubt William will be watching me, I'm not sure how to manage it anyway."

Kipp exhaled forcefully. "Well, I still think it's a good idea. But if you are afraid, I'll just push a deep dream state into Gilbert's head so that you can sneak in his room while he's dreaming."

"Can you do that?" I asked. Kipp could insert a notion into the head of a human, and he could also alter the course of a dream. But could he actually insert a novel dream into the subconscious mind of a person?

"Yeah, I've done it before."

"To whom?" I asked, almost afraid to hear the answer.

"I'd rather not say," he replied archly.

"Kipp, was it me?"

"I'm going to sleep now," he replied, closing his amber eyes. A moment later, he began to snore, but it was a fake snore.

# TWENTY-SIX

I f we were to do anything to effort the release of Robin, it would have to be that day, since he was scheduled to be executed on the next. Perhaps it was fate, but the weather, which had been relatively pleasant, turned fierce, and there was a savage storm pushing in from the northwest. Maybe the inhabitants of the castle were feeling a little lazy because no one willingly stirred to go outside, and it meant for a long day spent under the watchful eye of the sheriff and his seneschal.

For me, the hours crept past at a snail's pace because of what loomed ahead. When darkness fell, somehow, I had to get access to the key kept in Sir Gilbert's private chamber. I still had no idea how to manage that particular feat, but knew I had no choice since Robin and Timothy had little time left. My mind wandered to Elaini and Peter as a pang of emptiness washed over me. Where were they, I wondered? Maybe they'd gone home.

"No," Kipp replied. "I get a faint impression of Elani trying to reach me, wanting to know what to do."

"Why didn't you tell me?" I asked, a little bewildered since he'd communicated nothing to me.

"It is only like an early morning mist, elusive and tantalizing but not tangible. I tried, using everything I had, to project to her that they need to stay clear, and we'll come for them." He sighed, pushing his head up under my hand. "I only hope she could hear me."

We were in Lisette's room, where I listened to her reciting a fragment of poetry. Glancing up over the child's titian head, I let my eyes linger on the lovely tapestry Lisette's mother had woven for her. There was no doubt a great deal of love there.

"Madame," Lisette's voice grabbed my attention, sounding somewhat petulant. "Is my reading not to your liking?"

"Oh, no, on the contrary, my dear. You do it quite well." I glanced at Kipp, and for a moment, we made eye contact that carried within it complete understanding. I was only happy Lisette didn't see it, too, since I'm certain my facial expression would have revealed the depth and complexity of my connection with Kipp.

Through the thick walls of the keep, we could hear the storm as it lashed the side of the building. Occasionally the wind would whistle through the narrow apertures in the hallway, causing the candles to be extinguished, leaving behind the scent of burned tallow and beeswax and charred wicks. Jester had joined us, fearful of the thunder and occasional bursts of lightning, and he decided to nestle up to Kipp, much to Kipp's dismay. But the kind soul that he was, Kipp tolerated it for the sake of the poor dog.

My thoughts, however, were on the sheriff, since he'd decided to have a serious talk with me earlier that morning. He felt that waiting for my family to arrive from France could take months, and he was eager to get the show on the road, so to speak. Since he, of course, knew my heart in such matters, he'd discussed with the abbot that he would like to rush things along, and in fact, would like to marry me after the execution of Robin and Timothy. It would be a really big day for him, he thought, so why not bundle the planned events?

That left me with few options other than to help Robin and Timothy escape and leave at the same time or soon after. I would have preferred otherwise, thinking that the outlaws would have a better chance if not encumbered by me and Kipp, but there was nothing else to do. The sheriff would probably think I'd been kidnapped by Robin and would never stop looking for me. Or, if he held suspicions, he might think I had been part of a plot all along to infiltrate his castle. I hoped I wouldn't be around to have access to his thoughts.

"We can't control for all those unpredictable elements," Kipp said.

"We might end up causing more trouble for Robin if our leaving coincides with his," I pondered, not certain what to do.

"Petra, when they find out that Robin and Timothy are gone, I think there will be a lot of chaos in the castle. During that chaos, we could make our escape."

"What if there's not?"

"We may have to cause some. I don't want the sheriff to think you are connected to Robin's disappearance, because it will put Robin and his men in more danger. No, the more I think about it, we'll have to separate the events."

Kipp was right, and I knew it. As much as I desperately wanted to leave, putting Robin and his band of men in peril wouldn't help anything. We needed not to disturb the timeline anymore than necessary.

As the day drew to a predictable close, the anxiety I felt began to press in on me, almost making it difficult for me to take a breath. The notion I'd have to go into Gilbert's room and find the key was beyond alarming and frankly, I was afraid. Fortunately for me, the sheriff was occupied for the evening, and I didn't have to suffer through another awkward dinner, made even more so now that the sheriff had determined my fate without my input. A thoughtful and perceptive Peg brought food to my room.

"I understand the jitters of approaching a new marriage," she said, nodding her head with wisdom.

I wasn't sure how she knew, since she told me she'd never been married, but I just took her words to be kindly meant.

"The sheriff, he will be a good husband, as long as you allow him to guide you," she continued. "He knows that a man is meant to provide leadership for his wife, and he will want the best for you." Peg's eyes grew a little larger. "I'd listen to him," she finished.

I finally shooed her out of my room, wanting to be alone; I needed time to focus and settle my nerves. Kipp was stretched out on the floor, turning his mind and attention to the corridor outside the room. He'd know when everyone was quiet for the night. Hero had shown up at some point and was already in my bed, fast asleep. I hoped he stayed that way. If he awoke and found us gone and began to sound an alarm, it could be a short trip for us. I walked over to the small table and looked down at the piece of metal we'd managed to contrive using my large broach as the source.

"The sheriff is in his room, preparing for bed. He's tired, and I think he will fall asleep quickly." Kipp's remarks were hopeful. His ears flattened for a minute as he glanced up at me. He tried to make a goofy face to humor me, but it was lost. I managed a wan smile.

"Sir Gilbert, he's gone to his room, too," Kipp continued. "I think he had too much wine with dinner because his thoughts seem odd to me. They are discombobulated and kind of fuzzy. Does that sound right?"

"Could be," I replied. Not able to stop myself, I began to pace from one end of the room to the other. As much as I could, I kept my steps quiet so that Hero would stay in slumberland.

Kipp, to help me with my nervousness, began to tell me a funny tale from one of his classrooms. I could feel myself relax and sat, willing my pulse to slow. But it would start racing in the next moment when Kipp quit talking and just looked at me. Then he nodded his head. It was time!

After peeking at Hero, who was snoring, I went to the door of my room and gently pulled the latch up. The hinges were thankfully silent as I pushed the door open. Sticking my head out, I glanced in the corridor. Kipp had checked and certified the area to be human-free, but it was probably instinct that made me look. The corridor was shrouded in darkness, with only a couple of dimly lit torches in sconces on the wall to give any illumination. I began to walk, keeping against the wall and in darkness, creeping past Lisette's door, then that of the sheriff. Just out of whimsy, I put my ear close to the door of the sheriff's room. At least he didn't snore, and that would be a huge bonus for the future Mrs. Sheriff of Nottingham. Sir Gilbert's room was next. I paused outside and glanced around, even though my telepathy was in agreement with that of Kipp. There was no one watching me.

With care, I lifted the latch. There were no locks on the doors, and the latch was a simple device and fortunately silent. However, the hinges began to make a soft, groaning sound, and I stopped pulling the door while Kipp surveyed Gilbert.

"He's still asleep. I think we are lucky he had too much to drink."

I pulled the door back just enough so that I could slide past the slender opening, allowing my eyes a second to adjust to the darkness. The faint glow from the torch-lit corridor helped me to make out pieces of furniture scattered about the room.

"Okay, Kipp. Where does he keep his keys?" I asked.

"I followed him last night, pretending to be a friendly dog along with a couple of other mutts, and watched while he put them on the table beside his bed." Kipp paused, concentrating. "He has several that are in use in the keep, and those he has together on a large ring. The key to the cells—and there is only one—he keeps by itself."

Oh, great! I'd have to walk right up to him to try and find the key. The room was almost totally dark. There was a very large man in the bed, hopefully in a deep sleep, and I'd have to fumble around in an unfamiliar room to locate a bedside table to find a key. No problem!

Leaving Kipp to monitor the hallway, I began to creep close to the bed. Gilbert had not bothered to close his linen drapes, and I could see his huge body lying on top of the bed coverings. His back was turned towards me, or at least it seemed that way, and I reached down to the tabletop, letting my fingers rest lightly on the objects there. A moment later, I felt something slimy and moist and jerked my hand back with an involuntary start.

"I don't know what I just put my hand in, Kipp, but it was nasty." I felt my lips curl with displeasure.

"You're a real trooper," Kipp called out, feeling the need to bolster my resolve.

After wiping my hand on the back of my shift, I continued to work my hand over the table and finally felt metal. It was a single large key on a round hoop! It had to be the key, I hoped, saying a little prayer at the same time. With my eyes on Sir Gilbert, I began to carefully back out of the room, taking care not to knock into anything or make any noise. Finally, I got to the door and pushed it shut. A wave of relief that almost felt like nausea passed through me.

"Now, Kipp, it's your turn."

With that, I handed him the key along with the piece of metal we'd pried from my broach, which he grasped in his mouth, and said a silent prayer as his furry body disappeared down the darkened corridor. A second later, I could hear the soft ticking of his toenails on the wooden stairs that led to the great hall. With our telepathic connection, I felt as if I were there with him, experiencing his adventure in real-time.

"I'm past the hounds, which, since they know me by now, didn't raise a ruckus. One man was working, doing something, but he ignored me, too." Kipp paused as he began his descent to the level below the great hall. "People, for the most part, are asleep," he remarked. "I hope Robin and Timothy will be as lucky as I've been up to this time."

I had returned to my room by that time and sat on the edge of the bed. My legs were shaking, my feet tapping the floor with anxiety. Becoming aggravated at my lack of control over my feelings, I began to hum a tuneless song. Hero, who was lying behind me, awoke and began to nuzzle my hand, begging for attention. Turning, I glanced at his grizzled face. Hero would be long gone by the time I returned home … a forgotten dog lost to history. It was always so with us.

"Don't get morose, Petra," Kipp said, having remained in my thoughts while finding his path to the cells. "Think about the good things ahead."

"Such as?"

"Oh, a nice cup of tea with Fitzhugh or maybe a walk in Duke Forest with Philo."

I smiled to myself. "And how about you, Kipp?"

"I look forward to looking across our street when Peter and Elani arrive home. He'll open the car door, and she will jump out, vital, healthy, and happy. She'll look over at me; her tail will begin to wag." He paused, full of emotion. "The wind will be caught in her fur, ruffling it so that the sunlight picks out all the lovely colors."

After another hesitation, he added, "Elani sparkles if you've noticed."

If I'd ever heard a declaration of love, that was a good one. I stayed silent in my head, controlling my thoughts. Kipp needed to say those things and not feel embarrassed.

"I'm sure she will be fully recovered, Kipp, and ready for another adventure." I felt him relax.

"Okay, I'm at Robin's cell," he announced, returning to the business at hand.

I served as a listening post, trying as best I could to hear his dialog with Robin, who was still hesitant. But finally, they worked things out, and I could feel Kipp's relief as Robin and the boy began to stealthily find their way out of the lower level of the keep. We couldn't help them if they were caught again, so it was on Robin to use his telepathy and cunning to get past any humans who might be on guard.

"I'm on my way back," Kipp said.

As glad as I was his journey had been safe, I felt the anxiety began to escalate again as I considered my next task. I'd have to go back to Sir Gilbert's room and return that key. To say I was not happy would be an understatement. But I shook off my feelings and met Kipp outside my room.

"Good job, Kipp," I said, reaching down to take the key he was carrying in his jaws.

We walked down the short corridor, passing Lisette's room as well as that of the sheriff. All was silent, and neither of us could detect any active thoughts that might indicate a human was awake and in our immediate location. I carefully pulled the latch and grimaced once again as the door gave a quick groan before becoming quiet, as I pulled it open just enough to sneak inside. I'm not sure why I felt the need to tippy-toe, since my tread was silent upon the floor, but I did and had just managed to place the key on the bedside table when a large, powerful hand reached out and grabbed my arm.

"What are you doing?"

Gilbert's words were slightly slurred, an effect from both the wine he'd drunk as well as his brain being sleep-addled. The only good thing was that the room was so dark, he couldn't make out who it was he'd grabbed. I didn't resist, since I thought that would escalate the situation. In any case, his hand was so large it completely encircled my arm, and I wasn't going anywhere. Perhaps that was good because my knees had gone weak from the fear I felt and almost buckled.

Kipp then did something amazing. He entered the mind of Gilbert—and it was a forceful entry—and convinced him that he was having a dream, despite the sensations of having apprehended someone in his room. I stood quietly, willing Gilbert's vise-like grip on my arm to lessen, waiting for Kipp's coercive spell to begin to work. And after a few seconds, I could feel the seneschal's fingers begin to loosen. A moment later, he fell back against the bed, his arm dropped to his side. Kipp had done it! I began to back away, my steps silent, as I tried to control my breathing. All traveling symbionts have close calls, but that particular one was one of my most memorable, and I knew I'd be reliving that anxiety for many years when conjuring up the experience. I stepped out in the hallway where Kipp waited. He nuzzled my hand, trying to give comfort.

"You did good, Petra," he said.

"I don't ever want to attempt anything like that again, Kipp," I replied, as my breathing began to return to normal. "I think I aged by one hundred years, just in that moment. I can't recall when I've felt so afraid."

We quietly returned to our room without having disturbed anyone but Hero, who lifted his head and blinked sleepily at us before uttering a sigh and closing his eyes again. Kipp and I managed to crowd back into bed, working around Hero, who'd managed to take over most of the surface.

"And a few more things I'm looking forward to, Kipp."

"Yes?"

"Pop Tarts shared with Fitzhugh over the old dinette table … watching Lily chase you through the house and grabbing your legs, being generally annoying." I stopped, thinking for a moment. "I like our jogs out into the country and going to visit George, too. When the weather is beautiful, and we get to that silent hillside where everyone is at rest ... it is a good place from which to view the world."

Kipp pushed closer, snuggling, his jaw on my chest. "Ummm. Let's go the minute we get home."

He fell asleep almost immediately, but I lay there for quite some time. Had my life and the things that brought unexpected pleasure been boiled down to a handful? Maybe that was as it was supposed to be for humans as well as symbionts. I began to force my mind to turn itself off for a little bit; the morning would bring much excitement, during which Kipp and I would try to escape the castle. True, we could have time-shifted, but I was unwilling to leave Peter and Elani in an uncertain situation. No matter what, we had to find them ... and soon.

# TWENTY-SEVEN

The door to my room flew open the next morning, causing me to sit up with a start. Hero, who seemed to be offended by such a rude awakening when we were all slumbering so happily, began to growl and bark. Only Kipp remained silent, looking around, slightly dazed as he tried to awaken. His mental efforts at controlling Sir Gilbert the previous night had left him fatigued and sleep-addled.

"Thank goodness you are safe!"

It was William who stood over my bed, his face red with agitation. Of course, I knew he'd just found out about Robin and in that moment, realized how genuine were his feelings for me. He'd run to Lisette's room first, then mine. Pulling my shift closer for modesty, I sat up. With one hand, I reached out to touch Hero, quietening his barks. He had grown attached and loyal to me and probably would have moved to protect me if the need arose.

"William, what has happened?" I asked, trying to muster up something that sounded genuine in my voice.

"Robin Hood, the outlaw, has somehow escaped my custody," he said, grounding out the words as if it was impossible for him to consider such a thing.

"How?" I gasped. For good effect, I added, "Are we safe, my lord?" I knew my eyes were as big as saucers.

He managed to smile. "You will always be safe with me, my lady. The outlaw has managed to use a piece of wire to open the lock and has stolen two of my best palfreys upon which he escaped. But not to worry, I will find him!" The sheriff was clenching and unclenching his fists as if imagining what he would do with Robin once again in custody.

Robin and Timothy were free! Once Kipp had helped them leave the cell, they had been on their own. I could only imagine that Robin's telepathic gifts had helped him to avoid detection. It also worked to his benefit, as Kipp and I had found, that the castle was poorly guarded at night. Nottingham was not under siege, and there was no need to expend valuable men to watch every nook and cranny.

Peg was standing behind William, her eyes downcast, but I could read her thoughts. She was privately amused at the sheriff's agitation and was happy to see a Saxon had, well, got one over on the sheriff. She was waiting to help me prepare for the day.

"I need to get dressed," I began, speaking to William, who smiled and nodded his head.

"Yes, and as soon as you are ready, please meet me in the hall."

He brushed past Peg, not even giving her notice. She glanced at his retreating form before her eyes returned to me. "Oh, he's in a fine mood," she breathed, her cheeks a little pinker than usual. The morning routine at the castle had been infused with unexpected excitement.

I got out of my bed and walked over to the basin where she poured fresh water so I could wash my face. "I suspect Sir Gilbert is agitated," I remarked.

"Oh, my lady, you should have seen him. He showed the sheriff his key, which was in his room last night. Sir Gilbert found a piece of metal hanging out of the lock to the cell and believes Robin used it to free himself. I'm glad, because at first, they were going to question us, thinking someone helped Robin, him being a Saxon and all." Her blue eyes rounded. "It would have been bad, my lady, for some of us."

I breathed a sigh of relief. It seemed our plan, so far, had led William and Gilbert to think it was an escape completely under the control of Robin, and they would not harm any of the servants in trying to wring out confessions. Kipp caught my eye and nodded.

After I dried my face, I made a quick trip down the corridor to the garderobe then returned so Peg could help me assemble my layers of clothing and dress my hair. Her hands shook a little, and I realized how frightening the prospect must have been for the servants if they were threatened with an interrogation by the sheriff. I was thankful Kipp and I had managed to concoct an escape plan that left the servants blameless. With Kipp so close his shoulder brushed my leg, I went down to the great hall, uncertain of what lay ahead. The prominent thoughts of the sheriff had to do with the escape of Robin Hood, and anything else was layered beneath the agitation. Gilbert was standing next to William, a massive, glowering presence. I tried to avoid his stare and focused on William instead. Gilbert didn't know that I'd been in his room pilfering his keys the previous night, but the moment was still unnerving. William remained upset, but he smiled upon seeing me.

"My lady," he said, holding out both hands. Twisting his head, William glanced at Gilbert and ordered, "Prepare our horses." The seneschal turned and left, roughly shouldering his way past a couple of servants who were tending to the firepit. "My lady," William said again, his eyes on my face, "I regret to tell you we must postpone our nuptials. I am called upon to search for the outlaw, since containing him and seeing that he faced justice was my responsibility."

As he talked, I realized that his pursuit of Robin Hood was not based upon any malicious intent. He truly believed he was serving the people well by ridding them of a scourge. From his point of view, the forest outlaws preyed upon the innocent. Odd, I thought, that he didn't see the structure of the Norman society did the same to the Saxons. It was another reminder of how people can wear blinders and only see events and issues from one perspective. It takes a lot of effort to break past that barrier and take a more, uh, expansive view of the world.

"I understand," I replied, almost visibly shaking myself to pay attention to him.

Kipp and I watched as he left the hall. As the main door to the keep opened and closed again, a burst of cold air whistled through the large room, which even when empty seemed to be filled with echoes. I shivered, rubbing my hands against my upper arms to try and ignite a little warmth to my flesh.

"Time to get ready," Kipp said, looking up at me.

I almost took the stairs back up to my room two at a time; such was my haste. Lisette was still in her room where a servant had prepared a bath for the child. Since that was a lengthy process in medieval times, it was a good opportunity for me to try and get away. As I passed her door, I could hear her singing, and my heart skipped a beat. My allowing her to form such an attachment had been unintended and now had cruel results. I knew I'd always bear some level of guilt over hurting her innocent heart. Kipp nudged me with his sharp nose.

"Get over it, Petra. Time to go." His voice was harsh in my head, but I knew he spoke the truth.

I hastily donned my mantle, pulling it about my body and the hood over my head. As my hand reached the door latch, Peg stepped inside, her arrival unexpected. She took in my appearance, her eyes clouding with confusion.

"My lady?"

"Peg, you didn't see me leave." My eyes locked with hers. "Understand?"

"I was downstairs, trying to fetch some food for my lady. When I came back to her room, she was gone." Peg's voice was flat, her expression guarded.

"Yes, thank you." I reached out and touched her shoulder with my hand.

Probably due to the general agitation in the keep related to Robin Hood's escape, no one was watching the main doorway. The fact that William and Gilbert had left in such a hurry without giving a multitude of orders would work well for me, I thought. I walked quickly across the floor, my feet brushing the rushes in a soft rustle. Hero came down the stairs behind me, uncertain what to do.

"You stay here, old fellow. It's much too cold outside," I said, returning to pet him one last time. He blinked his dark eyes, once, before yawning sleepily to return to the nest of slumbering wolfhounds.

"Petra, hurry," Kipp urged, trying to keep my sentimental exchanges under some control.

As I slipped the latch to the main door, the air almost felt like needles of ice as it struck my face. I pulled the mantle securely about my body and began walking across the courtyard, which was busy with workers going to and from the kitchens and stable. The sound of the blacksmith working on heated metal pinged and echoed across the yard. Up ahead, I could see men guarding the main entrance to the castle. Thinking quickly, I picked up a basket that had been left and grabbed a piece of cloth to cover it as if I were taking something to the village.

"Where are you going?" One of the guards approached me. The little of his flesh that could be seen beneath his helmet was chapped and reddened from exposure to the cold air.

"Master said I need to go to the village and pick up some fresh bread," I said, reverting to Old English, tossing in some of the words which were part of the mixed stew of the two languages in use. "If you're nice to me, I'll give you some when I come back."

He could only see my eyes, since I was wrapped in the mantle, and like most of the inhabitants of England, he had learned enough of the languages in use to comprehend my purpose.

"I hope that's a promise, pretty girl." He grinned as he tried to grab my arm.

With a light laugh, I brushed past him, moving ahead of Kipp, who lagged behind. When the guards would be questioned later if they'd seen a woman with a large, reddish-colored dog pass, they could innocently say they had not. Since tradesmen and vendors routinely traveled into the castle proper to do business, who would recall one lone woman carrying a basket? I began down the steep hill that led to the village, and a couple of minutes later, Kipp bounded after me, joining me as I made it to the narrow streets of Nottingham.

"Well, that went okay," Kipp said, breathing a sigh of relief. "I was busy thinking of everything that could have gone wrong."

"Me, too."

Despite the early hour, the streets were filled with activity. The only people who could afford sloth were the extreme upper class, who allowed others to toil to keep them well-fed and comfortable. Everyone else was on the edge, always, of failing to survive. A couple of people pushed past me roughly, and Kipp had to step lively to keep his toes from being trounced upon. The streets carried with them the scent of food being prepared mixed with the stench of poor sanitation and unwashed bodies. As we turned a sharp corner into a dismal passage no better than an alley used for the disposal of wastes, a man driving a herd of swine almost bowled us down. In the process, I fell against a stack of wooden crates, and if it were not for Kipp protecting me from the charging hogs, I would have been trampled. It seemed the swine had a healthy respect for what appeared to be a big dog with equally big teeth.

"Are you okay?" Kipp asked as he anxiously licked the side of my face.

"Yes, just bruised. Let's go."

I staggered to my feet. With William and Sir Gilbert both gone, it would be some time before any alarms as to my absence would be raised. Or at least, there was no one left behind at the castle who would send a party of men to look for me. Yes, little Lisette would wonder where I'd gone and probably be asking that question, but would anyone be worried? For all they knew, I was down in the village, looking for fabric or spices. Hopefully, I'd be in Sherwood Forest long before that time.

"You need a horse," Kipp observed. "We won't make good time on foot."

We were at the southern edge of Nottingham. There were numerous horses either tethered or in small corrals. And we were about to pay a very savage trick on an unsuspecting human. But I knew nothing else to do. The walk to Robin's lair was too long, and I'd never make it without being detected.

A small palfrey, saddled, was tied to a post. Cautiously, I approached the animal, rubbing my hand along its neck. It seemed friendly enough as it bobbed its head, peering at me with a large brown eye while enjoying my caress. Glancing left and right, I didn't see anyone in the immediate area, so, well, I just stole the horse. It's nothing to be proud of, but I was desperate. Once clear of immediate danger, I'd set it free, and it would, most likely, find its way home. At least I hoped so.

It had been a long time since I'd been in a saddle, but I had ridden many times in the past. Pulling gently on the palfrey's reins—since he didn't seem particularly motivated—I managed to turn him, and with a brisk nudge of my heels, he began to trot. Kipp had no trouble keeping up and even outpaced us for a while. It was difficult to believe we'd managed to take the horse without being seen, but luck was with us.

The rolling countryside was beautiful, its appearance stark now that all the leaves had dropped, and what would have been early morning dew glistening on the dried grass was now a light layer of shimmering, pale frost that resembled fine lace. My mantle provided some warmth to my body, but the hood kept flying back, and before long, I could feel tears streaming down my face due to the cold wind whipping at my flesh. But as the palfrey galloped, I felt my hope return that we, along with Peter and Elani, could go home. It had been a close call this time, what with Elani's injury and the unexpected separation from each other.

"It will be okay," Kipp said, as he ran alongside the palfrey.

He didn't complain but seemed a little winded, so I pulled back, slowing the horse to a walk, allowing Kipp to get a breather. He glanced up at me with gratitude. Neither of us liked being out in the open, but the dense tree line of the forest was still ahead, and there was nothing we could do except keep moving towards that barrier between habitation and wilderness. Kipp's head went up, and when he took that particular attitude, I always knew something was wrong.

"Uh oh!" Kipp turned to look at me. "The sheriff is near, coming this direction. I think he's returning to the castle."

That was exactly what I'd hoped wouldn't happen. Quickly, I turned the palfrey and managed to get him to move to the other side of a hillock, where we found a narrow hollow. I could only hope William and his party would stay on the main roadway, and, if so, I would escape unseen. However, when he got to the castle and found me gone, he would immediately begin to search for me. I had to make haste!

Dismounting, I held a hand over the nose of my palfrey, hoping to keep him quiet as we heard the other horses draw near. My horse wanted to call out a happy greeting to his fellow equines, so I kept distracting him, rubbing his nose and resting my hand on his head. I didn't realize until William passed and we were clear of him that I'd been holding my breath the entire time.

"That was close," I gasped, glancing at Kipp, who nodded his head in agreement. Too close.

I remounted the palfrey, who was enjoying the respite and not particularly eager to run, and nudged his sides with my heels. We were off again, Kipp bounding along easily at my side after the pause. It was not long before we could see the darkened fringe of trees ahead signaling the forest and, I hoped, freedom for us. The woods were not particularly conducive to galloping horses, and it was only after I'd broken the barrier of the dense woods that I dismounted and turned the palfrey towards home with a gentle slap on his fanny. I saw his ears go flat as he began to run at a much faster pace than I'd been able to coax from him. What was that about, I wondered?

"He hadn't been fed yet today and is eager to get home to eat," Kipp observed, having determined the notions of the animal. "You disturbed his routine."

"Kipp, it's time for you to do your thing and find Peter and Elani." With his superior detection abilities, he could locate them easily, despite the size and breadth of the forest.

He began to focus and I didn't push him, knowing he needed space to, well, create. But at the same time, my anxiety was growing. We needed to be secured away in the event the sheriff returned since he would be looking for Robin in the same place in which I was hiding!

"I think we should go in that direction," Kipp finally said, pointing his long nose. It was nothing specific, just instinct that led him to make that decision.

That was good enough for me, since I had no idea, and we began to move quickly, with me jogging along when the thick growth of the underbrush would permit. It was not long before I became hot and stopped to remove my mantle. It was holding me back, anyway.

"Probably not good for you to sweat and get cold," Kipp advised.

"I can't run in this thing," I replied.

The forest became denser with old-growth trees and tangled thickets, and the darkness felt complete. It already had been overcast outside, with the clouds blocking any rays of sun. The tree limbs above us were bare of the leaves that had formed an almost impenetrable barrier between earth and sky during my last trip to Sherwood Forest. I stumbled once, falling to my knees, scraping my hands in the process. I found my footing and stood, ruefully examining my hands, which were pretty raw. Kipp glanced at my face, wagging his tail to keep me motivated.

"I think I'm getting something," he finally said.

I almost cried with relief. It seemed we'd run for hours; I was shaking with cold and my hands were throbbing.

"Think about going home," Kipp advised. "There will be sunshine, warmth, and a hot cup of tea."

I started to argue that we'd probably end up in the midst of a North Carolina winter snowstorm, but it seemed unkind to say such a thing when Kipp was just trying to help me feel better. Reaching down, I tugged on his ear.

"I will, Kipp."

He then turned his massive head slightly to the left. "I've got them!" he exclaimed.

I followed as he led, and it was only a few minutes more when I, too, could pick up on the anxious but joyful thoughts of Elani followed by Peter. They were safe, calling out to us, eager to go home! I stumbled, falling to my knees; exhaustion had overtaken me. Then I heard sounds echoing in the woods. It was the dogs from Nottingham! They were still at a distance but were moving quickly. The sheriff had brought them to search for either me or Robin Hood and they, no doubt, were following my trail since they were familiar with me and Kipp. Gasping, I got to my feet and pushed forward, Kipp staring at me anxiously.

"Kipp, let Peter and Elani know they must tell Robin to move to a place of safety," I said, knowing my telepathic messages would not travel as far as his. "Ask them to move towards us."

It was a short time later when we cleared a narrow stream that whispered a soft sound as it rolled over polished rocks. Directly ahead, we saw Peter and Elani, staring back as if they couldn't believe their eyes. My knees were trembling and threatening to buckle; I staggered forward and grasped Peter, pulling him to me, before I pushed him away again to inspect his appearance. His beard was untrimmed and full; his dark hair had fallen past his shoulders, and he had it tied in the back with a leather thong. But his eyes were full of the enthusiasm and curiosity that were a hallmark of his character. His hands were surprisingly strong, and I was aware he was almost holding me up so that I would not collapse on the ground.

"Petra!" He was giving me the once over, too, a shadow of concern crossing his face. "Are you ready to go home?"

"More than ready," I replied, trying to smile but my flesh was so cold all I could manage was a chilled grimace. "Is Robin clear?"

"Yes, it was only he and a couple of his men. There is a deep waterway close by with a fallen tree that makes a natural bridge. The dogs will not try to cross the tree as it is narrow and slippery; consequently, the dogs won't be able to find their trail."

Meanwhile, Kipp and Elani were touching noses, their eyes closed. I shut off my access to Kipp's thoughts, giving them a moment of privacy. Then, we heard the hunting dogs, baying as they came closer.

"Time to go," I said, my voice firm.

We sat on the cold-hardened ground. My exhaustion was such that I worried if I'd be able to manage the concentration needed for a time-shift while knowing Kipp could pull me along due to his strength of will and natural abilities. I lay back on the bed of fallen leaves, with Kipp next to me, his head on my chest. Peter and Elani copied us, and the last thing I remember was looking up at the bare branches of the trees overhead, marveling at the intricate patterns formed by the thick limbs which intertwined in the sky before they melted together into darkness.

# TWENTY-EIGHT

"Another cup of tea?"

I nodded, pushing my cup across the bruised surface of the dinette table. Fitzhugh smiled at me, enjoying the look of pure pleasure on my face as the steam rose off the surface of the tea. I was still trying to get warm, it seemed, even though I'd been back home for two days. Leaning forward, I let the vapor from the hot beverage tickle my nose while I inhaled the fragrance.

"I missed tea," I remarked, curling my fingers around the cup.

"Was the trip everything you thought it would be?" Fitzhugh asked.

"Yes, and more," I replied.

He sat back in his chair, his hand gently stroking his long beard. Fitzhugh had not asked me anything about the time-shift, wisely giving me time to decompress and work through events in my head. As a fellow traveler, he knew the impact of time travel on our minds as well as our bodies and gave me the space I needed. What information he'd gathered was given by me in fits and starts as the inclination struck. I looked through the kitchen windows, which offered a panoramic view of the backyard. Kipp was picking his way across the crisp, cold-hardened grass, followed closely by Juno, their lupine noses to the ground as they picked up more about the world through their senses than I ever would. Despite the contentment I felt, I was a mite pensive and moody.

"Aren't you relieved that it will fall upon Peter and Elani to chronicle the trip as well as make a report to the Twelve?" Fitzhugh smiled behind his mustache and beard. "I always dreaded that part, since I never knew whether or not to be completely honest."

"You, less than honest!" I widened my eyes. "Don't crush my impressions of you!"

He laughed softly and refreshed his tea. The smell of bergamot filled the room with a delightful cloud. Despite the fact it was quite cold outside, the kitchen was blissfully comfortable, thanks to the space heater, which was sending waves of heat across the room. I never was truly warm in the castle at Nottingham, despite the layers of clothing I wore. Well, I forget sleeping with Hero and Kipp! I was warm when their two bodies were curled up against mine. My heart squeezed as I thought of Hero and the trust in his brown eyes. No doubt he missed, perhaps, sharing my bed. Or was that just wistful vanity on my part to think I'd been loved?

"It was a tough time-shift," I began, needing to talk but also dreading it. "Elani could have been killed." My voice broke, and I could not speak for a moment. Taking a deep breath, I centered myself and continued. "I felt, as the elder of the group, my separation from them put everyone at risk."

Fitzhugh shrugged his shoulders. "Well, perhaps, but did Peter and Elani make it without your wise leadership?"

I looked up quickly, searching his face for meaning. "It's not that I think I'm indispensable or something, Fitzhugh," I replied, feeling defensive.

"And I meant what I said, Petra, with no sarcasm intended. You do provide wise leadership. That is your role as the most experienced of the group. And Peter and Elani managed to grow a little since they had to figure some things out on their own. So, that is a good thing, right?"

I smiled. "I'm sorry, Fitzhugh. I think I feel a little bruised, and I'll always feel a tinge of guilt over Elani's injury."

"And feel it with even greater impact since Kipp is in love with her, right?"

276

Fitzhugh laughed at the expression on my face. "I may be old, but I've been in love before and know all the signs. And with your bond to Kipp, you will feel all things that affect him with intensity."

Lily took that opportunity to make her presence known—in the way of a cat, insistent and self-assured -- and began to wind in between my legs, completing neat figure eights as she left deposits of hair on my black yoga pants. Reaching down, I picked her up and let her sit in my lap, where she curled into a ball and began to purr with contentment, her busy feet kneading my thighs. I scratched the top of her striped head, smiling at the expression on her face as her eyes blinked shut. I'd missed the little varmint.

"Finding Robin to be a symbiont was a surprise, to say the least. At first, I judged him, but in retrospect believe he was just trying to survive without the counsel of his peers. I think his intentions were actually good." I made a face. "At least I hope so."

"And the Sheriff of Nottingham?" Fitzhugh asked. "What is your assessment of him as a human?"

I took a deep breath as I recalled Sir William's handsome face and gold-brown eyes. He would never know what happened to me. And little Lisette! I'd allowed her to form an attachment that was ill-advised. I felt my throat tighten at the memory.

"He could be as ruthless as the times required of him. But he was capable of love and kindness, too. I believe in his role as the main keeper of the peace for the Norman nobility and the Crown he did what he thought was his job. In order to do that, however, he had to see the Saxon peasants as less than was he, and that is the fatal flaw that afflicts humanity at times, allowing people to do unspeakable things."

"He was able to love you," Fitzhugh remarked. "He was also able to overlook the obvious gaps in your story because he wanted to believe things about you that may or may not have been true."

"Another flaw in humanity?" I asked, smiling.

"And in symbionts," Fitzhugh replied. "We can all see what we wish to see and minimize anything that points to an unpleasant reality."

We sat in silence until a face appeared at the back door. It was Peter, smiling and waving at us to gain entrance. Elani had joined

Kipp and Juno out back. The sun was bright, despite the cold temperatures, and I was gratified to see the rays of light tangle in her lovely coat once again. Kipp was correct in his observation that she sparkled. She seemed whole, despite the danger she'd faced after her injury. Peter opened the door, bringing with him a rush of cool air.

"I'm headed to the store for a few things. Do you need anything?" He smiled, nodding at me.

Our travels together had created a close bond that felt like family. He could have been my little brother, I mused. As I glanced up at him, I thought he seemed taller, more filled out, his face pleasantly handsome with its adornment of the beard, which he decided to keep. He'd not cut his hair yet, and it was tied in a ponytail at the nape of his neck. It struck me he'd matured, and the process had been exacerbated by what had happened to Elani.

"We could use some honey," Fitzhugh grumbled. "Petra has been making a dent in our meager supply."

"Elani wanted to visit with Kipp," Peter said. He didn't need to ask if it was okay. Walking over, he gave me a little squeeze on my arm, smiling down at me. "Back in a few."

After he left, we sat in silence, watching the lupines cavort in the back yard. I'd backed out of Kipp's head, giving him privacy to experience his feelings about Elani without me hovering. The cold was not an issue for them, I thought, suppressing a shiver. And thinking about the weather made me revisit the time-shift to 1192 England; with that came thoughts of Robin Hood, the Sheriff of Nottingham, and even little Lisette. Something was nagging at me, and I wasn't sure exactly what. There was some loop left open, something needing closure.

"Fitzhugh, who was it that showed the artifacts to Ritson?" I glanced at him.

"How would we know that?" Fitzhugh asked, frowning as if my question was odd.

"He wrote his book based upon the artifacts, so I think it's important."

"Why?"

"It's bothering me. Isn't that enough?"

Fitzhugh's eyes opened wide. "If you are thinking it was Robin Hood who had the artifacts, I think the chances of that are pretty slim, Petra. Surely, it was some human who had the items passed down from generation to generation."

"But what if it was Robin?" I asked. "I want to know that."

"Why would it matter?"

"It would complete the story, Fitzhugh. It might help us understand the context of centuries of differing and evolving stories about Robin Hood." I sat back in my chair, momentarily disturbing Lily, who gave a meow of protest. Gently, I stroked her little head to soothe her; after a few moments, her eyes closed again. "Wouldn't that journey of a symbiont from before 1192 to at least the latter 1700's be a story within itself considering his impact on legend, lore, and written history?"

He began to fidget with his teacup. "If you don't register the trip with the Twelve, it would be a story you can't tell." Fitzhugh frowned, his gray eyebrows almost forming a straight line across his forehead. "What do you want to do, Petra?"

"I want to make a quick trip back to the time frame given to us by Ritson, which would be the first week of October 1793. He said the man had visited him on a Monday or Tuesday of that week. Kipp could manage that easily since we've made the trip to London so many times." I sat back in my chair, staring at Fitzhugh's face. It was clear he thought my reasoning was not particularly sound.

"And, do I correctly assume this trip will not be sanctioned by the Twelve?"

"I just thought Kipp and I would make a little hop and come right home."

Fitzhugh took a deep breath. "And you don't want me to, well, rat you out. Right?"

"Well, it would be really nice if you would just say I was out of town for a couple of days."

Fitzhugh stood, a little agitated. "And what if something happens to you or Kipp, Petra?"

"Aw, nothing's gonna happen," I replied, my fingers fumbling to move the teacup across the table. The action gave me something to do in the face of Fitzhugh's disapproval.

"That's what you thought about Elani, most likely,"

At his words, I cringed. Was I once again displaying my tendency to be brash, reckless, and fearless? I'd thought all those qualities had been tempered by age and experience. And here I was, acting like a young Peter, not considering how my actions might impact others or even the timeline.

Fitzhugh's dark eyes met mine. "Perhaps that was unfair of me, Petra. You have no responsibility for what happened to Elani. I'm sorry."

I took a deep breath. "No, as the leader of the team, I am responsible for the health and well-being of my members. And Elani could have been killed." I tried to smile, my lips quivering with emotion. "It was terrifying, Fitzhugh. I was separated from her as well as from Kipp and Peter and couldn't do anything to help them." As I spoke, I remembered the feelings I had when Tula had been killed, and I was abandoned in a time that was not mine. That had been terrifying, too. Glancing down at my teacup, I saw a few tiny leaves swirling in the amber liquid at the bottom of the vessel. My hands trembled slightly as I touched the fragile porcelain of the cup. "I don't want to be reckless now, but I just need to know if Robin or even another symbiont took the information to Ritson upon which he based his book. It's improbable, I think, that Robin would have survived all those years, but what if he did? He would have impacted the human timeline for centuries."

The frown on Fitzhugh's face began to relax. "And I think I am too old to appreciate what you are saying. Maybe I've become too careful." He paused. "I think my judgment is affected and influenced by my feelings for you and Kipp. Considering that, I need to back away and let you determine what is best."

"No, I don't want that."

I would have said more, but Kipp was at the back door, asking to come in. Crossing over the room, I opened the door as Elani, Juno and Kipp brushed by my legs, bringing with them the scent of dormant grass and fallen, damp leaves. Juno immediately chose a spot near the space heater; her arthritis made any cold weather a little more unpleasant. Kipp stretched out on his side, his tail thumping the floor as his eyes met mine. He shot a question mark to my brain in our private manner of communication. He wanted to know why I'd left his thoughts.

"Just giving you some privacy, buddy," I replied, closing one eye in a wink.

Fitzhugh had stopped talking about my proposed trip since he didn't want to share my thoughts without my consent, but I nodded at him. What he said was true in that if the trip was not sanctioned by the Twelve, none of what Kipp and I might discover would be reported. And for me to propose such a thing would be self-indulgent, to say the very least.

"Uh," Fitzhugh began, clearing his throat, "Petra was talking to me about a possible time-shift that would close the loophole in your recent trip."

"What loophole?" Elani asked. She was lying between Kipp and Juno, enjoying the heat from the space heater, as were they. Her dark eyes met mine, and despite her recent very close brush with death, there was no anxiety or fear. She was as confident and eager as ever and would have time-shifted right then and there if asked.

Kipp was staring at me, his head cocked to the side. "You want to find out who took the artifacts to Ritson."

What was intriguing about his statement—and it was a statement, not a question—was that he was not reading my thoughts to determine my intent. By that time in our relationship, Kipp just knew what made me tick and could predict my actions, it appeared, without breaking a sweat. As I wondered if that was good or bad, Fitzhugh threw back his head and laughed since he knew what had happened.

"Am I that transparent?" I asked, widening my eyes as I glanced at Fitzhugh.

"Obviously." Fitzhugh relaxed back in his chair, his alert eyes on Kipp and Elani.

"Well, I'm in," Elani began before Kipp cut her off.

"No way, Elani. You are still recovering and don't need to stress your body." Kipp huffed loudly, feeling outraged she would suggest such a thing.

"And you can't tell me what to do, Kipp," Elani replied with a toss of her head.

Juno, wise lupine that she was, leaned over and poked first Kipp, then Elani with her long, pointed muzzle. "Settle down, you two."

Kipp continued to breathe loudly and almost snorted a couple of times; Elani wouldn't look at him. It fell to me to be the peacemaker.

"Well, it isn't up to any of us, as Fitzhugh has helpfully pointed out to me." I pushed my teacup towards Fitzhugh for a warm-up. "I'd thought Kipp and I might just sneak away, but if we do that, anything we discover can't be recorded. So, I guess I'll have to approach the Twelve. And that august body will decide if any of us are permitted to go."

"Why do you think it is important?" Juno asked, her eyes on me.

"There are literally centuries of stories about Robin Hood," I said. "Was that just the natural evolution of tales created about a legendary figure, or was there a real, uh, person, in the midst of the action?" I smiled at Juno. "I need to know."

"And you also would like to reassure yourself that if a symbiont is involved, perhaps he avoided doing things that would negatively affect the human species." Juno wasn't asking. She knew it was important for us to clarify Robin's role in the mythology of England, if, indeed, it lasted for hundreds of years. She relaxed, closing her eyes for a moment. When she opened them again, they seemed clearer than usual, as if the opacities that clouded them had faded away and her view of the world was acute and penetrating.

"I agree with you, Petra. I think it is necessary. And I am glad to go before the Twelve and propose it myself."

As a very valued member of the Twelve, her words would go a long way in making the time-shift happen.

The door opened as Peter arrived.

"What's going on?"

Elani looked up at him, her eyes bright, her tail wagging furiously.

"We're going on a time-shift with Petra and Kipp!"

# TWENTY-NINE

E lani's words, though hopeful, were not realized. The Twelve—
perhaps wisely—didn't allow her to go. In consideration of her
recent brush with death, they felt the strain on her naturally resilient
lupine body would be too much. Yes, she would travel again, but just
not on this hopefully short hop that Kipp and I would make. Peter
showed maturity by supporting their decision. I wondered if he
privately chafed at the restriction but was just doing the right thing
so Elani would not feel bad that her physical considerations were
holding him back.

It did help things that the trip was approved by the Twelve, since
it compelled Karl to outfit me once again. He was in a bad mood,
irritable, and unpleasantly short with all four of us. Even though
Peter and Elani had not been approved to accompany us, they hung
out in Karl's workshop, making idle chit-chat as I tried on my gown
for a final inspection. Elani had gotten over her irritation at Kipp's
overly protective attitude, and the two were lying close together. I
was happy when Karl left to go retrieve something from his vault,
taking his bad attitude with him and leaving me to chat with Peter.

"I found Robin to be an honest broker," he remarked, his dark
eyes finding mine. "I hope that you don't conclude that he,
somehow, has damaged the human timeline in a way that is

deliberate or harmful." Peter glanced away for a minute, gathering his thoughts. "I mean, it's always an issue, and he lived amongst humans a long time, but I hope he tried to take a careful path and not overtly disrupt anything."

"I knew what you meant, Peter," I said, taking a sip of the bitter coffee that had been sitting on a burner in the workroom for who knows how long. I knew I'd be tasting it for hours as well as dealing with the feeling that the inner lining of my stomach was being eroded. "I liked him, too." Making a face, I set down the mug wondering why was I doing that to myself. The coffee was beyond salvation.

It was hard to consider that Robin had been dead for a long time, unless he was an exceptionally long-lived symbiont, such as Fitzhugh, and those were few and far between. Yes, we live much longer than humans but are mortal, and at some point, our timeline ends. It is true of all organisms, be they sentient or not.

Karl returned, and as he muttered words under his breath, I realized he was still upset that he didn't have to research the projected needs of my upcoming time-shift. The Twelve, in a miserly moment, had instructed him to take the gown I wore on the previous visit to Ritson and just make some alterations so that it would make do fashion-wise. I suppose economic realities strike all, including symbionts!

"Karl, I really like what you've done with the sleeves," I began hopefully. Maybe I could nudge him into a happy place. However, one glance from him made me dry up like a desert watering hole. My attempt was neither clever nor transparent, and all I'd managed was to irritate him to an even greater degree since he felt talked down to as if he were a child. I glanced at Kipp who was trying to cover the smirk on his face. No, you'd not think a lupine could manage that much facial mobility, but somehow Kipp always did.

Since we'd returned home, Kipp had distanced himself from Elani, emotionally speaking, and when I'd tried to query him, he only became grumpy and wouldn't talk for hours. His behavior left Elani confused, and after some careful consideration, I decided— wisely, I think—to stay out of it. I figured anything I said would be taken out of context.

Kipp and I decided to walk home, although the air was cold, the wind blustery. As I glanced at the gray sky that was undershot with a delicate lacing of pink, I realized that snow was on the horizon. Kipp said little; my hand drifted down to burrow in the dense fur along his shoulders.

"You okay?" I asked.

"Oh, yes," he replied. "I'm just getting focused for the time-shift since it needs to be precise, and I will be targeting a particular time of year."

A lateral shift, when one just made the jump to a corresponding date or season, was not as complex as the one we would make. But I knew Kipp could do it and had done so, with success, before.

"You remember last time I missed my mark." Kipp sighed.

"Not by much," I replied, scratching between his ears.

The wind was picking up, and I began to feel the first snowflakes brush against my face. Feeling energized, I picked up my pace. Peter and Elani had taken my garments to my house, and I planned to go ahead and make the jump later that evening. First, however, I was going to prepare a crockpot of soup for Fitzhugh in case I was delayed in my return.

"You like having Fitzhugh and Juno living with us, don't you?" Kipp asked.

"Very much, and the fact surprises me, Kipp. I never thought I'd want my little house crowded with others but now can't think of living any other way."

He grunted in response, and I knew something else was coming if I was only patient.

"I have been thinking about Elani," he finally said. "I'm not ready to break up, uh, this," he said, meaning his relationship with me. "I don't want to hurt her and care about her, but I'm too young to be saddled with a family."

"There are things you want to do in life," I remarked.

"Yes, oh, yes!" he said, relieved I understood his intent. "And I don't care less about her at all!" Kipp glanced up at me. "I think about her a lot."

"So, what do you plan on doing?"

"When we get back, I plan on having a serious talk with her. I'm thinking we could maybe, uh, go steady for a while but delay anything else."

I tried not to smile at his "go steady" remark, figuring he'd picked it up from a movie. Glancing ahead, I saw our house and felt happiness well inside me. There was a comforting glow of amber light in the front windows signaling Fitzhugh was in residence. How nice to come home to someone!

"And I plan on talking with her when we get back," Kipp resumed his pondering.

"I think that is good, Kipp. You don't want to leave her in suspense."

He grunted his wordless reply.

We found Fitzhugh in the kitchen, working on a pot of tea. Juno was in front of the infrared heater with Lily comfortably reclining on her back.

"I thought you might like some tea before you leave," Fitzhugh said, smiling.

We planned no leaving party this time. I'd said my goodbyes to Philo at work, expecting and receiving his usual kiss on the top of my head. Peter and Elani, likewise, had wished us well, as Kipp tried to ignore the lingering glances bestowed upon him by Elani. My garments were laid out, thoughtfully delivered by Peter. Tea seemed like a good idea. Fitzhugh settled in, making himself comfortable as he sipped on the hot drink while I assembled the pot of soup and set the timer.

"There, now you'll have something to eat," I remarked to Fitzhugh, who bowed his head and nodded. As I passed his chair, I almost leaned down to pull him against me in a chair-hug, but decided against such a brash move. I sat across from him, and we engaged in idle talk, most of it having to do with the upcoming Christmas holidays. Kipp enjoyed decorating almost more than did I, and we'd have to get a tree and pull the box of ornaments down from the attic when I got back. Fitzhugh still wore the sweater I'd once bought him for Christmas. As I thought of the occasional bad gift choices I'd made over my lifetime, I flushed with pleasure at the sweater and how much Fitzhugh had—and still—enjoyed it.

I felt we'd delayed enough, and Kipp and I returned to our

room, and he watched as I pulled on the altered gown. My backpack was lightly laden since we anticipated a short hop and return. If I was wrong, then there was Kipp's money collar, and I could buy things as needed. Kipp was quiet, and I realized he was simply trying to focus. If I'd been a betting symbiont, I would have wagered the money collar that Kipp was going to hit the mark squarely this time.

With the natural adaptation and abilities of symbionts, we arrived, unnoticed, early in the morning. I looked up at a set of brick-and-mortar buildings that towered nearby and realized with amazement that we were in the courtyard of Gray's Inn! I willed myself not to look at Kipp since I knew he was waiting for me to compliment him. But after a few seconds, I gave in to the inevitable. After all, it was an amazing bit of accuracy and one which I could not have managed myself despite my years of experience.

"Pretty good, huh?" Kipp asked, nuzzling my hand.

I had to laugh in response. "Let's wait for that conclusion when we know the date," I replied, arching my eyebrows at him. Of course, my love for Kipp is such that I wanted him to succeed in grand fashion and was only needling him just because.

It was daybreak, with the early light of morning beginning to fan out across the courtyard. A workman walked by, pushing a cart full of tools and other articles. He paused, taking a double-take as he glanced at me. It was clear he'd just traversed the area, and now a woman and a large dog were standing where there been no one a few seconds earlier.

"Beg pardon, miss, but how long have you been here?" His face was clouded with confusion.

"Oh, I just arrived," I replied, smiling as I watched the relief play over his features. He was not crazy, after all.

He tipped his rag hat and was preparing to leave, but I made him pause so I could ask the critical question. "Sir, I've become a little confused while traveling. Can you tell me the date and year, please?"

I'd learned to ignore the stares and looks of concern when making such an odd query.

"Why, miss, it's the last day of September 1793," he replied.

I looked down at Kipp; his eyes were bright, tail wagging. From our research, the first week of October began on a Tuesday; in Ritson's mind, the first week of October could include the last day of September, since it occurred on a Monday.

Kipp had done it with the most amazing accuracy yet. We'd arrived on Monday in the first week of October 1793! I glanced at Kipp and fancied I saw the same smirk I'd seen earlier.

"Proud of yourself?" I asked.

"You bet," he replied. "This stuff is not easy, although I make it look like it is."

"Well, we can only hope that your reading of his thoughts was accurate, or, at the very least, his own memory was not faulty."

Kipp turned away from me and gave a loud sniff. It was clear he wanted to chase his current feelings of accomplishment and success.

Our last trip to London to meet Ritson had taken place during the winter, with frigid temperatures and ice-crusted streets. Thankfully, the current weather was relatively mild, with almost no breeze. The street was busy with laborers going to work, meeting the needs of such a large city. A heavily laden dray rolled past, the weight of it seeming to make the surface upon which I was standing tremble and vibrate. A team of draft horses appeared almost bored as they pulled the dray with no effort expended. The driver glanced at me and politely tipped his hat, nodding as he passed.

I inhaled and picked up the usual scents of the city, which were a combination of coal fires, livestock, and a vaguely unpleasant and acrid chemical odor that was probably drifting from the east end of town where the tanneries were located. A couple of young boys were racing back and forth behind the departing dray, making their living by scooping up the piles of manure left behind. Kipp nudged my hand, knowing how sentimental I could get over the plight of children in a harsh world. I let him lead me to a bench that was located beneath the heavy limbs of a towering elm tree and took my seat. We could be waiting for hours, but since I was an observer of humanity in all its forms, both raw and refined, the notion of just sitting and literally watching the world go by was not a bad way to spend the day.

Six hours passed—just seconds in the life of a symbiont—when

Kipp sat up and turned his head down the street. It was moments later when I felt it, too, the stirrings of a symbiont mind. Of course, it could have been any symbiont occupying London in 1793, but I felt my heart leap with excitement! Could it be? A few minutes later, I spied a tall, lanky figure walking slowly towards us, leaning heavily on a walking stick and carrying a medium size valise with his free hand. His mind was familiar to me as I recognized Robin Hood! His head went up, too, and he paused for a second, almost stumbling, before continuing, leaving the sidewalk to cross across the grass to where Kipp and I waited.

"Petra and Kipp," he said, nodding his head and smiling. "Why am I not surprised?"

He was very old, with a face lined with creases, and blonde hair that had turned white over the years. But the charisma, the chemistry, was still there in full force, displayed with that smile. Without asking, he took a seat next to me on the bench, setting the valise down on the grass.

"You have come a long way and obviously have questions for me?" Robin's eyebrows lifted in query.

"I had to know if it was you who brought the artifacts to Ritson and why," I responded. With a nod of my head, I indicated the valise.

His eyes roamed over my face as if he was reacquainting himself with me. After he finished his inspection, he smiled.

"You have not changed at all," Robin remarked. "I, on the other hand, have turned old. I fear my time is short."

"Fear?" Kipp asked.

"Well, perhaps that is not the best word to use. My life has been good, richly spent, and full of adventure." He paused, his green eyes staring out at the humanity before us. "People can only wish for a little taste of what I've experienced." His eyes turned back to me. "I have no regrets."

"And the human timeline?" Kipp asked.

"Ah, no nonsense, as usual, I see," Robin said, smiling. "And you are right to ask." After a pause, he said, "I've tried to live out a lifetime and move on with as little disruption as possible, Kipp. There were people who became attached to me, and I did my best to minimize those attachments and move on so that the people could form new relationships and fulfill their natural arcs."

"And the generations of stories about Robin Hood?" I asked.

"They happened each time I remade myself. There was a Little John, a Will Scarlet, and Friar Tuck as well as a lovely Maid Marion. Their stories occurred after the time you and I were fleeing the Sheriff of Nottingham." At my look of confusion, he said, laughing, "Petra, there was more than one Sheriff of Nottingham and more than one set of adventures."

"But you were central to them all." Kipp was not asking; he was making a statement.

"In my own way, perhaps, I emboldened the humans to fight for their rights and dignity, and maybe I did disrupt what was naturally occurring. But who would know whether or not some other, uh, man, would have done the same? Is not the fight for rights the natural evolution of any subjugated people?" Robin's Lincoln green eyes met mine.

"You know there is no certain answer for that, Robin," I replied. After a moment, my curiosity overtook me. "What was it like after we disappeared into thin air?" I was referencing that last day in the forest when being pursued by the sheriff.

"Well, the sheriff did not find our, uh, hideout," Robin replied, smiling. "But we eventually pulled up stakes and relocated to the forest in Barnsdale. I think losing you almost drove him mad, and he made Sherwood unsafe for us for a while." Robin paused before adding, "He eventually resigned his position and took his daughter and disappeared."

I looked away from him, feeling my cheeks redden. I'd not asked for the attention from the sheriff and had, inadvertently, done the thing of which I accused Robin… and that was I'd precipitated a change in the timeline.

"And why are you here?" Robin asked, tilting his head to the side as he inspected my face. He diplomatically changed the tenor of the discussion.

"I had to put a period on the end of the sentence," I said. "I had to know."

We sat in silence for a few moments while we each gathered our own thoughts. Kipp had left the cozy spot he occupied in my brain and disappeared like a bubble popping in the air. He moved closer in the grass so that his body was resting next to my right foot. Eventually, he twisted his head and gazed at Robin.

"Are you lonely now?" Kipp asked.

Robin was quiet as he considered the question; his attention was caught, momentarily, by a bird who was in a tree nearby, scolding a tabby-striped cat which slunk in the grass at the base of the tree. A smile tugged at the corner of Robin's mouth.

"Maybe, just a little. But it never was so. I enjoyed the company of humans, although I admit when you and your group arrived, it was nice to visit with some of my own kind. And, yes, through the years, I would make another accidental acquaintance or two, but it was not something I sought." He turned to look at me. "I'm content with the life I've led."

I reached out, my hand finding his, which was still surprisingly strong despite his advanced years. The flesh, although mottled and wrinkled with age, was warm and resilient. His fingers tightened around mine.

"I think that is the best thing any of us can say," I remarked.

We sat with Robin for a while longer before he gently reminded us he had an appointment with Ritson. And we definitely didn't want to disrupt that assignation since it could impact the writing of Ritson's famous book, the one that had led us to this place and Robin. It was best to leave the timeline of humanity alone for a while. Finally, Robin stood, consciously straightening his posture until he resembled the vital, strong young symbiont we'd known. I stood, too, and after a moment, put my arms around him, letting him pull me into his chest. It was there I could breathe him in; he smelled faintly of pipe smoke, the odor sweet and lingering.

"Goodbye, Petra. And, Kipp, you take care of her, always. Okay?"

Kipp blinked his eyes, once. He had to lead me away and commanded me not to stare after Robin as he disappeared through the doorway.

"Let him go," Kipp said.

We found a small, ignored corner of the world, and with no

effort at all, I found myself swept back to my contemporary home. Blinking with the usual confusion, I looked around my small bedroom. Everything seemed as I had left it. Glancing at the clock, I noted the date had flipped to the next day, and we'd only been gone about eight hours total. The house had the stillness of late night or early morning, and the atmosphere and sounds seemed muffled. I instinctively knew if I peeked out the window, the land would be blanketed in snow. Kipp, beside me on the bed, began to stretch, his large ears flattened against his head, before he glanced at me, his tail wagging.

"How about that?" he asked, his jaw dropping in a lupine smile, remarking upon his accuracy.

There was a tap on my door before it swung open. Fitzhugh was there, smiling, too.

"Back so soon?" he asked. "I've already put the kettle on," he added. "I know it's late—or early—depending upon your perspective, but I had to know what happened."

When I didn't answer, he walked closer and finally sat on the edge of my bed.

"Are you alright, Petra?" he asked.

I looked up at his face and wondered how I could have thought it to be unkind or harsh. The face I saw was crumpled with concern and, yes, love.

"He is all alone, Fitzhugh." I began to cry.

Fitzhugh pulled me against his shoulder, and I think I felt his lips graze the top of my head.

"But you aren't, Petra. And you will never be."

# ACKNOWLEDGMENTS

The author values the support of her readers who enjoy following the exploits of Kipp and Petra. As always, she appreciates the validation from her husband, family, friends, and the publishing team at ePublishing Works!

# SUGGESTED READING LIST

*Life in a Medieval Village* by Joseph Gies and Frances Gies

*Life in a Medieval City* by Joseph Gies and Frances Gies

*Life in a Medieval Castle* by Joseph Gies and Frances Gies

*Medieval Underpants and other Blunders* by Susanne Alleyn

*Ivanhoe* by Sir Walter Scott

# ABOUT THE AUTHOR

T.L.B. Wood began her love of literature at an early age, encouraged by her mother who was an English teacher. She and her husband share a love of nature and animals, and more than one rescued dog or cat has found a forever home with the Wood family.

T.L.B. is an author in many genres: the inspirational romance *In the Eye of Hugo*, a paranormal history *The Way of Telitha*, the science fiction novels *The Last Child of Tole* and *The Ambassador from Tole*, and the epic fantasy *The Eagles of Arundell*.

She is best known for her young adult Symbiont Time Travel Adventure Series, which includes the books *The Symbiont, Tombstone, 1881, Whitechapel, 1888, The Great Locomotive Chase, 1862, Titanic, 1912, A Conspiracy To Murder, 1865* and the forthcoming Robin Hood, 1192.

In that series, time travelers with an eye for detail and a nose for trouble travel from the present era to investigate history's great mysteries. Humans think Petra is one of their own, a young woman accompanied by Kipp, her seemingly canine companion. But the reality is that Kipp and Petra are a bonded pair of telepaths in search of adventure.

T.L.B. has been described by reviewers as writing characters that "feel like old friends" with her "intelligent writing and research," and "improves with every book she writes."

www.ingramcontent.com/pod-product-compliance
Lightning Source LLC
Chambersburg PA
CBHW030959260626
47169CB00002B/611